THE CHASE

a novel

Susan Wales
and Robin Shope

Fleming H. Revell
A Division of Baker Book House Co
Grand Rapids, Michigan 49516

Published by Fleming H. Revell
a division of Baker Publishing Group
P.O. Box 6287, Grand Rapids, MI 49516-6287
www.revellbooks.com

Second printing, July 2004

Printed in the United States of America

Library of Congress Cataloging-in-Publication Data
Wales, Susan.
    The chase : a novel / Susan Wales and Robin Shope.
        p.   cm.
      ISBN 0-8007-5934-6 (pbk.)
        1. Investigative reporting—Fiction. 2. Women journalists—Fiction. I. Shope,
    Robin. II. Title.
    PS3623.A3585 C48 2004
    813'.6—dc22   2003024545

From Susan

To my family
My mother and father, Mr. and Mrs. Arthur Huey,
for the gift of storytelling,
my husband Ken,
and to my daughter and granddaughter,
Meg and Hailey Chrane.

From Robin

To my beloved husband, Rick,
who daily seeks God's heart and will,
and to our two children,
Kimberly and Matthew,
who are God's most gracious gifts to us.

1

Oh! How many times we die before death!
—Julie de Lespinasse

How could she have been so careless? Ordinarily when Jill worked late, she hailed a cab to drive her home, but tonight she opted for a late stroll to unwind before tomorrow . . . her big day. Maybe the biggest day of her career, if she lived to see it.

Heavy footsteps pounded the pavement behind her until she turned the corner of M Street. She listened intently for the sound of someone following her but heard nothing now. Desperately searching for any sign of life spilling out of the lighted doorways and on to the sidewalks of the business district, she saw there was none. Even the flickering lights of the corner liquor store seemed dimmed. The streets of Washington, D.C., were deserted, but Jill couldn't shake the feeling that some unknown pursuer was still out there and following her.

Chill! She forced herself to calm down and think of tomorrow. Soon visions of explosive headlines floated through her mind. A smile curled at the corner of her lips as she imagined the shock wave that would roll across America as its citizens unfolded their newspapers to read the words wielded by her pen. The story she had investigated for almost a year would not only change the course of history but also her life. By the next morning, lucrative job offers, media appearances, and seven-figure network deals would pour in across her desk.

But Jill's pleasant thoughts quickly faded when she heard the shuffle of feet again. Perhaps the late-morning edition might sport a different headline: "Top Senator Questioned by FBI for Reporter's Murder." She fumbled in her purse for her cell phone and felt it near the bottom. Cradling it in her hand, she pressed the on button, waiting for it to light up, but instead it flickered and died. *Why didn't I remember to put it on the charger last night?* Reaching down inside her purse again, she curled her fingers around the tiny canister of pepper spray that dangled from her key chain.

Whirling around in her head were all the "what ifs," tormenting her until she suddenly remembered that the presses had already rolled. *It's too late for the senator to get rid of me.* But this fleeting surge of confidence quickly vanished when three men emerged from the shadows and lunged at her. Attempting to back away, she realized it was too late. She was trapped.

Jill tried to keep her voice from quavering. "What do you want?" she demanded.

But the men remained silent. Breathing deeply, she commanded herself to stay calm. Hadn't she taken risks before and been in situations far more perilous than this one? Carrying large sums of money and meeting her shady informants in dark alleys late at night or in the wee hours of the morning? But then, she'd always had her cell phone in her hand and a taxi waiting. And even though she'd taken a couple of self-defense classes, there was no way she could fight off three attackers.

She began to scream. "Help me! Is anyone there? Help me, please!"

To her astonishment, the screams sent two of the perpetrators scurrying like rats into the dark alley. But the larger of the men hadn't flinched; he towered before her like a mountain.

"What do you want?" she demanded again.

With a look of arrogance the man uttered a deep groan, mockingly sending smoky clouds floating out of his mouth, permeating the cold winter air with the fragrance of cheap wine.

Muffling a faint cry, Jill searched his face, trying to determine her next move.

His dark eyes glared at her from underneath a red knit cap pulled down over his forehead. A bushy black mustache drooped down, hiding his lips, and he was clad in a pair of tight-fitting jeans and a shabby sweater riddled with holes exposing a tattooed chest. The man stepped toward her.

Suddenly, he pounced, grabbing her by the hair and trying to stuff her scarf into her mouth. Thinking quickly, she flung her briefcase at his groin, managing to spray hot pepper in his face at the same time. The man shook with rage and then staggered, enabling her to break away.

Adrenaline pumping, heart racing, Jill felt as though she had wings on her feet as she soared down the sidewalk to escape her tormentor, but goose bumps pricked her arms when she heard him cough. Turning slightly, she saw the man striding across the street after her. Frantically she hiked up her skirt and began to sprint even faster.

Jill gasped for air. Six blocks down and nine more to go. She figured there was no use wasting her energy by screaming for help, and focused every ounce of her strength on making her legs move faster toward home.

After a few more blocks her long strides had significantly widened the distance between her and the stalker. For the first time since the chase had begun, Jill believed she might make it home alive. But at the corner of Washington Avenue, she bumped into an empty newsstand. She clutched her left side as a sharp pain seared through her hip. Stumbling, she hastily struggled to get back on her feet, but she wasn't quick enough—the footsteps behind her came to an abrupt halt. A chill danced up her spine as she felt fingers coiling around her neck, dragging her backward toward a darkened alley. Biting, scratching, and screaming, she tried to escape from the attacker's powerful grasp, but his fingers squeezed even more tightly around her neck, causing her to sputter and gasp for breath.

Words from long ago sprang into her consciousness.

Yea, though I walk through the valley of the shadow of death.

Was that a Bible verse she had memorized in a long ago Sunday school class?

I will fear no evil.

The Twenty-third Psalm.

For thou art with me.

"God, please help me!" she whimpered as the lights slowly dimmed. Just at the moment she thought she would lose consciousness, a vehicle careened around the corner, screeching to an abrupt halt in front of her and her stalker. In slow motion, the attacker released his death grip; Jill's head flopped like a limp rag doll. Dizzily, she staggered toward the car.

"Need a cab, lady?" the driver called out the window. He released his seat belt and reached over to open the back door. "Get in."

Gasping for air, Jill couldn't speak but leaned into the cab and collapsed into the safety and warmth of the backseat. She glanced out the rear window. The street was vacant of any creature, alive or imagined. Turning back around, she leaned forward and let out a sigh of relief. "Sir," she rasped breathlessly, "did you see?" She paused to catch her breath. "Did you . . . did you see that man chasing me?"

"Nope, didn't see a thing. But you shouldn't have been out walking this time of night. A lot of bad stuff goes on in this town, but you can relax, lady, you're safe with me."

"Thank you," Jill mumbled. The driver's voice was reassuring.

Within moments she was stepping out of the cab in front of her apartment building. Henry, the doorman, stood waiting to let her in the building.

With a large white-gloved hand, the elderly doorman took Jill by the arm to help her out of the cab. Henry greeted her with a tip of his emblemed hat perched atop a silver Afro. Muscles bulging beneath his immaculate gray uniform, the retired FBI agent towered over Jill making her feel both safe and secure.

"You working late tonight, Miss Lewis?" Henry smiled at Jill, exposing a pair of dimples in his high-boned cheeks and a dazzling set of perfectly aligned teeth.

"Yes, a bit too late," Jill responded as she turned to pay the cabby.

But the cabby was gone.

"That's odd. He took off before I could pay him."

"Don't you worry, he'll be back for it, and I'll pay him. You get on upstairs."

Jill tried to slip money into Henry's hand, but he refused. "You can take care of it later."

"Thanks. Good night, Henry."

"It's morning," the doorman reminded her as they both

looked down at their watches to see the hands moving well past midnight.

"So it is. Uh, good morning, then, Henry."

Jill took the elevator to her tenth-floor apartment. Once inside, she dropped her purse and coat in the nearby chair and double bolted the door. Collapsing on her sofa, she put her head in her hands and sobbed into a wad of tissues.

How long she cried, she didn't know. But when the tears would no longer come, she stood up and dabbed her swollen eyes. Letting out a long sigh of relief, she walked over to the windows and looked out over the city. No boogieman looked up at her. The familiar sounds of night traffic, sirens, and voices floated up to her window. Feeling safe at last, she went to her room and dressed for bed, channel surfing to Fox News and then CNN to distract her but also half-listening to ensure that no late-breaking story would usurp her own morning headline. Within minutes her eyelids had grown heavy, and she nodded off with the lights on and the television blaring.

———

Startled awake by a noise, Jill groggily sat up in bed. There was a light tap at the door. Or was there? Reaching for the remote, she flipped off the TV and listened intently, but the room was quiet except for the distant wail of sirens and the hum of traffic beyond her window.

With shaking hands, she reached for her terry-cloth robe, pulling it around her and tying it tightly at the waist. She grabbed her tennis racket and cordless phone as she cautiously headed for the door. Straining to look through the peephole, she was relieved to see no one there. "Must've been a bad dream," she muttered to herself.

Figuring there was no way she could fall back asleep, she

headed for the kitchen and turned on the copper kettle to make a cup of chamomile tea. She stood at the stove watching the steam from the kettle rise into the air like a smoke signal. Calculating that it was still early enough on the West Coast to make a call, she dialed her boyfriend, David, who was in California.

The sound of his voice immediately began to calm the butterflies in her stomach.

"David!" she said, pouring the hot water into her china teacup. "How's your trip?"

"Hi, Jill. It's going great. We're being very well received here. The fund-raising events have gone beyond our expectations. If Senator Jacobs wasn't already slated for the party's next vice presidential candidate, I'm sure he could be elected governor in California."

Jill smiled. Everyone agreed that David had a bright future in Washington, but he chose instead to remain loyal to the man who had given him his first political post. She never ceased to be impressed by David's continued loyalty and admiration for his boss, a rarity in politics.

"Hey you . . . I miss you," she said.

"I miss you too. I was thinking that the two of us should maybe consider moving to California one day. It's eighty degrees out here."

"Sounds heavenly to me! We've reached a high of forty-five degrees here. When do I start packing?"

"You, leave Washington? I won't hold my breath," David replied. He knew her too well.

"But I doubt you'll stray far from Washington either, Mr. Chief of Staff. I'm thinking your boss will one day be our president."

"From your mouth to God's ears. Hey, what are you doing up so late . . . your investigation?"

"It's over. Finished. Morning headlines," she said proudly as she pulled back a strand of loose hair from her eyes and headed to her bedroom, carefully balancing her teacup and the phone tucked under her ear.

"Ah, so is this the big one that's changing the course of history?"

"Yep, this is the one." Jill Lewis's name had been a household word for over seven years. Even after only a couple of months at the *Washington Gazette,* she had broken a big political scandal by working with a street informant who had daily searched the trash of the president's mistress. Jill's future had been sealed with that story, but this one now was by far the biggest story she'd ever broken.

"Congratulations! You know that all the networks and cable news stations will be clamoring with offers for you, right?"

"They're wasting their time."

"Aw, come on, are you telling me that even a seven-figure paycheck won't lure you out of bed for those 4:00 A.M. camera calls?"

"I'm already up at 5:00 every day for an early morning run. I'm just more of a behind-the-scenes kind of gal."

David chuckled. "It must be nice to have such a rich daddy that you can do whatever you darn well please," he ribbed her. Then there was a long pause on his end of the phone. "Oh, Jill, I'm sorry. I just forgot. I'm such an idiot."

"Don't worry about it," she replied softly. "It's only been a year; sometimes it's even hard for me to believe my father's gone."

There was another long pause. "Come on, now, tell me who's going to be resigning in the morning?" he probed, obviously avoiding the subject of her father's death.

She laughed nervously. "You can read all about it in the paper along with the rest of the world."

"Can you at least tell me if I should be concerned about *my* job?"

Jill had always refused to discuss her work with him, and David knew this. She referred to it as a conflict of interest, considering his strong political connections. After an awkward pause she laughed. "Your job is probably safe."

Truthfully, after she had dug deeper and deeper into her investigation, the thought had crossed her mind that David's boss, Senator Jacobs, might be involved in the scandal. Much to her relief, Jacobs had come out squeaky clean. In fact, with Senator Burke's political ruin, she believed the party would elevate Jacobs from vice presidential candidate to the presidential slot.

"Good! If your story is put to bed, tell me, what are you doing up so late?" David's question jarred her back into the conversation.

"I . . . uh . . . I'm just nervous about tomorrow, I guess."

"Come on. What's wrong?"

Jill cleared her throat. "All right. I was walking home from the office, and some creepy guy came out of nowhere and started chasing after me." She fought tears as the memory of the terrifying attack came flooding back.

"Oh my goodness, Jill, are you okay? Were you hurt?"

"I'm fine—a cab showed up just in time. I feel very lucky."

"Well, you might not be so lucky the next time. What in the world were you thinking, walking home alone? You could've been killed!" He blew out a frustrated breath. "Dealing with all those shady informants, you know you have to watch your back all the time. How could you have been so stupid?"

"I guess I just—"

"Did you call the police?"

"I tried, but my cell phone was dead, and then when the cab came the guy took off so I figured he would be long gone by the time the cops arrived."

"How many times have I told you to carry a spare battery? It just astounds me that a woman of your accomplishments, especially one with your street smarts, can be such a flake!"

She began to get angry. He was grilling her like he was some hotshot prosecuting attorney. "I was just preoccupied with the investigation, and—"

"That's no excuse." He sighed. "Listen, Jill. I didn't mean to lecture you. You're safe and that's all that matters, but you've got to promise me you'll never walk home alone again."

"Okay, I promise."

"All right, then, let's forget about it. Today's your big day. I'll be back in a week, and we'll celebrate. I love you, Jill."

"Love you too, David. Bye." After putting the phone back in the charger, she climbed into bed and pulled her down comforter over her head.

So David thought she was a flake, huh? Well, he had good reason, she reckoned, suddenly trembling with the memory of her close encounter with death. If he had reacted so strongly over this little episode, how would he react if her story ruined his boss's political career, trashing his own in the process? She had been confident that Jacobs would be the party's nominee for president after Burke was ousted, but what if the public turned on Jacobs because of his association with Burke?

Jill tossed and turned; sleep was elusive. A flurry of thoughts whirled around in her head. The cab driver's sudden appearance saved her from the attacker. She was lucky to be alive! But was it luck? Perhaps God had intervened on her behalf for some divine purpose. Or was it a coincidence that the cab pulled up moments after she called out to God? Having ignored him for so long, she knew God didn't owe her any favors. Yet how else could it be explained?

Jill stared at the ceiling until her clock radio blared at 5:00 A.M. Silencing the alarm, she kicked off the covers and took a deep breath. The biggest ride of her life was only hours away.

2

The queen turned crimson with fury,
And after glaring at her for a moment like a wild beast,
Began screaming, "Off with her head! Off with—"

—Lewis Carroll

Towering over Washington, the steel gray building that housed the *Washington Gazette* commanded a breathtaking view of the nation's capital on one side and the Potomac on the other. Jill Lewis clutched her leather briefcase before pushing through the heavy revolving door to escape the blustery cold winds.

As she brushed the snow from her black cashmere coat, Jill entered the impressive lobby, rhythmically clicking her trendy Prada heels across the marble floor and talking on her cell phone. Although she hadn't slept much, she felt on top of the world. The events of the previous night were a distant memory. This was a new day—her day. The newspaper staff would throw a traditional celebration in her honor today.

"Rubric, not now, please," Jill begged. "I'll see you when I get upstairs. I promise. I have to go now; my publicist is on the other line." She disconnected from her editor and switched over to the other call. The *Gazette's* publisher, Annabelle Stone, had recently hired a publicity firm to handle the flood of media requests she had anticipated would follow the publication of Jill's explosive undercover investigation. Although Jill had balked at the suggestion, she was now grateful for Annabelle's foresight.

"Hi, I'm back. Sorry for the interruption. Okay, so I'm taping CNN this afternoon and then I take a train to New York to do *The Today Show* tomorrow morning, *Fox News* in the afternoon, and *Primetime News* in the evening? Great, got it! Thanks so much. Bye." Jill clicked off the phone and shoved it in her purse.

She paused to chat with Helen, who daily dispensed wisdom and warmth along with the papers at the small newsstand in the lobby.

"You go, girlfriend." Helen fanned her hand across the racks below her. "Every newspaper and network in the world is carrying *your* story, child."

A quick glance at the racks brought dozens of images of the tight-lipped, unsmiling Senator Tom Burke, one of the most powerful men in Washington. The senator icily stared back at Jill from the front page, a welcome change from the toothy grin that usually stretched across the width of the paper. Jill smiled; she was on the "A" list now.

Just then, a voice from *The Today Show* blared out of Helen's tiny television set above the counter. "Investigative reporter Jill Lewis of the *Washington Gazette* has alleged that Senator Tom Burke's foundation, Hope International, once believed to be a philanthropic organization that supported orphanages throughout the world and arranged for adoptions in the United States, is a multimillion-dollar clearinghouse that buys babies from Romania and other impoverished overseas countries . . ."

Recognizing the subject of the newscast standing in their midst, several patrons began to applaud. Jill bowed demurely.

"These children were sold to the highest bidder in the United States without any background investigations of the families who adopted them," the voice from the TV continued. "Only yesterday, the senator was his party's favorite for the White House, but today his political career lies in ruins, with the president calling for an FBI investigation. Tune in tomorrow when *Washington Gazette* reporter Jill Lewis will appear on *The Today Show*."

Jill turned away from the TV and picked up her usual stash of chocolate. Feeling pressured from Rubric's phone call, she hesitated whether or not to stand in the long, winding line, but since she hadn't slept, she figured the Hershey bars were worth the risk of his ire. Impatiently tapping her left shoe, she calculated that there were at least a dozen people ahead of her.

Rubric would be furious if he saw her in this line, but she figured the rest of her colleagues would be grateful for the extra time to set up the balloons, banners, and cake for her party. *Mmm. I hope the cake is chocolate.*

Her daydreams suddenly evaporated when a businessman swooped into the newsstand to grab a newspaper and then filed into the line behind her. Clearly as impatient as Jill, the man began to jingle a pocketful of change.

Suddenly a woman with big hair and big bosoms who was teetering precariously on stiletto heels bumped into the man. Ping, ping, ping. The coins he had been clutching in his hand scattered over the marble floor. Instinctively Jill stooped to help the man retrieve the change. Her blonde head bumped his sandy brown one as they simultaneously reached for one of the coins.

"Sorry about that," both said in unison.

Jill looked directly into cornflower blue eyes that crinkled at the corners. "Here you go." She smiled and returned the money to his hand.

"Thanks. I'd hate to lose this. It's a very sentimental coin." His smile dazzled her as he held a particular silver piece up in the air for her to examine. "I think you deserve a reward. How about a cup of coffee next door?"

"I, uh . . ." Jill stammered, looking down at his shiny new shoes. She wanted to accept his invitation, but she was anxious to get to the office for her big celebration.

"Are you feeling all right?" he inquired politely, reaching over to steady her with his hand.

"Perfectly fine," she said as she felt her face heat up. Struggling to regain her composure, she tried to think of something clever to say. *How ironic. The prolific wordsmith is speechless.* She focused on the coin. Pointing to it she asked, "What's so special about that one?"

"My grandmother wore this sixpence in her shoe on her wedding day," he explained.

She took the sixpence to examine it more closely. "Something old, something new, and a lucky sixpence in your shoe!" she impulsively sang out.

"You know more about all this than I do, I see," the stranger said. "I promised my grandmother I would carry on the family tradition and give this coin to the girl I'm going to marry."

"You're engaged?" Jill felt a slight wave of disappointment.

"No."

"Well, you really shouldn't be carrying something like that around in your pocket," she admonished, slowly regaining her composure. "What would your grandmother say if you lost it?"

Before the man could reply, she heard a voice calling out her name. "Hey, Jill! Jill Lewis!" Bob Alderson, a lawyer from the firm on the twenty-ninth floor, plowed up to her, tripping over people's feet and abruptly ending her cozy tête-à-tête with the blue-eyed stranger. Bob then managed to insert himself and his newspaper between Jill and the man whose sixpence she still held in her hand.

"Quite a spread about you this morning! How about a celebration drink sometime? Or is David keeping you too busy?"

Flashing Bob a look of exasperation, Jill pushed down his newspaper with her hand so she could see the man who owned the sixpence. But he was no longer there; the blue-eyed stranger had vanished.

Clutching the sixpence tightly, she abandoned her place in line and dashed about the lobby to find him and return the valuable coin. *Okay, Jill, what did he look like? Great blue eyes, shiny shoes. Not much to go on, but I've cracked cases with fewer clues.* Ducking into the nearby coffee shop, she perused the eyes of strangers but didn't find him. She wished she had concentrated on his face and not been so uncharacteristically bashful. Quickly whirling between the revolving doors to the outside, she saw no trace of the stranger. He was gone. Poof!

After walking back into the newsstand, she asked Bob Alderson, "Did you happen to see where the guy who was standing behind me went?"

Bob snorted. "Must not like reporters! When he heard your name he tossed his newspaper on the counter and ran out of here like his shoes were on fire."

"Very funny, Bob." Jill scowled and crossed her arms.

"Hey, what do you care, Lewis?" He bopped her arm with his newspaper. "Or is your love life heading south?"

"I have his heirloom coin. I only wanted to return it to him." She shrugged her shoulders and slipped the coin safely in the hidden compartment of her wallet.

"Lucky coin? Nice pickup line . . . I'll have to remember that one." He smoothed his beard thoughtfully with his free hand.

Jill turned away from him and handed Helen five dollars. "Did you see the guy next to me in line, the one who dropped the coins?"

"No, honey, I didn't get a look at his face," Helen said as she handed her the change.

"If he comes back to claim this coin, will you give him my number?"

"Sure, sweetie." Helen smiled, showing her white teeth outlined in orange lipstick. "If it's important to him, he'll be back. You go on now and enjoy your big day."

Jill glowed with the fresh congratulatory greetings she received upon entering the elevator as it sent the early morning office workers skyward. But when she stepped out on the thirty-seventh floor, she felt crestfallen when no one heralded her arrival. She hadn't expected a brass band, but a few balloons would've been nice. There wasn't even the usual bouquet waiting for her at the desk. Her highly anticipated "unexpected surprise" had fizzled. Or had everyone grown tired of waiting for her?

"Jill, they're waiting in the executive conference room," the receptionist explained between phone calls, nodding her head in the direction of the room.

"Aha, so that's where they're all hiding. Now tell me, who's waiting for me? Names, give me names!" Jill slapped the counter with her open hand.

The receptionist's reply was to shove a handful of pink messages at Jill.

"Come on, Landry," she begged. "Who's in there?"

"Oh, just about everybody from this newspaper, including the grande dame herself."

"Not Annabelle! Did you say Annabelle is here?" The newspaper publisher was taking Jill to lunch later, but they really must've planned a shindig if they got the boss lady to the office that early.

"Rubric said you were to go down there the minute you walked in the door," the receptionist added tersely.

"That man has the patience of an angry rattlesnake. Oh, well, I'm here now. Thanks, Landry!"

Jill hastily scanned the messages, happy she had decided on the pink fingernail polish that perfectly matched her mother's recent gift to her from Saks—an expensive black crepe Chloe suit featuring a flared skirt and a jacket piped in hot pink with a peplum waist.

As Jill hurried in the opposite direction of the conference room, a surprised Landry called after her. "Where do you think you're going? I told you, they're waiting for you! Get in there!"

"Have to freshen up," Jill replied flippantly. As she walked down the hall, several coworkers stared at their feet or suddenly became interested in a file they were carrying. Not a good sign. Jealousy was already beginning to raise its ugly head. Well, she would just prove to them all that she could be magnanimous in her fame.

Inside her office, Jill slid out of her coat and stood before the large windows, watching the heavy snowflakes fall gently around the White House. This was better than a birthday! Maybe after her party she would make snow angels all over Capitol Hill. And tomorrow the headlines would read: "Jill Lewis Declared Angel after Saving Her Country from the Evil Senator Burke."

She decided her admiring court could wait a few more minutes while she rehearsed her speech one more time. It was important to keep it short and simple. She had to remember to appear humbled by their admiration. One final look in the mirror, a puff of powder on her nose, a fresh swipe of lipstick across her lips, a smoothing of her hair, and she was finally ready to party.

Slowly walking down the hall, she savored every moment, each footstep, knowing there was nothing in this world that could compare to how she felt at this very minute. The world was hers if she wanted it. And she did. Reaching for the large brass knobs on the conference room's double doors, Jill twisted them. Flinging wide the doors, she stepped inside the room, smiling triumphantly with the right amount of surprise on her face.

A stony silence greeted her. Gazing about the room, she recognized several men and women from the FBI, a couple of aides to politicians, numerous colleagues whom she respected, and enough lawyers to populate a D.C. high-rise. And at the end of the table, facing her, stood Annabelle Stone; to her left stood Senator Burke's attorney, Mr. Chambers, who was attempting to fold his fat arms over his expansive midriff. Jill nodded her head in greeting, then gulped hard, feeling her staged smile of surprise sliding into true shock.

Tapping a thick folder of files with her long acrylic nails, Annabelle, resplendent in a red Armani power suit, spoke in snappy, amplified tones. "Good morning, Miss Lewis. Thank you for finally making time for us."

"What's going on?" Jill melted into the chair Rubric held out for her.

"I tried to warn you, but you hung up on me," he whispered sharply in her ear.

It finally sunk in that this was no party. It looked more like a lynching. Hers. But why? Looking down at her expensive suit, she felt ridiculously overdressed for the occasion. Fidgeting uncomfortably, her eyes scanned the room, searching desperately for a friendly face.

Yet when she caught Rubric's eye, he gazed down at his hands and began picking his nails.

Annabelle Stone stood at the head of the conference table with an ominous pile of documents spread out before her. She glanced at Jill then turned away, as though she were an executioner reluctant to look into the eyes of her victim. "You should find these documents very interesting, Miss Lewis. A good reporter would already have had these in her hands." Slowly and dramatically she slid them across the table.

An eerie silence pervaded the room. Jill, sitting straight, shoulders back, began flipping through the papers that supposedly documented every adoption conducted by the senator's organization. These documents had probably been meticulously prepared with each adoption and stashed in a safe, waiting for the day Senator Burke would be challenged. Jill was confident she could find something there to disprove their validity, but there was no time now, and besides, it was hard to concentrate with all eyes in the room glaring at her.

"These documents tell me that the paper has been put in an unfortunate position of accusing an innocent man. Tell me, Miss Lewis, how did that happen?" Annabelle demanded, snapping her fingers to elicit a rapid response.

Jill knew Annabelle would immediately suspend her; she had no choice. The young reporter's heart began to thump wildly. Why couldn't she find the words to defend herself? She knew Burke was guilty, and she had the evidence to prove it.

Her neck began to ache; the pain grew up along both sides of her temples. Glancing up, she hoped someone would jump to her defense. But no one moved. Sitting to Annabelle's right, the senator's lawyer appeared powerful despite his oversized stomach and thinning hair. He looked as if he was eager for a high-profile legal battle to defend his high-paying client.

Mr. Chambers' wry smile was her undoing as he spoke. "While we do not doubt that these sorts of atrocities go on all the time, Miss Lewis, you have implicated an innocent man. I believe these papers will show that Senator Burke did indeed receive several million dollars for his campaign fund, but you will also note that this . . . contribution . . . was from his family foundation that supports, not profits from their orphanages throughout the world. It's all here in the files. The senator has not profited one cent from the organization, and every adoption conducted through these orphanages is completely legitimate."

The world was spinning. Jill massaged her forehead, not willing to believe she had failed so miserably. Rubric sat next to her, breathing so heavily she could hardly hear her seething publisher speak.

"Two days ago Senator Burke's lawyers requested we delay the publication of your story until they could provide a documented rebuttal. Because you *were* a highly respected investigative reporter with an excellent track record, we refused."

"You did the right thing. I stand by my story," Jill proclaimed as she jumped to her feet.

"Please sit down, Ms. Lewis; I'm not finished."

"But I . . ." Jill hesitated until Rubric grabbed her arm and pulled her back into the chair.

"Later that day," Annabelle continued, "the FBI summoned our lawyers along with Burke's legal team. The agency not only compared your documentation with Burke's records, but they also conducted a mini-investigation of their own."

"Why wasn't I notified?" Jill demanded angrily.

Ignoring her, Annabelle motioned for a large muscular man

across the table to stand. "Agent Clark, will you please tell us the results of your investigation?"

Everyone looked to the large man, who looked more like a Redskins linebacker than an FBI agent, as he lumbered to his feet to speak. "After reviewing the documents and the financial records of the Burke family's foundation, the FBI has concluded that the practices and procedures of Hope International are impeccable."

"Aha! Then how do you explain that the adoptive parents are willing to refute that fact?" Jill spoke out of order again.

"Ms. Lewis," an exasperated Annabelle ordered, "will you please not interrupt?"

"I'm happy to address Ms. Lewis's concerns," Agent Clark offered. Annabelle nodded for the agent to continue. "A sampling of the adoptive families on your lists were contacted, Ms. Lewis, and while they admitted to meeting with you, they also complied with our request to FedEx their adoption paperwork. The agency has reviewed it, and everything is legit."

Sighs, gasps, and voices arose throughout the room. Jill leaned over and whispered sarcastically to Rubric. "After Burke threatened them with the loss of their children and then provided the necessary documentation to them."

Tapping her pen loudly on the table for order, Annabelle thanked Agent Clark and in a voice several octaves higher leaned toward Jill and said, "Too bad it was too late for us to stop the presses! Tell me, Ms. Lewis, how does a reporter with your background and experience overlook important documentation?"

"I . . . uh," Jill stammered. "Before I comment, I would like to wait until I've had an opportunity to review these documents." She flicked the thick file before her.

"No," Annabelle retorted. "But this is what I will do. I will have the paper print a retraction and formal apology in the next edition, and I will expect your resignation on my desk immediately."

"Resignation?" She had expected to be suspended without pay, but forced to resign? To resign would mean the end of her career—she would never work at a major newspaper again. She stared at Annabelle. Once this powerful woman had liked her, trusted her, and that was only yesterday. Jill knew that no matter what, business was always business with Annabelle—she would give her life for the *Washington Gazette* and would not hesitate to sacrifice Jill's either.

Finding a surprise burst of energy, Jill jumped to her feet. "This can't be. There has to be a mistake."

"Oh, it's a mistake all right—a mistake of inaccurate reporting. Yours."

"But I have proof, documentation!" Jill drummed her fingers on the table. "This is not the last of it."

"It better be the end of it!" Annabelle snapped, her voice at full volume as she cut Jill's inquisition short.

Jill could feel a flush creep up the side of her neck and blossom on her cheeks.

"Come with me, kid," Rubric mumbled sympathetically. He grabbed her by her wrist, leading her from the room and slamming the door behind them.

Jill stood on the rug in Rubric's office, grimacing as she surveyed the nine-by-twelve room stacked to the ceiling with banker boxes. She never knew what she might come across when entering his office . . . a dead body? Faded paperback crime stories and dog-eared murder mysteries crammed the bookcases that lined the walls, and all around the room ashtrays were heaped with soot and ashes and overflowing with old cigarette butts. Half-eaten sandwiches were drying out or molding in their cellophane wrappers.

Rubric slouched behind his large oak partner's desk and

grunted for Jill to sit in the only available seat in the office, a dark green overstuffed chair. Sinking down into the cushions, she felt the broken springs press into her backside. She tried to avoid leaning back or resting her arms on the sides of the dirty chair that was stained with no telling what.

"What's going on?" Jill demanded. "You examined all my documents throughout my investigation. How did this new documentation suddenly appear out of nowhere?"

Reaching across the cluttered desk for a pack of unfiltered Camels, Rubric tried to tap a cigarette out of the crumpled pack, but it was empty. Tossing it into his trash can, he frantically searched the piles on his desk until he spotted another pack. He grabbed the Camels and snatched a cigarette out of the foil with his teeth, struck a match from a book bearing the logo of Diamond Jim's Steak House, and lit up. After inhaling a deep drag from the cigarette, Rubric leaned back in his leather chair. "Ahh, I needed this." Sounding almost apologetic that he was ignoring the newspaper's nonsmoking policy, he added, "What I really need is a drink, but it's too early even for me."

Jill blinked her eyes as his smoke rings floated in her direction.

"Appears to me your source has framed you. Burke's foundation is totally legit. You bet your money on the wrong horse this time, or at least one too rambunctious for even me to handle."

"You're wrong, Rubric. My informant is on the inside. Senator Tom Burke is guilty!" Jill slid forward in the chair.

"Well, how come your informant didn't know these documents existed?" Rubric asked, propping his bad leg up on the desk.

"This documentation was probably fabricated and stashed in the safe for extra insurance against an investigation," Jill guessed. "I'll bet Burke and his lawyer were the only ones who knew about it."

"Sounds to me like your informant might have switched some names on you."

"No way. My informant provided copies of files on literally hundreds of adoptions that were illegal, and they all checked out. And the families confirmed that they were not investigated, that they paid over one hundred thousand dollars for each child they adopted."

"Do you know why these families betrayed you?" Rubric pondered.

"Duh. I told you . . . Burke's people likely threatened them with the loss of their children."

"But now because of Burke's documentation and the denial of those families, the FBI will put your files on the back burner and delay any investigation," Rubric surmised.

"Exactly. And by the time they get around to checking them out, it'll be too late." Jill sighed. "Burke will already be in the White House."

"Unless, of course," Rubric interjected, "you find another avenue of proof that will lead to Burke."

Jill knew Rubric was baiting her, and she jumped at the bait. "I know Burke's our man!"

"So *now* you've found your voice! Why didn't you speak up in that room! Shoulda showed more backbone."

Jill pointed at the doorway. "That was a lynching in there! In case you failed to notice, I was outnumbered and I couldn't think."

"Well, while you couldn't think, they had hard evidence. Jillie, you have made some very powerful people very unhappy, and you've made this paper look pretty bad on top of that. The Stone ain't happy. And when the paper's owner isn't happy, ain't nobody happy."

"I stand by my convictions. I know I'm right, but can I salvage this?" Jill's brain began clicking. "Rubric, get me a copy of Annabelle's report on Burke's documentation, okay?"

"Are you asking me to put my head on the chopping block? I'm too close to retirement to go there."

Jill couldn't help but chuckle. "Rube, no offense, but you are way past retirement!"

He winked. "Take your medicine like a big girl, and when this all blows over, we'll get our bad guy." He stood up to extinguish his cigarette.

"And what am I supposed to do in the meantime?" she fumed, knowing Rubric had been canned before too but always had a way of showing back up at his desk after a day or two. Well, she might not be so lucky. Whatever his magic was, she could use a dose of it now.

"Get a husband, take a vacation, whatever makes you happy," he said nonchalantly, swinging his bad leg to work out the kinks.

"But Rubric, *this* is my life, it's what makes me happy! I can't imagine doing anything else."

"Then get another life. You're not the first reporter to have your world turned upside down, and believe me, you won't be the last. It's out of my hands."

"I just can't sit back and do nothing! I checked and re-checked my facts! Senator Tom Burke is not Snow White!" Jill glared at her editor. "I'm going to nail him . . . eventually."

He held up his hands in protest. "All right, all right, I believe you." He paused for a moment. "Say, who was your informant?"

"You know I can't tell you that."

"Not his real name. What's his street name?"

"The Elf."

Rubric chuckled. "One of Santa's elves?"

"Well, he's small and wiry and seems to know everyone's business without anyone seeing him. Despite his size, he's a force on the staff. I trusted him."

"Well, my girl, it's time you learned there is no Santa Claus. Maybe the Elf man sold you a bill of goods."

"He would never do that." Jill stood up. Spinning, spinning . . . her head was spinning as she left Rubric's office and walked stoically down the hall. She was taken aback to see all the moving boxes that had been placed there in her absence. *Annabelle sure didn't waste any time.*

Collapsing in her desk chair, she dialed David's number, longing to hear his voice. Yes, his voice would make it all better. But she only got his recording. Slamming down the receiver with a vengeance, she looked around her office one last time. She wanted to get out of there before the movers showed up to carry her out on the street.

Pulling out a box of disguises that she had stashed for her undercover work, she selected a long red wig, a knit cap, and a pair of horn-rimmed glasses. She exchanged her sexy shoes for a pair of boots and slid into her black coat. Even Landry didn't recognize her when she walked toward the elevator.

As Jill passed Helen's newsstand on her way out of the building, she heard the television blaring still. "Late breaking news—Senator Tom Burke was cleared this morning of charges when . . ."

3

"Washington Gazette Retracts Story"
"Senator Tom Burke Cleared of Accusations"
"Noted Gazette *Investigative Reporter Jill Lewis Resigns"*

Fortunately no news reporter who recognized Jill awaited her at the steps of the *Gazette* building. She quickly blended into the crowd of workers streaming off to lunch and walked aimlessly through the park for an hour until she flopped on a park bench to try David's cell phone again.

At the sound of his voice, she burst into tears.

"Jill, I heard." He sounded irritated. "What in the world were you thinking? Why didn't you thrash this out with me first? I could have told you Burke is Mr. Clean. They're going to bury you alive."

"They already have," she said, trying to keep a sob out of her voice. "I've been . . . I've been fired."

"Fired?"

"After all this came down, I expected to be suspended, but not fired!"

David gulped. "This is worse than I imagined. What are you going to do?"

"Well, I plan to spend the rest of my days proving Burke is guilty."

"Don't waste your time," David snapped. "I know him. He's strictly legit. Whoever your informant was had another motive . . . maybe to hang you?"

Jill realized it was useless to argue with David. Like so many others, he had put Burke on a pedestal. Frustrated, she pulled out a hankie and blew her nose.

"I'm sorry, Jill. Whether you like it or not, Burke is going to be the next president of the United States. Why would you risk your brilliant career going after the people's choice . . . especially on something as insignificant as an adoption scandal? How on earth did you get into this?" He took a deep breath. "Oh, forget it. Is there anything I can do for you now?"

"Come home?" Jill sniffed, ignoring his previous comments. She needed him and couldn't afford to lose another supporter.

"What would I tell Jacobs? 'By the way, Senator, I have to leave to take care of Jill, the person who single-handedly tried to destroy your career.'"

"That's not true," Jill objected. "It was Burke I was after, not Jacobs."

"And who is Burke's proposed running mate?"

"Jacobs had nothing to lose and everything to gain if Burke was found guilty."

After a long pause he said, "Look, I'm sorry. There's no use arguing over this now. I'll get home as quickly as I can. In the meantime, is there anything I can do from here?"

"I can't go home. Reporters are staked out everywhere. I was wondering if I could hide out in your condo for a few days or at least until I can figure out what to do. Or where to go."

"Sure. You have a key. Make yourself at home."

Jill was reluctant to say good-bye. "When are you coming home?" she asked, needing to feel his arms around her.

"Maybe Friday. I'll call and let you know. Hang in there."

No "I love you. I believe in you. I'm sorry. I support you." Just a click of the phone had ended their conversation. She knew her story had upset David, and even more so the news of her firing. His greatest political asset had become his biggest liability overnight.

———

Struggling to unlock the door at David's condo, Jill couldn't recall how she got there. A huge sigh of relief left her lungs as she stepped inside the foyer. She tried to focus on her surroundings, but the room began to tilt this way and that way. With her red, swollen eyes closed, she steadied herself against the door and then slid down, knocking the light switch to off. Darkness enveloped her as she landed in a crumpled heap on the floor. Too exhausted to move, she pulled her arms out of the sleeves of her coat and folded it into a pillow and then cried herself to sleep.

It was after 9:30 P.M. when she awakened. Dazed, she rubbed her eyes and her stiff neck and slowly stood to her feet. Feeling famished for food and comfort, she checked her cell phone on the way to the kitchen. Still no word from David. Like everyone else in Washington, he was avoiding her. But he had to come home for fresh socks eventually, didn't he?

Opening the refrigerator door, she pulled out a container of nonfat, sugar-free yogurt. It tasted cold and delicious. She licked it off her lips and carried the container into the living room. Curling up on David's leather sofa, she pulled a luxurious cashmere throw around her shoulders and spooned the yogurt slowly until it was gone and she had scraped the container clean. She kicked off her shoes and dropped the empty plastic container on the floor, then stretched out on the sofa.

But sleep didn't return. After a half hour of tossing and turning she sat up and went back into the kitchen to find something else to eat. Perusing the contents of the fridge, she noted that all of David's designer foods were stacked neatly and in order of their nutritional value. Normally she considered David's fastidiousness a positive trait; today it irritated her.

Eyeing the alluring bottles of wine that were carefully arranged in the rack above the refrigerator, Jill considered this alternative. A glass of wine would relax her and put her to sleep, but drinking in a crisis to numb her pain could quickly develop into a nasty habit. She fought off the temptation.

So instead she wandered around the condo before stopping at the hall closet. Opening the door, she spotted a blue blazer with brass buttons engraved with David's initials. Holding a sleeve to her nose, she breathed in David's lingering scent, allowing it to intoxicate her senses with pleasant memories. She took the coat off the hanger and used it as a security blanket when she returned to the couch. Soon she was fast asleep.

She awoke with a jolt. "Please let this all be a bad dream! This cannot be happening!" she pleaded aloud to the empty room. *Not to Jill Lewis . . . ace reporter, former cheerleader, class president.* She'd sacrificed everything and everybody for her career, holding even David at arm's length. And for what? The poor guy had waited patiently for her all this time; surely he had done so because he cared for her and not because she was one of Washington's brightest rising stars. But now that her star had fallen, maybe he would desert her like her colleagues at the *Gazette*. Had he already deserted her? Where was he? Why hadn't he called?

The last time she had felt like an outcast was in the ninth grade when she stood alone at lunch, the victim of ridicule and gossip by a jealous classmate. The memory brought a familiar ache as she recalled the rumor about her, the football player, and the unmentionable things they had supposedly done behind the gym. Ashamed, Jill hadn't told her parents what was troubling her, but after weeks of misery it all came tumbling out at the dinner table one night. And her mother and father had known just what to do.

"You have done nothing wrong. Ignore them and go on like nothing has happened," her mother had advised.

"Hold your head high," her father had urged, promising her it would all blow over soon.

Well, maybe that advice was as good today as it had been years ago. She hoped so, because she was going to take it.

Pacing the floor, she began to study on a plan for her future. Without a job Jill couldn't support herself and afford to continue her investigation. The phone bills and travel expenses alone would devour her savings. With a job, there would be no time to devote to the investigation; it would literally take years for her to clear her name and reclaim her position at the *Gazette.* So what was she supposed to do in the meantime? Jill continued to pace like a lion in its cage . . . back and forth, back and forth.

Filled with a sudden inspiration, she stopped. "Haven't I just turned thirty? And how many times has David proposed to me?" His attempts to talk her into marriage had come so frequently, she hadn't been able to keep up with the number of his proposals. In the past her career had consumed her and there was never enough time to really focus on her relationship with David, much less plan a wedding. For the first time in her life, she had time, and she loved David. "Why not marry him?" *Yes, I will marry David now and live happily ever after,* she resolved. Who knows, maybe she would surprise him and be the one to propose this time. Being an Alexandria politician's wife wouldn't be so bad . . . would it?

Jill sat on the sofa and twirled her hair between her index finger and her thumb. She had put marriage off for so long, but finally there was time for it. Now she would focus on her personal life instead of her career. Her days would be dedicated to whatever job she could find—maybe a speechwriter? Then her weekends and evenings would be devoted to her husband. But each night when David fell asleep she would climb quietly out of bed, tiptoe to her study, and work until the wee hours of the morning to solve her case. The perfect plan!

And what about writing that great American novel after her name was cleared? An ideal project for a loving wife. Maybe she would even become the female Grisham. Then the shame of being humiliated and fired from the *Gazette* would disappear like yesterday's news. Of course, she'd have to come up with a pen name. Jane Livingston? Leslie Longtree? Who would want to read a book by Jill Lewis?

As she sat back down on the sofa, her mother's tender words suddenly popped into her head: "God doesn't close a door without opening a window. One day you will look back on this situation and say it was the best thing that ever happened to you." She doubted that was true, but she needed something to keep her mind on for a while, before she could even think about tackling Burke.

After showering, she hungrily consumed two more containers of yogurt and then raced off to catch the Metro—the luxury of a cab was something she could no longer afford. Emerging from the subway tunnel, she scanned the headlines at the newsstand. Seeing her name plastered on them made her feel sick. Maybe it was a good thing she was resigning from the rat race for a while. The perfect time to plan a wedding.

Although yesterday she had fumed when Rubric suggested marriage, today it seemed like a brilliant idea.

When she made a quick stop at the market to pick up groceries, she ignored the dairy and produce and went right to the chocolate. *No telling how long I'll be a captive in my home.* Then she stopped at several newsstands and a bookstore to buy bride magazines and a few wedding planner books. Although the chocolate was quite light, the magazines and books were heavy, and she struggled to carry her purchases down the street. While walking the last two blocks to her apartment, she called Henry to ask him to meet her at the side entrance so she could avoid the waiting reporters.

"Miss Lewis!" Henry motioned her to duck into the side door to avoid the throng of reporters. Then the kind doorman took her packages upstairs for her. Throughout Jill's career, Henry had become accustomed to the reporters who would occasionally come and take over the sidewalk. He knew the good ones and the bad ones, and all of them by name as well as by their antics. More importantly, he had become a pro at protecting Jill.

"I just want to tell you that I don't believe a word they're saying about you," he added before leaving.

Jill blushed. "Thank you, Henry. I appreciate that. Did the taxi driver ever show up to collect his cab fare?"

"No, he didn't." Henry didn't skip a beat. "It's none of my business, but if you ask me, you should settle down and find yourself a nice young man to marry."

She took the bags of books from Henry's arms. "Well, I might just do that." She paused before heading inside. "Aren't you surprised the cabbie never came back?"

"Nothing ever surprises me anymore, especially in this city. You take care, Miss Lewis. I'll be praying for you."

"Thank you, Henry." Jill smiled, tucking a twenty-dollar bill in his pocket. *Enjoy it, this is your last big tip.*

Later, she was eating a Hershey bar and thumbing her way through a bridal magazine when her unlisted phone rang. Noting David's number on the caller ID box, she grabbed it.

"David!"

"Jill, how are you?"

"Thank goodness it's you, and thank you for letting me use your condo to get my head together. I'm ready to face the world again." Of course, she didn't let on how irritated she felt that he hadn't bothered to call in the last twenty-four hours. *No man wants a nagging wife,* she reminded herself.

"That's my girl! Hey, I knew they couldn't keep you down for long. Say, I'll be home on Friday and was wondering if we could get together Saturday night to talk about our future."

So soon? Jill's heart quickened. She and David were obviously on the same wavelength. "Great!"

After she hung up the phone, she reached for a bridal magazine and hummed the tune of "Here Comes the Bride." Thoughts of reopening her investigation were fleeting. She was washing her hands of the whole thing. If the citizens of this country were stupid enough to elect Burke as their president, then they deserved what they got.

By the end of the day she had picked out her ring as well as china, crystal, and silver patterns, the flowers, her wedding gown, the bridesmaid dresses, and the wedding cake. She was searching the Internet for a honeymoon spot when Henry buzzed the apartment.

"I've got a large package for you down here, Miss Lewis."

"Who is it from?"

"Not sure. No return address on it. A fellow just dropped it off with only your name on it. I'll leave it outside your door, ma'am."

When the package arrived, she crept out into the hallway. She recognized Rubric's loopy handwriting—it was the copies of Annabelle's files that he had promised her. She walked back to her desk and set the package aside, continuing her search on the Internet for the perfect honeymoon spot.

4

Pussy said to the owl, "You elegant fowl!
How charmingly sweet you sing!
O let us be married! Too long we have tarried;
But what shall we do for a ring?"

—Edward Lear

It seemed as though Saturday would never come, but finally David arrived at her door for their big date. Jill took a deep breath and swung the door open, ready for a new chapter in her life.

"Wow! You look gorgeous." David's eyes looked as though they might pop out of his head when he saw her. Putting his arms around her waist, he nuzzled her and kissed her on the neck, maybe catching a whiff of the expensive perfume that the salesgirl at Saks had promised would render Jill unforgettable.

It's working, Jill thought to herself. She hated to shop, but the hours she had invested choosing the perfect black dress, the sexy Manolo Blahnik leather shoes, and the heavenly fragrance had obviously been worth the sacrifice. She had dazzled David.

David looked wonderful to her, too. The California sun had sprinkled a smattering of butterscotch freckles across his perfect nose that appeared to have been carved by a master sculptor. A blonde-haired, blue-eyed surfer who grew up in Malibu, he was tall and slender with broad shoulders and a movie star grin. When Jill was out with David, people looked enviously at her, but truthfully she was more attracted by his intelligence and ambition. First in his Harvard undergrad class, David had also attended Harvard Law School, where he made *Law Review* not once but twice.

He escorted her to the street, where Henry winked at Jill and summoned a taxi. Since several days had passed, most of the reporters who had gathered outside Jill's apartment building had scattered to the next scandal du jour. Yet she and David were still subjected to the stares of all the passersby who recognized her famous face.

"Ever feel like you're being stared at?" Jill whispered into David's ear.

"I can't take my eyes off of you either. You look ravishing."

"You're sweet, but we both know why they're staring."

David's body stiffened slightly, and his right arm, which was firmly ensconced around her waistline, dropped from her side. "Well, I guess you can't expect the public to be kind. Tom Burke is the people's choice. The country nearly lost their hero, and they probably see you as the reason."

Jill shot him a look, trying to decide if his voice was playful or critical.

Once inside the cab, David relaxed a little and reached over to hold her hand. Eyeing his pockets, Jill tried to figure out where he had stashed the little blue box from Tiffany's.

"One twenty-two South Fairfax. Old Town Alexandria," David ordered the driver.

Surprised, Jill sat straight up. "Your place?"

"I thought we'd have dinner at my condo. We need to talk. Remember?"

"About our future." She settled back down in her seat but was surprised David hadn't chosen a more romantic setting. Wasn't this the same guy who had rented a billboard on that busy stretch of Virginia highway to wish her a happy birthday a year ago? Closing her eyes, Jill tried to imagine what it would be like to be married to David and one day, have a family. At last she was ready to swap politics for the role of a proper political wife, and her deadlines for diapers.

Once inside David's cozy condo, she tossed off her high heels and folded her coat over her arm. Looking around she shivered as she recalled the state she was in the last time she visited his home.

"Have a seat." David motioned her to the brown leather sofa. He took her coat and hung it in the hall closet. His manners were impeccable, his taste, exquisite, and his blood, bluer than Rubric's collar. With a flip of a switch, romantic music floated throughout the rooms, the lights dimmed, and a roaring fire magically appeared in the fireplace.

It was no surprise that *Washingtonian* magazine had named David one of the city's ten most eligible bachelors. Not only did he have a bright future, but, unlike many of his peers, he also knew how to romance a woman, as evidenced by the two dozen long-stemmed Sonya roses, Jill's favorite, arranged in an exquisitely cut Baccarat crystal vase.

"Oh, David, how lovely," Jill cooed as she leaned over to smell the roses. "You remembered."

"I thought you could use a little cheering up." He winked

at her. "I'll be right back," he said as he disappeared into the kitchen.

She didn't need cheering up anymore. David was about to propose to her, and she would soon be a happy bride-to-be. Sonya roses would be perfect for the bridesmaids' bouquets, too. They would look stunning with the bronze silk dresses she had selected when she'd stopped by Saks yesterday.

Perched on the edge of his brown leather sofa, Jill fished an engraved compact out of her purse to freshen her makeup. Her heart skipped a beat when she spotted the sixpence. She imagined how the mystery man with the blue eyes and shiny shoes must have been searching all over to find it. She had been unable to erase those extraordinary cornflower blue eyes from her memory. For a brief moment that day at the newsstand, Jill thought she'd heard bells ringing, but poof . . . her Prince Charming had disappeared into thin air.

Jill clutched the coin in her hand and then dropped it back in her purse. *"My grandmother wore it in her wedding shoe."* How preposterous! Her mother and her sister might be hopeless romantics, but she was far too sensible to daydream about the coin's owner.

Besides, tonight she was primed to accept David's proposal. Of course, she had never really heard bells ringing when she was with David. He was like a cozy old pair of slippers—reliable, comfortable, and practical.

She inspected her perfectly manicured hands and lifted her ring finger polished with pink, awaiting the diamond that she and David had gazed upon in the Tiffany case for over two years. *What a fool I've been to put him off for so long!* Jill thought as David reappeared, smiling.

"Here you go." David handed her a glass of sparkling water with a lime gripping the rim.

Water? Where's the champagne? Jill sunk back into the down-filled cushions. David's mother was an alcoholic, and Jill's father had once suffered from the same demon, so together she and David had made a pledge to avoid alcohol except on special occasions. Certainly David would make an exception for tonight! Even a bottle of sparkling cider would've been more festive, and certainly not lethal. Maybe it was because he had just seen his mother while in California and found her drinking again.

But more surprising, David didn't sit beside her; instead he stood stiffly by the fireplace, far from his awaiting bride. He folded his hands behind his back in a lawyerly fashion and began his interrogation.

"Explain to me how this happened. I still don't understand how you could finger Tom Burke, one of the finest on the Hill."

Jill sighed. "Like I told you before, the case isn't closed yet." She looked over at him, wondering if he had learned this particular stance from one of his classes at Harvard Law School. *Maybe it would be too difficult for him to get down on his knee if he sat beside me,* she reasoned to herself.

"You look so beautiful, Jill, but tell me truthfully, how are you holding up under all this scrutiny?" David at last took the seat beside her and took her right hand in his. His voice had softened.

"Barely surviving," she confessed, pulling her embroidered shawl around her shoulders, as if it could hide her shame. "But please let's not dwell on the past. I'd prefer to talk about the future."

David got up and took his place by the fireplace. "Those who cannot remember the past—"

"Please, no quotes tonight." Jill raised her hand to halt him from finishing his sentence.

He stood silently sipping his water, staring at her.

Twisting the tassels on her pashima shawl, she suddenly felt obligated to explain further. After all, her actions could have cost him his job, just by association. If they were to marry, David's mind needed to be put at ease as far as her ethics and reputation were concerned. She cleared her throat and began. "Months of thorough investigation went into this story. I still stand by my facts. This is the biggest cover-up since Watergate."

"Even if Burke was selling babies, personally, I think the children are better off being adopted by couples who want to give them better homes and lives. I still don't see what you believe is so wrong with these adoptions." David argued as if he were reciting the senator's own words. "It appears to me that this is the only chance for the babies to have a decent life."

Jill could feel the blood creeping up her neck and into her cheeks until her face was hot and flushed. "Selling babies for a profit is a good deed? Honest, moral people may choose to call that slavery."

"Oh, don't be so dramatic! Don't you see? It's a win-win. Poor families receive the money they need to live on, the children are placed in good homes where they are loved and provided for, and the adoptive parents get to have the children they've so desperately wanted."

"I can't believe this! You're saying we should sell babies to the highest bidder! Do you realize that many of these adoptive parents aren't even investigated? Pedophiles, child abusers, criminals . . . anyone can have a baby as long as they pay the price."

"Well, maybe, but most of the children are better off in this country."

"You certainly wouldn't believe that if you read the case studies." Jill balled her hands into fists. "Besides, many of the biological parents loved their children but didn't have the money to care for them and were forced to sell them to survive. The men and women involved in our 'hero's' organization turned the selling of children into a highly profitable business by preying on these parents' desperation."

David gave her an icy glare. "I'm sorry, Jill, but your investigation fizzled and you can't prove it."

"I can sure try." She met his steely gaze.

A tense silence filled the room. Finally David spoke. "You know, it's a pity we're so far apart in our beliefs, Jill. I really cared for you. I was hoping you and I—"

"Cared?" Jill interrupted, confused by David's attitude. This wasn't the man she knew and loved. Or was it, and she had been too involved in her work to notice? She jumped to her feet.

"There's no reason to get hysterical," David replied, grabbing her wrist.

"No reason?" Jill jerked her hand from David's grasp. "I've lost my job, my reputation, and apparently the man I love, all in a matter of days. I'd say those are a few good reasons."

"Jill, you don't understand. I have to consider my career too."

"Is your career more important to you than me—than us?" Jill faltered.

"That's funny, coming from you, Jill. Wasn't it you who forced me to think in those terms? I work alongside Senator Jacobs, and you know how close he is to Tom Burke. He's a favorite for Burke's running mate in the next election. This election could be a huge step in my career. I can't afford to . . ." David halted, apparently not wanting to finish his sentence. "You've single-handedly tried to destroy Burke's political future, simultaneously affecting Jacobs's career and mine. Since I'm Jacobs's chief of staff, I think it would be inappropriate for us to continue seeing one another, or at least not until after all the dust settles."

"So the future you wanted to discuss was *your* future?" Jill said, lifting her glass off the coaster to take a sip of water, her throat hoarse.

"I am not going down with this ship." David tipped his glass toward her.

"I wouldn't be so sure about that." Jill tossed her water in his direction and ran out of the condo. She didn't look back.

5

Sweet is the hour that brings us home,
Where all will spring to meet us . . .

—Eliza Cook

Jill often imagined the triumphant return to her hometown of Delavan, Wisconsin, being heralded in the headlines of the local newspaper: "Famous Journalist Returns to Her Birthplace." The local high school band would march down Main Street, and she, perched atop a convertible and holding a bouquet of roses, would lead the crepe paper floats and lone city fire engine in a parade. Well, there'd certainly be no ceremony tonight; not even a Boy Scout with his silver whistle would welcome her. As she maneuvered her Ford Explorer through sheets of pouring rain, she went unrecognized.

WELCOME TO DELAVAN, POPULATION 8,000, the green sign read. It was her only greeting, but she was thankful for it. The rain diffused the light streaming from the lampposts, making it appear as if she were looking at a film clip of her past, awakening every cell of her body with memories, some pleasant, some sad. More than twelve years had passed since she had left for college, and ultimately, a job in the big city. But now she was right back where she had started from, amidst fields of corn, dairy cows, and a resort lake far from Washington. Not much had changed, but Arnold's Corner Drugstore was no more, replaced by a sign of the times, a Wal-Mart Superstore on the outskirts of town.

A familiar tune floated out from the radio. *"Have I told you lately that I love you . . ."* "Oh, no!" Jill cried aloud. "They're playing our song." She quickly pushed the button, turning off the radio. Losing her job had been one thing, but losing David on top of it had cut to the core of her being. It seemed the David she had known and loved no longer existed; his memory had been blotted out by a man who saw nothing wrong with selling babies, a man who chose to skulk away to save himself instead of standing by her. He hadn't even run after her the night she left his condo. Worse yet, he hadn't bothered to call. *Well, I guess it's better that I found out about him now rather than later,* she told herself.

The past seven months were a blur. During the week following her dismissal from the *Gazette,* Jill had numbed her pain by planning the perfect wedding; trying on dresses, looking at china, crystal, and silver patterns at Tiffany, making out guest lists, and selecting the script for her engraved invitations. She even spent time at the florist choosing flowers and bouquet designs.

When David's proposal never materialized, and worse yet, he dumped her, she'd gone into hiding. She spent an entire month eating chocolate and a mild sedative the doctor had prescribed for her. When she wasn't sleeping, which was most of the time, she watched old movies.

By May, the doctor refused to refill her prescription and suggested counseling, so she mustered up her courage to get out of bed. She checked her voicemail that morning, and to her surprise, there were a few phone calls of job offers from the tabloids. She'd starve first!

But the offers encouraged her enough to post her resume on the Internet and send a few to her newspaper contacts and her associates on the Hill. She responded to several speechwriting positions and even a corporate communication job. Yet the phone didn't ring. Jill had the plague; no one wanted to be within ten feet of her, much less hire her.

In early summer a voice from her past called. "Jill, this is Max Clark. I've heard about what happened to you, and I would love to have you back in Delavan to work at my weekly newspaper."

The Lakes News? Even though unemployed with her savings dwindling, Jill chuckled to herself. Circulation 15,000. She was desperate, but not that desperate. In a few weeks, she was working a temp job as a receptionist at a small law firm, the only job she'd been offered. Her life consisted of eating, working, and sleeping.

By the end of the summer with no prospects in sight, she received two phone calls that changed the course of her life.

"Jill, it's Mom."

"Mom. What's wrong?"

"Nothing's wrong. Fall is in the air, and as much as I love this time of year, it always makes me feel a bit melancholy. I guess I'm just lonely without your father."

"Would you like for me to come home for a visit?"

"Permanently?" Her mother's voice perked up. "Max told me you turned down the job at the *Lakes,* but I'm sure he'd make a spot for you anytime."

"Did you put him up to that, Mom?"

"No, I did not. It's just ridiculous for you to remain in

Washington when you'd have a free place to stay here and even a job."

"A job! I can't imagine working for peanuts on a small town newspaper."

"Have you considered how much less your expenses would be here? It sure beats being a receptionist. And it would give me a purpose to have you home again."

"A purpose?"

"I'd have someone to cook for and shop for again!"

"I wouldn't want to impose."

"In this big house? I'd hardly know you were here."

Jill shuddered. She couldn't imagine living with her mother again after all these years.

"I, uh, I don't know, Mom, but I'll think about it."

The second call was from Max. "Jill, would you consider joining us if I doubled that offer I made you?"

What Max thought was a generous offer would barely keep Jill in chocolate and Diet Cokes, but her mom had been very convincing, and Jill had to admit that her life in Washington was a big zero at the moment. It was awful being in the same town as David. In her weak moments she would go to Alexandria and walk around his neighborhood, praying she would run into him. She never did, so why not keep her mother company? She could get to know her sister, Kathy, and her family again, and it might be kind of fun to work at a small town newspaper. Plus, she'd have no social life in Delavan, so she could devote all of her leisure time to solving the mystery of her investigation.

At last she turned into the long gravel driveway of her family's estate, kicking up stones buried under a blanket of autumn leaves and splattering mud from the potholes. Pulling to an abrupt stop, she surveyed the two-story lake home ablaze in lights. Designed by Frank Lloyd Wright early in the century, the house had straight lines with sloping roofs, bespeaking elegance and notable wealth. Feelings of home-sickness flooded her. At that moment, she realized just how much she had missed her family.

At the sound of the car door slamming shut, her mother, Pearl Lewis, came rushing out of the autumn-wreathed door onto the screened-in back porch. "Jill, my sweet, you're home!" Her mother's welcoming words warmed Jill's hurting heart. "Hurry," she urged, "let's get your bags in . . . this rain is freezing."

Pearl hurried down the walkway toward Jill, pulling her camel coat about her shoulders. She looked striking with her freshly bobbed silver locks, sparkling blue eyes set off by a French blue cashmere sweater, and trim-fitting gray flannel trousers. Her svelte figure resembled that of a young girl's, but the accessories were those of a classic woman of means, from the simple strand of pearls to the matching pearl and diamond earrings to the stack of gold bracelets that jingled cheerfully as she moved.

"Mom, did you cut your hair?"

"I needed a change. Do you like it?"

"I love it!"

Hugging her, Jill thought her mom had lost too much weight since the recent death of her dad. Maybe being home would be good. It might lift both their spirits.

Pulling out the bare necessities from the Explorer, Jill felt the impact of the cold Wisconsin rain and air as it sent a nasty chill up her body. Her mother lifted out a small suitcase, and together they rushed up the path toward the house. For a brief moment Jill expected to see her dad appear at the door to welcome her home.

"Let me take these for you," he would say, employing a manner that meant carrying bags was a man's job.

Jill could feel her eyes begin to brim with tears. She had never needed him more than she needed him right now. As she entered the house, she looked over at his favorite chair. Its emptiness was a painful reminder he was no longer here. As if reading Jill's mind, her mom reached over and put her hand on her daughter's face and said, "I miss him too, darling." Jill quickly averted her eyes to the kitchen fireplace, crackling with burning logs.

"Mom, how are you?" She tried to keep her voice from quavering. "I know it's been really hard on you since Dad's passing. I worry about you."

Mom patted her hand. "My faith has been a great comfort to me . . . one day we'll be together again and then it will be for eternity."

Jill was glad her mother could garner so much strength from her strong faith. But to her, faith was for children, the elderly, and the weak. She hoped her mother wouldn't drive her nuts with all the Christianese.

The tall grandfather clock in the hallway began to chime. "Where have all the years gone?" Her mother sighed, making her question a comment. "Come on, let's take these bags up to your room. I put fresh sheets on your bed this morning."

Jill grabbed a suitcase. "I had such a happy childhood in this house," she said as she walked past a wall of family photos. "But after all that's happened this year, I wonder if I didn't acquire the coping skills I need. I mean, I just don't think I'm dealing with my situation very well." She sighed loudly. "I never thought I'd end up back home with my tail between my legs. Maybe you and Dad sheltered Kathy and me too much."

Her mom shook her head. "Well, you have suffered a huge blow, but I think you've done the best you could at handling things. And maybe it's true that you had a sheltered childhood, but we did equip you with a sustaining faith in God. He'll provide you with the strength to overcome any difficulty." Her mother's voice was warm and confident as she set down the suitcases in Jill's old room. "I'm here for you to talk to, whenever you're ready to talk. God is too."

Her mother's words slightly irritated her, but she had to admit that it was her mother's faith that had carried her through the tumultuous first years of her marriage to Jill's father, and ultimately through the difficult days following his death.

It seemed that her mom suspected but ignored Jill's estrangement from God. Should she tell her the truth? She decided it was best to just play along. She just hoped she could put up with all the church stuff. After her dad's death, she had wanted to scream when her mother quoted Scripture to everyone who walked through the door to pay their respects.

On the other hand, she reflected, *Mom built her house on a rock, while I built mine on sand. And now my house has sunk.* Maybe there was something to take from her mother's faith. Jill had traded her own relationship with God for a hot career, but she seemed to be getting burned in the process.

6

The writer must be willing above all else,
To take chances, to risk making
A fool of himself—or even risk
Revealing the fact that he is a fool.

—Jessamyn West

"May I have everyone's attention please?" said publisher and editor-in-chief Max Clark. "I want you all to welcome Miss Jill Lewis, a.k.a. Newspaperwoman Extraordinaire, formerly of the *Washington Gazette.* Born and raised right here in Delavan, Jill is the newest staff member of the *Lakes News.* I believe we are most fortunate to have her caliber of reporting with us." The beaming older man stood outside the pressroom in the center of a large room filled with desks, surrounded by his staff.

After he introduced her to each member of the team, an immediate hush fell over the newsroom. No one spoke, though everyone nodded pleasantly in her direction. Seeking comfort, Jill searched the room for a familiar face. Cornelia Southworth, the society editor, smiled back at her with twinkling blue eyes that gazed extra wide in a permanent look of surprise.

Obviously the work of an overzealous plastic surgeon. Reaching from ear to ear, her hot pink lipstick grin matched her mohair dress and a fuzzy beret that hid the silver roots of her bleached-blonde hair. The woman, probably in her late sixties, resembled a glass of pink lemonade complete with pulp as she tottered across the floor in her three-inch heels.

Jill knew that Delavan's venerable society matron had been writing for the paper for almost forty years. *Is this my fate too? To work in a small-town newspaper, clothed in outdated fashions?*

After what seemed like an eternity, Jill managed to break the uncomfortable silence. "Nice to meet all of you." She cleared her throat. "You heard Max say that Delavan is, uh, my hometown. I'm happy to be back after so many years away. And I'm looking forward to working with you all and getting to know you."

She was ill at ease with all those eyes resting on her and even more so with Max's flattering introduction. Once she would have reveled in the words. Of course, that was when she had been worthy of them.

"Miss Lewis, I think you will find yourself very much at home here. We certainly are not the hub of the United States as you are used to, but we are the heartbeat of our little town. I like to say that if we did not print it, the event never happened." He smiled at her. "That's a good thing to remember."

"Do you mean to say that if we don't capture it in print, the happening isn't noteworthy?"

"No, not at all. What I mean is that we record the history of Delavan. If we don't print the stories of this town, then it could not possibly have happened."

"I'll remember that," Jill replied politely, making a mental note to keep her thoughts to herself.

"You do that now. Here, these are your first assignments.

Show us what you're made of with that famous Lewis nose for news of yours," Max said, waving the papers in the air. He handed them to Jill and then went back into his small office and shut the door.

Jill looked at the assignments. "But these people are dead," she muttered.

"She's a quick study after all," said Craig Martin, managing editor. "Your reputation is only outshone by seeing your intuition and perception in the flesh."

Jill narrowed her eyes at this flippant remark. Where did he get off talking to her like that? Maybe he was envious that she had worked for a large city paper while he had been stuck in Delavan writing for this two-bit rag. Or perhaps he feared for his job. After all, given some time, she could replace him.

A short, stocky woman with wild red hair and big hips, lips, and heels chimed in. "Listen, honey, everyone who starts here, starts here." She took the list of names for the obituaries and tapped it with her long orange fingernails decorated with jack-o'-lanterns, as if that helped her to explain the point she was making. "Got it?"

"Got it," Jill said, grabbing the paper away from her.

"And if you do a good job on the obits," the redhead told her, "you could become my assistant for my advice column."

Jill sighed deeply and wondered if her decision to return home had been the right one after all. When she had signed her contract, she'd assumed she would be walking into a position more befitting her experience. Certainly she hadn't expected to start as a rookie working her way up again. Having an advice column to look forward to was not her idea of a future. Maybe she should have accepted that offer from the *National Enquirer.*

As if she could read Jill's mind, Marge, the redhead, clunked back over to Jill.

"It's not so bad," she offered, patting her on the back. "If you do a decent job with the obits, Craig might throw you a bone once in a while."

"A bone?"

"He might use you as a stringer, *if* he thinks you can handle it—to cover human-interest stories."

"Like what?" Jill could feel her hopes rising.

"Last year I covered the senior beauty pageant over at the local nursing home. On my next assignment I got to cover the square dance when a famous caller came to town, and a few weeks ago I even got to interview a few of the farmers who are entering the pumpkin contest. It's rumored that Mr. Gustafson's pumpkin will weigh in at 250 pounds, but I couldn't get a word out of him."

"Sounds fascinating," Jill gulped.

"Sure beats the obits." Marge patted Jill's back again and then trotted over to the reception area.

Jill stood in the middle of the room, alone, staring down at her feet. Twelve years ago she had wiped the dirt of this town off her shoes and headed for college, never looking back. After graduating summa cum laude from Northwestern University, she landed a plum internship at the *Washington Gazette* and quickly moved up through the ranks. In a matter of years Jill Lewis was revered as the city's brightest investigative reporter.

Now she was blackballed from the newspaper community at large—any newspaper worth its print, that is. Only this weekly newspaper with its small circulation of fifteen thousand would consider her, and it was becoming more obvious that they had given her the job not for her expertise but as a favor to her mother, who was an old friend of Max. Mom had probably been fearful her daughter would end up on the street and in the bread lines—which didn't sound too bad to Jill as she gazed around the dismal newsroom.

"Your desk is back there," Craig said, interrupting her thoughts.

Jill obediently walked over to the corner of the room where the light was bad. She took her seat at the oldest, shabbiest desk in the room, making a mental note to bring a desk lamp from home. As she sat down, she wished she were walking out. The computer was at least five years old, and her desk, marred by time, was missing several handles. An arrangement of fake poinsettias was placed on one side and a rickety in-and-out box on the other. A coffee mug that read "There's no place like home" was jammed with sharpened pencils, highlighters, and an assortment of pens, most of which didn't work. A pair of kitten-shaped bookends steadied an old dictionary and thesaurus, a King James Bible, an atlas, and an ancient copy of *The Chicago Manual of Style,* an inexperienced journalist's most trusted companion.

I have to remember this is a fresh start and I can do this, she thought, encouraging her heavy spirit as she settled in the chair and flipped on the switch of the computer. Peering over the top of the monitor, she studied the faces and mannerisms of this odd little shop of newsies. *Craig is kinda cute but definitely has an attitude,* she mused. Marge, the redheaded advice columnist, appeared to have lead feet. And a tiny handful of reporters who covered sporting events, social events, and historic events, as well as local news and advertising, seemed just about as eccentric, with Cornelia Southworth at the top of the heap.

Jill looked down at the list still clutched in her hand. For this issue of the weekly newspaper she had just five obituaries to write. Not much to keep her busy. She was definitely at the bottom of the heap in this little town. *"Oh, how the mighty have fallen.*" She could almost hear Rubric mocking her in his wry little voice. But she knew he would be proud of her too. She ached to hear from him; even his sarcastic comments would be welcome.

Since grieving relatives had already dropped off the paper's fill-in-the-blank form and a written synopsis of the lives of deceased loved ones, Jill tapped out the facts on her computer keyboard: birth and death dates, survivors' names, and the time of visitation and the funeral. The task was so easy the piece nearly wrote itself. Retrieving her copy from the printer, she walked over to the reception area to deliver it to Marge.

Jill gasped when she looked up to see a life-size poster of Elvis covering the wall behind Marge's desk. *Elvis is in the building!* She stifled a giggle as she imagined what would happen at the *Gazette* if someone hung a life-size poster of Elvis in the reception area. Searching for a vacant spot to leave her work, Jill noticed a plethora of self-help books of every shape, size, and description piled high on Marge's disorderly desk. Perusing the stack of books, Jill picked up one titled *How to Marry a Millionaire in Ten Easy Steps* and chuckled as she examined the pages.

She was startled by Marge's loud voice. "You can borrow that one if you like."

"Uh, no thanks." Jill blushed, returning the book back to the one vacant spot on the desk.

"No, I insist." Marge handed the book back to Jill. "On your salary, it might come in handy."

"You don't really believe this book can . . ." Jill ventured and then thought better of it. "And how do you know what salary I make? Aren't salaries confidential around here?"

"I had your job, remember?"

"Oh yeah, that's right." Jill then remembered why she had come over there. She proudly handed her finished copy to Marge and walked away. "All done," she said over her shoulder.

When she got back to her desk and sat down, she heard a loud shriek from across the room. "Oh my goodness!"

"What? What's the matter?" Jill sprinted across the floor, unsure of what she would encounter.

"This is just awful!" Marge yelped as she continued to read Jill's copy.

"I am so sorry. Did you know one of the deceased?" Jill asked sympathetically.

"No, it isn't that! The problem is the *way* you wrote these obits. They are so blah!" Marge said, waving the copy in the air. "Hey, Craig, I thought you said she was good."

Craig strode across the room and read over Marge's shoulder. "Huh. The facts, nothing but the facts. Marge, lower your voice and remember everybody has to start somewhere. Let's not embarrass Miss Lewis on her first day here." He shot an empathetic look in Jill's direction.

Jill was mortified.

"What happened to all that information I got from the relatives?" Marge pointedly asked her.

"I used it."

"No, you didn't. You left out the part about Mr. Whitely dying in his favorite chair. And you left out how it took three hours before his wife figured out he was dead."

"Why does that matter? Besides, how is that even possible?"

"It says so right here." Marge pointed to Mrs. Whitely's notes and read them aloud. "'I didn't realize that my James had passed on, since he always dozed off when we watched the soaps together in the afternoon.'" Marge held the paper up in the air and shook it. "And Mrs. Whitely also wrote, 'As soon as *Days of Our Lives* was over, I vacuumed right around him without knowing he had kicked the bucket.'

She also added that it was the episode when Bell found out that the baby Jan miscarried was not Sean's baby." Marge stopped her speech to inquire quickly, "Can you believe it wasn't Sean's baby? I'm still reeling over that one." She rolled her eyes, shook her head, and laid Mrs. Whitely's notes on top of her desk.

Fanning herself with Jill's copy, Marge gasped for air before beginning again. "Where is that per-tin-ent information, huh? All you have here are the names of all his relatives. Who cares?" She picked up Mrs. Whitely's notes again and thrust them at Jill.

Jill fought to keep her voice level. "Sorry to have to inform you, Marge, but those are the juicy tidbits you leave out of obituaries. You are to list just the facts, like how the news is handled. Only the cut and dry." She took back her copy and walked stiffly to her desk.

Craig followed her. Wiping his brow with the palm of his hand, he sat on the edge of Jill's old oak desk. "Look, Jill, things are a little different in small towns. People care about one another here; we aren't just statistics to each other. We already know who is related to whom and who the survivors are—what the people are genuinely interested in is how a person met his Maker."

"You mean people are more interested in gossip?"

"Not the kind of gossip that's mean-spirited. This is informational."

"Informational gossip? I'm not familiar with it."

"See it as a new area of reporting you have yet to learn."

"Max said that if we don't write it, it never happened. Well, here's a thought: Why don't we just not write about Mr. Whitely at all and tell his wife to vacuum a little longer? Maybe he'll eventually wake up from his afternoon nap."

He smiled into her eyes and then knocked his knuckles softly on top of her computer. "No."

"Okay, I'll rewrite the obits and make them interesting, with all the trifling details and information. I'll even add the fact about Sean not being the father of Jan's baby. Maybe that'll come in handy if someone missed the soap that day." She smiled, hoping she wasn't coming off with an attitude. "Thanks for your guidance here."

"Sure, no problem."

Jill watched Craig as he headed back to his office. Although he was very different from the men in Washington, Jill thought he was rather handsome in an old-fashioned sort of way. He wore slip-on loafers, khaki pants with a plaid flannel shirt, and one of those fancy sports watches on his wrist. He had that easy, small-town, I'm-in-no-hurry style. *The black-rimmed glasses are a definite fashion mistake for him though,* she thought. They detracted from his striking brown eyes that were so dark they appeared black. Craig's hair was so black Jill suspected that he might even dye it . . . to cover up some premature gray? A sure sign he was vain.

Marge stopped by Jill's desk to check on her. "Are we having fun yet?"

"What do you think?"

"Been there, done that," Marge replied sympathetically, "but it's not so bad. Just view the job as an opportunity to comfort hurting people. And listen, I'm sorry if I freaked you out before. I can be a little melodramatic at times."

"No problem. But I thought we ran a newspaper, not a counseling service." Jill could hear the note of sarcasm creeping into her voice. *I sound just like Rubric!*

"In a small town, the newspaper is everything to all people," Marge said as she walked away.

Jill rolled her eyes.

By 5:30 that evening, Jill had completed her obituary stories and sharpened every pencil in sight. She had even helped empty the trash. Grabbing her purse, sweater, and the self-help book Marge insisted she take with her, Jill headed for the door.

"Good night, Mr. Martin. Thanks for all your help and advice."

"You're welcome. And we're on a first name basis at the *Lakes,* Jill." He stood up from his desk to walk her to the door.

She looked at his nameplate before continuing. "Okay, good night, Craig."

Reading the cover on the book Jill held in her hand, he chuckled. "What is this?"

"Marge thought I might need this in light of my salary."

"She's got a good point there. Good luck; I hope you find your millionaire." He chuckled again.

"Yeah, me too," she muttered as she walked out the door.

7

We have our own front page,
as all people do who live in the country.
It is the sky and the earth, with headlines new every morning.
We wake to take in its news
As city dwellers reach across thresholds for their newspapers.

—Margaret Lee Runbeck

The Wisconsin landscape bore resemblance to a patchwork quilt done with fine stitching by patient and masterful hands. Children ran in yards, nudging one another playfully as their dogs bounded along excitedly beside them. A couple walked hand in hand as joggers, breathing evenly, quietly padded past them down the tar road. The autumn air was crisp and clear, having offered Wisconsin inhabitants the gift of one Indian summer day.

Jill drove down country roads toward the lake in the ancient VW Bug she'd found stored away in her father's multicar garage. As a matter of practicality, she had sold her sporty SUV the day after she arrived in town, when she discovered the VW was in perfect condition. Quite frankly, she needed to keep her cash flowing and her savings saved. The last thing she wanted to do after moving home at the age of thirty was to mooch off her mother. She was aware that her father had left a trust for both her and her sister, Kathy, but her mother had mentioned that they would be meeting with the lawyers to discuss the trust after all the legal work was completed. Pride kept Jill from inquiring or appearing too anxious.

She glanced at herself in the rearview mirror and brushed back the loose blonde hair that blew across her face from the breeze coming through the open window. Her almond-shaped green eyes stared back at her. Smiling at the woman in the mirror, she told herself for the hundredth time, "We did nothing wrong in D.C., and don't you forget it!"

She enjoyed traveling the familiar back road she was on, knowing she was heading for home. She giggled with the memory of how frequently she and her younger sister, Kathy, had sneaked their mother's keys and car late at night while in high school. Together they would drive up and down the country roads in search of some kind of adventure. Jill's idea of adventure was meeting new people and finding out where they were going. Kathy's included finding boys. Maybe that fact had defined them later in life as well; Jill headed away from home in search of new places and faces, while Kathy remained in Delavan to marry and start a family.

Jill dearly loved her sister and little niece, Marion. She admired her brother-in-law, Jeff, as well. For Kathy, marriage had been a good choice. And maybe she had been the wise one. Jill had gone a different route, and now she had no future—no career or man.

The car sped along the country road, winding its way between barren fields. Dairy farms dotted the landscape on distant hills. Jill could smell damp earth. At this point in the year, harvest crops were securely stored in metal bins in the outlying farm country, and dairy farmers were busily repairing their barns and fortifying their roofs for the expected onslaught of Wisconsin's infamous ice and snowstorms.

Turning into the long, winding drive of her family's estate, Jill grinned at the sight of Kathy's dark blue Lincoln Navigator. *If good can come from bad, then the opportunity to get reacquainted with Kathy is a bonus.*

She opened the back door, still half expecting to see her father. Each time she entered the house, she had to catch herself from calling out his name. Dad had died in a car accident on the lake road over a year and a half ago. She knew the heartache and lump in her throat would never fully go away—at times the pain would dim, but then it would come rushing back full force.

The late afternoon sun was pouring through the floor-to-ceiling windows that framed a view to the lake. Though a thin layer of crusty ice had begun to form on the water, the sunshine had melted the frost back into water again. Jill was glad she'd spent most of her growing-up years here. When her parents had decided to buy a summer lake home, her father had preferred a cottage, but when this majestic estate suddenly came on the market, her mother couldn't live without it. Dad thought it was far too extravagant for a summer home, but he purchased it anyway to keep peace in the family. He later agreed that it was a blessing to own one of Wright's precious architectural jewels, especially after they decided to make Delavan their permanent home a few years later.

Every summer when all the vacationers were in town, the Lewis family opened up their home for a week of tours, and every Christmas, many townspeople were invited to their Christmas party. Her father had hated it when all the summer residents tramped through the house, but her mother loved every moment of showing off their home. "Besides," she always explained, "it keeps the stragglers from knocking on the door and asking to see the house at all hours of the day and night."

Jill looked around the room that was familiar yet unfamiliar. Her mother had recently redecorated for the third time since Jill left home. Soaring up to the beamed cathedral ceiling of rare wormy chestnut, the massive stone fireplace was flanked by built-in bookshelves filled with carefully chosen leather-bound books and objects of art. Two new overstuffed couches and several chairs were separated by a large mahogany coffee table, and expensive, appropriately chosen antiques filled the room. Over in the corner was a familiar piece—the game table with four chairs, once used for their family's games, now used weekly by the members of her mother's bridge club.

Kathy sat on a couch watching as three-year-old Marion played on the floor. Mom, looking very much like a queen ruling her small kingdom, sat in the brocade wing chair with ball and claw feet.

"Hi, my darling!" Mom's voice was warm with love as she slipped her needle through the needlepoint canvas as though conducting the symphony in Handel's *Water Music*, which was melodiously filling the room from the sound system. Jill was amazed at how her mother could concentrate on three things at once without so much as missing a stitch.

"Tell us, how was your first day on the new job?"

Jill couldn't help but notice how her mother punctuated the words *first* and *new*. She felt as if she were sixteen and had just finished her first day carhopping at the local A&W Restaurant.

"Great," Jill fibbed. Maybe if they had remained close, Jill might have poured her heart out to Kathy, but now she seemed nothing more than a familiar stranger. Instead she gave her sister a quick hug.

"How does it feel to be living back at home after all these years?" Kathy asked her.

"Great!" Jill fibbed again. "You look beautiful . . . motherhood certainly agrees with you."

"I've never been happier," Kathy said as she gazed over at Marion.

"She's a great mom too," their mother interjected. "The best."

Even when she was a kid, all Kathy had ever wanted was a husband, a house surrounded by a white picket fence, and a minivan overflowing with kids. Her Prince Charming appeared in the form of a first-year law student; they married shortly after her high school graduation. Their marriage weathered her years in college and his in law school. But it nearly came apart when Kathy and Jeff found they could not have children. Adoption became a viable option, bringing precious Marion to their family at the age of five days.

"Marion, give Aunt Jill a big hug," Kathy instructed her young daughter. As Jill returned the hug of the curly haired child, she thought of how much fun she was going to have being an aunt who lived close by her niece.

"How's my Maid Marion today?"

"I fine," the cherub-faced little girl answered before wiggling away from being hugged any longer.

"You look great too." Kathy returned compliment for compliment. "Jeff and I are still stunned over the loss of your job, and David," she said, almost whispering his name. "Jeff thought he was an opportunist. He never liked him, you know."

"No, I didn't know."

"Mom told me that Dad didn't care for him either," Kathy added. "You're better off without him. I bet you'll meet someone else soon and wonder why you ever had anything to do with that arrogant . . . snob."

"Thanks, Kathy," Jill said, feeling the warmth of her family's support. Yet it was a surprise to her that they hadn't cared for David. Had they seen something she hadn't, like the character flaw that caused him to dump her at the time she needed him most?

"I cannot imagine what it must feel like to work at the *Lakes News* after the *Washington Gazette*."

"It's not so bad. After all, I get to work with Cornelia Southworth."

"The infamous Cornelia?" Kathy giggled.

Jill nodded. "She's now my new best friend—the only one at the paper who speaks to me."

"Does she still wear those dated outfits with the outlandish hats?"

"Yeah, only now they are at least three sizes too small," Jill quipped. "But she's a fashion legend in her own mind."

"Be nice, girls," Pearl warned her daughters. "If you can't say anything nice about someone—"

"Don't say anything at all!" the sisters finished with a giggle.

Their mom smiled indulgently and turned to Jill. "Kathy invited us to her house for dinner. We can hear all about your day then."

The idea sounded like fun, but Jill was too drained to even think about leaving the house again. "Kathy, you know I would really love to come, but the stress of this new job has zapped my strength. Another night?"

"Oh, but you must come!" her mother urged. "You haven't seen Kathy's new home yet! It's the most beautiful house in the Midwest, the largest too. Your sister has filled it with the most exquisite antiques, treasures, and art."

"At least one apple didn't fall far from the tree," Jill said, winking at Kathy. "I can't wait to see your new house, but not tonight. I have to be at the newspaper early in the morning, and I still haven't finished unpacking all my things."

"Are you sure?" Kathy said. "I had our cook make lots of the junk food you like—juicy hamburgers and cottage fries and thick chocolate brownies chock-full with nuts and topped with gooey chocolate icing for dessert."

"Ooh, tempting, but I'm going to pass. I'm a working girl again."

"All right, but just remember my door is open to you anytime. In the meantime, get some good rest."

A few minutes later, Jill watched them disappear down the drive. For the first time in her life, she felt a twinge of jealousy—not for Kathy's big house but for her husband and her child, something to come home to. Jill had no one waiting for her except her mother. How pathetic was that at age thirty?

Pulling open the refrigerator door, she saw a large pitcher of homemade lemonade with fresh lemons floating on top. She poured herself a tall glass and headed up the stairs to her room.

In her bedroom, Jill unpacked skirts and dresses from her suitcase and put the clothes on covered hangers in her closet. Having only been home a short time, she had much to unpack in order to make her old room feel like home again. When she had left for college, Jill had forbidden her mother to change the décor of her room; she'd wanted something familiar to come home to. Now Jill realized the room could use some updating. And her mother would love a new decorating project.

She pulled on the brass handles on the cherry-wood dresser drawers and transferred shirts, slacks, and socks from her suitcase into them. She lovingly took her antique collection of leather-bound poetry books from cardboard boxes and put them on the shelves of the bookcase, rearranging her collection of Hummel figurines.

Standing back to admire her handiwork, Jill thought of how fortunate she was that her room faced the lake—indeed, the water was only a hundred yards from her bedroom windows. She sat down on the cushions in the window seat. A seamstress had sewed the curtains and a large array of pillows from the coordinating fabrics her mother had let her choose from Pierre Deux in Chicago. Although the summer sun had faded the vibrant colors into soft pastels, she still loved the fabric. But it was time for a change. This had been her private spot to sit and read and dream. She would soon make use of it again.

Half undressed, she sat cross-legged on her four-poster bed with her laptop before her. Entering her password, she began to read through the files she had meticulously prepared and kept on the adoption investigations. She relaxed. *Something within the file will help clear my name . . .*

Jill had felt safe in the security of her childhood home, but looking back into her files, the old fears began to resurface. Hopping off the bed, she searched through her briefcase for a carton of zip disks and began transferring her files.

After a couple of hours of copying and perusing, Jill felt her brain turning to mush. She needed sleep. She took a hot shower; the water felt good against her skin. Reflecting on coming home, she decided she had made the right decision to move in with her mother.

Who was she fooling? The reason she came home to her mother's house was because it was the only place to go.

As she stepped out of the shower and into her room, Jill's eyes suddenly looked to her laptop and the disks lying in the folds of her monogrammed duvet that covered her down comforter. Next to that were the files Rube had delivered to her in Washington. She knelt on the floor in front of her dresser and reached beneath it, searching to see if she could still find the hiding place. Her hand struck the small empty space, and she slid the disks into the spot and then stood. Once a hiding place for her private diaries, it was now a hiding place for her computer files. Pacing the room, she viewed the dresser from various angles. "There, no one can see them."

Now she had to come up with a hiding place for Annabelle's hard copy. She took out the innards of a large lamp, rolled up the file, and placed it inside the light fixture. Just then she heard the downstairs door open and close and her mother's footsteps cross the wooden heart-of-pine floors. Jill jumped into bed.

"Jill? Jill, I'm home."

"I'm up here in bed," Jill answered. She didn't feel up to talking tonight.

Pearl opened the bedroom door and smiled at her daughter. "Kathy sent home some brownies. Is there anything I can get for you before I go to bed?" she asked.

"No, thanks. I'm just very tired. I need to get some sleep."

"Oh, I forgot to mention earlier, that the funny little man from the *Gazette* called this afternoon. What's his name . . . Reuben?"

"Rubric," Jill corrected, "and that funny little man is my editor, the only remaining soul in Washington who is still speaking to me. What did he say?"

"He said he wanted to check on you; it was nothing urgent," her mother explained. "But you can call him tomorrow."

She walked over to Jill and pulled the blankets around her more tightly, then sat down on the bed. She began to stroke Jill's hair, the same thing she did when Jill was in elementary school.

"When you were born, your father and I were so protective.

We prayed you would grow to be a strong, healthy woman. I don't know all the reasons why you lost your job—only what I read in the papers, and truthfully, I couldn't watch the news. Every time they mentioned your name, I had to change the channel. I know you aren't ready to tell me all the details, but if you need to talk or if I can help you in any way, I hope you'll speak up."

"Thanks, Mom. Thanks for not asking."

"I just want you to be happy."

"I know, but there is only so much you can do for your daughters. The choices I make are my own. I'm glad to be home for now . . . maybe not forever, but for now." She kissed her mother's cheek.

Her mom smiled. "I know it isn't easy to come home after being on your own, but it's nice for me to have you right here. It's been lonely since your father died. This is your home as long as you need it to be."

She turned out the light and left Jill to her thoughts. Jill turned over and looked toward her hiding place in the dresser.

"Dad would've known what to do," she whispered as her heart began to ache again. "I have to do this on my own, and I will solve it, sooner or later."

She remembered the bedtime prayer her mother had taught her as a child and began to recite it: "Now I lay me down to sleep, I pray the Lord my soul to keep. The angels watch me through the night, and wake me with the morning light. If I should die before I wake, I pray the Lord my soul to take."

At Jill's insistence, her mother had always left off the last line. Dying had always frightened Jill; she chose to avoid the word at all cost. However, with the reality of her father's untimely death, she reckoned it was best to put those words back in her prayer.

8

Only yield when you must; never give up the ship,
But fight on to the last with a stiff upper lip!

—Phoebe Cary

Jill awoke in a positive mood. She felt slightly ridiculous for hiding the copies of her files the night before. For goodness sake, she was in Delavan, Wisconsin, not the nation's capital. Here in her sleepy hometown, doors were left unlocked, windows opened wide. But she left the disks where they were nonetheless.

Slipping into her hunter green corduroy slacks, she reached for her large matching pullover sweater. Quickly she brushed her hair and clipped it atop her head. Last she pulled on her black boots. As she drove to work, she felt the shadows and concerns of the night before slowly dissolving. *Yes, it was just a good night's sleep I needed after all.*

When Jill arrived at the paper, she was greeted with a few smiles, to her surprise. Progress! On her way to her desk, she saw Craig in his office, going over copy. She sat down and got right to work on the new obituaries that had been dropped off overnight in the mail slot. She wrote the best short stories, with *all* the various facts, and then proudly handed them to Marge. Just as she reached her desk, she heard the advice columnist say, "Wow, this is great!" Others hurried over to read them, and all nodded their heads with approval. Finally curiosity got the best of Craig, and Jill thought she saw a hint of a smile as he read them. He gave her two thumbs up before scuffing across the room and heading back to his office.

When Cornelia Southworth came through the door to drop off her society pages, she spotted Jill and walked over to her desk.

"Hi, honey!" Cornelia said sweetly as she touched Jill's arm. "My arthritis is killing me this morning. It reminds me of how much I miss your daddy." She sighed dramatically. "He was such a good doctor. I've had arthritis since he died, and no one has been able to help me. You wouldn't know his secret, would you?"

Fighting back the tears, Jill responded, "No, but I'm sure Dr. Jenkins would be happy to check Dad's files."

"Don't bother. That young man doesn't have a lick of sense. I want your daddy back." Mrs. Southworth talked as if Jill could somehow magically make him appear.

"I know. We all miss him. And he thought a lot of you, Mrs. Southworth, and he really enjoyed your columns."

Jill was telling the truth; her father had slapped his knee in laughter plenty of times when he read the contents of Mrs. Southworth's society pages. It had been a weekly topic of conversation at their home. Since her parents often entertained, they made the society pages on a regular basis. After reading the detailed information printed in the *Lakes News,* her father had often wondered if he and Cornelia had attended the same party! "There must be another Dr. Lewis in this town," he had joked with his family.

Mrs. Southworth nodded with pride and blurted out, "Jill, we didn't believe a thing those people were saying about you on TV. I made my Herman turn it off every time your name was mentioned."

"Thank you, Mrs. Southworth. That means a lot to me."

The older lady reached into her bright-red patent leather bag and pulled out some frayed notes sprawled in fancy cursive on a stack of cocktail napkins.

"Jill, I understand from Max that you're writing the obituaries."

"Yes, ma'am," Jill replied, not knowing what Cornelia was leading up to. Maybe she had begun her career forty years ago writing the obits.

Cornelia continued. "I planned to run this in my society column but somehow it just doesn't seem in good taste. The society pages are supposed to be about happy times and to insert such tragic news . . . well, Max and I discussed it on the phone and we feel that this belongs in the obituaries instead." She plopped down the soiled napkins in front of Jill.

"If you have any problem reading my chicken scratch, just let me know. I'll be at my desk for a little while."

"Thanks for the news tip." Jill smiled appreciatively.

But after picking up Mrs. Southworth's notes to decipher, Jill could feel the smile fade from her face. Immediately she charged into Max's office, without knocking.

"Didn't they teach you to knock at that big city newspaper?" Max complained as he scratched his head.

Jill slammed the napkins down on his desk. "Sir, if you'll forgive me, I don't see the humor in including Betty Johansson's parakeet in the obituaries. I'll be the laughingstock of Delavan! Imagine how the relatives of the deceased will feel to have their loved ones' obituaries alongside one belonging to a bird."

Max calmly thumped his fingers on the stack of napkins. "People around here will want to know about Betty's parakeet," he assured her.

"What? That her parakeet, Petey Bird, met his untimely death when he drowned in her toilet last Tuesday?" Jill asked incredulously. "You've got to be joking! Do you really want the citizens of Delavan to know that the prim and proper Mrs. Johansson left the lid to her toilet seat up? Why, she won't be able to show her face around town! I wouldn't be surprised if the sheriff arrested her for negligence in Petey's death. And we'd be responsible, Max."

"Okay, I get the sarcasm. Aren't we overreacting just a bit?"

"You obviously didn't read the part about her burying Petey in her rose garden, ensconced in her velvet-lined jewelry box, along with his favorite mirror and bell."

"Just write the obit, Jill. We'll put it at the end of the column. Betty Johansson has had that bird for years. It was like a child to her, and we're going to honor that."

"So you're ordering me to include this?"

"Yep," Max chuckled. "You'll get used to things around here before you know it."

"I wouldn't count on it," she whispered on her way out the office door.

———

At lunch Jill rushed outside to make a call on her cell phone as she walked around. She didn't identify herself when Landry answered the phone; she only asked for Rubric.

But the receptionist immediately recognized her voice. "Jill, is that you?"

"Yes, it is," an embarrassed Jill admitted.

"How are you?" Landry said. "We miss you so much. You

got such a bum rap. But we're all on your side. You just hang in there. Somehow, you'll get your job back, I just know it."

Did Jill detect a condescending tone in her voice? "Thank you. I'm fine. I've found another job."

"You did?" Landry didn't do a good job of masking her surprise. "Who hired you?"

"My hometown newspaper in Delavan, Wisconsin. Can you believe it?" Jill laughed. "With a circulation of fifteen thousand."

"That must be a nice change," the receptionist replied too cheerfully. "Whoops—there's the phone, got to run. I'll ring Rubric."

A moment later, a voice growled into the phone. "Rubric here."

"Rube, how are you?"

"Who is this?"

"It's Jill."

He growled again. "Look, I've got a few good people out on the street quietly checking all this out to see if we can find out anything further about Burke's adoption organization. I'll let you know if anything turns up."

"Thanks," Jill replied. "I'm going crazy over here. Today I had to write an obit for a parakeet. Rube, I don't know how much more of this I can take."

She heard him muffle a snicker.

"I appreciate everything you're doing on my behalf."

"Don't get all mushy on me, now," Rubric scolded. "You know how I hate that."

"My mom said you called yesterday. I thought you might have some news."

"You haven't heard?"

"How could I hear anything stuck way out here in Delavan? I can't even get a copy of the *Gazette* until it's two days old."

"It's your Christmas Elf, your informant. Sorry, Jillie, but . . . he hung himself."

"Oh, no!" Jill let out a small cry. She propped herself up against the column outside of the newspaper office. "Surely he wasn't afraid I would ever reveal his name? Even if it did go to trial, I would go to jail before I revealed my source."

"He knew that. And personally, I don't believe the Elf, a.k.a. Edgar Lapointe, hung himself."

"Are you saying you think he was murdered?" Jill asked incredulously. "And how did you know he was the informant?"

"It doesn't take a rocket scientist to figure it out, especially with the news of his suicide. After all, Lapointe was an insider, one of Burke's closest aides."

"Well, why don't we go to the FBI and tell them he was my informant and that we suspect Burke had him killed? There's a motive there."

"The FBI would never buy it, especially since you have an ax to grind with Burke. Motive yes, but you can't prove a murder without a weapon or a witness, and you can bet that Burke has meticulously covered his tracks."

Jill clenched her fist. "Edgar Lapointe was a good man," she said with anger. "When he first approached me, he was horrified with the discovery that Burke was making money on all those adoptions."

"A really good man wouldn't have charged you so much money for the tip; he would have taken it directly to the FBI," Rubric reminded her.

"He may not have been perfect, but he was deeply concerned that innocent children were being sold to pedophiles and other abusers, or anyone who could pay Burke's price." She rubbed her forehead. "He wanted to save those children, and he paid dearly for it. And it's my fault. My fault. I should've protected my source better."

"You aren't blaming yourself?"

"Who else?"

"Well, do you ever recall being watched or followed to any of your meetings with the Elf?"

"You know how careful I am about that, Rubric!"

"Yeah, but do you recall meeting anyone who might have seemed odd to you?"

Jill thought for a moment. "Well, what about that creep who chased me when I walked home from work?"

"Nah, that guy was just some street punk, probably no connection. Can you think of anyone or anything else?" Rubric challenged her. "Did you ever receive a package, or a gift, or anything unusual, or did anyone ever ask you to hold something for them and then walk away?"

"I can't think of anything," Jill admitted, scratching her head.

"Something that could have contained a bugging device?" Rubric prodded.

"No, sorry, but if I think of anything, I'll call." She thought for a moment. "Wait a minute! Something like that *did* happen to me on the morning I was fired."

"Go on."

"I was waiting in the line at the newsstand to buy my chocolate bars when someone bumped into a man behind me and made him drop all his coins." Jill quickly relayed the details of the story, leaving out the part about her being attracted to the guy. She told Rubric how the man had quickly disappeared, leaving the coin with her. "He suddenly wanted to get away from me, so maybe that explains why. He was planting a bug on me."

"Do you remember what he looked like?"

"How could I forget?" she said before thinking. "Six feet, well dressed, sandy brown hair, blue eyes. He was wearing Gucci shoes, and I remember him as being very charming and sentimental."

"How long did you say you saw him?"

"Not five minutes."

"Must have made quite an impression."

Ignoring him, Jill continued. "The man made a point of telling me that this was a very special coin, quite sentimental; probably because he knew I would hang on to it, believing he would return for it. And Rube, that's exactly what I did! Are you thinking what I'm thinking?"

"That coin probably contains a bug. Do you still have it? Could you send it to me?" Rubric asked.

"Sure, but it looks like a perfectly normal sixpence to me," Jill remarked as she pulled it out of her coin purse, turning it over suspiciously.

"Yeah, but you can never tell about the devices they have out there today. My friend who's an operative agent released a fly in my office last week and it landed on the wall. Would you believe that the fly was actually a microphone?"

"Wow, now that's a clever idea."

"Yeah, your coin might be a clever idea too, especially if he thought he was able to convince you of its value and sentimentality, knowing you would hang on to it and expect him to retrieve it."

"I would've never dreamed that the coin was a bugging device. You're a genius Rubric!"

"Whatever. Check out all the photos of Burke's employees again; see if this guy's face pops up."

"I'm not sure I could remember the man's face," she admitted.

"Well, you remembered everything else about him."

"Yeah, but not his face. But wait . . . his eyes; I would recognize those eyes anywhere. Thanks for your help, Rube."

"Can you FedEx that coin to me so I can have it checked out?"

"I'll send it right now," she promised, heading back inside the office.

Rubric sighed. "You reeled in a big one this time, Jill."

Before she could reply, she heard the phone click and then a dial tone. She sat down at her desk and hurriedly prepared the FedEx forms, reversing the charges carefully. She reluctantly taped the sixpence to a piece of cardboard, popped it into the envelope, and sealed it before dropping it at the front desk. *So you're a bad guy too, Mr. Blue Eyes? Well, I guess you can't trust anybody.*

Even after hearing Rubric's voice, her life in Washington seemed like a lifetime away. She shuddered with the realization that her decision to return to Delavan had probably saved her life. Had she not left when she did, her obituary might have appeared in the *Lakes News,* too. Since she had left Washington and was no longer an obvious threat, she hoped Burke would leave her alone. With a sigh she walked to the lunchroom in the back of the building, joining Marge for lunch as though nothing had happened.

Marge ate dry tuna fish on rye with a pickle and three glasses of ice water with a twist of lemon. Jill gobbled down pastrami on sourdough bread, a bag of potato chips, a candy bar, and a Diet Coke.

"Where do you get off eating like that and keeping your trim little figure?" Marge protested as she gulped her water. "I never understood how I could eat like a bird and still have hips the size of Chicago, yet people like you eat like I do in my dreams and still look great!"

Jill stopped chewing the bite in her mouth and shrugged her shoulders. When her mouth emptied enough, she said, "Guess I'm blessed with a good metabolism."

Craig walked into the lunchroom just at that moment to pour himself a mug of hot coffee.

"That is shameless eating, Jill, with all the information we have nowadays about cholesterol. Sooner or later all this food will catch up to you." With that curt comment, Craig adjusted his glasses and exited the room.

"What's with him? Does he just live in an eternal bad mood?"

"Craig?" Marge said. "Surely you jest! He's the most upbeat, happiest, friendliest guy I have ever known, girl!" She shook her head in his defense.

"Surely *you* jest."

"I never jest. Craig has only been in a bad mood for two days."

"And I have been here for two days," Jill calculated as she clenched her teeth.

"Well, then maybe you're the reason he's in a bad mood."

Jill couldn't hide her hurt. "Why me? What is there about me that would put him in a bad mood?"

"I dunno, ask him!"

———

That afternoon, Jill helped Marge file photographs, then she read several back issues of the paper to get a feel for the events the town considered important, and time and time again she felt drawn to Craig's articles. Surprisingly, they were very good. Although he was not a guy who turned your head, he was somewhat attractive, and he appeared intelligent. She needed a friend. Should she go into his office and try to get to know him? Noticing he was alone, she took a deep breath and walked over to his desk.

"I see you liked my copy this morning."

"Yeah," he said without looking up.

"Have I done anything to offend you?"

"Now, how could you have possibly offended me? You just got here."

"Right. I just want to get along with the people I work with." She shifted from one foot to the other.

"Well, I'm planning to send you out on a big assignment in a couple of weeks." Craig smiled mischievously.

"Great! I'm hungry for a meaty story."

"I suppose you think anything would be an improvement over writing obituaries for parakeets."

"You heard about poor old Petey Bird?" Jill said. "I didn't really mind. It's just that I was stunned. I mean, I couldn't believe my ears. I just hope my reaction didn't upset Max."

"No, Max understands a small-town paper takes some getting used to, especially writing about parakeets when you're used to writing about presidents." Craig sounded sympathetic.

"Thanks for understanding. So, tell me about my new assignment."

"You're going to do a story about a dog show. I'll send a photographer with you."

"A dog show?" The blood rushed to her face, and she gritted her teeth.

"Yep, up at Lake Lawn Resort. Any problem with that?"

"Not a one," she replied, trying her best to fake a broad smile.

To mask her outrage over the assignment, she walked swiftly back to her desk and started researching dog shows on her computer. She needed background information anyway in order to know what to ask and how to write the piece.

When she left for home that evening, she made sure to smile and say good-bye to each person. Craig saw her smiling at him and flashed a small one in return. He held up his hand in a half wave just as he turned his back toward her.

Grumbling all the way to her car, she asked herself what his problem was. *What could he possibly have against me? Must have something against strong women,* she figured as she jerked on the door handle to her car. It came off in her hand.

"Great, just great! This is all I need now!"

"Having problems?"

She spun around to see Craig standing right behind her.

Finally, a smile on his face! Too bad it was put there by my misfortune. She wanted to yell at him, "Everyone else likes me, so why don't you?" She felt insecure when it came to popularity.

"What's the problem?" he asked as she continued to struggle with the door.

"Everything is just fine," she insisted.

"May I help you at all?"

Jill walked over to the passenger side, opened the door, and threw the handle inside. "No, I've got it covered," she said as she climbed over the seat and awkwardly sat herself on the driver's side. She just wanted to get away from the embarrassing situation as soon as possible. Waving a quick good-bye, she sped out of the parking lot.

9

There are some wiser in their sleeping than in their waking.
—Ralph Iron

Jill jerked up in bed screaming, palms sweaty, heart pounding. Where was she? Looking around in the morning light, she let out a sigh of relief when she realized she was in the familiar surroundings of her childhood room, safe in her family's home. Haunted by the news of the Elf's murder, she had tossed and turned all night, awaking sporadically in a terrifying panic. Pulling her knees into her chest, she rested her chin on them as she gazed out the window. A ginger sky crowned the treetops as the sun shone splintering rays of diamonds across the lake and poured through the lace curtains. Quickly she swung her feet to the floor and headed for the shower.

As the hot water pelted down her back, the terrifying scenes from her dreams began to dance around in her head again. So many ominous faces . . . Senator Burke, her Washington stalker, the Elf, David, the handsome stranger with the coin. For Jill there was no escape, even in her dreams.

Stepping from the shower to dry off, Jill suddenly recalled that her father had appeared in her nightmare too. How glad she had been to see him sitting in his chair by the fireplace. But when he had looked up to see her, a look of terror flashed across his face and he hurriedly shuffled her down the basement stairs. Was he trying to hide her? And from whom? Glancing at the clock on her dressing table, she realized she had to be at the newspaper office in less than an hour. Hurriedly she began to dry her hair.

She suddenly recalled that her new boss, Craig Martin, had been in her dreams as well, only she couldn't remember where, how, or why. She did remember the relief and giddiness she felt at the sight of him, however.

"Good morning, darling," her mother's voice rang out as she poked her head inside Jill's room. "Did you sleep well?"

"Fine." She didn't want to worry her mother with the truth.

"How about some French toast for breakfast?"

"My favorite. Thanks!" Jill replied, thinking to herself how living at home certainly had its benefits. "I'll be down in a minute."

After Pearl served her French toast with berries, she put the syrup container on the table and sat down next to her. "Is something wrong?"

"Last night I dreamed about Dad."

"I miss him too." Tears formed in her mom's eyes. "Nights are the hardest for me. In my dreams he's alive, and oftentimes in the middle of the night, I reach over for him, but he isn't there. The mornings aren't easy either; when I wake up, I forget he's gone until I open my eyes, and then I remember."

"I'm sorry, Mom," Jill said quietly. She embraced her mother, and both women dabbed their eyes.

After breakfast Jill got in the passenger side of her car and then slid over to the driver's seat. She sped off down the road in a hurry, swiftly shifting gears. When she attempted to roll the window down, the crank came off in her hand. "What else can go wrong with this car?" she muttered.

Glancing in the rearview mirror, she spotted a red sports car careening down the hillside behind her, seemingly out of control.

"Whoa! Did you hit a patch of ice?" she asked the other driver under her breath.

Managing to remain in its lane now, the car sped up, shortening the distance between them. Thinking they might be in an emergency situation, Jill began to slow her speed in order to allow the car to pass. It drove right up to her bumper and stayed there, only inches away. There was another hill around the next corner, and she wanted to fix this situation before then—the whole thing made her feel uneasy. Since the handle was broken, she couldn't roll down her window to wave him on. She tried waving to him from inside the car by pointing at the road ahead, but the driver either didn't see her gestures or was confused by them.

Jill slowed her vehicle to a crawl. The gauge on the VW barely registered at five miles per hour. *Surely that car could pass me now,* she thought anxiously, yet it stayed right behind her. She twisted the wheel, pulling off to the side of the road for the sports car to go around her safely. But the other driver didn't go around; instead the red car rolled right behind her, right up to her bumper. Though she readjusted her rearview mirror to get a better look, the sports car's tinted glass made it impossible for her to see inside. The motor behind her revved up, and then the car gently pushed her rear bumper.

Without further contemplation, Jill pressed her foot on the accelerator. Her little car took off, burning rubber on the cold road. The sports car followed, matching her speed easily as it began to bump her repeatedly from the rear. Her car was so much lighter that the jolt sent her head crashing into the ceiling. Pain radiated through her head. Her heart beat wildly in her chest, and her breath came in short spurts. She had never been good at driving on icy roads and was frightened she might crash into a tree or slide into the lake.

"Lord, help me!" she screamed into the air of the car. A voice inside her told her to go where the people were. A mile ahead she would come to the highway. Could she make it that far without further incident? Jill prayed and clung to the steering wheel as if it were her life preserver. At the end of the endless mile, she saw the stop sign where the highway intersected the county road. She put on her turn signal to the left. Then she snapped it off, not wanting to give the driver behind her a heads up.

Slowing slightly, she quickly looked to the left, then to the right, and then back to the left again. Her high school instructor would have called it a "rolling stop." She could see cars in the distance, so she gave the VW a bit more gas but not too much, not wanting to spin out on the icy road. The highway would take her directly to town, where there would be witnesses and the police station waiting to help her.

Jill kept a death grip on the steering wheel and her foot on the gas pedal, her eyes staring straight ahead and waiting for help. She could see the rooftops of the stores in the village just ahead, and traffic was beginning to thicken. Thank goodness for other cars!

She became aware of blue flashing lights. As she looked around, she could see no sign of the sports car—only the police squad car. She slowed her speed and pulled off to the side of the road with the patrol car following right behind her. She rested her head on the steering wheel, and in an effort to calm down, she began to talk to herself. *Get ahold of yourself. You are in Delavan, not Washington, D.C. Hang on to that thought. You are jumping to conclusions just because Rubric thinks that the Elf was murdered, but that hasn't been proven yet, and it doesn't mean someone's out to get you. You are not in any danger . . . probably it was just some kids on a joyride. Besides, your little VW Bug is no match for a sports car; if they had wanted to push you in the lake, they could have.*

The officer got out of his vehicle and tapped on the glass of her VW.

"Please roll down the window," he demanded, his classic mirror sunglasses reflecting the morning sunshine.

"I can't."

"Roll it down!" he repeated.

"See this thing?" She held up her window crank handle.

"Get out of the car," he instructed her.

She was able to open the door from the inside of the driver's side and held it open with one hand so she could squeeze back inside when the interrogation was over.

"You were speeding. I need your license, proof of insurance, and registration," he said as he pulled off his glasses.

"Officer, I can't believe I'm saying this, but I'm so glad you're here! Someone was trying to run me off the road back there on County 0." Jill began shaking and put one hand down on her car for support.

The officer peered at her. "Hey, is that you . . . Jill Lewis? Still driving the same old VW." He was smiling. "You haven't changed a bit."

She studied him more closely. "Chuck, Chuck Emerson!"

"I heard you were some big shot down in Washington, D.C."

"Don't believe all you hear," she said with a grimace. "I've moved back, and I'm working at the *Lakes News*. Listen, you won't believe this, but I think someone was trying to run me off the road."

"Did you get the license plate?"

"No. But it was a red sports car."

"What kind of sports car?"

"I don't know. I'm not that familiar with cars, but I think it might have been a Porsche."

"Well, I've gotta admit, that is the best excuse I have ever heard for not getting a ticket." Chuck grinned.

"It isn't an excuse! Look at my rear bumper if you don't believe me!"

Jill led Chuck around to the back of the car. Other than age, it looked perfectly normal.

"How could that be?" she wondered. Chuck looked at her and chuckled.

"He must not have hit me very hard. Maybe he was just trying to tap the back of my car and spin me off the road."

"Well, whatever the reason, I'll forgo the ticket for speeding. It was a very creative excuse. You get an A+." Chuck laughed. "You always were a smart girl. I guess some things never change."

"Give me the ticket." Jill held out her hand.

"Nope, I'm letting you go with a warning."

She put her hands on her hips. "I insist that you give me the ticket, Officer."

"Nope, sorry."

"All right, then. Thank you. Hey, Chuck, I mean Officer, are you sure you don't know anyone around here who might have a red sports car?"

"Only your brother-in-law that I can recall. He owns a Porsche, but it's not red and it's a fairly new model." Chuck scratched his head.

"Hmm, a Porsche. Jeff must be doing pretty well."

"You should know. He's your brother-in-law."

Jill blushed. She knew so little about her sister's life. But she would soon make it her business to find out.

At about that time, Craig pulled up in his truck and got out, cautiously walking up to them.

Chuck put away his ticket book. "Hey, just be careful on these roads, Miss Hot Rod. The next officer who pulls you over for speeding may not know you and give you a break."

"Anything wrong, Officer?" Craig sounded concerned and protective. "Jill and I work together at the *Lakes*."

"Hi, Craig. Nothing a little less foot on the gas pedal wouldn't cure." Chuck laughed and shook his finger at Jill as if it were an order. He got back into his patrol car and drove up beside Jill and Craig. "You look good, Jill. Real good. You and I should have dinner one night." Chuck peered over his sunglasses that had slid down his nose.

Embarrassed that Chuck had asked her out in front of Craig, Jill managed to smile and reply meekly, "Great."

"Oh, and Jill, I would suggest you get your car window and door handles fixed as soon as possible. Your inspection sticker is about to expire too. See you around." Pushing his sunglasses back up on his nose, he nodded at Craig and then pulled away.

"You two know each other?" Craig asked.

Jill's hands were still trembling and her pulse racing, but she took a deep breath and explained. "We went to high school together."

"What was Chuck like in high school?"

"Well, he had that same dark hair, those dark brooding eyes, but maybe that Adonis body of his isn't quite the same," she said with a shaky smile. "He was the star quarterback of the football team and the son of one of Delavan's most prominent families, and every girl in town wanted to go out with him."

"Including you?"

"Well, there was a time when I would've given my right arm to be his girl, but he was so wild that my parents would've never let me go out with him. Besides, when one of my friends told him I had a crush on him, Chuck told her, 'Jill's kinda cute, but she's flat chested.'"

Jill laughed; Craig blushed. She hadn't expected her comment to embarrass him, but he looked up to avoid staring at her chest. Finally he chuckled, "Well, now, after all these years, you've finally got your big chance."

"Very funny."

"I'm surprised that old Chuck was such a rebel in high school; he seems so straight."

"That's because after high school, his father made him join the army. To everyone's surprise he came back to Delavan as a model citizen and joined the police force to protect us from the bad guys." At the mention of "the bad guys," the image of the red sports car suddenly floated through her head. *Probably just a teenager like Chuck once was, just a dumb kid out having some fun harassing people.*

"You look upset."

"No, I'm fine." Jill crawled back into her car and turned around and smiled. "Thanks for coming to my rescue."

"Better be careful on these roads," Craig warned. "Driving is dangerous when they're slick."

"I am careful. I was—" She stopped suddenly and decided it was better not to mention the red car. "Yeah, sure. Thanks, Craig. See you at the office."

Later at the office Craig stopped by her desk and asked, "Can you finish up those classified ads and have them on Marge's desk by noon?"

"Sure." She tried to concentrate on the classifieds she had offered to do for Marge, but she thought about the little car trying to push her off the road. Was it connected to the senator and her investigation? Had her late-night stalker been connected to them too? What about the Elf's death? *But the senator's career wasn't damaged by my alleged inaccurate investigation at all, so why would someone want to harm me?* She decided again it had probably just been a kid out joyriding. She picked up her phone and dialed.

"Landry, is Rubric there?" Jill asked without stopping to chat.

"Here? Have you forgotten so soon? He sleeps here." The receptionist laughed heartily.

In a moment, Rubric picked up. "Rubric here."

Just hearing his scratchy voice was comforting to Jill. "Rube? It's me again."

"I'm waiting," he barked impatiently.

"Do you, uh . . . think I'm safe?"

"If you're worried someone's going to put out a hit on you like someone did on Elfie, don't. His death may have been suicide just like the police said. What did he have to live for after you left Washington, anyway?"

"That isn't funny!" Jill snapped, picturing the waif of a man swinging from a rope. "And besides, with a ruined career, what threat am I to the senator up here in Delavan writing obituaries? There's nothing to worry about, is there?"

"I'm sure you're fine." He hesitated. "Just be careful, Jillie." With that Rubric hung up, and the dial tone roared in Jill's ear once again. Slowly she replaced the phone back in its cradle and resumed work on the classifieds.

———

Jill was disappointed that Craig had stayed inside his office most of the morning. How was she ever going to make friends with him if he avoided her? By 11:00 A.M. she had the ads on Marge's desk, so she stuck her head in Craig's office to tell him so, but he was busily typing on his computer. Later he briefly stopped by her desk to thank her for meeting the deadline, but he made no attempt to converse with her. Jill had noticed lines of worry creasing his forehead this morning. She couldn't imagine what this man had to worry about. Women problems, perhaps?

At closing time, Jill cleared off her desk and mustered up the courage to knock on his office door once again.

"Do you need something?" he whispered, cupping his hand over the receiver.

"No, I just wanted to say good night."

He smiled a half smile and said, "Good night, Jill."

She returned his nod and turned to go.

Out in the parking lot, she shrugged her shoulders. Why didn't Craig like her? He was so standoffish. Maybe her success as a reporter had threatened him. Was he just pretending to be on the phone so he could continue avoiding her?

———

Later that evening Jill read a murder mystery that Rubric had recommended, probably not the best activity considering her recent experiences. He had called it entertaining, but it only left her unnerved. On impulse she got up to lock her window, then pulled the draperies shut. She decided to sleep with her bedside lamp on, something she hadn't done since she was a child.

Glancing about the room, she noticed the Bible her mother had placed on her nightstand. She reached over and opened it. Where to begin? Maybe the Psalms. People always seemed to quote from Psalms in times of trouble. She began to read but quickly became bored. *What does Mom find so intriguing about this book?*

Setting the Bible back on the nightstand, her thoughts turned to Craig. Why did she feel so drawn to him? Yes, he was cute, but not exceptionally so. There was nothing outstanding about him: dark brown, almost black, eyes, jet black hair, six feet tall, dull personality, and less than impressive clothes. He was a good writer; she had acquainted herself with his style and admired his talent. He truly had a gift for fashioning words and thoughts just the right way to make a subject interesting, yet he was completely objective. And he had fresh ways of looking at old ideas. But those awful black glasses! He needed to lose them before his next date. She wondered if he had a girlfriend.

Jill pounded her pillow and sat back in bed. She would have to have a really good sense of humor to offset all that moodiness going on with him. She wondered what that was all about. She wanted to see him laugh. Somewhere beneath his stuffy exterior there had to be a laugh, at least one good laugh. What would his laugh sound like? *Why am I even thinking about his laugh, anyway? Who cares about Craig Martin's laugh?* She was mending her broken heart over David. Wasn't she?

Her dad had had a good laugh. He would clap his hands and slap his side with a good belly laugh. She remembered how they'd laughed together on the phone the night before his death. She was teasing him about . . . what was it? Oh yes, about some new pet project he had taken up, a new cause. He told her she'd probably find it very interesting, since he was inspired by her investigative report. Jill had laughed, thinking her father was so sweet to try playing pup reporter to her. When she'd pressed him for more information, he told her he wanted to confirm several details before jumping the gun. Before hanging up she had told him that if what he was looking into was correct, maybe she'd put him on the *Gazette* payroll. Laughing, he told her he was sure he was going to solve her case so she could go ahead and write that check. Oh, how she wished she had taken his comments seriously, and questioned him further.

Suddenly Jill shot straight up in bed. A chill of terror slowly trickled down her spine. What if her dad was serious about a tie-in to her investigation?

10

It was as if I had worked for years
On the wrong side of the tapestry,
Learning accurately all its lines and figures,
Yet missing its color and sheen.

—Anna Louise Strong

The next morning Jill arrived at the paper by 7:00. Marge was already hard at work and plunking away at an old typewriter. She unlocked the door to let her inside the office.

"Did you forget it was Saturday?" Marge asked. "Hardly anyone comes in on Saturday except for the sportswriters."

"I need to read the obituaries from the week of March 28, a year ago," Jill said.

"Be my guest."

"Could you please get them for me?" Jill asked, opening her thermos of hot chocolate and taking a short sip. She grimaced. She had forgotten the vanilla.

"Nope."

"And why not?" Jill said, wondering why Marge couldn't be as efficient as Landry.

"Our back issues are stored in a warehouse outside of town.

Try the library. They keep the hard copies of the newspaper, and if they don't have that old a copy, they'll have it on microfilm for you to read."

"What time does the library open?"

"Not until Monday."

"But this is Saturday. You're not telling me they aren't open on Saturday." Jill set the hot chocolate down on a desk.

"This is the Saturday they clean and do their biannual inventory." Marge sounded apologetic, as if it was her fault.

"Where's Craig? What time does he come in?"

"It's Saturday," Marge repeated. "He's off today. He goes to his cabin up in Door County on Clark's Lake near Egg Harbor whenever he gets a chance."

"Does he have family up there?" Jill asked, trying to fish more information out of her about Craig.

"I have no idea if he has any family here, but I do know he's not married."

"He must have a girlfriend," Jill ventured, trying not to show any interest.

"So ol' Craig has a girlfriend. He ought to bring her down here so we can all meet her."

"No, I'm not *saying* he has a girlfriend, I'm *asking* if he has a girlfriend."

"Nope. No girlfriend, or not one that I know. Never talks about one. I've never seen him with anyone."

"Well, I guess it would be okay then to disturb him on the weekend. Do you have his number?"

"Nope. He goes up there to get away on the weekends."

"You must know how to reach him in case of an emergency," Jill insisted.

"In Delavan? You've got to be joking." Marge snickered. "But if you're so anxious to get ahold of him, why don't you call him on his cell phone?"

Jill felt near to exhaustion from talking to Marge. "Okay, will you please give me that number?"

After digging through numerous drawers, Marge finally found Craig's cell phone number on the Rolodex. She handed Jill the number, and Jill sat at her desk to make the call. After three rings he picked up.

"Craig here." Even on the weekend, he was all business.

"Craig, this is Jill."

"Jill? Jill who?"

Sigh. "Jill Lewis."

"Oh, the girl who I just hired to write the obits."

"Max hired," she corrected.

"I'm the managing editor. I have the final say."

She wanted to slam the phone on his ear. If it hadn't been so urgent, she would have. "So *you're* the one I have to thank for this job?"

"You're welcome."

"Craig, I need to talk to you right away about something very important."

"I'm listening."

"I think this is something I need to discuss with you in person."

"I'll be back on Monday morning. Catch me then."

"Not soon enough. This can't wait. May I drive up and see you there?"

There was a long silence, which indicated to Jill that he probably did have a girl with him. Despite herself, her heart sank. She even felt a hint of jealousy, and she had the green eyes to prove it.

"It's a long drive, and we already had snow and are expecting more, but yeah, if it can't wait and you want to make the trip, then come on up. I need to give you the directions though. Have a pen handy?"

She picked up a pen and said, "Shoot." After he rambled off two pages of meticulous directions, she voiced her next concern. "It's quite a drive, so I'll need to stay overnight. Are there any nice motels near you that are open in the off-season?"

"Nothing but a bed and breakfast in Egg Harbor that guarantees clean sheets and great food. But it's not too far from me; I'll call over there right now to reserve a room for you. Once you're settled, call me. Stay hungry; the seafood is great here. Over dinner tonight, we can discuss whatever is so urgent that it can't wait."

"What's the name of the place?" Jill asked.

"The White Gull Inn. It's right on Main Street in Fish Creek Village. Just follow the directions I gave you to Main Street and keep going straight instead of turning left. It'll be on your right. It's a white clapboard with blue shutters. Jennifer is the innkeeper."

"Jennifer . . . got it, thanks!"

———

At home, Jill packed a small overnight bag, thinking that it would be good for her to get away.

"Hmm, by the amount of clothes you're taking with you, I'd say you were planning on being gone for a week," her mother said as she stepped inside Jill's room.

"No, just for one night. I'm working on an assignment in Door County, and it's really cold up there. They've already had some snow, so I'm taking several layers."

"I hope you won't get snowed in. Do you have to go?"

"My managing editor lives up there. We're working on this together."

"How well do you know this man?" Her mother stood with her hands on her hips.

"I work with him, Mom. Besides, Max knows him. You have my permission to call Max and check Craig out if it'll make you feel better."

"Well, should I come along for company? I really don't mind."

"Mom, I'll be fine, and I have my cell phone," Jill assured her. "If there are any problems, you'll be the first to know." Jill felt a wave of love for her mother and hugged her. Losing one parent had made her feel all the more appreciative of the other. Suddenly she felt guilty about not being completely honest with her mother about her reasons for making the trip. But she hadn't wanted to worry her either; she loved her too much to add that burden. Knowing she'd better get started, Jill gave her mom one last squeeze and said, "Would you mind making a turkey sandwich for me so I won't starve on my long drive up?"

"I'll make it only if I can put the meat on whole wheat, not that preservative-filled white bread you normally like to eat."

"Deal. Thanks, Mom."

As her mother turned to go to the kitchen, Jill remembered feeling this way the first day of kindergarten when her mom dropped her off and walked away. Only now Jill was leaving, and it was her mom with the sad look on her face. Jill waited for her mom to go down the steps before she took the disks out of their hiding place. Reaching for another box of disks, she popped one in the disk drive and copied another set of files for Craig. She put the copies of the disks into her briefcase and returned the original disks to their hiding place. Pulling out the files from the lamp, she snapped those into her case as well and carried it downstairs with her suitcase.

Pearl was slipping the food into a small basket for her journey. "How long will it take you to drive there?"

"About five or six hours, I imagine. I should get there about dark. I'm staying at the White Gull Inn in Egg Harbor, and I'll call you the minute I get to my room."

"And what time will you be starting back tomorrow?"

"I'm not sure yet, but I'll call before I leave. Hey, do you think I could borrow your BMW? I'm having trouble getting in and out of my car. The door handle broke off and the window crank did too. Guess I shouldn't have sold my car, huh?"

Her mom burst out laughing. "I see you still need your mama's help, no matter how old you are. You can take my BMW, but your father's Range Rover is probably safer in the snow. The keys are on the silver tray on the chest in the foyer. I'll call Rich's Garage and have them tow the Volkswagen to make the repairs."

"I need a safety inspection too, while they're at it. Thanks, Mom; be sure to tell me what it costs you so I can pay you back."

"Forget it. The Volkswagen is fine to tool around town in, but I'm not so sure it's safe out on the highway. I've discussed this with Kathy, and it's fine with her—I want to give you your father's Range Rover."

"Mom, I couldn't!"

"Why not? I'll only lose money if I sell it, and you need a safe car," her mom insisted as a faraway look crossed her eyes. "I sometimes wonder if your father had been driving the Range Rover instead of his Jaguar, if he would've survived the accident."

Jill hugged her mother. Ordinarily she would have refused such a magnanimous gift, but after her incident with the red Porsche, she agreed with her mother—she needed a safe car.

"Drive carefully." Pearl kissed her daughter, whispering a prayer of protection over the top of her head. Jill flinched slightly at the mention of God. She felt envious that her mother could find such peace—there was no such peace for Jill. Yet she was determined to give more thought to the faith her mother lived by. After all, she had a long drive ahead of her, and what if she was right about the connection between her father and her investigation?

She would certainly need God in her corner.

11

In the depths of winter I finally learned
There was in me an invincible summer.

—Albert Camus

Jill enjoyed driving her dad's Range Rover after rattling around in her little VW Bug; her father's SUV was a luxury in comparison. It handled smoothly and had great power. She decided the long drive wouldn't be so bad; she might actually enjoy it.

After driving for a couple hours, hunger set in. Jill fumbled with the basket of food her mother had prepared for her and opened the lid. Inside was the sandwich on wheat bread and, instead of tasty potato chips, a large bag of Veggie Booty and a bunch of green seedless grapes. "Surely she didn't forget the brownies!" Jill dug a little deeper in the basket and found a brownie and two chocolate chip cookies. Nibbling her food contentedly, Jill glanced at her gas gauge. It was nearing empty. Unlike her little Bug, this baby guzzled gas. She pulled into the next gas station.

After filling up, she went inside to pay and buy a Diet Coke for the road. As she reached inside the refrigerated case, her eyes were diverted to the next case, which was stacked with rows of festive colored bottles of ice-cold juices. Her fingers fell from around the neck of the plastic bottle of Diet Coke. Maybe she should become a bit more health conscious?

While contemplating her decision, a booming voice took her by surprise. "Lady, do you plan to stand there all day?"

Turning swiftly she came eyeball to belly with a burly trucker. "Awwwgh!" she screamed as she jumped. Her face burned when she realized her overreaction. "I'm sorry," she said as she quickly moved out of the way. The trucker grunted and grabbed a six-pack out of the case and then headed for the cashier.

Opening the case door again, Jill pulled out two sixteen-ounce bottles of Diet Coke and fell into the back of the line, behind the trucker, to pay for her purchases. *Why try to kick the habit when I'm going through so much stress?*

Back in the car, Jill twisted off the cap of the Diet Coke and slowly put the icy-cold bottle to her lips, savoring every mouthful of the liquid. She gobbled the rest of her sandwich before pulling the Range Rover back on the highway.

Driving with one hand, she snacked on the brownie with the other, crumbs cascading down the front of her until she remembered she was meeting Craig for dinner. She returned the leftover food to the basket and closed the lid.

Would Craig be with someone up there? Maybe there wasn't a girl with Craig. Maybe he just hesitated because he wanted a peaceful weekend with no company. Surely he wouldn't have invited her to dinner if he'd been with someone. She found herself caring if he was involved in a relationship or not. It was a feeling she was not sure she liked having, especially after knowing him for only a few days. She had to focus on her mission, not Craig.

Jill wondered how much Craig knew about her professional past. She felt confident he knew it all. Maybe if she confided in him her suspicions that her father was somehow connected to her investigation, he could help her sort it out. Had she lost her touch for accurate reporting? Was she seeing phantoms? All the thoughts and suspicions made her feel dizzy.

Snow began falling, making the roads slicker as it began to accumulate. Trying to relax, Jill popped in John Grisham's latest book on tape and continued to follow the directions Craig had given. At last she arrived at the B and B.

"Welcome, I'm Jennifer," the owner said with a smile as Jill entered the lobby. "This time of year business is slow, so you have the place to yourself."

"That's fine. I just need my room and time to unwind."

Still covered in a light snow from head to foot, Jill took the key and lugged her belongings to her room. After she'd settled in, she called home to report her safe arrival. Her next call was to Craig.

"I've been cooking for us ever since you called," he proclaimed.

"Oh, I'm sorry, I didn't mean for you to go to any trouble."

"Forget it. I love to cook, and I promised you a dinner by the lake. Hope you're hungry."

She looked at her basket of half-eaten food. "I'm always hungry."

"You've had a long drive, so I'll come pick you up at the Inn. I'll be by in thirty minutes."

"Make it forty-five minutes, please. I have a steaming bath waiting for me, and I need to get my notes and thoughts together." *And have more time to get hungry again and calm down,* she thought.

Luxuriating in the footed tub filled with steamy lavender water, Jill sipped from a cup of hot apple cider, compliments of the B and B. After a good long soak with lots of bubbles, she dried off and pulled on her jeans and a white cashmere sweater. Onto her ears went cultured pearls; the matching necklace was already snapped around her neck. She brushed her hair until it shone and lay flat at her shoulders. A spray of perfume, and she was ready.

As she was sliding her arms into her leather jacket, she heard a knock at the door. She felt nervous again, as if she were on a first date with a guy she was crazy about. She reminded herself this was business and she must act professionally. She glanced down at her hands as she turned the glass knob on the oak door, feeling grateful that she had stopped biting her nails. She had grown them out for David's engagement ring, but when that had fizzled, she had resisted the temptation to bite them again.

She swung the door open. Craig's eyes traveled from her eyes down to her boots and then back up again to her eyes. "Wow, you look nice," he muttered.

"Thank you. Let me get my things," she said as she grabbed her briefcase and laptop from beside the bed.

"Looks serious," Craig said, obviously making an attempt to be lighthearted and hide his discomfort.

So you're nervous too! Could this mean you have a bit of a crush on me? She liked the thought but quickly pushed it out of her mind. There was a job to do, and she had come here for business, not a date.

"Shall we go?" Craig said. He held the door open for her and assisted her climb up into his pickup truck.

"I wouldn't have figured you for a pickup truck kind of guy," Jill commented after they were seated.

"There's a whole lot about me you don't know." Craig's brown eyes suddenly twinkled.

Yeah! A smile. Maybe a laugh too before the evening is through, please. Jill could only hope.

They chatted easily and comfortably as the truck treaded across the ice ruts in the road. It was still snowing, but not as hard. The wind was starting to blow a little.

"What kind of food do you like, Jill? Besides junk food?"

"Have you been speaking to my mother?"

"I've never met your mother, but she must be a smart lady," Craig replied. "I hope you like seafood."

"Love it."

"I bought a couple of fresh lobsters and steamed them and then whipped up a garlic sauce with linguine."

"Mmm." Jill licked her lips. "I didn't expect to be wined and dined. And I never figured you for a Food Channel junkie."

"I told you, there's a lot you don't know about me." Craig smiled. "I am anxious to hear what's so important you had to come all the way up here instead of waiting until Monday. But let's enjoy our dinner first, if that's okay with you?"

"Great," Jill replied with a big smile.

And then he laughed. It was a full-hearted laugh filled with spirit and joy. Better than she imagined.

The truck's headlights glared off the side of the cabin as they turned in to the driveway. So much snow! It had been plowed away from the house into large mounds. Off to the right she could see the lake framed by the snowy woods, the scene punctuated with an occasional cabin.

Another car was parked in the driveway. Jill's eyes caught a figure moving around inside the house. Her heart sank. She must have misread Craig. She wanted to go right back home to Delavan, but then she remembered the real purpose of her trip. She wanted to kick herself for letting the ridiculous thought of a romance sidetrack her.

Jill entered the lighted cabin filled with heavenly cooking aromas and warmed by a roaring fire. Craig carried her laptop and her briefcase inside and placed them on the pine coffee table. She noticed the table was heaped with hunting magazines and a large bowl of green apples. Looking around the cabin, she saw it had a masculine lodge look, yet it was comfortable and cozy with a large sofa and two overstuffed chairs piled high with Ralph Lauren pillows of western plaids. A life-size oil painting of regal spaniels with birds in their mouths hung over the stone fireplace that soared up to the cathedral ceiling. A hallway off the great room obviously led to the bedrooms and baths. There were two weight machines and a treadmill in the loft above.

Glancing at the dining area off the kitchen, she spotted a long pine table beautifully set for two. The logs burning in the fireplace and the strains of soft music playing softly lent a cozy atmosphere to the room. *"Okay, Jill, stop with the romance,"* she scolded herself.

She heard a voice from another room. "Craig, is that you home already? How were the roads?" In a moment, a strikingly beautiful woman walked into the room. Long, dark lashes framed her glistening hazel eyes. Her short, reddish hair only accentuated her turned-up pixie nose. She looked as if she belonged here in this cabin with Craig in her comfortable old pair of faded jeans and loose-fitting sweater.

"Hi! Craig tells me you two are having an important meeting, so I'll be on my way in a minute."

Who is this? Jill thought. She held out her hand in greeting. "I'm Jill Lewis."

"Oh, forgive me. I'm Caroline Jennings."

Craig stood with his arms folded over his stomach, smiling as if he had the answer to the universe and was not about to share it.

Caroline gave Craig a quick wink and scooted out the door. "Nice meeting you, Jill. See you later, Craig," she said as she breezed out the door.

Jill waved weakly as the beautiful creature disappeared into the snow.

———

Craig served her after they sat down to dinner. Gone was the easy conversation they had shared back in the truck. Jill couldn't help but wonder if she was eating Caroline's dinner.

"She seemed very nice. How do you know her?" Jill asked, pushing around the food on her plate, trying to be nonchalant.

Craig appeared to ignore the question; his eyes twinkled as he uncorked the wine.

"No, thank you." Jill covered the glass with her hand.

Craig turned and poured himself a glass. "Are you sure? It's a great merlot."

"I'm sure." She paused for a moment. "Uh, I asked who Caroline was."

"A good friend."

What did that mean? A girlfriend? A fiancée? Maybe a house sitter who kept the home fires burning while Craig was away in Delavan during the week? She wished he would elaborate, but his mischievous grin told her he was enjoying this little cat-and-mouse game.

Realizing Craig wasn't about to tell her who Caroline Jennings was, Jill opted to change the topic of conversation. "You know, Craig, there's something about you that seems vaguely familiar to me. Have we met someplace before?"

"Of course we have," he said while stirring the noodles on his plate. "I look familiar because we both work at the same place. You are *under* management and I am *upper* management."

"Very funny," she said, then took her first bite of pasta.

"Mmm. This is delicious! Where did you learn to cook like this?"

"Thank you. If you can read, you can cook."

Jill frowned, not liking that assessment, since she could hardly boil water.

A slow song came on the CD player. *"One look in your eyes and there I see . . ."*

"This is one of my all-time favorite songs," Jill remarked, waving her fork in the air to the music floating through the room. For a brief moment her mind went back to high school—riding in a car with her boyfriend-of-the-moment, listening to this song. "Do you know it?"

"Yeah, I remember this song from my senior prom." He smiled. "I can remember wanting so badly to ask my date to dance to this song, but I was afraid to put my arms around her, so we danced to all the fast ones and sat the slow ones out."

"Just what you mean to me . . ."

"She was probably dying for you to ask her too," Jill said, knowing that she would have wanted to dance with him.

"I know that now, but it's too late."

"Here in my heart, I believe your love is all I will ever need."

"It's never too late."

"Oh, it's definitely too late. She's married now with four kids!" He laughed, brandishing his fork in the air.

"Oh, you!" Suddenly an impulsive urge took hold of her. "Dance with me, Craig!" she begged, taking him by the wrist and pulling him to his feet.

"Now? But your supper will get cold," he objected, trying to sit back down.

"We'll reheat it." She took both his hands and dragged him to the center of the room.

"Nah, I'd feel too dumb."

"Here and now. I promise to love faithfully."

"Me too, but let's dance to this song, please," she begged. "You don't want to regret not dancing with me years from now when you hear this song, do you?"

"You're all I need . . ."

Without another word, he put his arms around her, and they began to sway to the music.

"Here and now . . ."

He had never touched her before. Well, maybe once his hand had brushed against hers when he handed a pencil to her the day she was busy sharpening all those No. 2s in the office. Having him hold her felt nice.

Just as they began to move in sync with the song, it ended and a fast one began.

Craig pulled away from her. "We'd better finish dinner," he said lightly.

Jill's heart was beating so loudly she thought he might hear it as they returned to the table. With shaking hands, she tore into her lobster. The hard shell cracked, and small pieces flew across the table, landing on his face, hair, and glasses.

Couldn't have planned this better. "You'd never know that my mother used to teach charm classes at the church," she giggled.

Craig laughed and went to the sink to rinse off his thick glasses. Jill followed him and snatched them up. She put them on her face to see how bad his eyesight was.

"Craig! There couldn't be a prescription in here!"

"Only a mild one." He quickly took the glasses away and went back to the table. As Jill passed by him to take her seat, she snatched the glasses off his nose.

"Give me back my glasses."

"Nope. Not until you tell me what or who are you hiding from behind these things."

Craig responded without any hesitation. "I wear those

glasses in conjunction with my contacts to correct a slight astigmatism. Would you like to examine my contacts too?"

"I'm sorry," Jill apologized. "I just thought maybe you wore them to keep people at a distance."

"They do come in handy for that, but unfortunately, they don't stop some nosey people," he chuckled, looking in her direction.

"Well, I think I know why you *really* wear them."

"To see," he retorted.

"No . . . you want to look like Clark Kent."

"Excuse me while I go into my phone booth and don my Superman cape," he said with a grin.

"Think we could convince Max to rename the *Lakes* the *Daily Planet?*"

"Only if you change your name to Lois Lane," Craig volleyed back. "You're a nut, did you know that?"

"I don't care. Leave the glasses off for dinner anyway."

"Okay, Jill."

When he said her name, she thought she heard music in his voice. Whoever this Caroline Jennings was, she must not be too important to him.

12

Seek and ye shall find.
—Matthew 7:7 KJV

Jill was disappointed. Craig hadn't made dessert. As she looked in the freezer, her voice resounded her dismay. "What? Not even any ice cream? What kind of man are you, anyway?"

"A healthy man," he said, tossing her an apple from a wooden bowl. "Eat this; it's better for you."

"Thanks." Jill sighed, catching the apple and taking a bite. "We have to get to work anyway."

"Show me what you got." His playfulness had evaporated, and now he was all business.

"Yes, my material. Let's sit on the couch." Jill tried to match his demeanor.

She booted up her laptop. Craig moved over on the sofa beside her.

"I really appreciate your inviting me to your cabin," Jill began. "I feel exiled in Delavan, and I really didn't know where or who to turn to."

"You invited yourself, remember?" He grinned at her.

She felt her face burning. She looked at him and saw the smile fade from his face.

"I'm sorry, Jill. I'm really honored you felt you could trust me. What's troubling you?"

"It's my Washington investigation."

"I've heard and read all about what happened to you in Washington."

"You and everyone else in the country."

"So what's your story?"

"Well, I was investigating a tip I got from an inside source who revealed that a prominent senator was at the helm of an overseas child smuggling ring. Since babies are hard to find to adopt in the United States, the ring was illegally taking babies from women or couples overseas for a small sum of money—or they would steal the children outright. The children were brought over here through Canada and then sold to underground baby firms for astronomical sums. The adoptive families weren't even investigated, meaning even a pedophile could adopt a child as long as the person had the money."

"It's hard to believe something so outrageous could happen in this country." Craig frowned with disapproval.

Unlike David's apathetic reaction to the scandal, Craig was horrified, much to Jill's satisfaction. "The senator was able to arrange for all the necessary papers for the babies to get out of these countries—all fraudulent, I might add," she explained.

"Who would want to deal with shady people like these?"

"People who are desperate to be parents will do just about anything for a baby. Others could not possibly pass the strict screening process for legal adoptions in this country. Many of the deserving parents probably didn't know they were dealing with an illegal organization. And maybe the papers looked legit to them and they didn't press it because they had a baby to bring home to fill an empty crib.

"Anyway, after the story broke, Senator Burke's office conveniently provided the necessary documentation to the FBI and the *Gazette*—legal birth certificates, thorough investigations and home studies of the adoptive parents, medical exams of the children, and the children's biographies, all of which indicated that these children were abandoned. It was all accepted and thus proved that his organization was totally legitimate. They also provided canceled checks of millions of dollars of donations that supported the organization."

Craig thought for a moment. "Pretty solid evidence, but what in your documentation proved otherwise?"

"I had verified every adoption in each of the files I was given. I even went so far as to confirm my documentation with the adoptive parents."

"Weren't they afraid they might lose their children?"

"Oh yes, but I've been at this undercover business a long time, and they not only talked to me, but agreed to testify after I had an attorney assure them their adoptions wouldn't be jeopardized."

"So what do Burke's people and the publisher at the *Gazette* say about your documentation?"

"That it's fabricated."

"Sounds like you got double-crossed by your source. Who was it?"

"You know I can't tell you that," Jill said. "But I know my source knew what he was doing. I've got the right man—he's Burke, and this is all a big cover-up. He got to those families and threatened them with the loss of their adopted children and supplied them with phony documentation and records."

"How do you plan to prove it?" Craig asked.

"For starters, my source hung himself a few weeks ago."

"Edgar Lapointe from Burke's office?"

Jill nodded, impressed that Craig kept up on the senator. "But Rubric believes he was murdered, and I'm beginning to agree with him."

"Who's Rubric?"

"My editor. My former editor."

"So how do you plan to prove that Burke is really at the helm of this adoption ring?"

Jill replied with conviction. "I need more evidence, some real proof, so I can force the FBI to conduct a full investigation."

"How are you planning to do that from here?"

"Well, Rubric has his informants out on the street in Washington, and I plan to do as much research, checking, and rechecking as I can from here." She hesitated. "And truthfully, I was hoping that you . . . that you might help me. I've been watching you around the office and you seem, uh, to have good instincts," she said, borrowing Rubric's compliment of her.

"Thanks." He smiled. "I enjoy dabbling in it." Her admiration seemed to please him. "Why did the FBI refuse to do an investigation?"

"Unfortunately, when Senator Burke's attorneys provided the necessary documentation before my story broke, they were apparently satisfied and closed the case. The next morning I was fired."

"That's not surprising."

"Yeah, I guess not. And if we don't do something soon, I'm afraid he'll be our next president." Jill jumped up and stood in front of the roaring fire. The warmth from the fireplace felt good on her back.

"Were you able to get a copy of Burke's documentation?"

"Right here." She held up the big envelope.

"Good girl. I may want to keep these for a bit to take time reading."

"Take all the time you need. So, do you think you can help me, Craig?"

"Yes, I'll help you, but you're going to have to give me my glasses back if you expect me to read all these files."

Sheepishly, Jill tiptoed over to the table to retrieve his glasses from their hiding place underneath her napkin.

Craig commandeered her laptop and read through some of the files for an hour. Jill sat across the room from him, pretending to read, but really she watched him. She noticed how he wrinkled his brow while he was thinking and scratched his head when he felt confused.

He finally shut down the computer. "It's late," he said when the clock chimed at 2:00 A.M. "I'd better get you back to the B and B."

Jill stood up and began gathering her things.

"Do you trust me enough to hold on to these disks for a few weeks?" Craig asked. "I want to read them more closely."

"They're yours. I made copies for you, but I have read and reread it and I can't find anything there."

"Maybe that's the trouble . . . you're looking too closely."

"Yeah, maybe." Jill bit her lip.

"Anything else troubling you?"

She was hesitant to tell him about the red sports car. "Do you believe I'm safe here?" she asked casually, not really wanting to hear the answer.

Craig stood up from the sofa and put his arm on her shoulder in a brotherly sort of way. "I think you're safe in Delavan, probably anywhere for that matter, since it would be too obvious to put out a hit on you. That would open up the mother of investigations."

"That's what Rubric says too," she sighed. "But what about a murder that looks like an accident?"

"Nothing's going to happen to you," Craig assured her. "Let's just focus on the next step."

"Okay. On Monday I want to get a copy of my father's obituary." She hesitated. "Strange as it may sound, I have this scary feeling that my investigation may have killed my dad."

"What?" Craig turned around. "Why would you think that?"

"Just before my dad died, he mentioned that my investigation had intrigued him and he was doing a little checking on his own."

Craig shook his head. "It seems highly unlikely that your father would have become involved in your investigation."

She sighed. "Yeah, I guess we'll never know. But I would like to rummage through his study to see if I come up with anything. And I want to check out his obituary to review the organizations he belonged to and any other affiliation that might connect him to Burke. I also want to review the police report of his accident."

"But your father was a physician, not a detective."

"Yes, but he had a very inquisitive nature; I think I got my curiosity from him."

"It's a good thing to have," Craig commented.

"Well, I may also have inherited his love of alcohol." The comment popped out before she could stop it. She had no idea why she said it; Craig was just so easy to talk to.

"So that explains why you refused the merlot tonight."

"Oh, I've never really had a problem with alcohol," she was quick to explain. "But when I first arrived in D.C., I was seduced by the martini power lunches, the elegant parties, the bars, and the whole Washington social scene. I must admit that I did my share of partying and drinking."

"That's pretty normal," Craig agreed, helping her pack her files as they chatted. "Was your father drinking at the time of his accident?"

"Oh, no. He stopped drinking before we ever moved to Delavan."

"And when did you stop drinking, Jill?"

"Last year, except for special occasions."

"Then you probably have nothing to fear," Craig assured her and excused himself to get her coat.

As she waited for him to return, Jill sat on the sofa and flipped through the magazines. Underneath a newspaper she discovered a well-used Bible.

Not you too. Jill sighed as she stood up to leave. She wished all this God stuff would go away—except when she needed him. She wasn't ready to surrender her life to God. There was plenty of time for that.

13

Borrowed illusions are better than none.
—Ellen Glasgow

On Monday at 10:00 A.M., Craig and Jill were at the library going through microfilm. Jill had convinced Craig that her documents were not only accurate but could in fact prove lethal to the senator. He agreed to help her confirm her suspicions.

"I found it!" Craig cheered as he scanned the document. "I don't see anything that will help, but let's make a copy and add it to the file."

Jill read the article, and it was as if she had written it on her first day on the job—the facts and only the facts. "So you wrote this obit?"

"Max asked me to write all the obituaries of prominent Delavan citizens when Marge was in charge." He shrugged his shoulders. "I wasn't much for storytelling either."

"Nothing to apologize for. I was just hoping for a clue. My father's death was probably just an accident. My wild imagination could very well be trying to make more of it. In a way I hope it was an accident or I would feel really guilty

. . . I don't know if I could live with that." She stared out the window for several minutes, watching mothers walk with toddlers through the snow on their way to story time at the library. "Well, I'm here in Delavan now, and this is my life. Maybe there's nothing more I can do about this case."

"What about all those babies?"

"I want to help, I really do, but I'm beginning to believe it's impossible."

"Nothing is impossible. Now tell me again why you think your investigation killed your father?"

"The night before he died, he said that my report had caused him to do a little investigating on his own."

"What kind of investigation?"

"Well, I didn't ask him. He mentioned it in passing, and I thought there would be plenty of time to talk to him about it," she admitted as tears welled up in her eyes.

"I'm sorry." Craig gently put his arm around her.

"I just feel like I may be putting the wrong puzzles together. I need a new piece—something fresh to go on."

They sat silently for several minutes. Jill was the first to speak. "The holidays are almost here. I don't want to think about this right now; I want to pretend I'm a normal person with an ordinary life. I want this Christmas to be nice for my mom. I want to celebrate with my sister, Kathy, and bake some of those gingerbread cookies with my niece, Marion. It seems like I've been on a crusade of one kind or another for a long time, and I've missed enjoying the holidays."

"Okay, political corruption is officially tabled for the holidays!" Craig hit the table with his hand.

"Good, I'm going to try to be joyful and celebrate the festive season," she said brightly, trying to convince herself.

"And the birth of Christ," Craig added. "People get so caught up in the holidays that they forget the true meaning."

"I figured you were a Christian," Jill mumbled.

"Are you?" Craig asked.

"Well—of course! I'm a good person, I believe in God, and I grew up in the church. But I've got to admit, I've had some doubts lately." *Like the past twelve years.* "I want to believe, I really do, but I can't seem to find my faith. God just seems so far away. Except . . ."

Craig seemed like the best person to talk to about this thing that was nagging her. Had she mentioned it to her mother, her mother would have gone overboard and called all the women on the prayer chain to say Jill was coming back to the Lord. She wasn't ready for that yet.

"Except what?" Craig encouraged her to tell him what was on her mind.

"I had this really weird thing happen to me back in Washington. I worked late one night and made the mistake of walking home, and I ran into a really creepy guy who attacked me. I was so terrified I was going to die that I cried out to God."

"And what happened?"

"Well, the streets were deserted, but then a cab driver came to my rescue at just the right moment."

"That was no accident," Craig said.

"I guess I'm not sure. But somehow I feel like it was God who really sent the cab. I can't explain it, but the more I think about it, the more I believe that to be true. I've often thought the cabbie was an angel. Do you think he could've been an angel, Craig?"

"An angel? Maybe; but I also know that God can prompt a person to turn down a particular street at just the right moment. That's what's so exciting about being a child of God; he comes to our rescue even when we've deserted him." Craig reached into his briefcase, pulled out a Bible, and handed it to her. "You're going to need this if you continue your investigation."

Jill hesitated. "I'm sorry, Craig. I can't. I guess I'm not ready. Besides, my mother has stacks of these if I need one." She returned the Bible to him.

"Then I'll pray for you."

"I'd like that."

Jill was surprised she meant it.

———

Near the end of the day, Jill sauntered into Craig's office. "I just want to let you know that I appreciate all your help. So how about my cooking some dinner for you tonight?"

"You cook?" he said as he tossed into the air the autographed baseball he kept on his desk as a paperweight. "I can't possibly turn down an opportunity to partake of this historical event."

Jill reached over and rapped his knuckles with her pencil. "Are you a good cook?"

"I'm a better reporter than I am a cook," she admitted, "but I think you'll approve."

"What can I bring?"

"Just yourself."

"How about an after-dinner drink?" he teased, tossing a bottle of Pepto-Bismol from his desk drawer.

"Very funny. Be there at 7:00," she ordered. "You can meet my mother."

"I've always wanted to see inside your house too. I'm a big fan of Frank Lloyd Wright."

"Good, I'll give you my nickel tour if you eat your vegetables."

"I know just what to bring," he said with a grin, leaning

his head back in his clasped hands and stretching his legs on his desk. "See you at 7:00."

Jill ran out onto the street and up to the corner where no one would see her and frantically dialed her mother on her cell phone.

"Hello," her mother answered cheerfully.

"Mom, I don't have much time, but guess who's coming to dinner?"

"What dinner? We're having split pea soup that I made yesterday. I don't even have any bread."

"Don't worry. I'll handle it. Just straighten up the house and set the table. I'll be there as soon as I can."

"Straighten up? I beg your pardon? We have the best cleaning service in the entire Lakes region. However, I will set the table."

Craig hadn't mentioned Caroline. Maybe they're only friends, Jill thought as she sauntered into the kitchen after driving home.

"Whatever possessed you to tell this man you would cook for him?" her mother fussed at Jill. "You have not made a real meal in your entire life. I thought you said you *liked* this man? And you're cooking for him? Just what is your plan?"

"And hello to you too, Mom. I do have a plan, and it's in these bags." Jill pulled out cartons of precooked food and smiled broadly.

"Oh, what a tangled web we weave when first we practice to deceive," her mom warned as she got out extra bowls. She peeked in the cartons. "Duck l'orange? Surely you jest. You think this young man is going to believe you cooked this all yourself?"

"I won't lie . . . I won't tell him I cooked it. But I won't tell him I didn't either."

Her mother raised her eyebrows.

Jill thought about all the gray areas she had allowed in her life since she left home. She had considered herself to be a generally good person, but was she really? "Well, maybe after tonight I'll take a cooking class or something."

"Right . . . and I'll be next door at the cake decorating class," her mother added, and both women started to cackle.

Jill was busy transferring the prepared food from heated cartons to her mom's exquisite Haviland china when the bell rang. Craig showed up at the door bearing gifts: a large box of Godiva chocolates and a half-gallon of ice cream.

"I thought this would be more welcomed than flowers," he said with a wink.

To Jill's surprise, her mother seemed to enjoy Craig's company as much as she did. Jill was amazed—her mom even laughed at all Craig's jokes. That was something else she was discovering about Craig; he told terrible jokes.

As Pearl led them in saying grace before eating, Jill noticed Craig had his head bowed and eyes squeezed shut, with both his hands clasped firmly together. Jill's heart melted. He exhibited the innocence of a seven-year-old, yet his manners were impeccable, which probably meant his upbringing had been similar to hers. Or maybe he had just gotten his hands on a good etiquette book.

After dinner Jill took Craig on a tour of the downstairs rooms of the home. His knowledge of antiques, art, architecture, and just about everything else impressed her. In addition to being intelligent, Craig was very refined. What a catch she had found right here in Delavan!

At 11:00 that evening, Jill slipped on her coat and black boots to walk him to his car.

"It's freezing out here. You should go back in," he told her.

Clouds of breath circled around them as they spoke.

"You're a good guy, and my mom likes you."

"That's 'cause I'm a good guy. And I like your mom too. Thanks for the delicious dinner."

"Oh, so you liked my cooking after all?"

"Excellent."

"Thanks."

"Yeah, great food. The Duck Inn is my favorite."

"You knew!" She playfully pushed him.

"Yep! It's one of my favorite restaurants, and I have that duck l'orange quite often." He scooped up a handful of snow and threatened her with it as he rolled it into a ball.

"Good night, Craig."

"Good night, Lois Lane."

Jill shivered, but not from the cold.

14

There are two times in a woman's life
When clothes are important:
When she is young and when she is old.

—Marcelene Cox

"Every woman feels better with a fresh wardrobe in her closet," Pearl told Jill and Kathy as they drove to the mall in nearby Janesville. Finding it too painful to gather around the dining room table where Dad had carved the turkey year after year, the family had celebrated a quiet Thanksgiving at Kathy and Jeff's magnificent new home. Today marked their annual mother-daughter trip to the Saturday after-Thanksgiving sales, and that was one tradition they weren't about to break. Jeff was keeping Marion, so the women had all day to Christmas shop.

Earlier that morning, Jill pulled her hair back into a tight ponytail and brushed a small amount of blush on her freshly scrubbed face. Wearing a pair of faded jeans for shopping comfort and a green sweater that accentuated the color of her eyes, she slipped into her old high school cheerleading jacket, which she had discovered in the back of her bedroom closet.

Jill couldn't help but feel like a schoolgirl whose mommy was taking her shopping. Somehow, deep down, it felt good to be taken care of.

"Mom, this is not necessary, but it is most appreciated. Other than the black dress I bought for David's proposal, I haven't been shopping for over a year."

"Hey," Kathy chimed in, "you mentioned his name without bursting into tears. I would say that is a major accomplishment."

"That's because she's got a new beau," Pearl teased.

"Mother, he is not my boyfriend. He's my boss."

"The lady doth protest too much, methinks," Kathy said. "What's his name?"

"Craig. His name is Craig Martin."

"Who is he? Is he from around here?"

"I don't know," Jill admitted.

"Don't know!" Kathy squealed. "Our little investigative reporter doesn't know?"

"He has a weekend cabin up at Egg Harbor."

"Why don't you ask Max? How long has Craig worked at the *Lakes News*?" Kathy wondered.

"Since the spring?" Jill guessed.

"What did he do before that?"

"I have no idea."

"Aren't you the super snoop of the century?"

Jill shrugged. "He's a private kind of guy. Besides, I've only gotten to know him better these past few weeks."

"You should've invited him for Thanksgiving dinner," Kathy scolded, but Jill simply shrugged her shoulders again. Secretly she had wanted to invite him, but she was afraid he might say no in favor of a turkey dinner with the beautiful Miss Jennings. Although Jill still didn't know how Caroline fit into Craig's life.

Jill couldn't get Craig out of her head. What would it be like to kiss him? How would it feel to be called Mrs. Craig Martin? Would he be a romantic husband? What kind of father would he be? Jill shook her head and looked around guiltily. She hoped her sister and mom couldn't read her thoughts. Even though David dumped her, she couldn't help feeling somewhat disloyal.

When they arrived in Janesville, the mall was aglow with Christmas lights and decorations. With throngs of shoppers scurrying about to the sounds of carols in the air, it was hard not to catch the Christmas spirit. The three of them breezed through several stores; Jill selected two pairs of warm slacks, a sweater, a pair of boots, two flannel nightgowns, and a new coat on the shopping spree. Her mother insisted on paying for all of it.

Pearl and Kathy laughed at Jill as she quickly flipped through sale racks. Little did they know that she had learned to be the queen of the sales, unlike the two of them, both extravagant shoppers. Jill's position at the *Gazette* had dictated what went into her wardrobe, especially since she was forced to mingle socially with the Washington "in" crowd. Her mother had exquisite taste, and Jill had loved to call her for fashion advice, but she was always embarrassed when a package full of clothes sent by her mother arrived after every phone call. She didn't want her mom to think she was calling to ask for things. So even though she abhorred shopping, Jill finally replaced her mother with a subscription to *W* magazine, which she read from cover to cover every month for the latest trends and fashions. Now it felt good to have her personal fashion consultant back again.

Kathy finished up her Santa shopping for Marion and bought presents for Jeff's office staff. Jill successfully picked up gifts for everyone at the *Lakes News* except Craig. Shopping for him would be a challenge. That afternoon, Pearl treated herself as well as her girls to a massage and a trip to the hair salon.

Jill decided to have her hair clipped shoulder length. She looked at her new "do" in the mirror and wondered what Craig would say about it—something humorous for sure, even if he approved. He seemed to love to tease her.

By the time they dropped Kathy off and drove home to the estate, they were exhausted but happy.

"Thanks, Mom, for such a special day. You've been an angel to me, not only buying me enough clothes for the next five years but making me feel so welcome at home again."

"The pleasures are mine, Jill. Just consider it part of your Christmas."

"You always say that, and then the tree is always loaded down with packages on Christmas morning."

"I can't help it. I love you. And by the way, I like Craig. He's a good man, I can tell."

"But you've just met him. How can you tell?"

"Woman's intuition. Besides, I called Max. He said there's not a finer man than Craig."

"Mother, you didn't!" Jill gasped.

"You told me I could, remember? When you were on your way up to Egg Harbor."

"Okay, I remember. But I need *you* to remember that Craig and I aren't dating. I don't even know if he's interested in me. Besides, I think he may have a girlfriend."

"Sure could've fooled me; I saw the way he looked at you at dinner that night. He's interested all right. I know a thing or two about men. After all, I was married for over thirty years."

Jill perked up. "You really think so?"

"Why shouldn't he be? You're special."

"But you're my mother," Jill reminded her. "You're biased."

The two began to carefully make their way down the walk toward the house. The day had been sunny with dripping snow, creating watery pools of mush. Now the slush had turned to sheer ice in the night air. Jill and her mother tried to balance their packages, laughing in the process. Suddenly they became aware of the security alarm going off in the house.

"Oh no, I'm going to get rid of that alarm," her mom complained. "It's going off again."

But Jill held up her arm. "Wait, Mom, leave the packages here on the snow. There might be a prowler in the house."

15

The weariest nights, the longest days,
Sooner or later must perforce come to an end.

—Baroness Orczy

Dropping the packages on the brick walkway, the two of them quickly hurried back to the BMW and locked themselves inside.

"Give me the car keys, Mom, and let's get out of here!" Jill said.

"We—we can't. I can't!" her mother cried out in distress. "I dropped my purse and keys with the packages."

Jill grabbed her cell phone and frantically dialed 911. They informed her that the security company had already notified the police, who were on their way.

Within minutes several squad cars pulled up behind them in the driveway. Policemen with guns drawn surrounded the BMW. Mom's eyes widened as they heard a voice yell at them.

"This is the Delavan police, get out of the car with your hands up!"

Pearl looked at her and quietly asked, "They can't be talking to us, can they?"

"I think so, and I think we better do what they say right now."

"In all my life I have never had this type of treatment. If your father were alive, he would tell them a thing or two!"

"Mother, I suggest we get out of the car with our hands up."

Both women emerged from the BMW with freshly groomed hair and their arms reaching for the sky. Jill heard her mother say, "Officers, we live here, please don't shoot us."

"Mrs. Lewis, I'm sorry about this," a familiar voice said as an officer walked up in a hurry. "It's okay, boys. I know these people; they're the owners of this house. Have a good look around in there. Something is causing the alarm to sound and I want you to find out what it is. Ladies, please stay here while my officers check the premises." The other officers headed inside.

"Who is this young man? Do you know one another?" her mom asked, looking back and forth from him to Jill.

"It's Chuck Emerson. I went to school with him, remember?"

Mom clapped her hands together. "Oh, Chuck, you've grown to be so tall." She looked him up and down. "How's your mother? I haven't seen her in ages."

"She's fine, ma'am. She and Dad love Florida."

"Do they spend their summers in their adorable little cottage on Egg Harbor? You remember that cottage, don't you, Jill? It was next door to the Parker's A-frame."

"Yes, of course. The one with the pretty rose trellises."

Chuck nodded. "They haven't used the cottage in years. They built a larger home on the other side of the lake after Dad retired."

"That's a shame. I thought that little cottage was the prettiest place on the lake," Mom protested.

"I agree," Chuck replied. "I keep threatening to go up there and fix it up on the weekends."

"You should, Chuck," Mom advised. "It would be a good investment for you. Property is really appreciating up around Egg Harbor. Lots of folks from Chicago are buying and renting summer cottages there."

"Thanks for the advice, Mrs. Lewis." Chuck excused himself and began talking with another officer who had just come from the house.

In a few minutes the all clear was given, and the women were allowed to enter the house. The police were courteous and helped to carry in the packages.

"Just place them over there by those two couches, young men," Mom instructed.

Chuck took down the report and then walked with the women around the house as they looked for anything that might be missing. While he was helping her mom, Jill sprinted up the steps to her bedroom and barged past the police officer standing at the door.

"Miss, you aren't supposed to go in there until Officer Emerson gets up here," the policeman called after her. Jill ignored him. Unlike the rest of the house, her room was a disaster.

"No! No! No!" she wailed.

Dressers were knocked on their sides, drawers pulled out and emptied, her mattress slit and the stuffing pulled out. Everything was emptied from the medicine chest in the bathroom. Even her garbage had been gone through. Afraid to look in her hiding place, she bent down with her eyes closed. With great relief she saw that her disks were still there, safe and sound.

But was Craig safe? Did he still have his copies of the disks? Jill picked up the phone to call him, but the phone wires had been cut. She ran down the steps two at a time in search of her cell phone. She found it and dialed his number. When she heard his voice, she felt calmer. After briefly filling him in, he asked, "Is everyone all right? Are you okay?"

"Yeah, I'm okay. Just a little shook up, I guess."

"I'm heading over. I'll be there in ten minutes."

"I'm okay now that you're here," Jill whispered when Craig arrived. "Let's go rescue the police officers from Mom. She probably has them hanging wallpaper in the family room by now." She shook her head.

They found her mother in the living room giving the officers a quick lesson on knowing how to tell original paintings from copies.

"Oh, Craig, it's so good to see you." Pearl waved her hand in his direction.

"Hello, Mrs. Lewis. It's good to see you're both okay."

"Everyone, this is Craig. I'm sure you all know one another. Nothing has been disturbed down here. The lock on the back door is broken along with the door frame, but we can get that replaced in the morning along with adding more security measures."

"I don't think anything important has been taken," Jill added. "Mom, why don't you stay here and tell the officers about your Majolica collection and how you came by it so I can take Chuck and Craig up to see the second floor."

"Run along then. . . . Now this blue piece has an interesting story to it. I call her my Blue Lady . . ."

Craig whistled as he saw the extent of the destruction in

Jill's room. The bed was set topsy-turvy in the middle of the room. The contents of the drawers were pulled out and flung about. Pictures were pulled down from the walls and ripped open from the back.

Chuck added to the report he was writing. "Is there anything missing that you know of at this time? What do you think they were after up here?"

"I can't tell if anything is missing right now." Standing in the middle of her belongings, she felt like one of those hurricane victims interviewed on TV.

Later that evening, after the police were gone, Craig did his best to secure the back door for the night.

"Mrs. Lewis?" Craig called out.

"You must call me Pearl. My, oh my. All this excitement and we don't even know what they wanted and who wanted it! Jill, maybe you can make this an investigation for Craig's newspaper."

"I don't mean to contradict you Mrs. Lewis, but it isn't *my* newspaper. I'm the managing editor."

"And a good one. There you go, setting the story straight."

Craig smiled and turned to Jill. "Would you ladies feel more secure if you checked into a hotel or if I slept here on the couch tonight until you can get that back door fixed?"

"Great idea." Pearl beamed. "Jill, please get your friend a blanket."

Jill was surprised when Craig pulled a pistol out of his coat and set it gingerly on the table. "I don't want to frighten either of you, but I think it might be a good idea to keep this handy."

Jill eyed the gun suspiciously. "Pretty fancy gun for a newspaperman. I suppose you're pretty good at shooting it too?"

"And how do you figure that?"

"I noticed your hunting magazine at the cabin."

Craig chuckled. "Very observant."

"Normally, I'd complain about you killing Bambi's mother, but tonight I'm glad you know how to shoot a gun."

"Hey, I resent that. I would never shoot Bambi's mother."

"I suppose you went out and *bought* all those antlers in your cabin?"

"Bambi's mother didn't have antlers." He laughed.

Jill blushed. "Well, his father then."

Craig rolled his eyes.

Pearl disappeared into her first-floor bedroom and came out with an ivory-handled pistol. "Look, I have one too . . . though I never thought I would use it," she said, looking quite pleased.

"Where on earth did you get that, Mom?" Jill said, trying to keep her jaw from dropping. "I'm a staunch gun-control advocate, and here my own mother has a pistol in the house."

"Your father bought it for me right before he died. He said, 'Don't ever hesitate to use it if you need it,' and I won't. I even took lessons down at the police station so I can protect us."

Jill rolled her eyes as Craig laughed and shook his head while he examined it for bullets. It was empty, and he handed it back to her without saying anything.

"Better get some sleep," he recommended. "We've got a busy day ahead of us."

"Will we be in more danger?" Pearl asked.

"No, Mrs. Lewis. Not as long as I'm around."

The idea of Craig staying with them made Jill feel safe, but she couldn't keep a nagging thought from her head. *Why on earth did Dad think Mom might need a gun?*

16

Accept the things to which fate binds you,
And love the people with whom fate brings you together,
But do so with all your heart.

—Marcus Aurelius

Craig and Jill spent hours trying to clean up her room, straightening the furniture and searching for anything that might have been left behind by the intruder, but they found nothing. When they became overcome with fatigue, Craig declined to use the downstairs guest room and fell onto the couch with some warm blankets and a pillow. Jill retired into the guest room.

She awoke in the red glow of early morning. She dangled her feet over the side of the bed and admired how beautiful the sunrise looked over the tops of the trees on the east shore. The sun's reflection off the ice only magnified the day's brilliance. The night before seemed like a nightmare melting away.

After a quick shower she got dressed and bounded down the steps to see how everyone was feeling. She was most anxious to see Craig and wondered how he looked first thing in the morning. She found him busily working on the door. Her mother apparently had already prepared breakfast for him. It lay half eaten on a dish on the counter near the sink.

"Am I the last one up this morning?"

Craig turned at the sound of her voice and smiled. "Yes, but I see you got your beauty sleep."

Jill's heart skipped a beat. *So is this how love feels? Every moment filled with anticipation, every day a gift waiting to be opened?*

She sat at the breakfast table with a sliced cantaloupe just as her mom walked into the room already dressed for church, though it was only 8:30. Jill felt exhausted and hoped the heavy circles beneath her eyes weren't too noticeable. Her mom's face and demeanor matched hers, but when their eyes met, smiles broke across their faces as if they were two young girls sharing a secret.

"You look great, but your face says you feel as bad as I feel."

"Worse," Pearl admitted as she poured herself a cup of fresh coffee, offering Craig a refill at the same time.

"Thanks, but I'm almost done with this section of the door. I think I'll wait."

Pearl sat down across the table from her daughter, placing the flowered china teacup and saucer on the table. The pink colors of the morning had faded into a rare sunny winter day. Outside the window an occasional snowbird pecked at the ice in the birdbath in search of a drink.

Pearl's eyes stared at her winter garden of frozen white. "Whatever story you left in Washington has obviously followed you home," she finally said.

"So it seems," Jill replied, feeling caught off guard. "Are you scared?"

Her mother ignored her question and concentrated on the birds fluttering around, the only color displayed in all the snow. "Just a few weeks ago it was Indian summer, and now look," she commented. "I suppose most of the birds are long gone for their winter holiday now."

"Mom, you aren't answering my question."

"Sorry, dear, I didn't realize you had asked one. What was it again?" She wiped her forehead with a linen handkerchief as if feeling fuzzy headed.

Jill felt mildly annoyed. She loved her mother, but it irritated her when she played cat-and-mouse games. She had been raised with proper, upper-class manners in a setting of careful order and decorum. Jill liked plain, quick answers and wasn't always comfortable with her mother's methods of communication.

"I just got off the phone with a crackerjack carpenter," Craig interrupted and sat down at the table with them. "He'll be here on Monday. I also got in touch with your alarm company—they're coming to assess your property and will let you know what more needs to be done to keep this house secure and safe. I rigged up your phone line so you can use the land line until the repairman shows up Monday morning."

"You're a handy guy to have around, Craig," her mother said, winking at him as she got up to pour him a mug of black coffee. She reached into the refrigerator for Jill's diet drink. She set both on the table.

"Well, at least you ate something that was good for you," Craig noted as he glanced at the remains of the cantaloupe.

"I'm glad someone around here agrees with me," her mother said, smiling. She looked at her watch. "Mercy! Jill, you better start getting ready for church." She turned to Craig. "We go to the Church of the Apostles. Would you like to join us?"

"I'd like that," he said. "What time does the service start?"

"Eleven o'clock."

"I'll do my best to make it," Craig promised as he returned to his carpentry.

"And afterwards I'll treat you and Jill to Sunday lunch at Millie's Cafe."

"You don't have to do that, Mrs. Lewis."

"After all you've done for this family? It's only a small way to say thank you," she insisted. "It's so nice to have a man around the house again."

17

Any God I ever felt in church, I brought with me.
And I think all the other folks did too.
They come to church to share God, not find God.

—Alice Walker

Her mother waited patiently for Jill, who tried on her new blue-and-black plaid skirt with a velvet vest. Standing in front of the full-length mirror, she asked, "Mom, what do you think?"

"You look like a schoolgirl."

No good. Next she went for sophistication with her mid-calf black skirt with the slit up the side and a tight-fitting cashmere sweater.

"Too much leg!" her mother gasped.

Jill finally settled on a simple dark blue wool suit with a pale blue blouse underneath the jacket.

"Simple but elegant." Her mother smiled approvingly.

Jill slipped on her classic black suede pumps and fastened pearls to her neck and ears.

Since Jill had spent so much time getting ready, she and her mother were the last to arrive at church. They pushed open the heavy, holly-wreathed doors just as a Christmas carol rang out from the congregation, signaling the onset of the advent season. It was Jill's first time going to church since she'd returned. Hoping to find a seat unnoticed, she and her mother slipped into the back pew of the church, but a rather large, red-faced usher bolted up the aisle to welcome them. His loud baritone voice floated over the swells of the organ.

"Welcome to the house of the Lord, Mrs. Lewis! And if this isn't our little Jill, all grown up." Everyone turned around to smile or nod at them. Suddenly remembering he was in church, the usher softened his voice into a whisper as he continued. "Jill, honey, I told my brother-in-law down in Grand Rapids not to believe one word of what those newspapers were saying about you—that you were a Lewis and the Lewises are fine folks and there couldn't be a lick of truth in any of it. Besides, even if it were, we still love our own around here."

Jill was relieved to escape the boisterous man when the minister called out, "Let us pray."

After the prayer Jill looked around the church for Craig. The hope that he would arrive at any moment made her heart pound and her palms sweat. It would be nice to have him join them in their pew. She slapped down her large purse to save the spot next to her.

Once the sermon began, Jill found it impossible to concentrate for glancing back at the door to watch for any sign of Craig. Even during the closing prayer, she couldn't resist peeking out of the corner of one eye. Her mother whispered, "Don't worry. He said not to wait for him. Something must have happened."

That was the problem. What if something had happened to him?

Just as the final amen was uttered, Pearl nudged Jill toward the front door. Suddenly the duo was swimming upstream with a throng of the townsfolk eager to welcome Jill back to Delavan. Afraid to face everyone, Jill had avoided church until today. She took a deep breath; the time to face her embarrassment had come.

"Glad to be home, Jill, honey?"

"I hope you'll come for tea soon."

"Is there a lucky young man?"

"Did you really meet the president?"

"We sure miss your daddy."

By the time everyone had thoroughly cross-examined her and then had a chance to brag about their own kids, their grandkids, and their successes, over half an hour had passed. Free at last, Jill ran for her mother's car to call Craig on her cell phone.

"You're not going to call him!" her mom admonished as she closed the car door.

"Mother, it's the twenty-first century."

"Better listen to me," her mom insisted. "I know about these things. Your father was madly in love with me right from the start, and I didn't call him on the phone until we were married. Instinctively, men are hunters; they're the ones that like to do all the chasing. Besides, I invited Craig to have lunch, so he's probably waiting for us at the cafe."

"Yes, and you invited him to church too, but did he show up?" Jill ignored the advice and resumed her dialing as her mother turned the car into the parking lot of Millie's Cafe.

In middial, Jill caught sight of Craig coming out of the restaurant with Caroline Jennings. She immediately turned off her cell phone and dove to the floor of the car so Craig wouldn't see her.

"What do you think you're doing down there?" her mom asked.

"Hiding," she moaned from below. "I don't believe it! First

he stands me up at church—and has me worried half to death—and then he shows up with his Barbie doll."

"He stood *me* up, you mean. I was the one who invited him." Her mother was quiet for a moment. "She's a very nice-looking woman."

"Do you really think she's pretty?" Jill asked as she peered with one eye over the dashboard.

"I cannot tell a lie. She's stunning. But you're prettier."

"Of course you think I'm prettier. You're my mother."

"Physical beauty only attracts a man initially. Remember, it's what's on the inside that counts. But even if that weren't the case, you have good genes . . . mine."

Jill wiped the beginnings of tears from her eyes. "I feel like such a loser."

"You get up from the floor right now," her mother demanded. "You aren't the one who should be embarrassed."

When Jill got out of the car, she noticed that Craig and Caroline were still standing in the parking lot, talking. She and her mom both nodded in their direction. He and Caroline smiled and waved.

Sitting in the red vinyl booth, Jill fumed as she fumbled with her menu, knocking over all the condiments. The waitress appeared and thumped her pencil on the pad. "What'll it be?"

"What's the Sunday special?" Pearl inquired.

"Turkey and dressing—Thanksgiving leftovers," the skinny waitress told them over the loud tunes of Christmas carols playing on the corner jukebox. "We're never gonna get rid of all this turkey."

"I'll have the Sunday special with a Diet Coke, please," Jill said.

Her mom chimed in, "Make that two, but replace the cola with nonfat milk for me."

The waitress didn't move but stood peering at Jill over her glasses. "You don't remember me, do you, Jill?" she asked.

"Of course I do," Jill replied, thinking frantically. "You're . . ."

"Judy Schipper. Chemistry class, remember?"

"Oh yeah. It's good to see you. You look great, Judy!"

"You've been gone a long time, but no one in our chemistry class will ever forget you. Remember the time you and Joe Fisher caused the explosion in lab?"

"Are you sure that was me?" Jill couldn't remember.

"Of course I'm sure. You must be suffering from posttraumatic amnesia." Judy clucked her tongue and shook her head. When the bell jingled, she turned to the door. "Oh, here comes Craig Martin again. I'd better go get another menu."

Momentarily stopping at the jukebox to drop in quarters, Craig then walked over to their booth. "May I join you two lovely ladies?"

"We would be delighted." Pearl smiled and patted the vinyl seat beside her. "You missed a good sermon."

"Sorry about that. Caroline had some urgent matters to discuss with me. I left a message for you under your windshield wiper that I'd catch up with you after church. Didn't you see it?"

"No," Jill said. Her voice sounded annoying to her own ears. She wanted to kick herself.

After an awkward silence, Judy came walking up to their table. "Twice in one hour, Craig?" She winked. "What can I get you this time?"

"Just a cup of your wonderful decaf coffee, thank you," he answered, and Judy disappeared once again into the kitchen.

"Would you ladies like for me to bunk at your home again tonight?"

"No," Jill said.

"Yes," her mom said at the same time.

"I insist," Craig replied. "It's just too risky for you two to stay home alone."

"We're staying with my sister, Kathy, tonight," Jill announced.

"We are?"

"We are." Jill glared at her mother.

Craig looked from one of them to the other. "Uh, good. I just wanted to make sure you're both safe."

Was it her imagination, or did Craig sound a little disappointed?

Just then Judy returned with his coffee. "Better watch out for her," Judy said, pointing to Jill. "She's dangerous."

"You aren't telling me anything I don't already know," Craig chortled, slowly stirring sugar into his mug brimming with black coffee.

Jill crossed her arms in front of her and gave Craig a look.

He caught her gaze and moved uneasily in his seat. "If you ladies will excuse me, I think I'll run along. Call if you need me." He stood up and left his coffee untouched, along with a big tip for Judy.

Jill and her mother said good-bye.

"Good-bye," Craig replied as he walked away. Stopping briefly to chat with the cashier, he disappeared out the door.

Jill craned her neck to get a more advantageous view of Craig's truck pulling out of the parking lot. She desperately wanted to run after him, but her pride nailed her feet to the floor.

"I hope Caroline Jennings knows how lucky she is," she finally blurted out.

"Listen to you!" Her mother clucked her tongue. "Aren't we the fickle one? Years of dating David, and a few months later, you're already pining over another man. Speaking of David, have you heard from him lately?"

"Not a word—and it doesn't bother me much anymore. I can't explain it. I thought I was in love with David, that I wanted to marry him. But that night in Washington when he revealed his true feelings concerning my investigation, I recognized something in him I didn't like. He was going for the easier choice, the more immoral one. I think he would sell his soul to be a part of the Washington scene. I want to be with someone who is a man of principle."

"And maybe that was the reason you put David off for so long—maybe it wasn't your career after all. You have good instincts."

"Maybe." Jill rubbed her head. "You always told me that I would know it when I met 'the one.' That I would hear bells ringing. With David, I never heard those bells ringing. I was tone deaf."

"And you hear them now?"

"Every time Craig walks in the room."

"It could be just a schoolgirl crush."

"It is not a crush," Jill protested.

Pearl smiled. "I felt exactly the same way when I first met your father, my Harold. There wasn't a day that we were together that I didn't feel that way. Even after more than thirty years of marriage, I never doubted he was the man for me, even during the tough times."

"Yes, but Dad loved you back. I just have to figure out a way to get Craig to fall in love with me."

"Trust God, darling. If it's his will for the two of you to be together, then you will be."

Jill shook her head. "I'm not leaving anything to chance. I'm taking control of my own life."

Her mother raised her eyebrows. "It's obvious you didn't

listen to the minister's sermon today. Free will can only get you so far. The rest is in God's hands."

Jill didn't like to admit when her mother was right, but she had to acknowledge that taking control of her own life hadn't worked so well for her lately.

When she and her mother returned to the car, Jill found the note Craig had left for them under the windshield wiper.

> Mrs. L. and Lois,
>
> Something came up and I can't join you for church. I'll catch up with you later.
>
> Forgive me?
>
> Fondly, Clark

She slipped it into her purse.

———

Jill and her mother decided not to go to Kathy's house after all. Instead they donned their flannel nightgowns and munched popcorn in front of the fieldstone fireplace in Pearl's bedroom while giggling like two schoolgirls, weeping over the men they loved, and watching old movies.

When Jill climbed into bed later that night, an eerie sadness fell over her as she looked out across the lake. It was dark and strangely quiet. The symphonic sounds of the past seasons were absent—the squeals of barefooted children when spring arrived, the summer night chorus of chirping crickets and grunting bullfrogs, and the Canadian geese honking as they fled the cold—all were silenced by the arrival of a brutal winter.

Filled with emptiness, feeling the loss of her father as

well as her career, Jill's heart ached. There were other empty places there—made by David's sudden departure and even Craig's absence, though he had only walked into her heart for a short while.

Smiling as she noticed the Bible her mother had left on her bedside table, she opened it and flipped the pages randomly, settling into Proverbs.

When you lie down, you will not be afraid; when you lie down, your sleep will be sweet. Have no fear of sudden disaster or the ruin that overtakes the wicked, for the Lord will be your confidence and will keep your foot from being snared.

Was God speaking to her? It was exactly what she needed to hear. Again she turned to the view of the lake. The lighted houses offered a small glimmer of hope through the darkness.

18

The voyage of discovery is not in seeking new landscapes
But in having new eyes.

—Marcel Proust

"Somebody's happy this morning," Pearl noticed as Jill walked into the kitchen. She handed her smiling daughter a steamy mug of chocolate.

"I am. I slept peacefully for the first time in months."

"Well, I have a surprise that I believe is going to make you even happier. Look out the window."

Jill pulled open the shutters, revealing a fresh blanket of snow sparkling like diamonds in the morning sun. "It's beautiful out there." She turned away from the window. "But I wish I got as excited about the snow as I did when I was a kid."

"Look a little closer," her mother coaxed.

Jill turned back toward the window and spotted Craig's pickup truck parked in the driveway. It was like a bow on the perfect gift that needed no ornamentation. "How long do you suppose he's been out there? He's probably frozen stiff."

"Judging by the snow that's accumulated on his truck, I'd

guess most of the night. Why don't you offer him a cup of coffee to thaw him out?"

Jill dashed into the powder room to inspect her appearance and apply lip gloss. On her way out the door she paused long enough to pull on her black boots and take the mug of fresh coffee from her mother. As she fought her way over the heaps of snow in an effort to reach Craig, her legs got stuck in the deep drifts. She yanked her legs to free them from the icy grip, but the snow sucked her boots right off her feet, and then plop! She fell flat on her face, with the contents of the mug spraying nature's white with brown teardrops of coffee.

Not to be deterred, she went back in and came out with another mug of strong coffee. Successfully reaching his truck this time, she knocked on the window. He looked up at her groggily.

Whew, Jill thought. *Thank heavens he missed my little ice capades.*

"Are you this perky every morning?" he asked, rolling down the truck's window.

"I was going to ask you if you always sleep in your truck!" She handed the steaming cup to Craig. He brushed her fingertips lightly with his hand.

"Thanks for the coffee. I thought you and your mom were going to spend the night at your sister's place, but when I drove to check on the house around midnight, I noticed you two naughty girls were inside the house. I couldn't risk leaving you alone or disturbing you at such a late hour."

The sunlight began melting the snow all around them, but it was his kindness and concern that melted Jill's heart. She stared at him as he took small sips of the hot, hot coffee.

"How about some breakfast?" her mother suddenly called out from the kitchen.

"Wouldn't want to wear out my welcome," he shouted back.

"Get in here before you freeze to death!"

"I'll cook for you," Jill offered. "What would you like?"

"I didn't know that the Duck Inn was open this early."

Jill playfully reached down and scooped up a fistful of snow and gave him a face full.

"You're in trouble now," he warned her as he peeled off his subzero down sleeping bag and got out of his truck and chased her up the walkway, pelting her with snowballs until she reached the inside of the kitchen.

Luckily for Jill, her mother had already made their breakfast and put it on the table.

"Thanks, Mrs. Lewis." He pulled out a chair for Jill. "Won't you join us?"

"Oh, thank you, but I've already eaten. I've got to go shower. By the way, we certainly appreciate all that you are doing for us, Craig." Pearl smiled at him and left the kitchen.

After stirring a heaping tablespoon of brown sugar into her oatmeal, Jill took a mouthful. "Aren't you going to eat?" she asked Craig, who sat silently unmoving beside her. Her cheeks reddening, she remembered they hadn't asked a blessing for the food. "Uh, Craig, wouldn't you like to say the blessing?"

Reaching for her hand, he asked the Lord to bless the food. She had no idea how long she clung to his hand, but she knew that if he hadn't let go, she would've held on to it forever.

"I really like your mom," Craig told her as he scooped up a big spoonful of oatmeal and fruit.

"You mean you really like her cooking?"

"That too, but I really like her. Your mom's a cool lady."

"She is pretty great," Jill agreed. "And what about her daughter? What do you think about her?"

Craig softly chuckled and then tugged at her hair. "I think

you're okay." He smiled but suddenly his smile faded and his demeanor changed. "I have something to tell you."

"Well, go ahead."

"I looked through your files after I left you and your mother at the cafe yesterday, and I think I've found something that could be very significant to your investigation."

"What?" She immediately shook off any romantic notions and was on her game in seconds.

"I know you didn't want to deal with this until after Christmas, but I think I've discovered an important connection."

"Well, what is it?"

Suddenly her mother peeked around the door to the kitchen and interrupted. "Jill, you're supposed to be at work in less than half an hour!"

"Oh my goodness," Jill mumbled with her mouth full of oatmeal. "I've got a meeting with Max!"

"And you don't keep the owner of the paper waiting," Craig reminded her.

"Never. He might have another parakeet obituary for me to write this morning!" She put her spoon down and folded her napkin, pulling it through the silver ring beside her plate before she got up to leave.

Halfway up the stairs she stopped and turned back to Craig. "We'll talk at the office. See you in a bit."

"I have some business outside the office this morning. How about if I meet you there around 1:00, and we'll go to Millie's Cafe for lunch?"

"I'll be counting the seconds," Jill sang as she floated up the stairs.

19

Where so many hours have been spent
In convincing myself that I am right,
Is there not some reason to fear I may be wrong?

—Jane Austen

Jill felt out of place at the office without Craig. She wanted him to tell her what clue he had found lurking in her files—maybe one she had overlooked. Over breakfast, she had also planned to tell him how the words in her Bible had comforted her, but news of the clue in her journals had sidetracked her.

Looking at her watch, she realized it was time for her meeting with Max and knocked on his door.

"Come in."

"Good morning, Max," she announced with a forced cheerfulness.

Max was dressed in a camel coat and wearing his trademark red and blue bow tie. He stood as Jill entered the office and then offered her a chair. Instead of returning to his desk, he took the chair next to hers.

"So how's it going? Everything to your liking here?" Max questioned in his small-town, folksy manner.

"I suppose researching dead people is preferable to digging their graves, but I can't say I enjoy writing the obits. But I have enjoyed getting to know the people in our office."

"Well, you won't be writing obituaries forever." He shook his head as though it were meant as an apology. "We do have a great bunch of folks in this office, don't we? And what do you think about our managing editor, Craig Martin?" Max folded his arms over his chest, stretched out his legs, and then crossed them at the ankles.

Surprised by the question, Jill blushed. *Has Max noticed my attraction to Craig?* She hesitated and then replied, "I think he's very bright, and I enjoy working with him."

"So do I, so do I. I'm glad the two of you have become friends." Max uncrossed his legs and leaned forward. "What do you have going on today?"

"It's been a slow week in Delavan," she replied wryly. "I don't have a single obituary to write, but I'm helping Marge answer a few letters for her advice column."

"I'll see if I can't dig up something around here for you to do. It's a shame to waste all that talent. Craig told me he's been on the lookout for some special projects for you; he has something in mind."

"Thanks, Max. I'm covering the dog show tomorrow at the Lake Resort." She tried to sound enthusiastic. "It isn't Washington, but it's a start."

"How are things down in Washington? Any new developments?"

"No, but I'm keeping up my investigation—in my spare time, of course. I expect to find the answers one day." She glanced at her watch.

"And you will," Max agreed as he stood. "Just wanted to check on you and see how you were getting along. And I must say, I'm really proud of you and the way you've made an effort to fit in around here. I know it couldn't have been easy, but you've been a real trooper."

"Thanks, Max. I appreciated you hiring me, especially when no one else in the world would even consider it."

"Well, the folks in Delavan don't turn their backs on their own. We're a family. I feel honored to have you here."

When she got back to her desk, she sat down and pretended to be busy. Every time someone would walk through the door, she'd jump and look up from her desk, only to be disappointed. As the clock inched closer and closer to 1:00, Jill became increasingly anxious. At 1:00 sharp her cell phone rang. She grabbed it up on the first ring.

"Rubric here," the gruff voice announced.

"Rubric! It's so good to hear your voice," Jill said. Her heart pounded as she stood up. She knew Rubric would never call to say hello. He must have news.

"I'm sure you assumed Burke was suing us?"

"Yes, thank goodness for malpractice insurance."

"Well, his camp has dropped the lawsuits against you and the *Gazette*," he informed her.

"What?" she screamed into the receiver. "Oh, Rube, sorry if I hurt your ears. That's great news." She paused. "We must be close to something they obviously don't want brought out at a trial."

"Now don't go off half-cocked," he warned her. "They may just not want to spend their time and money on a lawsuit."

"Maybe, maybe not. But Rubric, I think there is a significant clue in my files that I may have overlooked."

"What kind of clue?" Rubric asked, clearing his throat. Jill knew him so well—she could almost picture him shooting up straight in his chair at the news.

"I don't know just yet," she explained. "I gave a disk of

my files to Craig Martin, my boss at the *Lakes News,* and he actually found a fresh clue. I'm meeting him shortly so he can explain it all to me."

"You did what?" Rubric burst out so loudly that Jill had to hold the phone away from her ear. "How many times have I told you to trust no one?"

"Rubric, this is different," Jill explained. "I'm in Delavan, Wisconsin, not Washington, D.C."

"Things are never as they appear. If you didn't learn anything else from me, please remember that one thing."

"Rubric, you're getting all bent out of shape for nothing. You would really like Craig; he's a very smart guy."

"I guess that explains why he's working for a weekly newspaper in Delavan, Wisconsin?"

Jill froze. Rubric did have a point there. She found herself pushing uncomfortable thoughts out of her head and made a mental note to ask Craig why he'd chosen to settle in Delavan.

To assure him, and maybe herself, Jill said, "You always told me I had great instincts."

"Yeah, well, it seems you're out of my sight for a few months and already those instincts are fading. Must be the clean air up there." He coughed loudly into the phone. "Be suspicious, Jill, my girl . . . even of your own mother."

"You're wrong about Craig. You'll see."

"Just don't come crying to me when you get burned."

After Rubric hung up, she tried to make sense of what he'd said. She treasured his friendship even though he drove her to the edge at times. Except for Annabelle, the *Gazette*'s publisher, Jill was probably the only person at the *Gazette* whom Rubric respected—that knowledge validated her as a newspaperwoman. What exactly was Rubric thinking? Maybe she would fly down to Washington to see him one day soon.

Marge's shrill voice interrupted Jill's thoughts. "It's Craig on line one."

"Hi, Jill," said the voice that had become music to her ears. "I'm a little late. Want to meet me at Millie's Cafe in ten minutes?"

"I'm leaving now," she replied, pulling on her coat.

———

Jill was sipping her usual Diet Coke when Craig walked through the door. At the sight of him her heart began to pound and her palms began to sweat. Immediately their eyes locked. Craig stood smiling at her from a distance. Why hadn't she noticed how terribly handsome he was—perfect smile, perfect teeth, perfect everything . . . except those glasses!

As he came toward her, she wondered if he secretly wanted to reach out and hold her as much as she wanted him to wrap his arms around her. She rubbed her sweaty palms against her thighs and watched as he slid into the bench across from her. For a brief moment they gazed into one another's eyes, until Judy came running up to their table.

"You two together again?"

"Uh, yeah. We work together over at the *Lakes News,*" Craig said.

Jill felt like kicking his shin after this disclaimer. Her heart felt like a yo-yo spinning out of control. Falling in love was not easy.

"What's today's special?" she asked in an effort to concentrate on something other than Craig.

"Same as yesterday."

"Then I'll have a BLT with French fries and another Diet Coke."

"Too many Diet Cokes aren't good for you!" Judy scolded.

"You tell her," Craig said.

Judy turned and smiled at him. "And you, handsome?"

"The special, please."

"You had that yesterday," Judy said.

"I liked it."

Shaking her head the waitress headed back toward the kitchen.

"Such a creature of habit," Jill said.

"Judy?"

"No, you."

"What's wrong with that?"

"Not a thing, it's just that you're so . . . predictable."

"You say that as if you find me boring."

"You, boring?" Jill laughed.

"Oh, I forgot that women love a challenge, a man who keeps them guessing."

"Not me," Jill admitted. "I like a man who's uncomplicated and predictable. I don't like to play games." Too curious to wait any longer, she leaned forward and whispered anxiously, "I've been on pins and needles all morning. Now tell me about that clue you found hidden in my files."

Craig became serious and pulled out his notebook. "I was reading more about Hope International when I came across your file on Hope House."

"That's the orphanage in Chicago."

"Yeah, that's the one—Hope House. And for some reason, I thought it sounded vaguely familiar."

"Hope House was the headquarters of one of the orphanages that acted as a clearinghouse for a large number of the adoptions I was investigating," Jill confirmed.

"Right, but I couldn't recall where I'd heard of it before. Last night it suddenly hit me. When I researched your father's obituary, I remembered that he had served on several boards

. . . too many to include in his obituary. Look at this." He thrust a copy of his notes in front of her.

Jill quickly scanned the list of her father's curriculum vitae. There it was in black and white: *Dr. Lewis served on the board of Chicago's House of Hope.* Jill paused to think before replying. "Is there a connection between House of Hope and Hope House?"

"When I visited the Hope House web site last night, I discovered that the orphanage was originally called Chicago's House of Hope. This has gotta be one of the missing pieces to the puzzle."

"So what? My father lent his name to oodles of boards that he had no real involvement with at all."

"So you weren't aware that your father served on the board of this orphanage?"

"No, I would've caught it immediately. I mentioned Hope House to him on several occasions, but he never told me he was on the board." Jill suddenly became irritated. "Hey, what is this? Who do you think you are? The FBI or something?"

Before Craig could defend himself, Judy showed up at their table with the orders.

"Is there anything else I can get you guys?" She put the food down before them.

"Not for me; how about you, Jill?"

"No, thank you."

"Good! I have to go calm down Mr. Ripley. He's all upset about his meat loaf. I'll check back with you later." Judy ran off in another direction.

For a few minutes, Jill and Craig ate in silence.

"I'm sorry. I didn't mean to bombard you with questions, Jill, but I feel Hope House is a real significant clue."

"I agree, but you've got to remember this is my father we're talking about, not some criminal."

"Maybe your father didn't want to discuss Hope House or his connection to the case with you until he had a chance to check it out for himself."

"And it might've cost him his life?" Jill guessed, feeling on the verge of tears.

"I have no proof, but I do have a gut feeling that whoever framed you may have been responsible for your father's death. Or depending on your father's relationship with Hope House . . . he may have been involved long before you ever began investigating this case."

Jill felt her face flush. "You obviously didn't know my father. He was a man of integrity and would never have been involved in anything like this baby-selling scandal."

Craig was silent for a moment, then asked quietly, "Did you ever wonder where all your father's money came from?"

"He was a doctor. Doctors make lots of money."

"Doctors in small towns don't make that kind of money, Jill."

Her pulse was racing and her mind reeling. "How dare you? You know, this is actually none of your business."

"You asked for my help."

There was a long silence. Finally Jill spoke, almost in a whisper. "I'm sorry, Craig. You've just dumped a lot on me."

"It's okay. I know this isn't easy to hear, but if I'm going to help you, I have to get some answers. Do you mind if I go on?"

Jill nodded and squirmed uncomfortably in the booth. She could feel nausea rising from the pit of her stomach.

"And Jeff, your brother-in-law? Where does all his money come from?"

"Jeff?" Jill was incredulous. "Jeff's a lawyer in a successful practice." Suddenly she didn't want to hear any more about what Craig had found. She wanted to run and forget she was ever an investigative reporter.

"It's possible but unlikely that Jeff could make the kind of money that affords him the extravagant lifestyle he and Kathy enjoy," Craig pointed out.

Jill didn't respond but nervously twirled the red-and-white-striped straw in her drink. How did Craig know about Kathy and Jeff's lifestyle? He must have done some investigating over the last few days.

"So are you saying that you think my father and Jeff were involved in the adoption scandal?"

"I'm only speculating. First we have to establish a motive."

"Wouldn't that be ironic?" Jill sighed. "Of all the political investigations I could have become involved in, why did this one have to be connected to my family by some weird coincidence?" A terrifying thought struck her. "My father probably died because of my investigation. You think so too! Don't you, Craig?"

Craig nodded his head slowly. "There are still so many unanswered questions, but I do believe there is some connection."

Jill put her head in her hands. She wanted to scream.

"Why don't we talk more about this later?" Craig suggested gently, covering her hand with his.

She jerked her hand away. "You mean there's more?" She looked up at Craig; he looked unsure about continuing. She sighed. "Go ahead. It can't get much worse—can it?" she asked, nibbling on a french fry.

"Well, uh, I believe you may unknowingly have something the perpetrators want. Some kind of evidence that would incriminate them, and that's why your house was broken into—your bedroom ransacked."

"They can have anything they want!" she cried. "This has

already cost my family too much. I'm finished!" She tried to get out of the booth, but Craig grabbed her arm.

"Jill, wait." He held on to her. "You owe it to yourself to clear your name. You've worked too hard to walk out on your career."

At the expense of ruining my dad's name? Not a chance, Jill thought silently to herself. *Which is worse? Discovering that Dad might've been murdered and I'm partly to blame or finding out that he was somehow involved in an ugly adoption scandal?*

She composed herself and gently pulled back from Craig's grasp. "In case you haven't noticed, I'm quite content working at the *Lakes.*"

"Writing obituaries for dead parakeets?"

"I was hoping my editor might promote me."

"Maybe I could if I knew you were going to be around, but I'm telling you, Jill, these people will stop at nothing until they get what they want." Craig motioned Judy for the check. The waitress came right over and plopped it down on the table in front of Craig and then trotted away.

"Are you telling me I can't just walk away from this even if I wanted to? Are you insinuating that my life is in danger?"

Craig gazed into her eyes as he held her hand. "I'm not going to let anything happen to you. I promise."

His touch rendered her speechless. It ignited something deep inside of her that was both wonderful and terrifying at the same time.

"I want to go to Chicago soon and check out a few more things," Craig continued, dropping money on the table for their food and Judy's tip. They made their way out of the cafe. "I need to go through some public records."

"What public records?"

"I'd rather not go into it now. You've had enough to think about for one day."

"But Craig . . . hello, this is my investigation, remember?" She waved her hand in his face.

"Oh, I remember, which is why I want you to do a little snooping around your house. I need you to go through your father's possessions and see if you can find anything relating to Hope House."

"Have you forgotten to whom you are talking? I made a mental note to check it out as soon as you showed me my father's bio."

"So you're with me?"

"Yeah. Tell me what you expect to find in Chicago."

"It's only a hunch. I need a chance to check it out first."

Jill felt irritated. Craig was giving her orders and not disclosing all he knew about *her* investigation. She paused, suddenly recalling Rubric's suspicions.

"How long have you been at the *Lakes*?"

"About half a year. Why do you ask?"

"Just curious. When I was in Washington, Mom would send me your editorials; she found them most interesting and agreed with them. I did too, actually. How did you end up in Delavan?"

"When I saw Max's ad in the *Chicago Tribune,* I said to myself, 'Now that's the perfect place to raise a family.'"

Under normal circumstances, Jill would have been delighted to hear that Craig was thinking of raising a family. But Rubric's comments kept popping into her mind. *Besides,* she told herself, *at this point Caroline is the most likely candidate to be the mother of his children.*

"But how did you know that about Delavan?"

"My family had a vacation home near Egg Harbor."

"Who are your folks?" she asked, suddenly metamorphosing

into an investigative reporter again. *Am I crazy? I trust Craig. But Rubric was right. You can never be too careful.*

"Elizabeth and Bill Martin. My mom died of cancer and my dad still lives in Chicago."

"I'm sorry," she apologized. "I've been so wrapped up in my own troubles I lost sight of the fact that you have a life and family too."

"No need to apologize. My mom's been gone since I was a teenager. I'll never stop missing her, but I have gotten used to her being gone."

"Oh, Craig, that must have been awful for you."

"It was, but I'm comforted by the fact that she's no longer suffering and is in a much better place now. And I know that one day we'll be together again."

"That's just what Mom said about Dad."

Craig spoke with such confidence, such faith—Jill envied him. She wanted what he had, what her mother had, and yet she wasn't quite sure how to get it. But at least she was beginning to try. Rubric was wrong about not trusting anyone. *I trust Craig with all my heart. And it was me who asked him to get involved with this investigation in the first place.*

"After work today," Craig said, "go home and get a good night's sleep. You'll need your strength for your big assignment tomorrow." He held her hand as they tramped together through the snow back to the parking lot.

"Oh, I almost forgot, the dog show!" Jill mustered her enthusiasm and managed to flash Craig a phony smile.

20

When you feel really lousy, puppy therapy is indicated.
—Sara Paretsky

After arriving at the Lake Lawn Resort just a few miles from town, Jill trudged alongside and in between the hundreds of people milling around Lake Delavan. Huge dogs with large feet and floppy ears were walking on leashes, running free, lounging in cages, panting out of car windows, and sitting on snowmobiles with their owners. Jill wore a stocking cap atop her hair that was tucked neatly behind her ears. With her beige corduroy slacks she wore a heavy cable-knit sweater for warmth beneath her jacket. The Bernese mountain dog club of America's National Specialty Show had come to town, and she was the investigative reporter sent to cover it. She secretly hoped that someone might kidnap a dog so she would have a crime to solve.

"Seven-thirty A.M. and look at all these dog nuts!" Fred, one of the photographers at the *Lakes,* muttered in disgust. "You know, you could've gotten the story and called me to come out later for the shots. I could've gotten a few more hours of sleep."

"Not a chance, Fred," she told the older man as she pulled on his sleeve. "From all the research I've done, I can tell this is a *big* deal for Delavan. There are daily events all week long, and I need you right here by my side."

"I'm touched."

She ignored the sarcasm. "Okay, we're supposed to meet a Mary Muelling by the receptionist desk. She's the show chairperson and my dog-story mentor for the next six days of doggie events."

Upon entering the lodge, Jill spotted a woman in her fifties with silver hair reaching to her waistline. The woman was standing by the front desk, scanning the crowd. She wore black jeans and a plaid shirt underneath a down-filled vest. Jill couldn't help but think of her as a fading flower child who finally found her purpose in life—dogs.

"Mary Muelling?" Jill asked.

The woman smiled and shook her hand with a firm grip.

"I'm Jill Lewis and this is our photographer, Fred Wallace. We're from the—"

"The *Lakes News,* I know," said Mary. "You'll be following me around for the next six days, and I'll answer all your questions and give you a quick lesson on dog shows. By week's end you'll agree with me that the Bernese mountain dog is the best. Just stay in the background and follow my lead!" She waved a finger in their faces.

Even though she was twenty-some years younger than Mary, Jill found herself having a hard time keeping up with the petite woman.

"Registration lasts all day, and we have daily events with training and other specialty seminars in the evening. People from all over the world are here; they stay at hotels and motels for a hundred miles around. Some came in their campers," she said as she waved at a huge field across the road that was lined with parked RVs. Many more were trying to work their way into the stream of congestion.

"One of the best events, although all the events are good, is the obedience segment. Many times these dogs are used for therapy."

"What do you mean by 'therapy'?" Jill asked, feeling genuinely curious.

"Dogs who are especially calm and good with people are trained to go into schools, nursing homes, children's wards at hospitals, and so forth. They help bring back the 'spirit' of hurting people. One of the best of God's creations are these furry little animals."

"They don't look so little to me," Fred said.

"Just a figure of speech, of course. Their height is anywhere from 23 to 27 inches at the shoulders, and they can weigh anywhere from 80 to 110 pounds when they are fully grown."

"They look like teddy bears to me," Jill said as she watched owners working with their animals. She scribbled notes on her pad: *soft, long, shiny black coat, and markings of white spots.*

Looking over Jill's shoulder, Mary corrected her. "Blaze. They're not called 'spots' but 'markings of white blaze,' and they have those on their chest, feet, and tail tip."

Jill and Fred trailed at Mary's heels all day, taking a lot of notes and pictures. And Jill found herself falling in love with the breed. She was also amazed at how much fun she was having. She might be able to tell Craig she had actually enjoyed the assignment.

———

By week's end, Jill felt relaxed. For a short while, she had managed to put the investigation on hold as she tackled the dog show with the enthusiasm of a rookie reporter. She had even picked up a little breeder and dog talk. She found she could fit right in with the Bernese mountain dog people. And even Mary had begun to grow on her.

After all the competitions were awarded and the food from all the banquets devoured, the week's *Specialty Dog Show* was done. Jill was kind of sorry to see it end.

As Jill and Fred were packing up to leave, Mary walked up to her with a six-month-old puppy on a leash. "Here, for you," she said, handing the leash to Jill. "From my female dog's last litter. You're a Bernese lady at heart, I can tell."

Jill thanked Mary profusely and knelt down in front of her new little friend. "I just love you!" she told the puppy, who in fact seemed to understand her. Jumping up on Jill, it gave her a rambunctious wet kiss, knocking her backward. Jill laughed joyously.

———

Struggling into the house that night, Jill held a bag of puppy food in one hand and a leash with an exuberant puppy at the end in the other hand.

"What on earth are you bringing into my house?" her mom asked as Jill entered the back door.

"Craig's Christmas present."

21

The large white snowflakes as they flutter down, softly, one by one,
Whisper soothingly, "Rest, poor heart, rest!"
It is as though our mother smoothed our hair,
And we're comforted.

—Ralph Iron

Even before the sun came up on Saturday morning, the furry puppy's frantic yipping startled both Jill and her mother out of deep slumber. "It's just like having a new baby in the house," Jill's mom said as she peeked inside Jill's room and saw her kneeling at the crate, cradling the puppy in her arms. "Bye, sweetie. Can you handle this little troublemaker by yourself?" she asked, reminding Jill that her mom was volunteering as a pink lady at the hospital for the morning.

"Who would deliver flowers and magazines and pour juice for the patients? You go ahead, Mom. Gracie and I will manage just fine."

After her mom left, Jill headed for her father's study and began leafing through his files. Finding nothing an hour or so later, she searched his closet and discovered an old file box labeled "House of Hope" at the back of the top shelf. Pulling the box down, she carried it over to her father's chair. She settled down into the leather cushions and flipped through the yellowed pages. Then she discovered the minutes from a board meeting. She froze as she studied the documents. To her shock, there alongside her father's name was that of good old Senator Tom Burke. Both were listed as board members and attendees. She sprung from her father's chair to phone Craig.

"I found the Hope House files!" she blurted out. "They have both Senator Burke's and my father's names listed as board members."

"Good girl! I've got the later part of the day free. Why don't you drive up here? The roads are clear."

"I'm there." She made sure the puppy had plenty of food and water and left a note for her mother.

Hours later she walked into the restaurant where she'd told Craig she would meet him for lunch. When she caught sight of him wearing faded jeans and a flannel shirt with a navy blue down-filled vest, her heart fluttered. He was already seated at the table for two in the dining room, sipping coffee. "Let's have lunch and then drive to the cabin in my truck," he suggested.

After an enjoyable lunch, Craig transferred the heavy file box from Jill's car to his truck. He smiled with a grin that stretched ear to ear. "Do I have spinach in my teeth?" he queried, laughing as he saw her staring at his mouth.

"No, just a nice smile. And I appreciate you taking the time to help me again."

"Think nothing of it, Lois Lane. I think you and old Clark Kent here make a pretty good team."

Jill smiled in agreement.

When they arrived at his cabin, she tramped behind Craig, stepping into his footprints in the snow. Since this was the first time she had visited him in the daylight, she hadn't noticed the cabin next door, set back from the road. It was smaller and not as nice.

"Looks like you have neighbors," Jill observed as she saw smoke curling out of the stone fireplace next door.

"That's my cabin too. I was over there this morning doing some work. That fireplace is the only source of heat. It's really only a one-room cabin, but it should bring a good price with all the hunters and fishermen that come up here from the city."

"How much work do you plan on doing to it?"

"Well, I need to finish the plumbing, and then I want to put in a heater. Maybe by the end of next summer it'll be complete."

"May I see it?"

"Nope, it's a mess."

"All the better. I can compare the before and the after."

"Forget it. It's too cold over there. Let's go inside and get to work."

Once inside the larger cabin, Jill made herself at home. "Have any Diet Coke in your refrigerator?"

"Nope. You must have Diet Coke running through your veins," he teased. "How about some of my famous hot chocolate instead?"

"Chocolate? Did someone say chocolate? I love a man who learns about the important things in life. Hand it over!"

As Craig disappeared into the kitchen, Jill sat cross-legged on the floor at the coffee table. She lifted one of the picture frames. There was Craig with Caroline holding a big fish between them. The next photo she picked up was of Craig and Fred, the photographer at the paper; they were skiing. Next she spotted Craig and Caroline smiling in a group of campers. *Ugh, he's a real outdoorsman. No woman in her right mind could possibly enjoy the great outdoors this much—or is Caroline just pretending to please Craig?* Unfortunately, Jill's idea of roughing it was spending a weekend at the Ritz without room service.

Craig caught her off guard when he entered the room. Startled, she hurriedly repositioned the frame, but it fell to the floor. Ever the gentleman, he pretended not to notice and handed her a steaming cup of chocolate.

"It's going to be a long afternoon," he said, eyeing the large box overflowing with her father's files. "Spread out this stuff while I go outside to get a couple of monster logs."

By the time he finished adding logs and stoking the fire, she had the frame back on the table and all the hard copy files spread out on the floor. He joined her on the floor, but she moved to a more comfortable spot. Perching on the edge of the overstuffed denim sofa, she helped Craig dig into the files, and together they spent the afternoon making notes over the material while sitting in front of the roaring fire. Although absorbed in the information, Jill was still very much aware of his presence.

"So far, nothing—only the name of the illustrious Illinois senator, but it leads nowhere," Craig announced.

To Jill's disappointment all the other business in the files was fairly routine. Senator Burke's name, which she had found this morning, appeared to be the only clue in any of the files. "I hope I haven't wasted your Saturday," she said.

"Don't be ridiculous; we had to go through these files sooner or later, and today was as good a day as any. Besides, it is a significant clue. It connects the dots, proving that Burke and your father knew one another and had some association. By the way, have you ever considered talking to your sister or Jeff about Marion's adoption?"

"No." Jill was afraid. "Oh, Craig, I couldn't bear to think that Marion was one of the illegal adoptions. I just cannot go there . . . not now, maybe not ever. If I find out that my investigation resulted in my dad's death, I'm not sure I could ever forgive myself. And I couldn't bear to bring any more pain into our family by implicating Kathy, Jeff, and Marion in some manner."

"But Jeff could hold the key to your entire investigation."

Jill sighed. "I suppose broaching the subject of the adoption with Jeff might fill in a lot of the blanks. But Craig, you've got to promise me you'll drop it if we uncover anything, anything at all that would endanger Kathy, Jeff, Marion, or the adoption. Besides, this revelation that my dad was on a board with Burke doesn't prove anything. I mean, so were a lot of other prominent people from the Chicago area. We're just jumping to conclusions here."

"You're probably right."

She looked at her watch. "It's 5:00. Guess I'd better be heading back to the B & B." She stood up, hoping he would invite her to stay for dinner.

"Let me help you with your coat," Craig offered as he quickly got to his feet.

Is he anxious to get me out the door? Is Caroline biding her time next door until I leave?

When they stepped out onto his porch, she was shocked to discover his truck had disappeared under an avalanche of snow. There was no sign of a driveway either; it was now hidden under layers of white powder. Heavy snow flurries were still swirling through the cold air, blinding the two of them.

"Looks like the weatherman goofed again," he said. "We had better get back inside." Shivering, he added, "We're lucky to have power. From the looks of things, there's no way we could make it over to the B & B, even with my super-duper snow tires and four-wheel-drive truck." He grabbed the remote and quickly scanned the weather channel. "Looks bad. You might be here for a while."

Feigning upset on the outside, Jill was secretly smiling on the inside. She scanned the shelves flanking the fireplace and saw a neatly stacked group of games. Grabbing one, she said, "Want to play Scrabble? Before you accept, I must caution you, I rarely lose." She stood with her hands on her hips.

"But you've never played with me."

Ignoring her mother's outdated advice to let the guy win occasionally, Jill beat Craig at Scrabble for over two excruciating hours. After watching more snowflakes fall from the skies, they made peanut butter and jelly sandwiches and ate them by the fire.

"So what are your dreams, Craig?" Jill ventured after she had finished the last bite of her sandwich. "Surely you don't plan to stay at the *Lakes News* forever?"

"I hope to," he replied a bit defensively. "I love my work there and I love living in a small town. Anything wrong with that?"

"No, nothing. I just thought you might have other ambitions. What are your plans?"

"Well, besides working at the newspaper, I want to have a loving relationship with a godly woman and at least four or five kids, three dogs, maybe a goldfish, if that's God's plan for me."

Suddenly she felt as if this was all she wanted in life too. *Five kids? I've lost my mind!*

"My mom believes that God has a plan for our lives too," she ventured pensively. "I'm not so sure. If he's given us our own free will, how can he have a plan for us when he lets us make our own choices?"

"Just a minute," Craig replied as he disappeared into the hallway. In a matter of seconds he returned carrying a well-worn Bible and took the seat next to Jill on the sofa. Turning to Jeremiah 29:11, he read aloud, "'For I know the plans I have for you,' declares the LORD, 'plans to prosper you and not to harm you, plans to give you hope and a future.'"

"That's beautiful, but how do you know what God's plan is for your life?" Jill asked the question she had wanted to ask her mom if she hadn't feared a sermon.

"Personally, I pray about every decision I make, no matter how small, and I ask God to close the door on anything that is not in his plan or his best interest for me." He turned in his Bible to Proverbs 16:9 and read, "In his heart a man plans his course, but the LORD determines his steps."

"But what if there's something that really matters to you, and it doesn't appear to be part of God's plan for your life?"

"That's where obedience comes in—being willing to give your plan up for God's plan for you. 'Not my will but thy will be done,' is what Jesus says. And you know what, Jill? God's plan is always so much better than any plan we could devise for ourselves."

Jill nodded. "My mom read the Bible to me every day as a young girl, and when I was a teenager I continued the habit, but I've got to confess that I drifted away from God when I was in college. All the people in church seemed like such hypocrites to me. Yet I've been through so much lately . . . I really want to believe that all things truly work together for good. I guess maybe that's why I ended up back in Delavan. Now I just have to find out what the rest of the plan is."

"You will, Jill. You will. Just ask him, have patience, and persevere until you discover that plan."

"I think maybe it was part of his plan for me to meet you, Craig," she said bravely.

"Me too—to help you solve this investigation." He got to his feet to look out the window. "Still snowing."

Jill glanced down at her watch. "Oh my goodness! It's after 11:00. Mom will be sleeping now; it's too late to call her."

"She thinks you're staying at the B & B; she won't worry."

"You don't know my mother. She might wake up in the middle of the night and try to call me. I think I'd better phone her."

For a moment there was an awkward silence. She felt uncomfortable staying in the cabin with Craig. After all, her mother had always warned, "Avoid all appearances of evil." And here she was in an awkward position with a man. Surely snowstorms were the exception!

"Here," Craig said as he handed her his cordless phone. "Use the land line."

Jill dialed the phone. After a few rings, her mother picked up. "Hello? Jill, is that you? Is anything wrong?"

"Just thought I'd better let you know that Craig and I are snowed in at his cabin. But don't worry," Jill quickly added. "Craig will be staying at the cabin next door."

Her mother chuckled. She obviously wasn't worried.

"Thank you for calling, darling," her mom said. "Tell Craig I said he'd better take good care of you and make sure you're safe. Don't even consider driving in this weather."

"I won't take any chances. I love you, Mom. See you tomorrow."

"Love you too, darling. Tell Craig I said hello."

Jill hung up and turned to Craig.

"Was your mom upset?"

"No, she understands. She just said hello and that you'd better watch over me and keep me safe."

"I'm afraid you are stuck here, but you'll be perfectly safe in the guest room." He left the room and soon returned with a stack of plush towels and a pair of his pajamas for her to sleep in. He led her down the hallway and pointed out the private bathroom and then led her to the guest room, pointing out the flashlight by her bed.

"Good night, Lois. If you get scared or anything, Superman's only a scream away, okay?" He touched her face gently with his fingers.

Jill slowly puckered her lips, thinking he was going to kiss her. Instead, he said good night and closed the door behind him.

Oh well. I guess it's a good thing Craig didn't kiss me. I don't know if I could have trusted myself alone in the cabin with Craig on a romantic, snowy evening.

After changing into the pajamas he'd given her, Jill knelt by her bed and said her prayers, something she hadn't done in years. She almost guiltily included a cry for help to snag Craig once and for all. "I want to be his wife, Lord. Pure and simple. I want to have his five babies and I want to live in Delavan with him and grow old together. Lord, I guess I've lost my mind. Who would have ever dreamed that Jill Lewis would be asking to have five babies? Not me!"

She reached over to turn out the lamp before climbing into bed. Her hand rested on the switch when she spotted another photograph. It was her again, Miss Egg Harbor, and this time she and Craig were playing tennis. *Lady, is there anything you don't do?* She turned the picture facedown and looked around the room.

Suddenly, Jill, the super snoop, had an inspiration and sat up in bed. She realized this was the perfect opportunity to look inside Craig's room for clues to see if he and Caroline were in fact living together. Craig had high standards, and it seemed unlikely that he would share a room with Caroline before they were married. Maybe she was nothing more than a house sitter for him in his absence, or truly just a friend.

Jill felt a little guilty, but nothing was going to stop her. Tiptoeing down the hallway with the flashlight, she tried to open the door of the next room. It was locked! Didn't Craig trust her? She went down the hallway to the next room. That door was locked too. What? Craig obviously had a privacy issue. Just what was it he was trying to hide? She walked out into the great room and climbed up the stairs to the loft. She had never seen so much exercise equipment outside a gym in her life. This explained Craig's great body, although he didn't seem preoccupied with fitness, like some men. She figured she might as well go back to bed. She wasn't going to find any answers here.

She didn't awaken until the sunlight streamed through the windows the next morning. She could hear Craig moving around in the kitchen and smelled fresh coffee brewing and bacon frying. As she came out of the bathroom, she heard a car pulling up in the driveway. Looking out, she saw Caroline walking toward the cabin. What would Caroline think of Jill's overnight stay? Jill panicked. What to do? She could answer the door with a Cheshire smile and try to throw a wrench in Caroline's relationship with Craig, or she could do the honorable thing. She chose the latter and hid in the hall closet.

"Jill?" She heard Craig call her name softly and then close the bedroom door. She didn't answer. Jill heard them talking in the next room: a male voice, a female voice, both twirling together like snow in the winter air. Then there was a long silence followed by laughter. The cabin door opened and closed and a car started again in the driveway. Footsteps came down the hall toward her. The closet door opened, and Jill looked up at Craig's face.

He burst out laughing. "What in the world are you doing in there?"

"I was doing you a favor. How would you have explained me to Caroline? Snowstorm or not, it doesn't exactly look proper for me to wake up in your cabin, in your pajamas."

"Don't be ridiculous. I told her you were here, and I went to find you. We figured you must've gone out for a walk."

She sheepishly emerged from the closet. Craig burst out laughing again. He removed a wire hanger dangling from the back of her sweater and a big fuzz ball sitting atop her head.

"I really don't appreciate you laughing at me," she said defensively. "I was only trying to be sensitive."

"Well, thank you," Craig said, "but Caroline is very mature and she didn't think anything of it. Things like this happen in life." He smiled.

When he smiled at her, the glow of his smile melted her anger away. She just couldn't be angry with him anymore.

22

Christmas Eve was a night of song
That wrapped itself about you like a shawl.
But it warmed more than your body.
It warmed your heart ... filled it, too,
with melody that would last forever.

—Bess Streeter Aldrich

A fresh blanket of snow and a little help from the town's decorating committee had transformed Delavan into a winter wonderland overnight. Evergreen wreaths with trailing red velvet bows had been hung from the lampposts that lined the cobblestone streets, and every storefront was ablaze with twinkling lights. Crowned with a brilliant star, the traditional forty-foot blue spruce stood at the center of town. And churches at every corner proudly displayed a nativity scene on the lawn to celebrate Christ's birth.

It may have been the dead of winter, but Jill had a spring in her step. Maybe it was because Craig had told her he was planning to attend her family's annual Christmas party. She walked around the streets of town singing carols, loaded down with packages, looking forward to this particular party more than she had any others in the past.

Lost in her daydreams, she imagined her grand entrance over and over in her head. Craig would look up at the winding staircase and see her floating down in a vision of red silk, like the movie legends she had mimicked in her childhood. She hoped her grand entrance would not only take Craig's breath away but capture his heart as well.

Jill was jolted out of her daze when she bumped right into Craig and Caroline at the entrance to the Ben Franklin store. "Is this my Christmas present?" Craig teased her, pulling at a package while holding the door for her.

"As a matter of fact, I—I just put in an order with Santa for a bag of switches for you, Craig," Jill stuttered, trying to get her thoughts together, trying to act normal, as if she didn't feel as though someone had stabbed her in the heart with a dagger.

Caroline stood by, smiling. Her exquisite profile, framed by the fur on the hood of her parka, reminded Jill of the image of the snow princess that had graced the cover of her childhood book of fairy tales.

"We'll see you tonight," Craig said.

Jill nodded dumbly. She couldn't avoid watching the two of them blend into the crowd of last-minute shoppers. It should've been no surprise that Craig had said, "*We'll* see you tonight," meaning not just him but Caroline too. How could she have been so stupid to think he'd come alone?

———

That evening Jill soaked in a sudsy tub scented with rose water, scheming of ways to upstage Caroline so Craig would be sorry he brought her to the party. For weeks she had searched everywhere for the right gown. She'd finally settled on a tea-length emerald taffeta skirt with a pale green cashmere strapless sweater and a matching cardigan studded with rhinestones. While trying it on at home, she'd borrowed her mother's opera-length pearls with the emerald and diamond clasp to complete her fashion statement.

"You look like a little princess," her mother had effused when Jill modeled the outfit for her. It wasn't exactly what she'd wanted to hear, so she had returned to the shop and purchased a slinky red silk chiffon gown with a plunging back that clung to her every curve. Her mother had gasped when Jill modeled that dress, and this was just the reaction Jill was looking for, but she had held on to the green outfit in case her courage to wear the red dress faded.

Scrubbing her back with the loofah, Jill considered the two dresses and decided on the red. *Isn't all fair in love and war?*

An hour later, Jill was putting on the red dress. She didn't remember it being quite so revealing. For modesty's sake, she was glad the gown came with a shawl. She pulled her blonde curls back from her face with a rhinestone clip and looked through her mother's jewelry cases to find the ruby and diamond earrings. As she sifted through the piles of jewelry, she found herself growing more and more astounded. She knew her mother had an impressive collection, but this stash rivaled Queen Elizabeth's royal jewels. *Where did it all come from?* She began to feel uneasy. She didn't want her thoughts to go there, not tonight. Quickly fastening the earrings she'd found, she then took one last glance in the mirror. Jill was determined to outshine Caroline Jennings.

Many of the guests had already arrived when Jill slowly descended the stairs. She searched for Craig's face in the crowd. There was no sign of him or Caroline. She felt ridiculous. All those grand entrance rehearsals were a total waste of time. No one in the room even looked up at her.

Christmas carols played softly throughout the candlelit house as friends, acquaintances, and previous business partners gathered around tables laden with holiday fare. The smells of Christmas—evergreen, cinnamon, a fire in the hearth—all conjured up thoughts of holidays past, and she blinked back tears for those memories of her father.

When the doorbell chimed, Pearl asked Jill, who was standing nearby, to welcome the latest arriving guests. Jill's heart pounded at the sight of Craig with Caroline. The two were standing outside with snow swirling around their heads, as though they were posing for a Currier and Ives painting. Scrutinizing the handsome couple from head to toe, Jill had to admit she had never seen Caroline look more beautiful nor Craig so handsome as he did tonight in his tuxedo and midnight blue overcoat.

"Merry Christmas," the stunning couple sang in unison.

"Happy Holidays," a dazed Jill said quietly, clinging to the door for support.

"This snow is coming down pretty hard. They won't be able to find us if you don't let us in soon," Craig teased her.

"I'm so sorry," Jill stuttered. "Please come inside."

Craig and Caroline entered the house, and he helped her with her coat. When Caroline turned around, Jill could feel her eyes widen.

It can't be possible. It just can't be.

Both women gasped as they looked over at the other's gown and then down at their own. They couldn't be . . . but yes, they were wearing the very same red dress!

Jill mustered a smile. "I thought things like this only happened in the movies." She hoped her voice sounded cheerful.

"What great taste you have, Jill!" Caroline seemed amused at the coincidence.

Trying to keep a straight face, Craig finally managed to say, "You are both a vision of loveliness—a double vision!"

Jill tried to be discreet while looking Caroline over. The woman sure filled out her dress in all the right places; Jill was painfully aware there was no way that she could ever compete with Caroline's buffed body. Heads turned in admiration as Caroline and Craig made their way through the party with ease. Even Jill had to admit they were a striking couple.

Walking to the piano, she hoped to hide her feelings of despair beside the group of carolers, but the beautiful couple seemed to follow her everywhere. As she glanced to her right, she heard Caroline singing in a sweet soprano and then Craig's voice singing "Away in a Manger" in a resonant baritone voice. They sounded as if they had been singing in perfect harmony for a lifetime.

Deciding she had had enough of the happy, harmonious couple, she headed for the wassail bowl, poured herself a generous cup, and gulped it down. While lingering at the bowl, she overheard two men talking about Caroline.

"Did you see that gorgeous siren in the red dress?"

"I sure did. Who is she?"

"I don't have a clue, but I'm going to persuade Craig to introduce me."

I just can't escape that woman! Jill wanted to scream, until the words of a song caught her ears and slowly began to sink into her heart.

The words spoke of a baby who was laid in a manger. No gift beneath the tree could ever compare to the one of eternal life. What were her priorities compared to that? Suddenly she felt ashamed of herself. The reality of Christ's birth seemed to speak to her at that moment, and for the first time in a long time, she felt the warmth of the love of a heavenly Father. After all, Christmas was a time of new birth and new beginnings.

Jill lifted her skirt and walked up the stairs toward her bedroom. As she stood in front of the mirror, she cried out to God. No longer was Jesus the babe in Bethlehem's manger. He was her risen Savior and comforter, and he was right beside her. It was time to totally surrender.

Her soul weary, Jill realized she no longer wanted to be a control freak; she was tired of running too; it was time for her to surrender, to give the reins over to him, to rest, to come home. *I surrender, Lord. Here I am. I have nothing to give you but a messed-up life. Forgive me and come into my heart. Change me into the person you want me to be. Whatever your plan is for me, I'm yours.*

Jill stepped out of the red dress and tossed it over the back of the overstuffed chair. She was relieved she had kept the green taffeta after all. She slid into the skirt, pulled on the sweater set, and fastened her mother's opera-length pearls with the emerald clasp.

When she returned to the party she found Craig and Caroline standing in the hallway by the Christmas tree, posing for Fred, the photographer from the *Lakes*. Next to him was Cornelia Southworth.

To Jill's surprise, Craig tapped her on the shoulder. "You look lovely—this dress is much more your style. Very elegant."

"Thank you." Jill blushed.

"Have you been avoiding me tonight or was it just my imagination?"

"Of course not," she said coyly. "Who would ever want to avoid you?" Then it was as though God had whispered into her ear, reminding her that if she wanted to change her life, she had to avoid all the gray areas. "Actually, Craig, I've been ignoring you tonight because you brought a date."

Craig smiled sheepishly, reached inside the pocket of his tuxedo, and pulled out a small wrapped package tied with a gold ribbon. "Well, I have a Christmas present for you."

Jill tore off the paper, revealing an antique volume of Elizabeth Barrett Browning's poetry bound in gold-etched leather.

"Craig, it's lovely!" she said breathlessly. She smiled as she opened the cover and saw the inscription written in his neat, precise handwriting.

> To Jill,
>
> "Those who bring sunshine to the lives of others,
> Cannot keep it from themselves."
> —James M. Barry
>
> Merry Christmas, Craig

Suddenly the whimpering of a forlorn puppy reminded her of the Christmas gift she had tucked away for Craig in the den.

"I've got a present for you too," she said happily, "but I'll bring it to the office tomorrow."

23

How much is that doggie in the window?

The following morning, Jill parked her car around back of the office so no one would see the dog crate. As she tossed the puppy a nylon chew toy, Jill promised she would come back for her soon.

Other than Marge, who unlocked the office, Jill was the first to arrive.

"Great party, Jill!" Marge said.

"Uh, thanks. Will you let me know when Craig gets here?" Jill said as she scurried away. She didn't want to get stuck discussing the party details with Marge.

Settling down at her desk, she thought about the spiritual awakening she'd experienced the night before. Last night she had given her life to Christ, but this morning, other than feeling hopeful, she didn't feel any different. Pulling out the small devotional book her mother had given her years before, she read today's entry, but even those words didn't sink into her heart. Had last night been real? Had she really connected with God? She closed the book and slipped it into her top drawer.

Jill looked around the office. One by one the staff began arriving. Miss Cornelia came in with a flourish, and although Jill tried to appear busy, the society editor stepped over to her desk. "Oh my! I can hardly wait to write about your mother's soirée. It was her most divine Christmas party ever, but first I'm going to phone Pearl to tell her what a wonderful time Herman and I had last night. Simply sublime!"

"Thank you. Mom would love to hear from you." Jill forced a smile.

"Stand up, honey, and let me get a closer look at that outfit!" Cornelia examined Jill up and down, smiling all the while.

Suddenly Jill felt ridiculous in her holiday threads. She must look a sight in the plaid skirt with the Christmas sweater covered with holly and bells! She realized it was exactly the kind of getup Miss Cornelia would choose for herself. *She must be rubbing off on me.* But if she had to acquire Cornelia's poor taste, she hoped she would also gain her sweet spirit.

Within the hour everyone had arrived and was working at their desks, except Craig. Jill began pacing the floor and watching the big clock that hung over the door. She had asked Marge at least a dozen times if he had come in yet. If Craig didn't arrive soon, she'd have to bring the puppy inside the office.

Finally Craig called in, and Marge connected him right away to Jill.

"Craig, where are you?" she demanded.

"Jill, I had a great time at your party last night. I just wanted to call and thank you. Caroline is sending a note to your mother from us both."

"Thank you." She conjured up a painful vision of Craig sitting by a crackling fire with Caroline and watching her pen the note on her elegant stationery.

"I've decided not to come in today," he announced.

"What do you mean?" Her heart sunk. *Maybe Caroline decided that he should stay at home with her.*

"I drove Caroline back up to Egg Harbor last night, so I'm not going to drive all the way back down there today. I'll telecommute from here."

"Telecommute?"

"Surely a city gal like you knows what that means," he teased.

"Of course I know what it means, but Craig, did you forget I was bringing in your Christmas gift today?" She imagined Caroline rubbing Craig's neck as he talked on the phone.

"Seems like I remember something about it."

"Don't you want your Christmas present?" She envisioned Caroline shaking her head no.

"Can't it wait until after Christmas? With all those last-minute shoppers out on the road, traffic is terrible."

"No, it can't," she said firmly, thinking of Gracie in the car.

"Pop it in the freezer, and I'll thaw it out after Christmas." She didn't respond.

"Jill? Jill, are you still there?" He paused and sighed. "Okay, if it's that important to you, I could be there about 3:00."

"Oh, would you, Craig?" Suddenly she felt guilty for making him drive all that way.

"Meet me at my apartment."

When Craig finally pulled up to his apartment, it was 3:15. Jill was pacing up and down the sidewalk.

He looked apologetic as he got out of his car. "I'm sorry to have kept you waiting. Traffic was terrible, and I couldn't even get through on my cell phone. Bah humbug! So where's my present?"

Jill beamed as she opened the crate. The large puppy bounded out at him, knocking him to the ground.

"Craig, say hello to Gracie."

He was speechless as he stopped to rub the dog's ears. Finally he spoke. "I haven't had a dog since I was a kid. What on earth made you decide to give me one?"

"I got her at the dog show. I don't know, something just told me you'd like her."

"Uh, thanks . . . I think."

"You're welcome. Hey, since you're here anyway, how about dinner tonight? We've got tons of leftovers from the party."

Craig shook his head. "Sorry, but Gracie and I have to head back. My dad is driving up from Chicago for the holidays, and I've got lots of stuff to do before he gets here."

Jill tried to hide her disappointment. "Oh, that sounds great. It'll be nice for you and your dad to have a visit. I hope it's good driving weather for him." She turned quickly and got the puppy situated on the front seat of the truck while Craig loaded the dog's crate into the back. Jill hugged Gracie good-bye. "I'm going to miss you so much, girl. If your new owner doesn't appreciate you, come back to me." She kissed the pup on her wet nose.

"Okay, I'm off then. Merry Christmas! See you next year!" Craig waved heartily.

Jill watched him as he sped away in his truck and disappeared into the snowfall.

24

Celebratin' New Year's Eve is like eatin' oranges.
You got to let go of your dignity t' really enjoy 'em.

—Edna Ferber

It was New Year's Eve at last. Jill told herself that if Craig came to the office party that Max and his wife, Char, were hosting, she wouldn't complain even if he brought Caroline. Just to see his face, hear his laughter, look into his eyes, and if she was lucky, brush his hand over the punch bowl, would be enough for her.

Jill pulled out the brown dress she had worn last New Year's Eve. The hanger bounced against the wall and onto the floor. She couldn't recall ever being this nervous, not even for her first date, her first kiss, or her first day of school.

David had loved this Armani dress. She wondered if he would miss escorting her to the by-invitation-only supper at Annabelle's exclusive penthouse. More importantly, would he miss her? She realized with surprise that she didn't care. If she directed these questions at herself, the answers would be no.

She couldn't remember any New Year's Eve she had anticipated more than this one. It would be a quiet evening with friends, a night void of famous people, stimulating political gossip, and fireworks over the capital. Maybe she had reached a pinnacle in her spiritual life, a point where she could thank God for allowing her troubles. *The old things have passed away.*

Glancing at the clock, she realized she no longer had time to daydream. No, the brown dress she had on would certainly never do. Off with the old and on with the new. After choosing the new black dress she had recently purchased, she pulled the gown over her head. She fastened her pearls and earrings and swirled down the steps and into the kitchen, where her mother sat reading the mystery novel Rubric had recommended.

"Happy New Year, Mom!"

"Ahhh!" Startled, her mother jumped an inch out of her chair.

"Scary book, huh?" Jill giggled. "Sorry, I didn't mean to sneak up on you." She made a mental note to share her mother's reaction with the sinister Rubric. No doubt he would relish the fact that the book had terrified someone.

"Chilling!" Her mother shuddered. She took off her reading glasses and spun her finger in the air, indicating that she wanted Jill to turn around. After she saw all angles of Jill in the dress, she said, "I told you to get the blue one." She put her glasses back on. "But now I'm glad you didn't listen to me. You look stunning in the black." Smiling coyly, she went back to her reading.

Jill hugged and kissed her.

"You never told me how Craig liked your Christmas gift," her mom said, setting her reading glasses straight on her face after Jill had displaced them with her sudden show of affection.

"He fell in love with Gracie as soon as he saw her. I wish things had been that easy for me."

"Give it time. If it's meant to be, it will be."

Jill sighed melodramatically. "I was hoping for a ring by the New Year."

Shaking her head, Pearl shot Jill a questioning look.

"Are you sure you don't want me to stay home with you, Mom?"

"No. I want to finish my book. I turned down plenty of invitations for this mystery. And don't come home on time; stay out late," she called after her daughter.

Jill's stomach fluttered on her way to Max and Char's home. *Am I really attracted to Craig? Or is it just the thrill of the chase?* That had to be the reason. Every time she was attracted to a guy, she lost interest as soon as they started dating. Never failed. Except with David. She'd stayed with him a long time . . . too long? Was she incapable of true love?

Jill pulled into the gas station, turned the car around, and headed back for home. "No, I'm not going to that party," she said out loud. "I'm going to stay home and keep my mom company." She wasn't sure she could handle Craig's rejection of her. Instead, she'd beg her mom to make that delicious apple strudel and see what was on TV.

But once she got halfway home, she laughed at herself. How ridiculously silly she was acting. Many of her brand-new friends would be disappointed if she didn't go to the party. Besides, seeing Craig was worth the rejection. She pulled into a driveway, backed around, and headed on down the road toward Max's again.

It was New Year's Eve, and so what if she didn't have a date? Maybe she would meet someone interesting tonight. Thinking of all the guys at the paper, she wrinkled her nose. *Nah! If I'm going to be a single lady, I might as well get used to going to events alone.*

And I won't let Caroline ruin my evening.

Jill walked into the festive gathering and saw many new faces of spouses and friends she had never met before this evening. Jill mingled politely as she kept an eye out for Craig.

At last he walked in the front door with a group of people. That ache in her stomach began again. Quickly finding the powder room, she closed and locked the door, leaning against it for good measure. Taking deep breaths, she noticed her hands were trembling. No wonder she never made time for romance! It felt terrible. Gathering her courage, she mumbled a prayer and walked out, her head held high.

And there he was. He seemed taller and even more handsome, his dark eyes glistening in the candlelight. He wore a brown tweed jacket over a blue button-down shirt and a pair of wool slacks. Had he arrived alone? Jill told herself to be brave as she walked toward him.

"Jill, don't you look like the little princess tonight." Cornelia appeared out of thin air and stood as a flashing roadblock.

"Hi, Miss Cornelia. You look stunning yourself," Jill said, eyeing the woman's red and green sequin dress.

"I see at least three unattached people standing here tonight," Cornelia said.

"Oh?" Jill hoped she wouldn't make the headlines in the next *Lakes News* issue: "Jill Lewis Begins the New Year Dateless."

"Yes, but I don't count, since my Herman is at home in bed with a tummy ache." Cornelia laughed and then stepped aside, smiling broadly at Craig and then back at Jill. "I like men in tweed. My guess is you like yours the same way?" She gave a knowing look to Jill and swept away.

"Happy New Year, Craig. Where's Caroline?"

"She went home for the holidays to see her family, but I'll tell her you were asking about her."

"I'm so glad," Jill blurted out without thinking. "Uh, I'm

so glad you're here," she quickly recovered. "I'm anxious to hear how Gracie and you are getting along."

"She woke me up crying the other night," Craig answered, rocking back and forth on his heels and sucking on a piece of ice from his glass.

"What? Who woke you up crying?"

Craig looked at her as if she were trying to be funny. "Gracie."

"Oh, *Gracie* was crying." Jill laughed. "I mean, poor little thing. She must be missing her mom."

"Nope, she was crying because she wet her bed."

"What did you do?"

"I let her sleep in my bed."

"How sweet."

"Yeah, she wet that too," he said, grabbing a handful of cashews. "So we had to sleep in the guest room together on that double bed, and that was no easy matter." He laughed. "I hadn't planned on owning a dog until I had a family, but I have to tell you, Jill, being a pet owner has changed my life. Thank you!"

"I'm so glad you're enjoying Gracie." Her eyes met his. "Did you have a nice Christmas with your dad?"

"Yes, very relaxing. He left yesterday."

They both reached for a potato chip and picked up the same one.

"Here, you can have it. I know how you love the taste of greasy food that's high in cholesterol," Craig said, as seriously as if he'd told her he loved her for the first time.

"That's really considerate of you, but you can have it," Jill answered as if returning his words of love.

"Hey, guys, get a grip! It's only a potato chip. Look, a whole bowl, see?" Snapping her fingers, Marge said loudly, "Here, take the whole thing." She shoved the glass bowl into Jill's chest. Jill coughed uneasily and set the bowl back down again, noticing a grease mark left across her bodice.

"Let me introduce you to my date!" Marge beamed proudly, grabbing the shy, skinny fellow behind her by the hand.

"Jill, Craig, this is Daniel Boneski, my date. And this is my boss, Craig Martin. And Jill Lewis here is my charge." Marge chuckled with an air of superiority and pointed to Jill. "I'm her boss."

"Nice to meet you, Daniel." Craig offered a firm handshake. "You look so familiar to me."

"That's because . . ." Daniel cleared his throat. "I deliver your mail. I'm your postman."

"Of course. I didn't recognize you without your uniform," Craig apologized.

"I couldn't place you without the uniform either," Jill said.

"Not supposed to wear it unless I'm on duty, but I told Marge I'd take her to lunch in my uniform."

"I have a *thing* for a man in a uniform," Marge demurred, batting her false eyelashes at Daniel.

"Yeah, and I have a thing for Marge, too. I hope ya'll appreciate her down at that newspaper. It wouldn't last a day without her."

"Oh, we do." Jill smiled. "Marge does a great job, and she's a wonderful boss. By the way Marge, I suppose you're the person I should talk to about a raise?"

"Yes, and my answer is no."

"Ah, come on Marge, give the girl a break," Craig begged playfully.

"Not until she's written at least a thousand more obituaries."

Jill gasped. "But that could take years in Delavan."

"Maybe you'll get lucky and a serial killer will move to town," Daniel interjected.

Marge perked up. "Think what that would do for subscriptions. They'd fly through the roof. I'd have to hire a whole battalion of paper persons for deliveries."

"Are there any openings now?" Daniel asked.

"Are you thinking of moonlighting as a paperboy, uh, person?" Craig asked.

"Actually, no. I make a good salary at the post office." He smiled at Marge. "I was thinking of Ms. Lewis, to help her make ends meet until she gets her raise."

"That's a much better idea than the serial killer." Jill scrunched her nose.

"You've got to be joking. She'd never be able to hit the porch," Marge hooted. "I'd get complaints all day long; the phone wouldn't stop ringing. Well, good-bye, you two." She winked and strutted off like a peacock, dragging Daniel by the hand. "Be good now and don't do anything I wouldn't do! If you do, I'll read all about it in Miss Cornelia's column."

After Marge left with Daniel in tow, Craig turned to Jill. "That was very gracious of you."

"But it's true. I do report to Marge."

Craig looked at her intently. "There's something different about you."

Jill replied quietly. "I had an amazing encounter with Christ over Christmas, and I don't think I'll ever be the same." She looked up at him, afraid she had shared too much.

But the look in Craig's eyes told her otherwise. "Jill, that's great news! I'm so happy for you," he said as he hugged her. For a brief moment Jill thought he would kiss her, but then he pulled away. Yet he looked into her eyes as though he were trying to decide what to do next. He just stood there staring at her, and she at him. Jill could hardly find her breath. Before either one could find their voice, the magic of the moment was interrupted by their host.

"Let's have our toast and prayer for the New Year right now! Get yourselves a drink and gather around everyone, it's just a few minutes until midnight."

Jill poured a glass of sparkling cider as Craig picked up a glass of champagne.

Max bowed his head. "Lord, you have given to us good friends, good neighbors, and a good way of life. May we appreciate what we have right in front of our eyes and not be thinking about all the things we do not have. And bless these my many friends. Guide us in this new year. Amen." Max held his ginger ale glass high in the air, and all his guests followed his example. "Happy New Year!"

The whistles and horns and clapping became deafening. Jill turned to Craig, but he was gone. Maybe he had gotten away from her in order to avoid the inevitable New Year's Eve kiss. She became acutely aware of her breathing and the sound of her own heart beating above the revelry in the house. She walked from crowded room to crowded room, pushing between the bodies of celebrating people, desperately searching for him. *Did he leave already? Could he have turned and gone home just like that?*

The mistletoe ball dangling from the archway caught her eye as she stood beneath it. *What a lonely place to be at the stroke of midnight on New Year's Eve,* she thought.

Suddenly she felt arms catch her around her waist. "Happy New Year, Jill," Craig murmured. Taking her into his arms, he kissed her, a kiss that took her breath away. Then he whispered her name softly in her ear. "Jill."

25

I am glad it cannot happen twice, the fever of first love.
—Daphne du Maurier

The milky morning light fell across Jill's sleeping form, rousing her from a peaceful slumber. A cloudy vision of the night before, of her under the mistletoe, embraced by Craig's arms with the touch of his soft kiss upon her lips, floated through her mind like a scene from an old movie.

Had last night really happened or was it only a sweet dream playing over and over in her mind? Not daring to open her eyes to discover if it was all make-believe, Jill hid her face from the morning sun in the folds of her pillow.

It had happened! It wasn't a dream at all. Last night Craig had surprised her with a kiss, and it remained fresh on her lips still. As she snuggled into her crisp bedsheets that she was thankful her mother still insisted on ironing, she replayed the touch of his hands around her waist and how he'd caressed her face. She thought about the softness of his clean-shaven face against her cheek. Beginning to awaken, she wanted to replay the long-awaited moment of that first kiss; she wanted each detail planted firmly in her memory. Twining a curl around an index finger, she recalled the touch of his black hair against her face as they held on to one another beneath the mistletoe.

Finally Jill opened her eyes, gazed around the room, and jumped out of bed. Her circumstances were still the same, but somehow she saw her life through different eyes. If she never went back to Washington, it wouldn't matter—her life was taking on a new direction.

She was just stepping into the shower when she heard the phone ringing. "Jill, telephone," her mother called up to her. Wrapping a towel around herself, Jill dashed to the phone.

"Hi," she said with anticipation as she picked up the phone. "Happy New Year!"

"Happy New Year to you," the familiar voice said.

David, not Craig. Her heart sank as she sat down on the edge of the bed. "Thank you. To you too."

There was a silent pause.

"I've missed you, Jill. New Year's Eve wasn't the same without you." David sounded sad. "How are you?"

"Fine," Jill replied curtly, interpreting David's remark to mean that he had missed attending Annabelle's party. Without his attachment to Jill, he wouldn't have been invited. David hadn't minded her Washington connections one bit.

"You've moved on to new investigations there, haven't you? Or are you going after the local dogcatcher?"

"Very funny. It's not really any of your business anymore."

"Jill, give me a break. I'm attempting civility."

"Hmm. I like the word *civility*, especially since I haven't heard a word from you since the night I left your condo."

"You have to understand my point of view. My career and future were at stake."

"Yes, and mine had just washed down the drain."

"I miss you, Jill. I was wondering if I could come up to

Delavan and see you so we could work this out? Maybe have a nice long talk?"

"You're welcome to come to Delavan."

"I hear a 'but' coming."

"You should know before you come, there's no future for us."

"Can't you forgive me, give me another chance?"

My thoughts exactly when you dumped me several months ago. "I forgive you, David, but those words aren't some hocus-pocus phrase that magically turns us into a couple again. The fact is, you abandoned me when I needed you the most, when I was alone without anyone in my corner."

"And I regret that, Jill. People make mistakes all the time, but it doesn't mean the relationship is over; they work things out, put the past behind them, and try to make a fresh start."

"That's true of a marriage, but not always in a relationship."

"Is there someone else?" David's voice quavered as he asked the question. "If there is, I still want to see you again. I need closure."

Jill hesitated, struggling for the words. Craig's kiss under the mistletoe had said, "I love you" and by tonight she was sure his mouth would deliver the same, but at the moment, he wasn't officially her boyfriend.

"Someone kissed me under the mistletoe last night." Jill tried to be honest with some humor. "But I haven't dated yet."

"Well, I kissed someone under the mistletoe last night, too." David began to lighten up. "Let's call it even. Truce?"

"Sure, I forgive you, but unless you make some major changes in your life, I couldn't trust you, knowing that you are capable of abandoning me."

"I'm happy to make any changes in my life. Like what do you have in mind?"

"Like getting right with the Lord."

David paused. "Sounds to me like you've been hanging out with your mother," he finally mumbled.

His comment provoked Jill. "We'd both be lucky to have my mother's faith."

"Aren't you the one who always complained that your mother was nutty, that she was a religious fanatic? Jill, you've changed."

"I'm a totally changed person . . . a new person in Christ."

"Jill, you've been through a lot; you're not thinking clearly. Christianity is for weak people; when you're strong again, you'll come to your senses."

"I don't think so, David."

"Well, when you decide to snap out of this little religious phase you're going through, give a call and we'll try to work things out."

"Don't hold your breath." As soon as the words left her mouth, she wished she could take them back. She didn't want to be rude to David. "David, I'm sorry. I will pray for you."

"Thanks, but no thanks."

"Well, thank you for calling, David." She ignored his sarcasm. "It's really wonderful to hear your voice again. Please know that I will always cherish the good times we shared together."

"Whatever." Then the phone line suddenly went dead.

For months she had waited for this call, but when it finally came, it no longer mattered. Jill wanted a husband with character . . . she wanted Craig Martin. She galloped down the stairs to tell her mother that David had called.

It was a new year . . . a time of new beginnings. She was a new creature in Christ, not perfect but forgiven, and she was anxious for her new life to begin.

"Happy New Year, sleepyhead," her mom said, setting down her teacup when Jill walked into the kitchen.

"Happy New Year to you, Mom."

"You are positively glowing. Must have been Craig on the phone?"

"No, but last night Craig kissed me, and let me tell you, it was no ordinary kiss!" Jill sipped her green tea. "Yuck! This is awful, how can you stand drinking this?" She pushed the cup and saucer away with a clatter.

"This tea is good for you!"

Before Jill could tell her mother that David had called, Kathy walked into the room with little Marion. "How would you know an ordinary kiss from a non-ordinary kiss?" Kathy ribbed her.

Jill was surprised to see Kathy and Marion. "What are you doing here so early?"

"Early? It's afternoon, my dear older sister! I heard you in the other room with all this talk about kissing."

"Kisses, I love kisses. Kiss me, Auntie Jillie." Marion raised her arms to Jill, who was more than happy to fulfill her niece's request.

"Now may I have one of your kisses?" Jill asked Marion, pointing to her cheek.

"Nope. No kisses for you."

"And why not?"

"I only have two kisses left and I have to give them to my daddy." The little girl ran off to look for her favorite doll.

"What happened to the beautiful Caroline Jennings?" Kathy asked.

"I have no idea and I'm not about to ask. I'm not even sure they were a couple . . . maybe just friends. Who knows?"

Before Jill could tell them about her phone call, the phone rang again, and Pearl went to answer it. "Happy New Year!" A frown clouded her face, and the lines between her eyebrows deepened.

"Thank you. It is a happy one with our Jill back home," she replied coolly. "How are you, Annabelle? Yes, she's right here."

"Happy New Year to you!" Annabelle's voice rang out in the phone.

"Happy New Year, Annabelle."

"We miss you, Jill. And Rubric isn't the same since you've left. Maybe I should hire you to come back and put you on the payroll as Rubric's friend. Since you've been gone, he's gone around with such a long face and those sad puppy dog eyes."

"I miss you and Rubric, too." Not having spoken to Annabelle since that day in the conference room, Jill felt wary of the call. "How was your New Year's Eve party?"

"Fabulous, wonderful, marvelous! The only thing that was missing was you. How was your New Year's Eve up there in that little town of Devilish, darling?"

"It's Delavan," Jill corrected, "and yes, I had a nice New Year's Eve." It was really the best ever, but Jill wouldn't risk insulting Annabelle, who believed her New Year's Eve party was the best on the planet earth.

"Well, take care of yourself, Jillie darling."

"Uh, thanks, Annabelle. Good-bye." She hung up the phone. "Well, if it isn't old home day," a surprised Jill told her mother and sister. "First David calls me, and now Annabelle."

"Did you say David?" Kathy's mouth flew open.

"Yes, David. He wants to come and see me and work things out."

"Well, I hope you said no!"

"I told him we had no future."

"That must have come as a shock to him. With his ego I'm sure he never expected a woman to refuse him."

"Kathy, he wasn't that bad. David has some good qualities," Jill defended.

"But loyalty is not among them," Pearl chimed in.

"And it took me six years to discover that," Jill admitted. "Truthfully, I was more surprised to hear from Annabelle than David."

"Do you think she's going to offer you your job back?" Kathy asked.

"She can't do that, but at least she's still thinking of me. Said she just wanted to wish me a happy New Year. Come to think of it, this is so uncharacteristic for Annabelle to make a friendly phone call. Why would she keep our lines of communication open? First David and now Annabelle. Something's going on . . . but I'm not sure what yet."

"You wouldn't take the job if it were offered to you on a silver platter, would you, darling?" her mother ventured.

Kathy shook her head. "One never knows what one will do until it actually happens," she said.

"No, Mom is right. I wouldn't go back."

"Are you crazy?"

"Jill has made some real positive changes in her life since she returned home, don't you agree?" Pearl asked, looking at Jill.

"I do, Mom," Jill answered. "I've sacrificed a lot for my career, and I have to admit that being here has changed my life. I should tell you both that I recommitted my life to Jesus over Christmas."

Her mother's eyes lit up. "Why didn't you tell us before?"

"I guess I just wanted to make sure it was for real," Jill replied as Kathy gave her a hug.

"We've been praying for you a long time, sis," Kathy told her. "We suspected you were running from God, but we never doubted you'd find your way home."

Jill could feel her eyes misting over. "Even with all my problems, I'm on a much better path, and I know that God will make those paths straight, eventually. I just want to find out God's plan for my life. Now, if that kiss last night meant what I thought it did, I think I can guess part of it." Jill smiled.

"This is about Craig Martin, isn't it?" Kathy lifted an eyebrow. "I'm surprised. The guy is a bit of a nerd."

"But he's a nice nerd," Pearl said.

"Hey, that's not a very nice thing to say!"

"But those glasses he wears!" Kathy turned up her nose.

Mom smiled. "Well, I've always told you girls to marry a nerd. They always seem to make the very best husbands."

Suddenly, overtired little Marion began to cry in the next room.

Kathy sighed and headed toward her daughter. "Come on, sweet pea. You've got to take a nap." She scooped up Marion with her doll in her arms and brought her to Jill.

Jill leaned over to kiss her niece on the forehead. "I know he's not that attractive, but I think it's mostly his glasses and the clothes he wears. I think he's handsome in an intellectual sort of way."

Kathy shook her head and carried Marion up the stairs.

Pearl stood up from her chair. "I'm cooking a traditional New Year's Day dinner, and I'd like you to ask Craig to join us. Kathy, Jeff, and Marion will all be here. It'll be a nice family gathering. Tell him I'm missing Gracie and that she may come as well."

Jill jumped at the chance to have a legitimate excuse to call Craig and quickly ran for the phone and dialed the number to his apartment in town.

"Hello," he answered.

How wonderful his voice sounded! She felt her heart pounding. "Hi, Craig, this is Jill."

"Jill? Jill who?"

"Craig, stop teasing me."

"Is this the same Jill who's responsible for giving me a Christmas gift that has yet to be housebroken?"

"Another bad night?"

"Yep, and there was a present under the tree this morning—definitely not left by Santa."

"Sorry, but take heart. I've heard that Bernese mountain dogs are easily trained."

"Enough about Gracie; how are you? I was planning to call but figured you weren't up yet."

Jill's heart fluttered, and her hopes soared. Craig had been waiting to call her. "I'm fine. In fact, better than fine. I'm absolutely great! Mom is cooking a New Year's Day dinner. Jeff, Kathy, and Marion will be here, and you're invited."

"That would be great." He paused. "We need to talk. Think we could manage some time alone?"

"We can sneak away to Dad's study after dinner and have all the time alone that we need."

"Okay. Anything special I can bring?"

"Mom said to bring Gracie."

"Your mom may be sorry she said that!"

"We're looking forward to seeing you both," Jill said. A long, uncomfortable silence followed.

"Maybe this would be the perfect opportunity to chat with Jeff too?" Craig ventured.

Suddenly the spell of last night's kiss was broken. Back to business as usual. "Sure. Come over about 4:00."

"I'll be there."

Feeling uneasy about the phone conversation, she tried to convince herself she was being silly. Only a few minutes ago, she was floating on cloud nine. Now she felt as though she'd toppled off and landed on earth with a resounding crash.

Being in love wasn't easy.

26

Think one thought, a soul may perish;
Say one word, a heart may break!
—Adelaide Anne Procter

Jill raced down the curved stairway when she saw Craig's truck turn into their long drive. In the foyer she glanced at the clock. *Right on time,* she thought to herself as she stood before the double front doors anticipating the doorbell. No sound. What was taking him so long? She pressed her ear against the door. Nothing.

Impatiently Jill marched out on the porch. She laughed at the sight of Craig meandering up the walk while trying to keep Gracie under control. She ran through the snow to greet the two, not worrying about her new suede pumps. She patted Gracie affectionately as the dog barked loudly and wagged her tail fiercely. When they stepped up on the front porch, Craig gave her a friendly hug. He didn't seem to want to let her go, and she was hoping for a kiss, until she spotted Marion through the crack of the door. Her mother ran out of the house, wearing an organdy apron, and took Marion's hand.

"Hello, Craig," Pearl said.

"Hi, Mrs. Lewis." He handed her the roses that were tucked under his arm. "It's nice to see you again."

"Thank you. Roses in January. My, my, they're lovely!"

Craig crouched down to talk to the little girl. "Hi, Marion, I'm Craig, a friend of your Aunt Jill's. Want to play with Gracie?"

You'll make the most wonderful father, Jill thought to herself as she took Craig's coat and scarf. Marion shyly scampered away. Jill took Craig's hand and Gracie's leash and led them into the kitchen to say hello to everyone. After a few minutes of friendly chatter, Pearl invited everyone into the formal dining room.

"Craig, would you honor us by saying grace?" she invited.

"I'd be delighted."

He invited everyone to join hands around the table and prayed eloquently. Everyone joined in the amen. Mom's lips curled with a smile, signaling that Craig had passed her test with flying colors.

Kathy quietly nudged Jill. "Sweet blessing."

"Amazing, isn't he?"

"Yeah, and tonight he even looks pretty handsome . . . when you look beyond those glasses."

"Girls! Stop that whispering between yourselves or I will insist that you tell us what you are saying," their mother admonished.

"Here, here," Jeff said.

"Here, put food here." Marion pointed to her plate.

Jill noticed how at ease Craig was in the formal surroundings, sitting beneath the crystal chandelier, eating with sterling silver, and wiping his mouth on monogrammed cloth napkins. The more they ate, the more the conversation became comfortable and easy. At times it was downright joyous. Jill kept smiling at Craig over the candlelight and was glad he fit in with her family so well. She could see the light dance in his dark brown, almost black eyes.

"Where did you go to school, Craig?" Jeff asked.

"The Naval Academy. Then I got an M.B.A. at Kellogg."

"I didn't know you were at the Academy," Jill said. "Did you enjoy living in the Washington area?"

"Loved it," he replied. "It's an exciting city."

"How long were you in the navy after you graduated?" Jeff asked.

"I was discharged about five years ago."

"Where were you stationed?" Jeff asked.

"Everywhere. What about you, Jeff? Where did you go to school?"

"I haven't wandered far from home—University of Wisconsin for both my undergraduate and my law degree. But I am curious, after a stint in the navy and such an impressive degree from Kellogg, how did you end up at the *Lakes* in Delavan?" Jeff wasn't about to let Craig deflect the conversation.

"Craig grew up in Chicago, and his family summered up at Egg Harbor," Jill cut in, feeling she had to explain.

"Let the man speak for himself," Jeff scolded.

"Well, it's simple, really. After living all over the world, I longed for a simple life in a small town, and since I knew and loved this area, I jumped at the chance when I saw Max's ad in the *Chicago Tribune*."

Appearing satisfied with Craig's explanation, Jeff replied, "I agree with you. We love living in a small town."

Pearl looked around the table at everyone's empty plates. "All of you go into the living room while I get the dessert ready," she ordered.

Dessert was served casually in the living room before the

roaring fire. Pearl reigned in her easy chair with her grand-daughter on her lap at the far end of the room, reading to the child. Jill sat close to Craig on the sofa as he and Jeff discussed business, the rise and fall of the stock market, ball games, and the friends in Delavan they had in common. It was the perfect family gathering.

When everyone finished their desserts, Kathy cleared away the plates and went back into the kitchen. Pearl followed her, and Marion stayed behind, climbing up between Jill and Craig.

"Hi, Marion," Craig said.

"Hi," Marion chirped.

"Hey, your Aunt Jill didn't eat all of her chocolate mousse. Is she sick?"

"Her tummy hurts."

Gracie got up from her spot in front of the fireplace and stuck her cold wet nose up into Jill's face.

"What a sweet girl you are, Gracie. This is Marion. Say hello to Marion." Jill patted the puppy's head.

Shyly, the child pulled back. Gracie yawned and walked over to the coolest part of the room and flopped to the floor. Craig took Marion by the hand to introduce her to Gracie. Marion pulled away when the puppy licked her hand.

"That's a doggie kiss, Marion," Craig told her. "Gracie loves you."

"I wuv you too, Gracie," Marion scrunched her nose up, reaching out her hand to pet the dog again. When Pearl came in with a plate of warm cookies, Marion ran over, grabbed a cookie, and came running back.

"Tank you, Mimi," Marion said rhythmically as she held her cookie in the air. At that second Gracie raised her head and snapped the cookie right out of Marion's hand, frightening the little girl so that she began screaming at the top of her lungs.

"Sorry, Marion," Craig explained, "Gracie likes cookies too. And she's a baby and hasn't learned her manners yet."

Everyone laughed as Marion took another cookie and toddled to the kitchen with her grandmother to eat her cookie far away from Gracie. Craig returned to his seat beside Jill.

"You're great with kids, Craig."

"Don't act so surprised," he said with a laugh. "I love kids."

Once the others had left the room, Craig didn't waste any time questioning Jeff. "You know, Jeff, Jill told me that you're really blessed to have adopted little Marion; she looks just like you. How old was she when you adopted her?"

"We got her as a baby. She was only five days old."

"Did you get her through Hope House?"

"Hope House? Where on earth did you get that idea?"

"Just guessing. I noticed when I wrote Dr. Lewis's obituary that he was on their board when he died."

"We didn't need his help. It was a private adoption and that's how it will remain—private." He seemed irritated.

"I have a cousin who waited for a baby for ten years. You must have a special connection with some people," Craig pressed.

"Being a lawyer, I know how these things work. God is good to us. He blessed us with Marion at just the right time," Jeff answered with a touch of pride.

"Will you ever tell her she's adopted?" Jill asked.

"We already have told her that fact, and we'll explain it to her on her terms as she is able to understand the details." Jeff's demeanor now almost seemed hostile. "I'm curious. Why are you so interested in Marion's adoption?"

Jill knew he was trying to hide something, which fueled

her curiosity, so she continued to probe as innocently as she could. "Jeff, you know I was away in Washington when you got Marion, and I never heard all the details. Did you get any medical history or find if the family had any special talents that could have been passed along genetically to Marion?"

"Yes, of course, I did."

When silence followed, Jill continued. "What do you know about her parents?" She figured that if Jeff knew a lot of information about Marion's background, then the adoption would have more credence for being legitimate.

"As adopted children grow older, they often want to contact their birth parents," Craig jumped back in. "Will you allow her to do that?"

He ignored the question. "If you two have finished giving me the third degree, I think it's time to take Marion home and put her to bed." Jeff abruptly stood to his feet, ending the conversation. "Marion, Kathy, time to go!"

Craig and Jeff stood face-to-face.

"I assure you, Craig, and you, Jill, that Marion's adoption is legit. Please don't concern yourselves with it anymore."

Kathy rushed in from the kitchen. "What's wrong, Jeff?"

"Nothing. It's just time to go on home. We've got to get Marion to bed," Jeff explained. "It's been a lovely evening, but I've got a big trial starting at the courthouse in the morning. I want to turn in early, too."

Kathy stood there for a moment, obviously surprised at Jeff's sudden desire to leave. Then she turned around and left the room to collect Marion.

"Craig, do you play golf?" Jeff asked, trying to diffuse the uncomfortable situation.

"Tennis."

"You're in luck. I can hit a few balls. That's about all, but I did have a championship tennis court built in our backyard for

Kathy. I'm willing to give it a try if you can put up with me. Here's my card; let's make a date soon." Jeff said this as though he were making amends for his previous evasiveness.

Craig pulled his card out of his wallet and said, "Call me when you have some free time."

When everyone had said their good-byes to Jeff, Kathy, and Marion, Pearl headed to the kitchen and said, "I'm going to finish up here and then go on to bed. Good night, you two."

"We'll help you," Craig volunteered, jumping to his feet.

"Oh no, you won't. No men are allowed in my kitchen tonight. Kathy and I have already done most of it. You two enjoy one another's company in the family room. Oh, and thank you for the lovely roses. I'll enjoy them for days. Hope to see you again soon, Craig."

"Me too, Mrs. Lewis. Thanks for the dinner. I had a great time."

"Good night, Mom," Jill said after giving her mother a hug.

Craig and Jill were left alone in the family room. They sat silently for a few seconds as they watched Gracie snooze beside the fireplace.

"Gracie's such a sweet doggie," Jill said.

"Yeah. . . . Do you think we came on a little too strong with Jeff?"

"Maybe a little. But I'm beginning to think he has something to hide."

"Like the circumstances of Marion's adoption."

"Do you think Marion is illegally adopted and could be taken from them? Oh, Craig, our family just would not be able to get through something like that. Anyway, Jeff's a lawyer, and he would know better than to do something shady with his own daughter! I mean, I've known Jeff all my life, and it's hard to imagine he would stoop this low to break moral and national laws. I just can't believe he would betray his faith either. I know he can be arrogant at times, but he's always struck me as sincere." She was silent for a moment, trying to get her thoughts under control. "Now, tell me, is there a relationship between my investigation in Washington and little Delavan, Wisconsin?"

"We don't have enough to go on yet," Craig answered thoughtfully as he took the seat across the room from her.

"There's no doubt the senator is at the helm," Jill replied, noticing that Craig had chosen to sit as far away from her as possible.

"Think about it," Craig began. "We hear about smuggling exotic animals into this country all the time. If people are willing to pay top dollar for them, how much more will they pay for a baby? Infertility is rampant in this country. Once the babies come into the country, there are many others wanting to cash in on this product, but it means reaching into small towns across America. It's an active underground railroad. The money is astronomical. I think Jeff may be one of the nameless people you were investigating in Washington. It's so ironic that whoever was behind chasing you out of Washington chased you right into the heart of it here." He walked over to where Jill sat. His voice softened as he moved aside a strand of hair that had fallen across her eyes. "This case has tentacles that can stretch across all the states. Tell me, does Jeff ever travel to Washington?"

"I really don't think so. For all the years I lived there, he never visited me once, and Kathy never mentioned any trips."

For a few moments they sat in silence. *Go on,* Jill thought. *Kiss me!*

"Jill," Craig began.

Anticipating a kiss she moved toward him, looking him in the eyes. He suddenly moved away from her. Her brow furrowed. Where was this evening going, anyway?

"Jill," Craig began again, "we need to talk."

"We have talked." An alarm went off in her head. She'd heard this line before. It was as if someone had yanked her heart from her chest and was squeezing it in their fist, not wanting to let go. This talk was not about holding her, kissing her, or professing his undying love.

"Jill . . . I, uh, I'm sorry. This is a little awkward. I hope you'll understand."

"Understand what?"

"Jill, I hope you can forgive me. Last night I got caught up in the moment under the mistletoe. It was New Year's Eve, music was playing, you looked beautiful, you smelled nice—and hey, I'm a guy! What can I tell you?"

She popped up from the couch and walked to the other side of the room. "Oh, don't worry about it." She desperately tried to sound nonchalant. "It was nothing. Friends always kiss on New Year's Eve. I'd already forgotten all about it."

"Good. I didn't want to lead you on; I'm glad you feel that way."

She gathered her wits about her before turning around to face him again. Praying silently that God would give her strength to handle this heartbreak, she also asked his forgiveness for lying. But a girl had to have her pride, didn't she?

Craig fidgeted uncomfortably on the sofa with his long legs outstretched. He clasped his hands behind his neck and leaned back. "I treasure your friendship, but I really can't see you on a personal basis." He sounded businesslike as he stood up and walked over to the fireplace. "Look, I enjoy working with you, and I want to help you with your father's case and to help you clear your name, but it's impossible for us to go out as a couple."

They both stared at the dancing flames. Tears stung her eyes, and she fought against them as they careened down her cheeks.

"So this is a 'Dear Jill' letter spoken out loud?"

"I'm sorry."

"Does Caroline have anything to do with this?"

He sighed. "Maybe a little, but it's a lot more complicated than that. There are just some things going on in my life right now I can't talk about. Besides, we both work at the same paper and I'm your boss; we really shouldn't be going out. It's unprofessional."

"Craig, I said to think nothing of it. Really. I got carried away in the moment too. I understand." Her legs felt wobbly. She prayed he would leave before she fell down. "Caroline was out of town, you came to the party alone, and I just happened to be the only available female."

"Jill, stop. It wasn't like that."

Gracie lifted her nose in the air, yawned, and then whined. She ambled off the floor and wagged her tail before beginning to bark as though she were talking to them.

Jill patted the dog. "Gracie tells me it's late and she needs her rest. I think you do too. Come on, let's call it an early evening, and I'll walk you to the door."

Craig leaned down to give her a peck on the cheek, but she drew back. "Now, now . . . let's not get carried away again." She feigned laughter.

As soon as Craig left, she ran up to her room. She was washing away the tears when the phone rang again. Reaching for the phone, she mumbled, "Hello." She hoped it was Craig calling back to say he'd had a change of heart; her heart sunk when she heard the voice on the other end of the line.

"Hiya, Jillie! Sure missed a good party here in D.C. last night."

"So I've heard. How are you, Rubric?"

"Great as a jellyfish in the coral reef. Happy New Year."

"Happy New Year to you. Hey, as long as you're on the phone, I have a question for you."

"I'm all ears."

"What did you ever find out about that sixpence I sent you? Surely by now you have an answer for me. Was it a bugging device?"

"Nope, it was clean. Call me next week."

The phone went dead.

Jill was relieved that Rubric hadn't spoiled her fantasies by revealing that the blue-eyed stranger was a spy, especially since she'd just gotten the boot from Craig. She needed something else to think about. Who knew . . . maybe one day Prince Charming would return on a white horse to reclaim his coin. Despite her heartaches, she still believed in fairy tales.

27

Whatever our souls are made of,
His and mine are the same.

—Emily Brontë

How am I supposed to act around Craig now? Jill wondered as she pulled into her parking space at the *Lakes*. *Act as if nothing happened when his kiss is still lingering on my lips?* Maybe being in Delavan wasn't God's plan for her after all. Maybe God had brought her back to her hometown so there were fewer distractions to bring her back to him. Annabelle called her yesterday; maybe she was supposed to go back to Washington as soon as her name was cleared. Maybe her blue-eyed prince was waiting for her there, or maybe she was never meant to marry at all. Maybe she was supposed to change the world instead.

With her head up, chin out, and shoulders back, she walked inside the office and was greeted by total pandemonium.

"Guess whose job it is to clean up after Gracie?" Marge griped to Jill as she came in the front door. "If I find out who gave this oversized puppy to Craig, I am going to get them!" She eyed Jill suspiciously.

Craig appeared in the doorway to his office. Looking around at the destruction, he shook his head and then caught sight of Jill. "Glad to see you. Keep your coat on, you're coming with me."

"What's this all about?"

"I have an idea."

"What?"

"I've been thinking of you, as your boss."

"Oh?"

"I think you need a promotion."

"With more pay?"

"Maybe."

"What are you promoting me to?"

"The bottom line is you're a good reporter, although I have to admit you are an excellent obit writer too." He winked. "I want you to cover accident reports and police reports. If anything interesting shows up, go after it."

"Are you telling me in an offhanded way that I can do investigations?"

"If you can find anything in Delavan worth investigating. But keep in mind we're a small-town newspaper. Don't get carried away making mountains out of molehills."

"You sound like Rubric."

"Thank you, uh, I think."

"What about accidents that are not really accidents but murder?" she said, lowering her voice.

"Especially those. But you'll have to double as the obit writer too until I can hire someone to take your place." Craig donned his coat and tucked his muffler inside his lapels and pulled a wool cap on his head. Then he grabbed Gracie and headed for the door. "Come on. Let's go."

Jill breathed deeply as they opened the front door of the

office to step out into the January air. "Mmm, fresh air! And how are you, Gracie?" she asked, stroking the pup's head.

"For your safety, I want you to know I'm keeping it a secret who gave me Gracie. But I must advise you—you're at the top of everyone's list."

"Ha ha." She folded her arms across her chest. "Okay, tell me where we're going."

"For a walk with Gracie."

"I have a feeling this is a walk with a purpose."

"That's my girl! You have good instincts."

"Are you talking to me or Gracie?"

"Both my girls."

Okay, this guy is hard to read. No, not hard, impossible! He was acting as though New Year's Eve had never happened and the two of them were picking up their friendship where they had left off before that fateful night under the mistletoe. But "my girls"? What was that supposed to mean?

She wasn't complaining, of course, because she longed to remain in Craig's presence. There was something so familiar about him; she truly believed they were soul mates. *Step aside, Caroline Jennings, my catcher's mitt is out and ready!*

Waiting for the light to change, they stood close together as Gracie ran circles around them, wrapping their legs together with her leash.

That's my doggie, Jill thought to herself. *Gracie is doing everything in her power to get the two of us together.* But she was engulfed with disappointment when they untangled themselves, and his body was no longer near hers. She wondered if he cared for her too and was just fighting his feelings. After all, he was a fine man and probably wanted to stay true to his commitment to Caroline. Jill knew she should respect that, and she prayed that God would give her the strength to do so.

"Let's go to the police station." Craig hesitated, untangling Gracie's leash. "Are you sure you can handle this?"

"What, being with you?"

He blushed, wiping snowflakes from his black glasses onto his coat sleeves. "I'm not that stuck on myself. I mean, your father."

She looked away from him. "This is something I have to do sooner or later. It might as well be today with you," she finally said.

"No matter where it leads?"

"Yes."

"What if we discover your dad was murdered?"

Even though she'd thought of the possibility, to hear the word *murder* spoken out loud made her nauseated. "I guess I've been suspecting that. I'll want to go further to find out why and who. And if he was murdered, I want to see my father's killer brought to justice."

They walked the few remaining blocks to the police station in silence. Craig tied Gracie to a post and gave her a chew toy he pulled from his pocket. With his hand on the doorknob of the station, Craig suddenly stopped and turned around to face Jill and said, "Take a deep breath."

She took his advice before they went inside and spoke with the officer. Soon another policeman appeared with the files. Seated across from one another at a wooden table, Jill and Craig spread the official papers and photographs across the width and length of the table.

"Are you thinking what I'm thinking?" she asked, no longer speaking as the daughter of Dr. Lewis but as a seasoned reporter.

"Yeah. There's too much information here for an accident. The roads were dry, it was a straight stretch of lake road, and it happened during the daylight hours. He went right into a tree, and there were skid and breaking marks for at least thirty feet. And the back end was smashed in as badly as the front bumper where it hit a tree. This picture shows it clearly."

Jill had a hard time imagining her dad sitting in the front seat of the car, hurt and dying. She felt helpless all over again and asked, "How did this happen?"

Craig slid his glasses off his nose and set them on top of the notes he had been taking. "Jill, what do you think?"

"I don't want to think. You tell me, Craig."

He shook his head no.

Jill took a deep breath. "Okay, my dad was driving home on a sunny spring day, on a stretch of lake road that was straight. Someone came up from behind him and rear-ended him. Most likely, he tried speeding up to get away from the other car that hit him, but then the other driver probably sped up too. The other car hit him again, but this time that other car didn't pull back. He kept right on pushing Dad's car forward as Dad applied his brakes, leaving tire tracks burned in the road. He was pushed into the tree, where he died from the impact."

She covered her face with her hands. "No, I can't cry. I will not cry. I have to be strong. Craig, there's something else you should know. Remember when Officer Emerson stopped me on the road that one day?" She made a fist.

Craig nodded his head.

"I never told you, but on my way to work, a car bumped me and attempted to push me off the road. It was a little red sports car, a Porsche, I think. It pushed and bumped me only slightly, so it wouldn't leave any marks on my fender. It was just enough to spin me out on the road. Only God kept me from harm."

"Why didn't you tell me about this before?"

"Well, I thought maybe it wasn't a big deal, just some prank by a kid. But now, after reading this report and looking at the pictures, I'm not so sure."

"Jill, promise me you will not ever keep information like this from me again. Promise me!" His voice was tense.

"I promise."

"After the break-in at your home and everything, you should've known this was no coincidence. All of this is important to your investigation."

"Yes, to the investigation." She looked down at the table again.

"And to me."

She looked up into his eyes to see if there was still hope for them.

"As a friend," Craig added as though he had read her mind.

"As a friend, of course." She swallowed her disappointment.

Craig cleared his throat. "Are you ready to talk to the officer who investigated the accident?"

"I think so. . . . Yes, I'm ready."

Officer Barrows wasn't very helpful. He was a large, burly man with a round face, carrot-colored hair, and little patience for explaining his report. His answers were curt and to the point.

"I made my report, and it's all here."

"How do you think Dr. Lewis's car got smashed in from the rear?"

"Car must have spun around, clipping other trees."

"But the tire marks don't say that," Craig pointed out.

"And," Jill added, "there are no marks on any of the other trees. The only damaged tree is the one the car crashed into."

The officer flipped carelessly through the various photographs with his large hands, trying to find a picture they knew was not there.

"Nope, don't see it. Somebody must have misplaced it."

"Convenient." Craig nodded and stood up. The officer followed suit.

Jill stood up too and held out her hand in pretend politeness. "Thank you, Officer, you have been so very helpful." She turned to Craig. "Come on, Gracie is waiting for us outside."

Craig stuffed his notes into his pockets and steadied Jill with his arm around her waist as they left the police station. Gracie wagged her tail, happy to see them again. Craig untied her leash, and the three of them headed back toward the newspaper.

"Let's get my truck and take a drive," he said.

"Where are we going?"

"This isn't going to be easy Jill, but God will give you the strength."

28

I would rather feel the sword than behold it suspended.
—Regina Maria Roche

The couple drove to the spot where Dr. Lewis's car went off the road and into the tree. They got out of the truck and walked over for a closer inspection. Jill lovingly ran her hand over the damaged part of the tree.

"You know, I haven't been able to visit my dad's graveside since the accident," Jill said. "The thought of it is too painful."

Together they walked forty feet up the road, looking at each and every tree on the way back for any damage. Not only were there hardly any trees that close to the road, but there were also three houses standing in plain view along that particular stretch of pavement where the accident occurred.

"Let's see if they remember anything," Jill suggested.

Craig stood back by his truck in the drive and allowed Jill to knock on the first door. Jill knew she had that friendly look that people instantly warmed to and trusted, which usually led them to talk freely. The first house had a bright green door. When she knocked, an elderly man answered and smiled at her.

"Excuse me for imposing on you, sir. My name is Jill Lewis. About a year ago, at 4:00 in the afternoon, my father, Dr. Harold Lewis, was killed in an accident when his car ran into that grove of trees over there. I was wondering if you happened to remember that or if you might have seen anything?"

"No, I didn't even live here at that time," the man politely replied. "I just moved in, oh, about a month ago."

"I see."

"Could you tell us the name of the people who lived here before you and where they might have moved?" Craig called from the driveway.

"Yeah, the guy's name was Robert Schrader, and he moved to the brand-new apartment complex in Fontana, about five miles from here."

"Yes, I'm familiar with Fontana. Thank you. I appreciate your help," Jill said. She headed for the next house, a small one with a covered porch. When she knocked, three little children answered.

"Hi, is your mom or dad home?" she asked the kids.

"No," a dark haired boy of about six answered.

"When will they be home?"

The older boy punched his younger brother.

"Oh, I forgot, she's in the shower right now, and Dad is taking a nap," the little boy said, correcting himself.

The sound of their giggles over the pretend excuses made her smile.

"Can you tell me how long you've lived here?"

"About one hundred years," the blond boy of about nine piped up.

Jill handed the older boy her card. "Please have your mom or dad call me as soon as they get home," she said. But somehow she knew she would never get the call because the parents would never get the card.

Turning around, she noticed Craig knocking on the door of the last house, a large cedar home that was situated farther back from the road. Jill stood at the hedge that divided the two properties. She watched from afar as a pretty blonde woman in her mid-thirties, clad in tight-fitting jeans and a clingy white shirt with a plunging neckline, greeted Craig. The woman shamelessly batted her eyelashes at him.

"Hi, there," Craig said.

"Hi, yourself, handsome," the woman answered, eyeing him up and down. Jill thought maybe she should rescue Craig from this flirty woman, but his broad grin indicated he didn't seem to mind. Men! But she knew Craig would be able to get answers from this woman.

"About a year ago, there was a fatal car accident over by that tree. I noticed it's close to your yard. Did you happen to see what happened?"

"Oh, I think I might remember something about it." She smiled and pushed her chest forward. "Why don't you come inside and I'll pour you some coffee and tell you what I know."

To Jill's surprise, Craig stepped inside the woman's house as she opened the front door to him. "Going in for some coffee!" he shouted over to Jill as she waved back.

Jill went back to sit in the truck. She was fuming when he finally jogged back.

"I drank so much coffee, I really have to find a men's room," he said urgently, turning the key in the ignition. "Sorry, were you cold sitting out here?"

"I'm fine, but why didn't you use Miss Hospitality's bathroom?"

"Well, I didn't feel safe in there," Craig said, rolling his eyes.

"What did you find out?"

"That her husband left her three months ago."

"Anything else?"

"She heard the crash but was afraid to look."

"Hmm," Jill murmured and thought how stupid men were to allow themselves to be trapped by these types of women. Or maybe they weren't so stupid after all; maybe they enjoyed these situations that pumped up their egos.

They drove into Fontana and found Robert Schrader in his apartment watching TV. They explained they were from the *Lakes* and were conducting an investigation of the accident.

"Sure, I remember that accident." Mr. Schrader belched before wiping his mouth with the back of his hand. "Ol' Doc Lewis had been my doctor since I moved here from Iowa ten years ago. The sight of him all crumpled up inside that car really tore me up. I was glad when my house finally sold so I could move out of there."

"Wanted to leave the bad memories, huh?" Craig sympathized.

"Nope. The taxes got too high being so close to the lake, so I couldn't afford to pay them anymore."

"Can you remember anything that might be helpful to us?" Jill asked. "What you were doing when the accident happened?"

Robert Schrader shifted in his chair. "I was watching TV when I heard this big crash and felt the house rock a bit. I looked out my window and saw a car out in the trees. I called the police and the ambulance right away. Then I ran out to the car to see if I could help, but I couldn't; he was already dead." Mr. Schrader shook his head. "Never saw a dead man before that day."

"So you called in the report? Were you interviewed by a police officer?"

"Yep, I called in the accident and I talked to a policeman. He was a nice fella."

"Do you remember the name of the police officer?" Jill asked.

"No, but he was a good-looking young fella with dark hair."

Dark hair? Jill thought with surprise. "If you can think of anything else, Mr. Schrader, please call me at this number on the card."

"I sure will call if I can think of anything else," Mr. Schrader promised.

As they were driving back to Delavan, Jill asked, "Would you describe Barrows as a 'good-looking young fella'?"

"No, I would not."

29

Think of the storm roaming the sky uneasily
Like a dog looking for a place to sleep in,
Listen to it growling.

—Elizabeth Bishop

The following weekend an unseasonably warm front blew across the southern Wisconsin landscape. Afternoon fog shrouded the snow, casting an eerie shadow reminiscent of an old man's sleepy memories. By nightfall, easterly winds coming in at a higher altitude formed clouds, feeding them with moisture. Evening thunderstorms raced into the area, dissolving the fog and eating away at the snow. News broadcasters boasted it was one of the warmest days in January on record. It seemed every TV news show featured an expert who discussed the effects of global warming.

Craig headed north to Door County with Gracie for the weekend. He said he wanted to ice fish and needed to work more on his cabin. Of course, Jill figured he was probably spending time with Caroline. On Sunday night she curled up under a quilt to read a good book. Her mother was rattling around in the kitchen making what she termed a simple dinner of rosemary chicken and Caesar salad with anchovies.

Jill heard the roar of thunder as flashes of lightning tore across the sky. The dramatic change in weather unnerved her. She watched as the small trees got quite an aerobic workout with the rain pelting down upon them, bending their tender boughs almost to the ground. Branches cascading from the larger trees looked as though they might touch their toes as the water forced them to the ground. A loud clap of thunder and a spark of lightning that set the night sky ablaze not only made Jill jump but also illuminated the shore of the lake. In that split second, she saw the figure of a man moving cautiously and purposely, as if he were trying hard not to be seen by anyone.

Were her eyes playing tricks on her or was she really seeing a man? Another bolt of lightning lit up the sky. There! She saw him again, but it was a fleeting view, maybe less than a second. Could it be a dog? Or was it a man? Lightning flashed in quick succession across the sky once more, and she saw the movement again. She felt her stomach churn.

On instinct she walked through the house, making sure all the windows and doors were securely locked and the alarm system armed. After securing the first and second floors, she forced herself to check the basement. She picked up a flashlight in case the power went out, not wanting to end up in the dark cellar without light. She opened the creaky old door to the cellar and remained at the top step for a moment to gather her courage. Smelling the cool dampness, she did not relish going into the dank hole beneath the house.

Carefully and slowly she stepped down the long wooden stairway to make sure the root cellar door was still bolted from the inside. Step-by-step she clung to the wooden railing and crept downward in her stocking feet until she could feel the chilly cement floor. She flailed her hand around, finally finding the pull string to turn on the light. She tugged it until it lit up the room. The basement smelled musty like an old trunk filled with dirty socks; the room was creepy when no light came in through the small windows. Checking the eight small panes of glass, she found none were broken or open. She shined her flashlight into each of the dark corners of the room, where the single bulb's light did not reach, and shuddered at the sight of all the cobwebs.

Suddenly a loud pop rang out in the cellar. Jill screamed and dropped the flashlight, causing the fragile bulb inside to shatter into many small pieces. She heard the noise again and realized it was the freezer's motor kicking in. After jerking on the handle, she wondered why it was locked, since her mother came down to retrieve meat from it all the time.

With the flashlight now broken, Jill quickly headed for the stairs and pulled on the light string, sending the room back into total darkness except for the small light at the top of the steps. Imagining all kinds of creepy, crawling things licking at her legs, she made a dash up to the main floor of the house.

Out of breath, she made it back into the serene light of the hallway and slammed the basement door shut behind her. With her heart racing, she gulped deep breaths in order to rid herself of her shakiness. She turned to look outside again through the front windows and felt satisfied that whatever or whoever had been in the storm had now found shelter.

For an extra measure of safety, Jill searched for her mother's ivory-handled derringer. She found it where her mother kept all her important things, in a lingerie drawer between stacks of silk slips.

Jill thought it was a good time to hear Craig's steady voice, even if he was with Caroline. After all, hadn't he said he still wanted to be her friend and help her solve these crimes? She held the weapon in one hand and picked up the phone with the other. No dial tone. The phone was dead. She grabbed her cell phone from her purse. The cell service was out too. Just her luck! Suddenly the lights in the house went off, leaving Jill in total darkness. A few moments later her mom appeared carrying a silver tray with a lighted candle into the living room and set it down on the coffee table. The tray was filled with their chicken and salads and tall glasses of iced tea.

"My dear, you look like you've been through a haunted house with all those cobwebs in your hair. What on earth have you been doing?"

"Locking doors, checking windows, searching the basement, finding out our phone line is dead and that I have no cell service," she said, expecting her mother to leap to hysterics.

"Oh, that happens when it rains; the lines get wet and bog down. Once they dry out they'll be working again. The cell tower will go back up too. Happens all the time. Here, bless the food and let's eat."

"What do people around here do when there's an emergency?"

"They do what they did before we had phones," her mother replied. "They go fetch some help."

"Any reason you keep the freezer locked?"

"Of course there's a reason. I got in that habit when you girls were kids, and I mustn't stop now that I am a grandmother. Children have died because they climbed into a freezer and then got trapped when the door slammed shut."

"That's awful."

"In case you ever need the key," her mother instructed, "it's on the hook inside the breaker box. Is anything else frightening you, my darling?"

"I thought I saw a man outside walking along the lake."

"Oh, Jill, I'm sure you did. Other people live all up and

down the lake. It was either a neighbor or one of their dogs, or your imagination." Pearl took a bite of her chicken.

"You're probably right, just my imagination. Where are the bullets for this?"

"Jill, I will not allow a loaded gun in my house. I worry about Marion getting ahold of it."

"I promise to take the bullets out in the morning."

Her mom hesitated a moment, then gave in. "I keep the bullets in the same place I keep the batteries, with the orange juice in the Sub-Zero freezer in the kitchen." She shook her finger at Jill. "But I want that gun emptied first thing in the morning."

Jill found the bullets and was fiddling with them, trying to get one in the gun, when she heard a loud crash and breaking glass, making her jump and drop the bullet. It rolled beneath the refrigerator. Mustering a brave look for her mother's sake, Jill burst out in laughter as she caught sight of her armed with the broken flashlight, looking ready to clobber a criminal over the head.

"Sounds like it came from the solarium on the south side of the house," Pearl whispered. Together they groped down the dark hallway, Jill with the empty derringer and Pearl with the broken flashlight for a weapon in one hand and a smaller working one for light in the other.

As they neared the solarium, Jill whispered a strong warning, "Let's not act scared." Her mother's eyes grew wide.

Arriving at the solarium they discovered one of the glass panels had been broken.

"Don't move," Jill mumbled under her breath. "There's a man standing at the corner of the house."

"Who is it?" her mother whispered excitedly.

"It looks like Chuck . . . yes, it's Chuck Emerson." Jill's voice grew louder as she recognized him and opened the door.

"Chuck, come on in," she shouted over a blast of thunder. "What are you doing here on a night like tonight?"

"Got a report on my radio that someone was snooping around your house."

"But the phones are out. How did anyone get through?"

"On a cell phone," Chuck hollered above the thunder.

"I should find out what service they have. Mine's not working."

"Don't just stand there. Come on in out of the rain," Pearl insisted. She helped Chuck peel off his police slicker and led him to the seat nearest the fire. She handed him a bath-sized towel to dry off.

"You're soaking wet." She shook her head. "I have some of Harold's shirts in the guest room closet."

"No, thank you. I'm fine."

"Well, just sit there by the fire and dry off."

"I should check the house. You and Jill stay in the kitchen, but scream if you need me," he instructed them.

Chuck returned after going through the house room by room with his standard-issue police flashlight.

"Everything is in order," he announced. "There's no sign of anyone in the house or basement. I think someone must've scared your prowler away before he got inside."

"That's a relief." Jill sighed. "Chuck, you're always coming to my rescue. I don't know what I would do without you."

"Get that glass fixed on Monday, and until then, dead bolt the solarium door from the inside," Chuck said as he rubbed his hands together from the chill.

"How about some dinner? I made more than enough for all of us," Pearl insisted. "I want to hear about your mother."

"I'm on duty, Mrs. Lewis. I can't," Chuck explained apologetically. "I have to fill out a report too."

"Sit right here to fill out your report and have a cup of

coffee to get the chill off your bones before you go out in that nasty rainy weather again. Oh, heavens to Betsy . . . what am I thinking? I can't possibly brew any coffee, there's no electricity. How about a glass of iced tea? We're having some with our dinner; it's quite refreshing. It's that new-fangled Passion Fruit iced tea from California." Obviously more frightened than she had let on to Jill and Chuck, Pearl chattered nervously.

"Thank you, Mrs. Lewis, I'd like a glass of tea."

Pearl reached around for a crystal glass, filling it with ice, and then poured the tea to the brim. Adding a lemon wedge to the side of the glass, she placed it on a silver tray with sugar and artificial sweeteners and a starched linen napkin rolled into an ornate silver napkin ring. Jill was embarrassed that her mother always made such a production out of everything, even something as simple as serving a glass of tea.

"Jill, go to the living room and get our trays, and we'll have supper in here."

Jill obeyed her mother and left the room to get the trays.

"Did your folks drive up from Florida for the holidays?" Pearl asked.

"No, ma'am," Chuck said while sipping his tea. "They're only up in Egg Harbor in the summertime; they spent Christmas in Fort Myers."

Jill set the trays down on the breakfast table and took her seat.

"Did you go down to Florida to see your folks over the holidays?" Pearl asked.

"No, ma'am. I was too busy down at the station."

"What could possibly keep you so busy at the Delavan Police Department?" Jill wondered aloud.

"I get double time when I work holidays," Chuck explained.

"Did you ever get around to fixing up your sweet little cabin at Egg Harbor?" Pearl inquired.

"I'm waiting until springtime, when the weather clears. It's going to be a big job. It's been abandoned for years."

"Yes, but it'll pay off. I can't believe the price of the property for sale up there." Pearl rolled her eyes. "How about some more iced tea?"

"Thanks, ma'am, but I've got to go."

"You can stay a little while longer, Chuck," Jill urged. "Pour him some more iced tea, Mom."

Her mother filled his glass again and passed him the sugar. She seemed excited to have a guest. Jill suddenly realized how her mother appeared to long for company since her husband's death.

Chuck made some small talk with the women and finished his tea. "Guess I'd better move on. Usually when the storm knocks the power out, we get lots of calls. Folks have accidents, and the noises jangle their nerves and their imagination."

Jill nodded her head. "Chuck, may I see you in my dad's . . . in the study before you go?"

Mom began to clear the table as Jill led Chuck away into the room and shut the heavy doors behind them.

"Chuck, do you have any idea what's going on?"

"What are you talking about?"

"First I was run off the road by the red Porsche, then we had the break-in and my room was ransacked, and now this." Jill shrugged her shoulders.

"That road incident was probably just some kids out joy-riding," Chuck assured her, "and I don't even know if today's little incident is related to the other break-in. Probably just some bum looking for shelter in the storm. We can have a patrol car assigned to keep a watch on you if you're worried."

"I'm not sure that would make me feel any better."

"What's that supposed to mean?" Chuck appeared offended.

"It's not you. You're like family. It's Barrows. There's just something creepy about that guy."

"How do you know Barrows?"

"He investigated my dad's accident, so I dropped by the precinct to ask him some questions."

"That's new to me. I investigated your father's death."

"You? Then why's Barrows' name on the report?"

"My name is on the report. I signed it."

"That's odd. Check it out when you get back to the office," Jill suggested.

"I will. I'll pull the accident report as soon as I get back to the precinct. I can't imagine why Barrows would say he investigated it."

"He showed us the report with his name on it too," Jill continued. "Why would he switch the reports?"

"I have no idea, Jill, but I will sure find out." Chuck seemed upset. "Barrows is a bit of an opportunist. For all I know, he could be changing reports to get that promotion he's been vying for the past couple of months. Or he may have misplaced my report and substituted it with one of his own. I can assure you that there's a simple explanation."

Jill decided to drop the report and ask some more serious questions. "Chuck, do you think my father's accident was really an accident or was it murder and then made to look like an accident?"

"We're talking about Delavan, not Washington, D.C. Of course it was an accident."

"How can you be so sure?"

"Because I got the call. A resident by the name of Robert Schrader heard the crash and saw the car wrapped around a tree just to the right of his property."

"Were you the first squad car on the scene?"

"Yep. I was exactly one mile away and the only patrol on the south shore at that time. When I drove up, I noticed the skid marks. I ran to the vehicle and saw it was your father and knew right away he was dead."

"How could you tell that?"

Chuck heaved a deep sigh. "His neck was broken, and the impact of the accident caused the steering wheel to penetrate his chest cavity. I also checked for a pulse. There was none. His eyes were fixed and dilated. Sorry to put you through the gory details, Jill, but you asked for it."

Jill tried to harden herself. "I need to know, Chuck."

"It looked like an accident to me," he repeated. "I'll pull a copy of my report for you."

"But what happened to the air bag in his car?" Jill wondered. "He was driving a brand-new Jaguar. Why didn't it inflate and release upon impact?"

"It should have," Chuck agreed, scratching his chin, "but it didn't. You know how these new cars with all those elaborate systems often malfunction."

"Or someone tampered with it."

"How could someone tamper with an air bag without your father noticing it?"

"I don't know." Jill's stomach tightened.

"How do you explain that his car was rear-ended?"

"That's simple; your father's car was spinning out of control and hit a tree and then he spun again, this time hitting that large tree with the front of his car."

"But I searched every tree in that vicinity, and there was only one scarred tree."

"It's been over a year since your father's death, Jill. The tree could have been removed in the interim. Besides, have you ever considered that he could hit the same tree twice? Whatever, I can assure you it was an accident."

As Chuck continued, Jill was swayed by his sincerity. "Remember, I was the officer at the scene. It was really devastating for me. I'd known your father all my life. He saved my father from dying of a heart attack."

"I'd forgotten that."

"I'll never forget it. The big house wasn't finished yet, and we were spending the weekend at our cabin on Miller's Creek Road. Your family was visiting the Andersons' next door when it happened, and your father risked his life to swim out to the spinning boat to save my dad."

"I remember now. It was very dramatic."

"I'll say. Dr. Lewis administered CPR and gave my father an injection that kept him alive until the rescue units arrived. It was a good thing, because it took the paramedics forever to find Miller's Creek Road." He paused. "I guess what I'm saying is that if I had any inkling your father's accident was suspicious, I would go to the ends of the earth to find out who rear-ended him."

"I'm sorry, Chuck, I wasn't doubting your expertise as a police officer, but there are just so many things that don't make sense to me."

She wished Craig were around to hear this too. How comforting it would be for him to hold her hand and tell her everything would be all right. Hearing the details of her father's death was almost more than she could bear.

By the time Jill and Chuck got back into the kitchen, the lights had come on and Pearl was seated at the table with three mugs of steaming hot chocolate and a plate of oatmeal cookies. The phone rang, startling all three of them.

"Service has been restored," Jill said as she picked up the phone. "Hello?"

"Jill, are you and your mom all right?" Craig asked.

At the sound of his voice, Jill sighed with relief. "Why do you ask?"

"Just a feeling. I heard about the storm and I was concerned."

"Glad you called. We had an attempted break-in during the storm."

"Are you and your mom okay? I knew I should've been there this weekend."

Craig's voice sounded so comforting that Jill immediately regained her composure.

"Yeah, someone reported a prowler outside our house and called the police. Chuck is with us now."

"Put him on the phone."

Jill handed Chuck the phone. "It's Craig."

Chuck spoke to Craig in hushed tones and then handed the phone back to Jill.

"Chuck is going to have a patrol car drive by the house throughout the rest of the night," Craig said. "You're as safe with Chuck as you are with me."

"I know. Thanks."

After she and Craig said good-bye, Jill walked back in the kitchen.

"Why would you investigate your father's death?" Pearl asked as she held Jill's gaze.

"I'm just asking for answers to some unanswered questions."

"It was an accident," her mother said firmly. "You'll save yourself a lot of time and heartache as soon as you can accept this."

"Listen to your mother, Jill," Chuck agreed. "It was an accident. I've got to get going. I'll be patrolling the area myself."

"Thank you, Chuck," Pearl said. "It's a comfort to me that you'll be outside."

"And what about you, Jill?" Chuck surprised her. "Do you feel safe with my guarding the house?"

"Of course, Chuck. Just don't let Barrows come near this house."

Chuck laughed. "Barrows is pretty intimidating, but he's a decent cop."

Jill flashed him a look of doubt. She wished he would leave so she could call Craig and tell him Chuck had confirmed that he investigated her father's accident, not Barrows. "Well, good-bye. Be careful in this weather." She stood by the door, but Chuck lingered, acting as if he had something to say.

"Is there something on your mind, Chuck?"

"Are you and Craig Martin, uh, seeing each other?"

"No," Jill said nonchalantly. "We work together, that's all. Why do you ask?"

Chuck smiled. "I thought the two of you might well, uh, be an item. If not, I was wondering . . . maybe you and I could drive over to Janesville for dinner and a movie?"

"Sure, Chuck. That would be nice."

To Jill's surprise, Chuck then leaned over and brushed her lips with a schoolboy kiss. She was so taken aback that she didn't push him away. Hoping he wouldn't misread her lack of resistance as an interest in him, she issued a disclaimer as politely as possible. "Chuck, Mom and I both cherish the friendship we've had with you and your family all these years." Chuck was not someone Jill wanted to alienate at this point in her life. "Call me on Monday, and I'll check my calendar. Good night."

As she watched him walk back down the long drive, she dialed Craig on the cordless phone, but there was a busy signal—the storm had reached Egg Harbor, and the phones in his area, even his cell phone, must've been out of order.

30

When I am dead, my dearest, sing no sad songs for me.
—Christina Georgina Rossetti

Jill couldn't ignore her mounting suspicions that her father was murdered and that maybe her investigation was the cause of it. Guilt kept her awake at night. At midnight she tiptoed down the stairs for a glass of hot milk to help her sleep. Peeking out the transom at the front door, she made out Chuck's silhouette sitting in the patrol car. To her surprise she startled her mother, who was sitting in the kitchen curled up in Dad's chair.

Jill walked over to her. "Don't worry, I know in my heart that this will all be over soon."

"I don't believe you," her mother replied. "It will never be over. Not for me."

Jill hugged her. *What does Mom know that she isn't saying? Wait a minute. Am I suspicious of my own mother?* Delavan was a small town, where the worst thing that could happen was a car accident. This was home—small-town U.S.A. The burglars who had ransacked her room were most likely from Washington, but they hadn't been back. Maybe they had realized she was no longer a threat to them writing obits at the *Lakes.*

———

On Monday morning Jill had to wait for the glass repairman to arrive before leaving for work, since her mother had an early hair appointment. After the window was repaired, Jill mustered enough courage to go to her dad's grave in the country. Her car tires made the stones on the narrow road to the cemetery crackle and pop as she slowly drove over them. Despite the noisy gravel, the place seemed quiet and serene, befitting its unseen residents. Jill parked the Range Rover. She could see the grave with the mammoth marble headstone, so ostentatiously done it seemed to scream "This is the spot."

She walked over to the headstone. "There are no flowers in my hand, Dad," she whispered. "But they are here in my heart. There isn't one moment of one day since you've been gone that you haven't been in my thoughts. I dashed off to college to make you proud of me; I became an investigative reporter because you always told me to do what made me happy. I wanted to be of service to others, but then I became caught up in my ego and pride and chased all the prestigious awards. I was convinced that I was unstoppable, invincible, unsinkable, only I stumbled over my pride and fell hard into a brick wall. I bragged to you about the case I had been working on, never listening to what you were saying, and because of that I wasn't there to help you. I feel so guilty. I'm sorry." She hastily wiped the tears from her eyes. "I love you, Daddy."

When she arrived at work, it was already 10:00.

Craig was waiting for her at the door. "Glad you decided to show up today." His voice sounded angry, but his eyes gave him away.

Matching his playful mood, she smiled a hopeful smile and said, "Out of my way!"

He rolled up the paper he was carrying and bopped her on the head. "I have a new desk for you by the window so you can watch everything that goes on in this town."

"And I was just getting used to my old desk."

"We hired another woman for the obits. So you can have both feet in investigations now."

"That's great news! When do I meet this woman who set me free?"

Craig beckoned to her. "Follow me."

Jill could feel her face flush when she saw the new hire typing away at a desk in the front room.

Craig looked sheepish. "She needed a job—I told you, her husband left her three months ago. Who'd have thought she was an English major in college with a minor in journalism?"

"Ah, Miss Hospitality, the woman who plied you with coffee when we were questioning the residents about the accident." *Better discuss the dress code with your new employee, Mr. Martin. She's practically poured into those spandex pants.*

"I was hoping you might mentor her," Craig suggested. "Come on and let me introduce you." He led her to the new obit writer. "Jill, this is Laura Hall, and Laura, this is Jill Lewis." Craig stood between the two women.

"Nice to meet you, Laura. Welcome to the paper."

"I can't believe I'm meeting *the* Jill Lewis! This is so exciting. You're the first famous—or should I say, infamous—person I've ever met." Laura giggled and jiggled as she jumped to her feet and shook Jill's hand vigorously.

"Uh, please let me know if I can ever help you with anything."

Craig grinned. "Take her up on that offer, Laura. Jill's a pro."

Laura waved her hand and batted her eyelashes at him. "Oh, I have no interest in becoming a career woman; I'm only helping you out until I find Mr. Right."

Jill narrowed her eyes suspiciously as she and Craig walked away; she couldn't believe he had hired this shallow woman. "I bet she can't write a good obit."

"Well, you and Marge can help her with that. Come into my office for a minute."

With the door closed behind them, Craig asked, "Were things okay last night after we spoke?"

"Sure. Chuck Emerson spent the night outside our house in his patrol car." She hesitated.

"What's the matter?"

"I'm not sure. It's just that the Delavan Police Department . . . there's something going on over there. Even Chuck was surprised to find out that his name wasn't on the accident report."

"You told him?"

"No, he told me he was the officer who investigated the accident."

"And what did you say?"

"That Barrows's name was on the report. But he told me again that he investigated the accident and signed the report. This proves that Barrows tampered with the reports." She saw the frown on Craig's face. "Are you upset with me for mentioning this to Chuck?"

"No, Chuck's a good guy; you can trust him."

"That's good to hear. I've agreed to go out with him."

Craig turned and looked out the window. "You should go, Jill. Have some fun and get your mind off the investigation."

"Yeah, you're right." Jill felt crushed. Apparently Craig couldn't care less if she went out with Chuck.

She returned to her old desk and cleaned it out for the new obit girl. By the afternoon, she was settled into her desk by the window. Though now in a faraway corner, Jill had a bird's-eye view of Craig and could keep an eye on the new obit girl from her new desk—at least he couldn't catch her staring at him.

Jill took a deep breath and held her thoughts inside as he walked out of his office toward her desk. "There's something I want to show you." She followed him to his office; once inside, Craig slid a manila folder over to her. She pulled out a long list of computer printouts.

"What is this?"

"That's what I went to research in Chicago. Have you seen these before?"

"Yes, of course," Jill admitted as she quickly scanned the list of individual contributors to Burke's last senate campaign. "I had one of my associates review the list. He found nothing out of the ordinary."

"So you didn't review it yourself?" Craig said slowly as he scratched his chin with the eraser at the end of a pencil.

"Only the contributions that were made by corporations and foundations," she admitted. "I spent hours researching those, but the individual contributions hardly seemed significant enough, especially since my associate reported nothing out of the ordinary."

"That explains it."

"Explains what? Is there something on here I should be aware of?"

"Had you reviewed them, you would have most likely noticed the two names that I have highlighted on pages 182 and 338."

Jill began flipping through the computer printouts. She was stunned to see her mother and father's names on the list for a sizable contribution of $100,000 and even more stunned to discover Kathy and Jeff's name listed for an equal amount.

"Doesn't it seem odd to you that two fine Wisconsin citizens would contribute so heavily to an Illinois Senate campaign?" Craig probed.

"I—I think I can explain," Jill stammered nervously. "You know that my family lived in Chicago until we relocated here. My father had a lot of ties there."

"What about Jeff?"

"Because of my father's connections, Jeff has clients there too."

"Would you feel comfortable discussing this with Jeff?"

"Since I've been away over twelve years, we really aren't that close. Kathy told me he was offended over the way we grilled him about Marion's adoption, so no, I'm not sure I feel comfortable approaching him with this."

"I understand. Why don't you start by asking Kathy some questions?"

"Jeff doesn't share a lot with Kathy, especially when it comes to business. But I guess I could do a little probing."

Jill's lip began to quiver. She feared they had inadvertently opened a can of worms that might jeopardize Marion's adoption. Her family had suffered enough. Would they ever forgive her if there were more pain and heartache to uncover?

"You know, Craig, in spite of how all this looks, my father was a very fine man."

"I know that, Jill. Your father was a fine Delavan citizen who was loved and respected by all who knew him."

"There must be some explanation." Jill folded her hands and fought back the tears. "I believe we're close to discovering just what it is."

"Me too, Jill. But the question is, are you prepared to hear the answers?"

31

It was a perfect spring afternoon
And the air was filled with vague, roving scents,
As if the earth exhaled the sweetness of hidden flowers.

—Ellen Glasgow

Winter had thawed into spring, and Jill had finally mustered the courage to confront her sister. A stretch of sunny days had melted the ice on the lakes. Dampness still clung to the morning air, blanketing everything with a cold covering of thick dew. By afternoon, the wetness had been absorbed by the warmth of the sun. The gentle breeze swept Jill and Kathy's faces as they sat together on the limestone patio, taking in the breathtaking view while sipping their hot tea. The huge expanse of forested ground spread before them with the peaceful lake below.

Jill smiled uncomfortably, hoping her suspicions about baby selling and racketeering were wrong. "This view is awesome. Jeff must be doing really well."

"He is!" Kathy gushed. "He's a full partner."

"The perfect life."

"It's a good life, not a perfect one." Kathy frowned slightly.

"Nobody has a perfect life, Jill. Unfortunately, Jeff spends lots of time at the office working on extra cases; he said I needed to have a great view to distract me."

"I can only imagine the beauty of the trees during the fall when the leaves turn colors. I'll have to bring my camera and capture it on film."

"Yeah, we'd like to do the same thing. We're commissioning an artist to paint Marion and then the three of us together as a family. And we're going to sit outdoors to do it."

"Wow, that's expensive."

"Jeff said not to worry."

"Does he take care of all the finances?"

"Yeah. Just like Daddy did with Mom. Is there something wrong with that?"

"No. I just can't imagine not knowing about the financial situation when I get married someday."

"Well, I feel quite secure."

"I'm glad." Jill decided to change the subject. "Do your plans include having any other children?"

Kathy smiled. "We'd love to adopt more children. I'd like to adopt a son, but Jeff insists he would be just as happy with another little girl. It can take so long for your name to come up to the top of the list for adoptions. We put our name out there and just have to wait."

"Are you using an adoption agency?"

"We're working with three adoption agencies as well as putting feelers out for a private adoption. Whatever door the Lord opens first is the one we'll go through." Kathy shrugged.

"Where is Maid Marion, anyway?" Jill asked, looking around for her little niece.

"She's with Jeff's parents at the Milwaukee Zoo. She'll probably come home tired and all sticky with cotton candy."

"Was Marion's adoption private, like Jeff said?"

"Yes, of course it was private, just like he said. Jeff has no reason to lie to you, Jill."

"What kind of 'private' do you mean? Did you meet the birth mother's parents?"

"Jeff really doesn't want me to discuss this." Kathy whispered as if Jeff would walk in on them at any moment.

"Even with your own sister?"

Kathy looked embarrassed and didn't respond.

"Well, if it was all legal and everything, why not tell me? It's just between us sisters," Jill coaxed.

"Jeff calls this 'family business.' Ever since our dad paid for Jeff's way through law school, he's felt that the Lewis family owns him, and he hates that."

"Right, the Lewis family is so bad, it gave him all this," Jill said, waving her hand around at the scenery.

"No, the Lewis family gave him the education so he could *earn* all of this," Kathy said. "And Jeff wasn't the only young person from Delavan that Dad sent to college."

"No, but he's the one who married Dr. Lewis's daughter."

"If you're insinuating that Jeff stays with me because he feels obligated since Daddy paid for his education, you're wrong," Kathy snapped. "You probably think that because I've suffered some emotional problems that I'm a burden to my husband. But Jeff has always stood by me and supported me every step of the way."

"That's not what I was trying to—"

"Shut up and let me finish!"

Jill was shocked. She had never seen her mild-mannered sister react in such a hostile manner. *There must be something she's trying to hide.*

"I couldn't have asked for a better husband." Kathy trembled as she continued. "Marriage is no picnic, but it's worth every effort. We are committed and love each other very much."

"He loves you so much he would even buy you a baby—isn't that right?" Jill dared to ask.

"What? You think Marion was a bought baby? You're crazy, Jill!"

Jill put both her hands on the table. "Am I? What is all this 'don't tell anyone' stuff about, anyway? Why can't anyone know the truth behind Marion's adoption?"

"Because it's private. You don't know what that was like for me while you were off pursuing your hotshot career."

"Where I've learned things about adoptions. More than I ever wanted to know."

"What do you know about it? The only things you know come secondhand from your investigative reporting. Well, I've lived it! I live with it! You talked to and reported on women who couldn't get pregnant. I *am* a woman who can never have a biological child of my own!"

"I can imagine it was hard for you." Jill hoped using softer words would calm Kathy. She knew she had touched a raw nerve.

"You couldn't wait to get out of town as soon as you graduated from high school, and you never looked back. You ran off to find a big, important, flashy life. I wanted simpler things, and my life was right here, so I stayed. In college you hardly ever came home or even called to talk to any of us. Do you know how much Daddy missed you? Do you even care?

"Then you ran after your precious journalistic career in Washington. We saw you even less," Kathy seethed. "How many times in those years did you even bother to call me? Maybe twice a year! And when we did talk, I could tell you weren't really listening to me. You only wanted to talk about what you were doing."

Jill felt ashamed. She didn't know what to say. "I'm sorry I wasn't more in tune with your needs," she ventured.

"Yeah, right. You've gotten everything you ever wanted! I have too, except for the one thing I wanted most—a baby. If you don't have enough money, you can get another job or work harder and make more money. If you're sick, you can get well by going to the doctor to get medicine. But if you can't have a baby . . . there is no fixing that problem. My arms ached from loneliness. I began to hate all pregnant women. And I became so angry with God too. Why did he let this happen to me? All I ever asked for was a baby.

"I thought I would go crazy. Jeff would sit up nights with me as I cried my heart out. Sometimes Daddy had to come over with medications to help me sleep or calm my hysteria. Marion saved my life. If God hadn't brought her to us when he did, I don't know what would've become of me."

Jill had tears flowing down her cheeks now. "Kathy, I'm so sorry I wasn't there for you. I had no idea you were suffering like that. Can you forgive me?"

Kathy nodded, handing Jill a tissue, and both sisters wept as they hugged one another fiercely. They cried for their lack of understanding for each other, for the past hurts they had inflicted, for the father they had both lost.

After a few minutes, Kathy motioned for Jill to follow her into the house. They walked through the long hallway, up the winding staircase to the second floor, and into the master bedroom. Jill looked around at the room lavishly decorated in too much money and too little taste while Kathy walked over to her ornate, marble-topped desk gilded in gold. She unlocked it and looked through some papers. After a moment Kathy found what she had been hunting for and brought it to Jill.

"Here. You've got to promise never to mention to Jeff that I showed this to you," Kathy said as she handed Jill the papers.

Jill quickly went through the paperwork on Marion's adoption. It was a private adoption after all. "The baby was born to Jeff's unwed younger sister," she whispered.

"Craig mentioned on New Year's Day how much Marion looks like Jeff, and that's why. In actuality, Marion is Jeff's niece, born to Jeff's sister. Jennifer didn't want to abort her baby, but she couldn't raise the child herself. She knew we could not, or rather that I could not, have a baby and asked if we would take this child and make her ours. We did. And every night we thank the Lord for our daughter."

Jill handed the papers back. "So Jeff hid the business of Marion's adoption to protect you all, just like he said. It is 'private family business.'" She felt numb. She felt ashamed and vowed to be nicer to Jeff. "Kathy, are you aware that I was investigating Senator Burke?"

"Me and everyone else in the country."

"Did you know that Dad and Jeff contributed heavily to his last senate campaign?"

"No. Jill, I was honest when I told you that Jeff handles *everything*."

"What if something happened to Jeff?"

"We have a financial advisor."

"But you can't trust everyone. You should make an effort to find out more about your finances."

"I'll try," Kathy promised. "I know it's a good idea."

"It's a necessity. Look at Mom. She always made it a point to know what was going on with their affairs, and now that Dad's gone, she's in a position to oversee the financial advisor's decisions."

"Then why don't you ask her about the contribution she and Dad made to Burke's reelection campaign?"

Jill sighed. "I had hoped to avoid that. Kathy, you would've made a good investigative reporter too."

Kathy laughed. "No thanks, I'm happy doing just what I'm doing."

The sisters hugged. Jill had prayed that God would restore the closeness she had once shared with her sister. It appeared that this was the beginning of their healing, and God was answering her prayers again.

"Oh, and Jill, please feel free to ask Jeff about the contribution too. He has nothing to hide. He's really a good person. I so want the two of you to get to know one another better and become closer. We are a family, after all."

"I'll try," Jill promised, fishing the keys out of her purse. "Kathy, there's one more thing. Did Jeff ever make any trips to D.C. that you know of over the past few years?"

"Washington? Never." Kathy put the papers back in her desk. "But Daddy went all the time. You must know that though. Surely he visited you when he was there?"

32

Jill watched as Craig stared with intensity at the computer screen in her father's home office. After hearing her shocking news that her father had frequented her old city, he had jumped right in and checked the flight schedules of Dr. Lewis in the previous years.

"Hello? Did you forget about me?" Jill waved a folder in his face.

"Forget about you? Never!" His smile was disarming.

Her heart fluttered. "Finding anything on that computer about Dad's flights to D.C.?"

Craig pulled up the information and read the screen to Jill as she took notes. "One, two, three, four, five . . . a dozen trips to Washington, D.C., each year for the last four years, including the year before he died."

"But he never visited me or even phoned."

"He obviously didn't want you to know he was there. Hey,

look at this: one, two, three, nine trips out of the country in the last six years before his death."

"What?" Jill jumped to her feet and pressed closer to see for herself.

"Yes, here he has four trips to Canada, and the rest are to Romania, Russia, and Bosnia," Craig said as he pointed to the computer screen.

"These trips were made long before my investigation even began." Jill was trying to let the new information sink into her brain. "What does this mean?"

"Maybe your dad and Jeff worked together on this 'project' of theirs. Jill, you didn't pique your dad's interest with your investigation; he was one of the men you were investigating."

"No, that's not possible! He must've gone on all these trips for medical purposes."

"When your mom gets back from her shopping spree in Milwaukee, you should ask her what she knows."

"So now you're implicating my mother! Why don't you just accuse me too while you're at it and put the whole family behind bars?" Jill tossed down her notes.

Craig leaned back and folded his arms across his chest. "Think like a reporter, not a daughter."

"After talking to Kathy, I was beginning to think Jeff was innocent, but if Dad is guilty, maybe Jeff is too. Craig, I cannot believe my father, this man whom I loved and idolized my entire life, could be such a monster! Why would he do such a thing?"

"Why does anyone get into illegal practices?"

Jill tapped a pencil on her forehead. "We always had lots of money, but you had a good point a few months ago—a doctor in Delavan couldn't make that much money. Moving from his lucrative practice in Chicago to Delavan would've drastically reduced my father's income. But maybe when he made a lot of money in the city, he invested it well."

"Why did your family leave Chicago in the first place, if your father was doing so well there?"

"Until my dad died, I'd always believed it was because my parents wanted to raise Kathy and me in an idyllic small town, away from the big, bad city. At my dad's funeral, one of my aunts asked my mom, 'Pearl, was Harold drunk when he had his accident?' That night I confronted my mother, and she confessed that when we lived in Chicago, my dad had a serious drinking problem; so serious that the partners in his Chicago medical practice booted him out. Because we spent our summers here, we had good friends in Delavan who offered my father a position at the local hospital—if he would voluntarily enter a treatment center first. He did, and since then he never had another problem with alcohol."

"You had no idea? That must have been a terrible shock."

Jill nodded. "My mother could've won an Oscar for her performance to convince us, and the world, that we had the perfect family. I was angry with her and devastated to learn the truth when it came out."

"She was only trying to protect her children."

"Yes, she was. I knew that, and it was easy to forgive her, and now I have to admit that I think we have officially established a motive for my father." She sighed. "He obviously needed the money," she concluded sadly. "My childhood was a lie. My dad was obviously not an honorable man."

Craig put his arm around her. "This doesn't change your childhood, it just explains things. Nor does it erase all the honorable things your father did as a husband, a father, a doctor, and a friend." He handed her his handkerchief to dry her tears.

"Thank you, Craig." She sniffed into the hankie. "He may

have been a bad man, but he was a good father. I just can't bear to think about Dad not knowing the Lord."

"You don't know that for sure," Craig reminded her. "One never knows what occurs in those last few minutes of a man's life." He gently took her hand and helped her stand up. "Let's get to the bottom of this once and for all. Let's go visit Jeff." Pausing, he smiled at her a bit quizzically.

"What are you thinking?" she asked.

"How much I enjoy working with you."

———

When the secretary escorted Jill and Craig through the door of Jeff's elegant office, Jeff saw their faces and frowned. Immediately he replaced the frown with a tentative smile.

"Should I call my lawyer?" he joked as he stood and tapped his pen on the side of his desk.

"Why would you say that?" Craig asked as he slid into an expensive brown leather chair.

"Sheesh! I'm only joking. You have a very serious boyfriend there, Jill."

Jill looked around his office: walls of leather-bound legal books, a mahogany desk adorned with ornate silver-framed photographs of Kathy and Marion, thick, lush Oriental rugs, and a butler's tray at the side of his desk holding a cache of sparkling crystal decanters of Scotch and expensive brandies. This was the office of a prosperous attorney.

She took a seat beside Craig. "Jeff, I need some answers—and this is off the record and personal."

"Sounds like newspaper jargon to me," he laughed, dropping his pen. He got up from his chair and came around the desk and leaned against the front of it with his arms folded across his chest.

"I know my dad was involved in international adoptions

of babies on the black market. I just can't prove it yet. Can you tell us anything?"

Jeff's stare bored down upon Jill so intensely that it made her squirm in the expensive Chippendale chair. To avoid his glare, she looked down at her hands.

Jeff's amusement had quickly turned to anger. "You think you know so much, and you know dirt!"

Jill knew what he was thinking. "I'm not talking about Marion's adoption."

"Right, do not talk about Marion," Jeff reiterated, slamming his fist on the desk. "Marion is not your concern."

"Come on, Jeff, cool it," Craig warned him. "Jill only wants to find out who killed her father."

"You obviously don't know Jill like we all know her," Jeff mocked. He unfolded his arms and walked back around to the other side of his desk and sat down, leaning back as far as the chair would take him. "Jill doesn't fool me for a minute. She would sell her mother for a story."

"Jeff," Craig interjected, "please don't say anything you'll regret later. You know Jill loves her family."

"This is all about clearing her name, reclaiming her throne in Washington. You poor sucker." He pointed toward Craig. "She doesn't care how many people she destroys and leaves behind in the process—her sister, her mother, her niece, or me—and that includes you too, buddy. One day you'll wake up and poof! Jill Lewis will be gone. She'll use you just like she has the rest of us, including her dad."

Jill's head was pounding and she felt dizzy. Were Jeff's accusations true?

Craig reached over and took her hand, holding it tightly in his. "Hear her out," he advised. "You know about the break-in at the Lewis home?"

Jeff nodded, appearing to soften some as he bent forward and placed his arms on his desk.

Leaning forward in his chair, Craig continued. "I'm concerned for Jill and her mother's safety. There have been other incidences too."

Jill leaned forward as well. "I just want to know for my own mental well-being. If it's true that he was murdered, I would like to bring Dad's killers to justice," she pleaded. "And I have to know why and for how long Dad was involved in the racketeering of babies. And also if you were involved, Jeff."

"I was not involved at all. Off the record, your father was another story."

"Why?" Jill cried.

"For money."

"Jeff, if you weren't involved, how do you explain the six-figure donation you made to Burke's campaign?" Craig asked, holding up the list of donors.

"That's easy. I have several corporate clients in Chicago who encouraged that donation."

"Those clients you're speaking of, would they happen to be referrals from Dr. Lewis?"

"A few, but not all."

"How do you explain that it was the same amount of money as Dr. Lewis's contribution?" Craig asked.

"I discussed it with him. Dr. Lewis was my mentor in many ways. But I refused to join in his shady business deals."

Jill sat quietly, feeling numb. She wanted to disown her father, but she couldn't—he was already dead and buried. "How much did Mom know?"

"If she knew anything, she suffered in silence."

She wasn't satisfied with this answer. "With all the trips he took, why didn't she question him?"

"He made up a lot of excuses when he left town: medical

conferences, consultations with other doctors, a witness for the insurance companies, learning new methods of medicine, etc. Your mother never doubted him."

"Good ol' Mom," Jill sighed.

Craig peered at Jeff over his glasses. "How can we take your word for anything?"

"My word is all you have at this point. Dr. Lewis invited me in on the adoption deal with him. He needed someone in an official position in town to help with legal work, to help make the illegal stuff appear legal. He promised he could fill our bank account with money and our house with children. When I refused his offer, your dad got so angry with me that we stopped seeing your parents for several months."

Dad, how could you? "Jeff, I'm so sorry. Does Kathy know?"

"No, she knew your father and I had a disagreement, but she doesn't know about this. I suppose I'll have to tell her now, won't I?" He looked accusingly at Jill and then softened. "She loved her dad too."

"I thought Dad's interest in adoptions was piqued when I began my Washington investigations."

Jeff's eyes narrowed. "Leave Marion out of this. You know, I never liked you, Jill. I always thought you were a trouble-maker. I think I like you even less now."

Craig held on to her hand, but the words Jeff had hurled at her struck her heart like a spear.

Jeff continued. "I read the police report about the accident myself. It didn't make sense to me, nor did the fact that the air bag on his brand-new car didn't inflate. But then after I considered the risk, I felt it best to let any suspicions of murder disappear, no questions asked."

"But Jeff, he was our dad, your father-in-law." Jill fought valiantly against the tears that were forming.

"What good would it do? Your father is dead; nothing can bring him back, and I sure don't want to risk putting my family in jeopardy. I love Kathy dearly, and Marion is the light of our world. You may not have much to live for, Jill, but we do."

Feeling hurt and confused, Jill lashed out. "If you don't mind me asking, where did you get all your money to build your house and live so grandly?"

"You just don't quit, do you? It's none of your business, but since you are family and a super snoop, I'll tell you. The firm is doing great, and I made senior partner a couple of years ago." He leaned back with a smile. "I've also taken on some very well-to-do clients out of Chicago."

"How very nice for you."

Jeff smirked. "Didn't you ever wonder where all the money came from when you were growing up? Small-town doctors don't make that kind of money. Your father lavished you, your mother, and your sister with designer clothes, trips to Europe, priceless antiques, and anything else your little hearts desired."

"I've never thought much about money and things, Jeff. I've focused more on books and learning."

"And I admired that about you, Jill."

Jeff's words sent Jill riding back up her emotional roller coaster. *Was he actually offering me a compliment?* She glanced over at Craig, who sat uncomfortably by her side, to check out his reaction. He looked surprised but relieved that Jeff had pulled back his attacks.

Jeff continued. "But you aren't blind; you must've noticed that your mom and Kathy care very much about those things."

"But they're both very generous too." Jill felt defensive

toward her family, whose image had taken a very bad hit that day.

"Can you imagine what it's like to have to support your sister's insatiable, extravagant taste that she learned from your mother?"

Embarrassed by what she knew to be the truth, she glanced at Craig out of the corner of her eye. What must he think of her and her family? Her father appeared to be a criminal and an extortionist. Jill was a workaholic who would stop at nothing to get her story, even if it meant destroying her family in the process. Her mother and sister were greedy, extravagant, and materialistic. And Jeff, well, he was an arrogant egomaniac.

A deep pity for Jeff suddenly swept over her. She'd had no idea her father had tried to run his life and that her sister was pressuring him to live well beyond their means. This was her perfect family?

"I'm sorry, Jeff," she said quietly.

"Don't be. Fortunately for me, the firm is doing very well, and there's always plenty left over, even after one of your sister's spending sprees."

Jill and Jeff sat staring at one another. Jill shifted slightly in her seat, wondering if her mother's extravagant tastes had driven her father to crime.

Breaking the uncomfortable silence, Craig jumped in to rescue her. "Is there anything else you can tell us, Jeff? Names? Dates?"

"I've told you all I know," Jeff responded curtly, standing up to signal the end of the interrogation. He escorted them out of his office.

"Have you ever discussed any of this with Mrs. Lewis?" Craig said at the door.

"I've stayed as far away from the Lewis's business as possible, but I do know that Pearl is of the generation where these things aren't talked about. She was raised with the belief that all that mattered was keeping up appearances."

Jill knew exactly what Jeff was talking about. Her mother had always taught her that family business was not to be discussed outside the home. The fact that she hid their father's alcoholism from even her daughters was another sign of her obsession to hide the family's imperfections.

As though he suddenly pitied her, Jeff looked over at Jill and added, "There may be a lot of things that weren't as they appeared, but I do know that the love your parents had for one another and for you and Kathy was very real. Your parents had a great marriage, and if I learned anything from them, it was about love."

"Thanks for sharing that, Jeff," Jill said softly. "It means a lot to me."

"Yes, thank you, Jeff," Craig said as the two men shook hands.

Without speaking, Jill reached over and hugged her brother-in-law tightly.

Jeff patted her back awkwardly and added, "I'd like to help, but I hope you understand my concerns about the safety of my family. If you are going forward with this, please leave me—us—out of it."

"You have our word," Craig promised.

On the way out, Jill stopped briefly in the ladies' room to splash cold water on her face.

"Feeling better?" Craig asked sympathetically as she emerged.

"As well as anyone can feel when the family skeletons are out of the closet for all the world to see. Let's go talk to Mom."

33

We cannot destroy kindred;
Our chains stretch a little sometimes, but they never break.

—Marie de Rabutin-Chantal, Marquise de Sevigne

Jill and Craig walked through the unlocked kitchen door to find her mother singing as she sorted and cleaned her jewelry, oblivious to the impending confrontation that would affect her life and the lives of her loved ones. She looked up and smiled.

"Mom, you're supposed to keep these doors locked at all times," Jill scolded.

Her mother's face looked so happy and radiant, so full of life and spirit. How could she crush all that now? But she had to have answers; answers would lead to the truth.

"Hello, darling. Sorry, I just forgot. I've lived here for years and never locked these doors."

"Well, it's time to start now," Jill said while locking up. "How was your shopping trip with Vickie?"

"Marvelous. Vickie and I both found these linen jackets in these bright spring colors . . . we bought every color. And you should see the fabrics in Chanel's new spring line. I found a couple of darling things for you . . . they're hanging on your closet."

"Mom, you really shouldn't have." Jill felt more irritated than usual.

"Oh hush, you'll be glad I did when you see them."

"Mom, please, you've got to stop treating me like I'm a teenager."

Ignoring Jill's protests, her mom asked, "Would you two like to join me for dinner tonight?"

"That's kind, Mrs. Lewis, but Jill has agreed to have a working dinner with me tonight at the country club."

Jill looked at him in surprise. "That's news to me. I thought we were going to use our usual office—the back booth at Millie's Cafe."

"Tonight's special. As your managing editor, I want to take you to celebrate your promotion at the *Lakes*."

"Another promotion, how wonderful! Well, if you two will excuse me, I want to take my jewelry back upstairs to the safe."

Jill grabbed her arm. "Not so fast, Mom; please sit down. We need to talk."

Her mother hesitated and looked at Jill with concern. She motioned for them to sit. Craig sat in her father's chair, but Jill followed her mother to the love seat in the breakfast room.

"Mom, you know I was investigating a story about babies being brought into this country illegally for placement with families, yes?" Jill asked gently as they sat together on the love seat.

"Yes," her mom answered quietly, gazing at her daughter with worried confusion.

"This is a difficult question to ask, but do you think Daddy might have been involved in any way?"

Her mom looked over at Craig. "Jill, this is family business. If you're going to question me, I would prefer you do it in private."

"Mom, Craig knows everything. He's our friend, and he's going to help us." Craig smiled at Pearl assuredly. She seemed to relax as she sat back on the sofa and folded her hands in her lap. For several moments she did not respond; it was as though she was searching for the words to say. She pulled her handkerchief out of her pocket and folded it neatly in her lap. Then she answered flatly, "Yes, your father was involved."

"You knew, Mrs. Lewis?" Craig asked.

"I found out near the end, before his accident. I suspected he was having an affair because he left town so often."

"Dad would never have had an affair," Jill reassured her mom. "He loved you too much."

"I'm not proud to admit this, but I was so sure he was seeing someone else that I decided to follow him on an airplane right to Washington, D.C. He had no idea. I traveled economy; he traveled first-class."

"Mom, do you know if he met with anyone from the capitol?"

"He did. He met our dear friend Tom Burke's son, Senator Burke, and they had an argument over lunch. I was so relieved it wasn't another woman that I didn't care what he was doing there! When your dad left the senator, he seemed so upset I thought he would need more of his stomach medication. You remember how his tummy would get when he was upset? I confronted him right on the street outside the restaurant."

"What did you say to him?" Jill asked, picturing the scene in her mind.

"I said, 'Harold, what are you doing here?' He looked

at me in shock and said, 'Pearl, what are you doing here?'
I told him I had followed him because I thought he was
having an affair. He told me I was crazy to think such a
thing."

"Then what happened, Mom?"

"Your father rented a car, and we drove back to Wisconsin together, and he spilled out his heart to me. He
and Tom Burke Sr. had been on the board together from
early on at Hope House, and Tom was very aware of your
father's financial situation before we moved to Wisconsin.
Tom asked him if he would like to become involved in a
lucrative project. The project needed a physician on board
for medical exams and records, so that's how your father
got involved."

"I wonder what Dad must've thought when he realized
I was investigating Tom and his son, and that eventually it
would lead right to him?"

"When your father heard you were investigating the adoption operation, he said it was only a matter of time before you
found out about him. He was so upset."

"How touching." Jill couldn't keep the sarcasm from her
voice.

"Oh, Jill, your father was not a bad man. He was so ashamed,
and he didn't want you to find out." Her mom grabbed on
to Jill's hand. "That's why I asked if you were investigating
anything to do with your dad's death. I always wondered if
his sinful life would catch up with him, but you assured me
that you weren't, so I felt better. I hoped you would never
find out the truth about him. He loved you so."

"Was Jeff involved too?" Craig asked.

"No! Harold tried to persuade Jeff to come in with him
on several occasions. He wanted Jeff to have money so Kathy
could have everything she ever wanted, but Jeff refused; he

wouldn't accept a penny from your dad. I never knew what was going on between the two of them until later. I assumed your father was one of those men who believed that no one was good enough for his daughter."

"What would Dad have done if I'd found out about him before his death?"

"When your father heard that the case you were working on was his, he naturally became very upset. He didn't want you to think badly of him and knew you would. He wanted to make the wrong places right in his life, so he went to the FBI and told them all he knew. They said they would cut him a deal if he could provide proof to bring Senator Burke down. Well, Jill, you know how close your father and Tom Burke Sr. had been all these years. The thought of turning on his old friend, and especially ruining his son's presidential bid, repulsed him. But after much thought and prayer, he decided if he was going to get right with the Lord, he had to do this."

"The FBI was involved?" Jill asked incredulously. "Why didn't you tell me, Mom? Didn't you realize how this might have helped clear my name?"

"I'm sorry, Jill. It was one thing for your father to take the risk at his age, but you have your entire life ahead of you. It was so dangerous that the FBI even offered your father the witness protection and relocation; that's when they give you a new identity and . . ."

"I know what it is, Mom, please go on."

"Your father chose to live with the risks. He told me if anything ever happened to him not to say a word to anyone, to let the FBI handle it."

"So you knew Dad was murdered?"

"Not for sure, but I suspected. A few weeks after we buried

your father, the FBI showed up at my door with a search warrant looking for the tapes, and they told me."

"What tapes?" Jill asked.

"Your father wore a wire to some important meetings with Burke and others. He was anxious to hand them over to the bureau immediately."

"So that's what everyone's looking for . . . those tapes. They aren't looking for my files at all."

"After four or five searches, Keith Strickland, one of the agents your father had been working with, told me to call him right away if I found anything. He scribbled his number on a little piece of paper."

"Do you still have the paper?" Jill asked.

"Of course, but let me finish. After you were home last Christmas the FBI returned for another search and suggested that I have you move home with me. I laughed and told him, 'That'll never happen.' But here you are!"

"Why would they want me to move home with you?"

"Probably because your mother was afraid to live alone," Craig said.

"I was afraid, but the FBI promised me they were keeping an eye out for me."

"They didn't do a very good job, did they?" Jill frowned. "We've had one break-in and another attempted one, plus someone trying to run me off the road and no telling what else you haven't told me. Mom, why didn't you and Dad discuss this with me and give me copies of the tapes? I could've helped you."

"Yes, but you'd be six feet under," Craig reminded her. "Compared to your father, you were just a harmless little fish in a big sea of sharks."

"Well, they're after me now." Jill shook her head and then regretted worrying her mother.

"Probably because they think you've found the tapes, or maybe you're just in their way of finding the tapes," Craig said.

"But I could've cleared my name if you and father had let me in on this." Jill looked into Pearl's eyes.

"I'm sorry, darling, but I'm going to make this all up to you. I have something to give you now."

"The tapes?" Both Jill and Craig guessed in unison.

"No." Pearl jumped to her feet, reached under the sofa cushion, and pulled out some large envelopes. "These documents. I was going to call Agent Strickland, but I'm going to give them to you instead. These should clear your name." She handed the envelopes to Jill, who ripped them open.

She gasped. "There are dozens of canceled checks from a holding corporation, the Tom Thumb Corporation. The checks are made out to Dad, and some of them are signed by Senator Burke and some by Tom Burke Sr.," she said as she handed Craig another envelope containing documents and letters to Dr. Lewis from Senator Burke.

"We've got him!" he announced after scanning the material.

"But what do these checks prove?" Jill asked. "Except that Dad was in cahoots with the Burkes?"

"These checks and documents are your ticket back to Washington," Craig said, holding a stack in the air.

Jill's mother tried to smile through her tears, but Jill was not smiling. She was still in a state of shock.

"What about me, Mom? My career? Didn't you care?" She was still reeling from the fact that her mother had known important information all along and kept it from her.

"For selfish reasons, I was glad you lost that awful job. I

wanted you to settle down in Delavan and meet a nice young man." She paused for effect and looked over at Craig. "I wanted you to have a life, a family, a nice home, pretty things, and pretty clothes—all the things a mother wants for her daughter."

"Mother, please, that's so shallow! This was my life, what I had worked for all those years. Didn't you care?"

"Of course I cared, but what kind of life did you really have?"

"I had a great life," Jill defended. "I hate to think that being surrounded by money and so much *stuff* is somehow better than what I had. Besides, I would like to think that my investigations made the world a better place."

"Offending people at every turn, some of them nice people? Ruining lives and careers? Living in that cramped apartment near the bad section of town? Associating with criminals? You call that a great life?"

"Any people I offended were guilty—they deserved it! You reap what you sow."

"Only God can judge," her mother replied quietly.

Jill was finding it difficult to control her anger. She stomped her foot. "Have you ever considered that maybe God called me into this profession for my ministry?"

Her mother didn't respond.

"I think maybe Jill has a point there, Mrs. Lewis," Craig said. "Jesus said, 'What is done in darkness shall be revealed in the light.' Isn't that what Jill's job is all about?"

"That's an interesting viewpoint," her mother mused, "but there was hardly a night that your father and I got a good night's sleep for worrying about you."

"And here I thought you were proud of me all this time."

"We were, but we were praying that you would get all those

crazy newspaper notions out of your system and come home one day to settle down and live a normal life."

Jill sighed and looked around her family's palatial home. She shook her head. "So *this* is a normal life?"

34

Nothing in life is to be feared.
It is only to be understood.

—Madame Curie

Just a handful of weeks before, Jill had longed for a hot romance. Now, after the shocking events of the last few days, she felt off balance; romance was the last thing on her mind.

Embarrassed and humiliated, she asked Craig, "How about a rain check for that dinner at the country club? I'm afraid I wouldn't be very good company tonight. I need some time alone."

"Why don't you take tomorrow off? Take a whole week if you need it."

"Thanks, I do need a day off, and since you hired Laura, you don't really need me."

"Of course we need you, but there's nothing pressing. Let's talk later."

After Craig left, Jill went upstairs, locked the door to her room, and allowed herself to sob into her pillows. *Why am I crying? I should be happy,* she thought as she fluffed her pillow and sank her face back into it. The documents and checks would put Burke in prison and clear her name in the process. Her job in Washington would once again be hers, but did she really want to put her family through this madness, muddying her father's name in the process? No one would forget the fact that Dr. Lewis was a criminal, and that the Lewis fortune had been gained from the suffering of others. Hadn't her family suffered enough at her hands? The realization that it was her investigation that had killed her father was more than Jill could bear. He would be alive today if it weren't for her.

Her mother lightly tapped at her door, interrupting her thoughts and prayers.

"Mom, I love you, but I really need to be alone right now. Could we talk tomorrow?"

She heard a muffled "Fine," and then her mother's feet shuffling down the hall. She felt sorry for her mom, but she was still very angry. She didn't want to risk saying hurtful things that she would regret later.

Jill wanted to escape from Delavan as fast as she could, but where would she go? The only job she could get was the one she had at the *Lakes*. Before she had returned to Delavan, she hadn't prayed much except when she was in a tight spot. Now her life had become a continuous prayer. She would do some serious talking to the Lord tonight about her needs and his plan for her life.

———

By morning, Jill felt that God had answered her prayers. Feeling peaceful, she was ready to leave the troubling case behind. And that wasn't all she planned to leave behind. She had also decided it was time to let go of her feelings for Craig. Since New Year's Eve, he hadn't shown the slightest romantic interest in her. She was just fooling herself to think she could take him away from Caroline. Nor did she really want to. She would put closure on her past and look toward the future.

Not everyone was destined for marriage and children. Hadn't she once believed this? She had refused to marry David when she had the opportunity. Her life had been filled with far too much excitement to even think of settling down.

She frowned. If she never saw another senator it would be too soon. Politics were dirty and dishonest. And digging deeper might collapse the foundation of her family even more. She finally agreed with one of Jeff's points—the family was more important than salvaging her career.

Although most of her anger at her mother had dissipated through her prayer time, Jill was still hoping to avoid her, so she tiptoed down the steps to the kitchen for some breakfast. Her mother was nowhere to be found, but she had left a note.

> *Dear Jill,*
>
> *There is so much to say, but all I am going to say this morning is that I am truly sorry. I know you need some time alone, so I have gone to spend the day with Kathy and Marion. Hope you can have dinner with me tonight.*
>
> *Love, Mother*

Jill knew she had to forgive her mother even though she didn't feel like it. Besides, didn't God promise that if she would forgive, he would change her heart? She tucked the note into the pocket of her robe. She would have dinner with her mother tonight.

But what to do before then? She didn't know what to do with her time off. She wandered the house aimlessly for a while, then sat down with a few newspapers. Flipping through the pages of the *Chicago Tribune,* her eyes stopped on the help-wanted ads. There was an ad for a corporate business writer in Oak Park, and another for a research position at a company downtown. Jill had the qualifications for both. Circling the ads, she had a sudden inspiration to head for the city to check out the job market, have her hair trimmed, and spend at least one afternoon perusing the Art Institute. Hurriedly, she picked up the phone to call Craig. Thankfully, Marge was busy on another line so she didn't stop to chat but put Jill right through.

"Craig, it's Jill. If your offer still stands, I'd like to take the week off. I've decided to drive over to Chicago to get away for a few days." She held her breath, hoping Craig hadn't changed his mind.

"That's a great idea. I'm glad you're getting away, but could we have dinner tonight? There's something urgent I have to discuss with you that can't wait a week." He spoke with some urgency. "I need to see you right away."

"Craig, I'm sorry, but my mother has already asked me to have dinner with her tonight." Jill felt relieved to have that ready excuse. She wasn't so sure she wanted to see Craig right now. It would be difficult to let go of her feelings if he was sitting right across from her. Time away would give her strength.

But it looked like he wouldn't let her off the hook that easily. "How about breakfast tomorrow?"

"Well, I don't know. Is 6:30 A.M. too early for you? I want to leave for Chicago midmorning."

"Nope. I'll meet you at Millie's at 6:30 A.M. sharp."

After a nutritious breakfast of her mother's Bran Buds cereal

and some fresh fruit, she responded to a couple of the classified ads by e-mailing her resume. She would follow up with
some calls today to set up job interviews. Next she called to
reserve a room at the Embassy Suites for Wednesday, Thursday,
and Friday nights. With her plans in place, her spirits slightly
lifted. Next she lugged a couple of her suitcases out of the
closet and spent her entire day sorting, organizing, packing,
and throwing out things she no longer needed.

Jill left a voice mail for Chuck on his phone at police headquarters, explaining she had to cancel their date since she was
going to Chicago. By late afternoon the packing was done;
she decided to go out for a run around the lake. By the time
she returned, she felt relaxed.

That night, over quiche lorraine and a salad, the two
women made small talk about the weather, Pearl's upcoming
trip to Europe, and the latest fashions, until Pearl mustered
up the courage to broach the more serious subject on both
their minds.

"Darling, I hope all these new revelations concerning our
family haven't turned you away from God. I was so pleased
that you were rediscovering your faith."

Jill said nothing.

"I hope you can forgive me, Jill."

"Mom, I do forgive both you and Dad, but it's going to
take me some time to recover from the shock of all of this."

"Take all the time you need; I'll be here for you when
you're ready to talk some more." She tucked a check into
Jill's hand.

Jill cautiously opened the check. It was for $15,000. "I
can't take this," she protested. "I won't."

"But it belongs to you. It's a stock dividend. I've been in-
structing our financial advisor to reinvest all the dividends,

but I thought you and Kathy could use a little mad money. I gave Kathy hers today too."

"But Mom, I know how Dad earned this money. I could never take this." She pushed the check away.

"No, this money is from my family's trust," Pearl explained. "I signed over the trust to you girls a few months ago, and all the legal work should be completed soon. Your grandfather earned this money legitimately in our family lumber business, so you can take it in good conscience."

"Mom, I don't understand. Why didn't you and Dad use this money when he lost his job in Chicago?"

"Because your father refused it; he was too proud. He wanted to support his family with his own hands, and he insisted that I save my money for you girls to have one day."

Jill sighed. "With that noble attitude, it makes you wonder how he ever got mixed up in this adoption scandal, doesn't it?"

"I don't think your father knew clearly just what he was getting into when he first got involved. He trusted Tom Burke Sr.; the man was your father's lawyer when we lived in Chicago. After a few years of being involved, when your father realized what was happening, he wanted to get out, but it was too late—he was in too deep. It was your investigation that gave him the courage to do the right thing."

"Yes, but it was also my investigation that killed him."

"Jill, stop blaming yourself. Your father knew he was putting his life at risk, but the Scriptures tell us it is better to lose your life doing the right thing than to live in sin. Your father died a noble death," Pearl said proudly. "He had gotten his heart right with the Lord, and he was ready to meet his Savior. I find great comfort in that, and I have you to thank, darling." She wiped the tears from her eyes. "Your father knew he was putting his life at risk."

Jill wiped her eyes too. "Poor Dad."

"Darling, he's in a much better place than we are. And it will make you happy to know that your father set up a foundation with most of his money to take care of the families overseas who were wronged by this adoption scandal; he also helped begin several Christian and community charities. Now go on and take this check," she insisted, handing it back to Jill.

Jill reluctantly took the check. It would come in handy, if she were to be honest with herself. Maybe she would use a portion of the check for a deposit and pay the first month's rent on an apartment in Chicago if the job market looked promising.

"Thanks, Mom. I'm leaving for Chicago in the morning, and this will come in handy. I'm planning to spend the rest of the week there looking for a job."

"But darling, Craig seemed to think that those copies of the checks and the letters in the files would help you get your job back at the *Gazette*."

I just can't figure this woman out! "Mom, I'm surprised you would want me to go back to the *Gazette*!"

"Until last night when you and Craig explained it, I just never understood what you really did before," her mother admitted. "But it's obvious you're using the talents God gave you to change the world. It's true that your father and I wanted something different for you, but I don't want to risk getting in the way of God's will."

Jill got up and hugged her mother. "I can't tell you how much this means to me. I'm not even sure I want my old job back, but it's so great to know that I would have your blessing if I did. And if I do resume my career, it doesn't mean I can't also have all the things you and Dad wanted for me."

"Like love, marriage, and a baby carriage." Pearl winked.

"And in that order," Jill teased. "Truthfully, I'm not sure I want to use that evidence to get my old job back."

"But what about Tom Burke Jr.? Surely you aren't going to let him get away with all this. If you don't stop him, he will likely be elected president. Didn't Craig say those copies of the checks and the letters would be enough evidence to stop him?"

"Yes, that would likely do it, but I'm not sure, with our family's name and safety at stake, that I want to be the one to expose him. Eventually, Burke will hang himself."

"Maybe so," Pearl worried, "but have you prayed about this?"

"I'm going to pray some more before I make my final decision, but right now I'm feeling led to close the file on this case."

"Have you told Craig?"

"No. I'm meeting him for breakfast tomorrow, and I plan to tell him then."

"Does he know you're going to Chicago?"

"I told him this morning."

"And he didn't try to talk you out of leaving?"

Jill shook her head. "He thought it was a good idea for me to get away for a while, but I didn't tell him I was job hunting. I'm going to wait until I have a solid offer and can give him my resignation and two weeks' notice."

"I'm sure he'll try to talk you into staying," Pearl guessed as she stood up to put the dishes away and straighten the kitchen.

"Well, he can try all he wants, but I'm not staying. It's just too painful for me." She got up from the table to help her mother carry the dishes to the sink.

Pearl looked at Jill sympathetically. "You've got an early morning breakfast meeting and a long drive to Chicago tomorrow. Go to bed, darling."

Jill headed for the stairs, but she hesitated a moment at the kitchen door. "Mom, do you believe every person is supposed to marry?"

Pearl folded her dish towel, put it down on the kitchen counter, and thought for a minute. "Genesis 2:18 says, 'It is not good for the man to be alone.' It was God who first saw man's need for companionship; he was the author of love and marriage. So, yes, I do believe that for most of us it *is* his will for us to marry. God is the one who put that longing in our hearts for a partner in the first place."

"But there are some people called to be single. Look at Mother Teresa and Corrie ten Boom."

"Yes, but God had another plan for them. They were filled with passion for the job he had given them to do, and they were totally fulfilled doing it. Do you believe you are one of those people?"

"I did. Truthfully, I never cared about getting married or having a family when I was working in Washington," Jill confessed. "Every time David talked about marriage, I avoided the subject."

"But that's all changed, hasn't it?" Mom prodded her.

Jill couldn't answer; she bit her lower lip and fought back the tears.

"It's Craig Martin, isn't it?"

Jill hung her head and sighed. "If only I had come back to Delavan sooner, before Craig Martin was spoken for."

"But remember, darling, God's timing is perfect." She put her arm around Jill, brushing the hair out of her eyes just as she had done when Jill was a child. "God brought you back to Delavan at just the right time."

"I wish I could believe that."

"Maybe you shouldn't be in such a rush to run off to Chicago. Perhaps you should just stay at the *Lakes* a while longer? To see what happens."

"Seeing Craig every day is just too painful for me. He's told me he has no romantic interest in me."

"But maybe things could work out between you and Craig if you stayed. Don't give up five minutes before the miracle happens. And believe me, if things don't work out, God will have someone even more special than him waiting for you somewhere."

"Yes, and that special someone might just be waiting for me in Chicago."

35

I don't think secrets agree with me.
I feel rumpled in my mind since you told me that.

—Louisa May Alcott

Jill felt an air of excitement as she loaded her bags into her Range Rover. Glancing at her watch, she realized she only had fifteen minutes to get to Millie's. Just as she stepped out the door, the phone rang.

"Jill, darling, it's for you!" Jill's mom ran out the door in her terry-cloth robe. "It's Annabelle, and she says it's urgent."

"Annabelle? Mom, would you please call Millie's Cafe on the other line and ask to speak to Craig? He's waiting there for me. Tell him I received an urgent phone call and that I'm running a few minutes late."

Mom nodded as Jill picked up the phone. "Hello?"

"Hel-lo, hel-lo, Jill!" Annabelle Stone's familiar singsong voice came through the phone loud and clear. "Hope I'm not calling too early, but this couldn't wait a minute longer. I set my alarm early just so I could make this call. Ready to come back for another turn at D.C. life and the paper?"

"What are you talking about?"

"Let's just say our solid-as-a-rock Senator Burke won't be going to the big white house on the hill as he'd hoped. More like he'll be moving into another big house and wearing stripes. They're arresting him as soon as the paperwork is completed. Can you jump on your laptop right now and bang out a story for me in the next couple of hours for tomorrow's edition? I had your assistant e-mail you all the pertinent details of the indictment that's being handed down. I want your byline on the story in the early morning edition. You deserve this one, kiddo."

"You must be joking," Jill felt the blood rushing to her face. "What happened?"

"The FBI paid me a little visit yesterday and gave me all the copies of your updated files with implicit instructions not to contact you until this morning. I set my alarm so I could get to the office early and personally offer you your old job back, with a promotion, of course, as soon as you get here. And I hope it's soon."

"I—I don't know what to say."

Jill could feel Annabelle's impatience through the phone. "You aren't going to hold a grudge, are you, and go to work for someone else? I'll double whatever they offer you. Rubric and I argued over who would call you. Finally we flipped for it, two out of three. Well, he won all three, but I convinced him that I had to do the dirty work and fire you so I should be the one to tell you the good news."

"Rubric always wins those tosses." Jill's head was spinning. "Did you say the FBI had copies of my files?"

"I have copies of your files right on my desk. Rubric and I spent most of the night poring over them. Wow, but you are the thorough reporter I remember. I'm right now ankle-deep in files containing your documents, pictures, interviews, police reports, news clippings, and suppositions; you've done some dynamite investigating right in your home state. Rube and I are so proud of our little protégé."

Jill clenched the phone in her hand. "Let me get this straight. The FBI gave you copies of my files? But how on earth did the FBI get my files?" She was silent for a moment, thinking. "Hmm. They must've been the ones who ransacked my room. They left the original files in their hiding place, but they must have copied them."

"They told me that *you* gave the files to them."

She snorted. "A likely story."

"But who cares how they got them?" Annabelle babbled. "The important thing is that the files and especially those canceled checks from the Tom Thumb Corporation and Burke's correspondence to your father are here. Your name is cleared, Senator Burke is going to jail, and I'm getting my ace reporter back! And it was the *Washington Gazette* that once again changed the course of history."

"Wait a minute—did you say canceled checks? And Tom Thumb?" she asked. "But Craig Martin was the only one who had copies of the canceled checks and those letters. And he was the only other person who knew about Tom Thumb."

"Yes, and that Craig Martin is the bureau's crown jewel. You made quite an impression on him."

"Craig Martin—not my boss at the *Lakes*?" She was stunned. "So he gave my files and those checks and letters to the FBI?"

"Jill, calm down," Annabelle ordered. "Listen to me. Didn't Craig explain all this to you at dinner last night? He promised he would."

"He invited me to dinner, but I had to cancel. I was just on my way over to meet him for breakfast when you called."

"Uh-oh," Annabelle mumbled.

"Exactly what was Craig supposed to tell me? That he handed over my files and those canceled checks to the FBI? Because if he had told me, I wouldn't have allowed it! I can't believe he betrayed me like that."

"Jill, Craig didn't give those files and checks to the FBI. You did."

"I most certainly did not! The only person I gave my files to was Craig Martin."

"Jill, Craig *is* the FBI."

Jill laughed. "Craig Martin, the FBI? Now I've heard it all."

"Yes, Craig is FBI. He's been working undercover in your hometown. He was sent there over a year ago to investigate the case—first your father, and then to work with you. By the way, I'm really sorry to hear about your father's involvement. I cannot imagine what this tragedy is doing to your family."

Jill couldn't speak for a moment. She didn't believe she'd ever felt so angry. "And all along I thought Craig Martin was my boss. He sure fooled me. He's even a decent writer."

"You can't tell a soul that I told you this. The bureau really didn't want to bring you in on this yet, but Craig insisted you could be trusted, and I want you back at your job so you can break the headlines. Of course, the FBI orchestrated this whole mess in the first place, getting you fired and then luring you back to Delavan. But you had no idea, did you?"

"But why?" Jill fought tears and wondered if the adoptive parents had never betrayed her. Was it all a sham arranged by the FBI?

"For a number of reasons. First of all, they suspected that you might have copies of your father's tapes, but when you were fired and didn't try to defend yourself, that theory was blown. They also figured if you were off the case, Burke's gang would let their guard down, but most importantly, they wanted you fired so they could force you back to Delavan."

"Well, it worked, but I don't understand why they'd want me in Delavan."

"If the killers hadn't confiscated the evidence from your father when they murdered him, you'd flush them out to look for it again when you showed up in Delavan and started snooping around. Also, you're much easier to keep tabs on in a little town like Delavan."

"And if they find the killers, the FBI will offer them a bargain in exchange for testimony against Burke," Jill surmised.

"You've got it, girl! Burke's dreams of living in the White House will dissolve into nightmares of living in another federal building . . . prison."

Jill didn't reply.

"We'll talk about this in more detail when you get here. In the meantime, I need my ace reporter back on board as soon as possible. The FBI is still desperately trying to flush out another guy who they believe is responsible for your father's murder. Until they do, Craig is still your boss and the managing editor at the *Lakes News*. Forget everything I've told you. Got it?"

"Ex-boss. He's my ex-boss."

"Does this mean you're coming back?"

"Annabelle, I think maybe you are an answer to prayer."

Annabelle laughed. "I've been called lots of things in my life but never that. I'll be looking for you sometime in the next week, okay?"

"I've already started packing. I could be back in a few days."

"Yahoo! Oh, but Jill, please tell Craig I'm sorry for blowing his cover."

"Oh, I'll tell him. Good-bye." She hung up the phone and immediately began pacing the floor. She just couldn't believe

Craig had been involved in this right from the beginning and had lied to her the entire time. Rubric was right; she should've trusted no one. *Wait a minute. Is that why Craig had wanted to be so close to me—so he could solve this case?*

"What on earth is wrong with you?" her mother asked when she saw her pacing back and forth in the kitchen. "Aren't you supposed to meet Craig?"

"Mom, my name has been cleared, and I'm going back to my job at the *Gazette.*"

"I was afraid of that."

"Hey, you said last night that you would be happy for me if I got my job back."

"I am." Her mom's smile looked forced. "I just didn't know it would be so soon. When do you leave?"

"This morning."

"But what about your trip to Chicago?"

Jill shrugged her shoulders. "Change of plans. There are a few loose ends I have to tie up first. I'll be back after my meeting with Craig to get my article written for the *Gazette* and pack the rest of my things."

Her mother sighed and poured herself a cup of tea. "I knew it was too good to last."

36

You have delighted us long enough.
—Jane Austen

Jill dashed out the door, hopped into her Range Rover, and sped down the road to Millie's. Her anger was so intense it frightened her; her heart was racing and her head felt like it was going to explode. Tapping the steering wheel to keep her hands from shaking, she wondered how Craig would tell her he was with the FBI. He would probably assume she would be happy to hear that her name was cleared and that she could return to the *Gazette*. Ha! Would he ever be surprised!

Arriving at Millie's, she parked the car and got out. Pushing the door to the cafe wide open, she stood there, huffing and puffing and looking for Craig.

"Where is he?" Jill called out in a voice at least three volumes louder than normal. With both hands planted firmly on her hips, she stomped around, searching the cafe.

Finally spotting Craig, she stood over his table and stared down at him. He gave her a sheepish grin and was about to say hello when his cell phone rang.

"Uh, excuse me just a moment, Jill." He flipped open his

phone. "Hello?" he said with forced cheerfulness as he motioned for her to sit down.

She remained standing, tapping her foot.

"Oh, hello," he said. A long pause followed. "I didn't think it mattered."

Jill just stood there staring at him.

"I know," Craig said into the phone as he looked up at her. "Yeah, there's not much traffic in Delavan, and she's . . . uh . . . she's standing right here." Another pause. "Okay, thanks. Good-bye."

As soon as he was off the phone, Jill slammed her hand on the table. "Why did you have my files and those copies of the checks sent to Annabelle without my permission?"

"You, uh . . . we, us together have done a crackerjack job discovering and putting pieces together. I wanted your editor to have the pieces so you could clear your name. And so you could get your job back."

Jill reluctantly slid into the booth across from him. "Maybe, just maybe, I decided I no longer wanted the investigation solved. Those files and canceled checks and letters were not yours to send. This is *my* family and *my* life that you feel you can just do whatever you want with! You betrayed me, Craig Martin." Her voice lowered to a whisper. "I trusted you, and you gave the FBI all my documents. And now Annabelle has them too! I didn't want the investigation to continue. And now it's too late."

"But, Jill," he said, "you had no choice. This is a federal investigation."

She bent over and hissed into his ear so no one could hear. "And furthermore, why didn't you tell me you were with the FBI?"

"I, uh . . . you know the answer to that," he whispered.

"You're an investigator. You know I had no choice. I was working undercover."

Jill knew that was the truth, that he didn't really have a choice on that count. "Okay, I can accept that." Taking a deep breath she continued more calmly, "But you've ruined my life and the lives of my family in the process."

Craig spoke between clenched teeth. "Your name is cleared. You got your old job back. When this case breaks tomorrow, Senator Burke will eventually land in jail for a long time, and you'll go back to being America's heroine. Isn't that what you wanted all along?"

"What I wanted? This is obviously what *you* wanted. I guess it's a good way to get rid of me too, huh?" she said loudly, causing all eyes in the cafe to stare at her.

"Let's step outside." Craig got up and led her out of the restaurant and into the parking lot. Once outside, Jill saw Max walking toward them. She could feel Craig tense at her side.

Max tipped his hat. "Well, if it isn't my two favorite reporters. Good morn—uh . . ."

Jill saw Craig and Max exchange an odd look. The newspaper owner stopped quickly and walked past them and into the restaurant.

She shook her head as she watched him disappear through the doors of the restaurant. "So Max knows too?"

"Yes, and there is more I have to tell you, to explain to you." Craig reached out for her as he opened the door to his truck. Jill flatly refused his invitation to get inside. She stubbornly leaned against his truck as he continued to explain.

"I care about you."

"Interesting way of showing it. The first man I ever loved and trusted was my father, and he betrayed me. Even my own mother wasn't honest with me. Now you've betrayed me too.

Good-bye, Craig." She turned around and began walking away. "I'm on my way back to Washington as soon as I can finish packing my things," she tossed over her shoulder.

"Jill, please listen to me," Craig pleaded. "You're in a state of shock. If you'll let me explain everything, you'll understand."

Jill couldn't stop the words from coming out of her mouth. "Tell Caroline I hope she's happy," she spat out. "Now she can have you all to herself. I suppose she was in on this too, huh? Let's just get rid of Jill, send her back to Washington. You want me out of the way so you can hide your guilt for leading me on, pretending to care about me so you could gain my trust."

"Jill, that's not true—"

"Not true? Are you going to lie and say that your behavior toward me was appropriate? I'll bet your big boss in Washington would like to know what went on under that mistletoe on New Year's Eve."

"Everyone kisses everyone on New Year's Eve. It's a custom," Craig said lamely.

"Not the way you kissed me, Romeo!" She felt crushed, realizing that their kiss had meant so little to him.

She looked over at him. His face was reddening. "Okay," he said, "then who drove up to Egg Harbor the first weekend after we'd met and begged me to dance with her?"

"So now you're accusing me of seducing you?"

"I'm sorry. I didn't mean that. You get me so tied up in knots when I'm near you." He tried to touch her arm, but she pulled away.

"I hope you're happy, Craig. Tell Caroline I hope she's happy too." With that, she turned on her heels and stormed across the parking lot.

37

Some of the biggest failures I ever had were successes.
—Pearl Bailey

Jill's new position and salary at the *Gazette* afforded her a classy apartment with a view of the Potomac River. It was difficult for her to imagine that she had been back in Washington for only two months. Her time in Delavan seemed like a distant dream. At night she stood at her large windows to watch the lights of boats moving up and down the water; the view brought back memories of the lake outside her bedroom window in Delavan. She could also see the car lights moving in easy streams along the highways. So fast, so busy, they were all going places to see people—loved ones, families, friends—while she sat alone with a large box of Godiva chocolates and an extra large Diet Coke. Squishing each piece of candy, she prevented herself from devouring the whole box by eating only the ones containing nuts.

There was one positive to being alone: It brought her closer to God. She had more time to pray and study the Word, and she had recently joined a Bible study. She had learned that the more she quieted her feelings, the better she was able to hear his voice speak to her heart.

Of course, if she didn't want to be alone, there was always David. Since she had returned to Washington, he'd left messages for her every week at the *Gazette,* trying to persuade her to see him. But she never returned his calls. There wasn't much of a past and no future with him.

There had been no phone calls or e-mails or letters from Craig. *Maybe he and Caroline are on their honeymoon by now,* she thought sourly. It was painful to accept that every word Craig had spoken to her, every compliment he had given her, every kindness he had ever shown her, were all part of a deeper motive.

⸺

When she arrived at the office one morning, Landry told her, "Rubric is waiting for you."

Jill grabbed her messages. "Uh-oh. What could be wrong now?"

Landry smiled. "Don't be so negative. Maybe he has good news for you this time."

She slapped her palms on her forehead. "Does he ever have good news for me?" Still wearing her coat, she hurried down to Rubric's office.

"I've been waiting for you," he announced when she poked her head in the door.

She looked over at his green chair; it was dirtier than ever, so she decided to remain standing. "Good morning to you," she said.

"Where's the story? You said it would be ready last week."

"I know, I know." She sighed. "I'm waiting for one more piece of evidence as a backup."

"Do you even know where to find it?"

"My informant has already promised it to me. I'm expecting his call any day now."

"Good girl. Just make sure we're first to break the story." Rubric rapped his knuckles on the desk.

Jill nodded as she stepped back toward the door.

"Not so fast, I've got something that belongs to you." Rubric grinned as he fumbled around in the top drawer of his desk. "Hold out your hand."

Puzzled, she quickly removed her cashmere gloves and held out her hand. Rubric dropped a tiny silver coin into her palm.

"It's the sixpence!" Jill smiled. "Thanks, Rubric."

"Well, you've only asked me for it about a thousand times," he grumbled. "Sorry. I just kept forgetting to look for it and give it to you. Ran across it last night."

"What would've happened if the sixpence had been a bugging device?"

He frowned. "Your case may never have been solved, and you would never have gotten your job back either. You would probably be six feet under by now, if you really wanna know the truth."

Jill flipped the coin in the air. "Heads or tails, Rubric?"

"What are the stakes?"

"If I win the best two out of three, I get some time off. If you win, I'll take you to dinner," she replied.

"I knew there had to be a reason, but you're on," he said. "Heads."

Jill flipped the coin three times, and each time Rubric won.

"Okay, where do you want to go to dinner?"

"I'll have to think about it."

"How about if I cook for you? Did you know I'm taking cooking lessons?"

He made a face. "You want me to be your guinea pig? Not a chance. Let's go to Diamond Jim's Steak House."

"Yuck." Jill crinkled her nose. "The last time we were there, you found a bug in your salad."

"It was only a roach; they still have the best and the cheapest steaks in town."

"How would you know? You've never eaten anywhere else. Can't we go to Blackies' Steak House instead?"

He waved his hand in the air. "Get out of here, get to work," he ordered. "I'll decide where we're going to collect my steak dinner when you finish your story."

Jill tucked the sixpence into her pocket. It brought a smile to her face, reminding her of the handsome stranger who had left it with her. At the end of the day she rode the elevator downstairs and posted a note in the "Found" section of Helen's bulletin board at the newsstand. She truly hoped the handsome stranger might happen by and contact her.

"Helen, call me if he shows up. Here are all my numbers." Jill handed the proprietor her card along with the money for her chocolate. "The man who owns this coin is probably long gone, but maybe one day when he decides to get married, he'll remember his lost coin and come back to look for it."

"I wouldn't hold my breath, girlfriend!"

"Now, Helen, I never figured you for a pessimist."

"Somebody's been reading too many romance novels. Good night, Jill."

"Good night." Jill chuckled. She'd never read a romance novel in her life.

———

At work the next morning she stopped by Rubric's office to discuss her latest ideas for a new investigative assignment, but she began by sharing a bit of her newfound faith with him. She desperately wanted him to see his need for God.

"I never figured you for some religious nut, kid," he replied, "but you've driven me crazy since you came back from Delavan."

"I'm not a religious nut. I've found the truth."

"Why should I want to be a Christian when you're so miserable?" he teased her.

Jill figured he did have a point, since she wasn't exactly the poster child for joy. "I know I haven't appeared very happy," she tried to explain, "but because I trust God, I know that he is working in my life right now. I know that everything's going to be all right—that things are going to turn out no matter what, because God has a plan for my life. The goal is to get our stubborn wills in line with the heavenly Father's."

"Please save your sermons for the sinners."

"But we're all sinners," she persisted. "You, me, Annabelle —all of us."

"Annabelle wouldn't appreciate being called a sinner."

She sighed in frustration. "Rubric, I can see we're getting nowhere here. Could we talk about this later? I was wondering if I might be able to have a couple of weeks of vacation."

"You lost the coin toss—no days off. I won fair and square," he reminded her.

"Rube, please!" she begged.

"What about the new story?"

"I'm waiting for a call this afternoon to pick up my last package to write the story. I can finish it while I'm away."

He grunted. "Okay, what do you have in mind?"

"My mom leaves for Europe for a month in a couple of days, and I thought this might be the perfect opportunity to go home and snoop around the house for any clues or for my father's tapes, the ones everyone is looking for. It's virtually impossible to search the house while she's there."

"Isn't the FBI still working on the investigation? Why can't you leave it to them?"

"I have a personal agenda here. I lost my dad, and I want his killers brought to justice. I want Burke locked away for a long time."

"But they already have enough evidence to put him away till he's a hundred."

"Yes, but can you imagine what a conspiracy murder rap would do to that jail sentence? We wouldn't be subjected to that toothy grin again until we were in our rocking chairs on the front porch of a nursing home."

Rubric grunted again. "Are you sure this trip doesn't involve a certain FBI agent?"

"I won't see Craig while I'm there. Besides, he's probably gone back to wherever it was he came from. So what do you say? Think I could have some time off?"

"You know how excited Annabelle is over this new story; you have my blessing if you can persuade her."

Jill jumped up from her chair and flung her arms around the older man. "Thank you!" she called back as she walked toward the door.

"But you have to promise me you'll see that young FBI agent when you're there."

The comment was so unlike Rubric that Jill stopped dead in her tracks.

"I'm going home for one reason and one reason only," she replied haughtily. "And that is to discover who killed my dad. As far as Craig is concerned . . . he betrayed me, and I want to put all that behind me and get on with my life. And I told you, he's probably long gone from Delavan by now."

"A good reporter knows better than anybody that there's

often more to a story than meets the eye. Go home and find out the rest of the story before it's too late. And if you have the sense I think you have, you'll stay there."

She walked back toward him. "Wait just a minute. An old newspaper dog like you is telling me to walk away from the most powerful rag in the world?"

"I've actually thought about this. Do you want to end up like Annabelle and me? Aging and alone with no one to go home to every night?"

"But Rubric, you and Annabelle love what you do."

"If I could turn back the hands of time, I would've married that sweet little blonde who loved me. Instead she married the manager of a tire store, and together they bought a little house out in the suburbs and had five kids. There's not a day that goes by that I don't envy the guy and wish I could trade places with him. That would be happiness: To have someone to go home to who is happy to see you, glad you're alive, and can't do enough for you. That's life." He threw his hands up in the air.

"Rubric, I had no idea. And Annabelle? Was she in love once too?"

"In love? She was crazy in love, but she let him get away with that foolish pride of hers. If you ask her, she'll tell you the same thing. Get out of here, kid, before you have regrets like us, before it's too late."

"But what if it *is* too late? I mean, for all I know, Craig and Caroline may be married."

"Maybe not." He shrugged his shoulders. "In case you run off and get married and don't come back, I might as well give you this now." Opening his desk drawer, he reached in and fumbled around until he found a small black velvet box. He shoved it across the piles of paper in Jill's direction.

"For me?"

"Open it!"

Jill gasped when she looked inside. She couldn't believe her eyes—the most beautiful diamond cross she had ever seen. "Rubric, I can't possibly accept this."

"It belonged to my mother," he said gruffly. "I want you to have it."

"Oh, Rubric, I love it! This is the nicest present anyone ever gave me, and the most exquisite cross I have ever seen." Her eyes widened as she examined the antique necklace embedded with diamonds and seed pearls and hanging from a delicate gold chain.

"My mother loved that cross. She prayed for me every day. She would want you to have it since you're taking over for her . . . praying for me and harassing me."

"I won't let your mother down," Jill promised.

"Yeah, I'm sure of that."

Knowing Rubric despised displays of affection, she gave him a quick hug and told him good-bye.

When she got back to her office, she buzzed Jake Weber, Annabelle's assistant. After speaking to his boss, he summoned Jill to Annabelle's office.

"Save your breath. Rubric called," Annabelle explained, motioning Jill into an exquisite French chair covered with an imported silk fabric. Jake flipped papers on the desk for Annabelle's signature.

"Do you really think you'll find those files?"

"I do. And the timing is everything; my mom will be out of town."

"You can go, but if you blow this new story, I'm warning you, you'll be looking for another job for good this time." Annabelle pointed a shiny red nail at her as Jake rolled his eyes.

"You'll get your story. Thank you, Annabelle—you won't be sorry."

Jill went back to her office and thought of Craig and everyone else in Delavan. She even missed the newsroom. She laughed fondly, thinking about Miss Cornelia and Marge and Petey Bird. They'd all taught her so many wonderful things about good reporting and what was important. And Delavan had brought her back to the Lord too.

She jumped when her phone rang.

"Hello?"

"Jill Lewis at the *Gazette*?" the husky male voice asked.

"Yes."

"I have some information about a situation on the Hill concerning the donkey farm. Are you interested?"

It was the call she'd been waiting for, the call that would put the finishing touches on her current story. "I'm interested. There's a little pub on the corner of Fourth Street and Fifth Avenue. I'll meet you there in twenty minutes."

"Right," he answered.

"Wait, how will I know you?"

"I know you."

Then silence.

———

Twenty minutes later, Jill was sitting at a corner table, repeatedly checking her watch and glancing toward the door. Finally a lumpy-looking man strode over to her table. He dropped a large brown envelope in front of her.

"I'm the one who called you. Sorry I'm late, but just as I was walking out of the house, my kid's dog got hit by a truck and died. I got sidetracked."

"Oh my goodness! I'm so sorry to hear about your dog. It must be hard on you, Mr . . . ?"

"Yeah, yeah," he said while waving his arms in the air. "Just call me Roy."

"What was the dog's name?"

"Princess."

"Princess? What a cute name. I have—had a dog named Gracie."

"Listen, do you want this information or not?"

"Yes, of course." She took the envelope filled with the documentation she needed to uncover the scandal. "Here's your money." She handed him an envelope containing a stack of large bills.

The man quickly stuffed the cash into his jacket pocket. "Where are you going in such a hurry?" he asked curiously as Jill snatched her purse from the table.

"Home. I'm going home."

38

True knowledge comes only through suffering.
—Elizabeth Barrett Browning

Jill hopped on the Metro and didn't look back. When she returned to her apartment, she began throwing things into her suitcase while she dialed her mother's number, hoping she hadn't left for Paris yet.

"Hello," her mom answered.

"Mom, it's Jill."

"Darling, you just caught me. I'm leaving in an hour."

"How would you like to have a house sitter?"

"Anyone I know?"

"Me! I'm coming home for a short break. I thought it would be nice and quiet there."

"You wouldn't be coming back for any particular reason, would you?"

Jill rolled her eyes. "If you are thinking of Craig, no. I have no idea where he is."

"He's here in Delavan. Never left. He's still working at the paper."

He won't be there for long, Jill figured.

Several nights later, Jill's car splashed into town on the wet streets. When she turned up the long drive of her family's estate, she felt truly lonely. For the first time in her life, no one would be waiting to welcome her home. Lugging her bag up the stairs, she remembered the last time she had come home almost a year ago. So much had happened since then.

The house creaked and groaned. After she said her prayers she collapsed into bed, allowing herself to think of Craig and then falling into a dreamless sleep.

The next morning she awoke at the crack of dawn with boundless energy for the task at hand. She began her search for information—the tapes she hoped her father had hidden somewhere in the house. Besides bringing her father's killer to justice, the tapes she desperately sought would help Jill restore what was left of her father's reputation, as well as restoring the family name. These tapes would likely contain other names of individuals involved in the scandal. In all her career, there had never been another story Jill had wanted to break more than this one.

She stopped at 8:00 A.M. and worked on the story for Annabelle until noon. It was moving quickly, so she was confident she still had a job. By the day's end the house was in shambles. She would give her mother's cleaning lady a call to come and put it all back together after she was done.

On a mission to discover the truth, she continued going through the house for days, but nothing turned up. By the end of the week she had come to terms with the fact that she would probably never find the missing tape; maybe they were at the bottom of a garbage dump or had been turned to ashes and lay in an incinerator. Or maybe her dad had the file with him when he was murdered, and the killers took it.

After her fruitless search, her thoughts turned to Craig. Wanting to put their relationship to rest once and for all, she picked up the telephone.

"Hi, Marge, this is Jill."

"Hi! It's good to hear from you. We miss you sooo much."

"I miss you too. Is Craig in?" She held her breath and closed her eyes as if wishing over a birthday cake.

"Right here."

"Engaged or married yet?"

"He is? I didn't know that!" Marge breathed with surprise. "He never said a word. To whom?"

"So he's not married yet?" Jill's heart soared.

A male voice suddenly spoke into the phone. "Hello?"

"Hi, Craig, this is Jill." The sound of his voice brought tears to her eyes.

"Jill who?"

Same old Craig. "Very funny. Listen, I'd like to see you."

"Sorry, I don't have plans to visit D.C. anytime soon."

"But I'm here in Delavan." She gathered up her courage. "How would you like to come over for dinner tonight? I'm cooking, and it's not from the Duck Inn. I've actually been taking culinary classes back in Washington."

There was a long pause. "Sorry, but I'm busy. Deadlines."

"You have to eat somewhere. I thought you might bring those files of Senator Burke's contributors. You don't have to stay. I need to see you, Craig. I want to tell you I'm sorry. I was so angry when I left, but I'm back at my job and I'm very happy now."

"You're happy?" He sounded surprised. "I'm glad, Jill. You deserve to be happy."

"Never been happier in my life." She winced at the lie. She missed him terribly, and she missed everyone in the little shop of newsies. But a girl had her pride.

"Okay, I'll try. I need to ask your forgiveness too. I didn't mean to hurt you, Jill, and I can understand why you were so upset, but you have to understand the position I was in at the time. I got a little too personally involved, and I'm sorry for that."

Jill bit her lip. "I know. You're only human, after all. So let's be friends again. Stop by whenever you finish. I'll be up late anyway, and I can heat something up for you."

"I'll do my best. If I can't make it, I'll have someone else drop off your files."

"Great."

She hung up the receiver. It was hopeless; Craig had been less than enthusiastic at the sound of her voice. Well, she would go to the grocery store and fix dinner anyway.

On her way back from the store, she decided to stop by Kathy's for a minute. Her mother must've told Kathy that she was going to be in town, but her sister hadn't bothered to call. Jill decided she would drive over to make amends.

———

Pulling into the grand estate's drive, Jill could see Kathy's gardeners hard at work, landscaping the grounds. She parked the car and slowly walked up to the front door. She was about to ring the bell when the door flew open and Kathy appeared with a look of surprise.

"Jill! Mom told me you were visiting."

The two wrapped their arms around each other. Kathy led her out to the garden patio, where they sat and enjoyed the view of the river.

Turning to face her sister, Jill spoke from her heart. "Kathy, I am so sorry for all the hurt I dredged up. Please forgive me."

"You're forgiven! I just want to put it all behind us. We're sisters. We're family."

Kathy paused and then surprised Jill when she added, "You know, I'm glad they got Burke. Dad would've been pleased."

"Thanks." She decided to drop any more talk of the newspaper or the investigation. She was sure the copies of the canceled checks made out to their father and featured in all the newspapers across the country had been a major source of pain and humiliation for Kathy and Jeff, as well as her mother.

"Today's our anniversary," Kathy spoke up, snapping Jill out of her thoughts.

"Kathy, happy anniversary. I'm sorry. I forgot."

"You always forget."

"I know, I know. One thing God has shown me through this whole ordeal is that the greatest things in life are him and my family—not my career."

"That's something I thought I'd never hear!" Kathy smiled. "So how are you, Jill? How is it to be back in Washington?"

"Great. I actually got a promotion and a raise, and I've moved into a gorgeous new apartment that overlooks the Potomac. Even Mom would approve. I wish you could come down to help me decorate."

"I would love that. And I know Marion would adore spending a couple of days with her favorite auntie. Maybe the next time Jeff has to go out of town, we'll fly down."

"Please do. We can show Marion the Smithsonian."

"She's a little young for that, but we'd really enjoy just visiting with you."

Jill nodded. "So, what are you doing for your anniversary?"

"Well, we were going to drive down to Chicago for dinner

at the Ivanhoe Restaurant, then see a show at the Steppenwolf Theatre and stay overnight, but our baby-sitter just called to cancel."

"I'll do it. Why don't I keep her at Mom's house overnight so you and Jeff can have a nice night in Chicago?"

"Oh, that won't be necessary."

"I know it's not necessary, but I'll be going back to Washington soon, and I'd love to spend the time with Marion. Consider it an anniversary present."

"Actually, Marion's not feeling very well. She's been running a fever."

"Nothing serious, I hope?"

"Just a cold." Kathy thought for a moment and said, "I suppose it would be all right. I'll pack some Tylenol you can give her later. I'll go get her bag."

Later that afternoon, Jill drove the short distance back to her mother's house with little Marion and her bag for the night. She settled Marion and her favorite doll on a quilt on the floor in the breakfast room. Then she popped in a *Veggie Tales* video and checked her messages.

She had a message from Kathy saying that Jill had left the Tylenol on the counter and that she and Jeff would drop it off on their way to Chicago. Jill hurriedly dialed her sister. "Kathy, it's out of your way. Don't worry about the Tylenol, I'll bundle Marion up and run out to the store. Have fun tonight!"

"Thanks, Jill. That would be great," Kathy replied. "See you tomorrow."

On her way out of the driveway, with Marion sitting in the back in her car seat, Jill noticed a car with two occupants that slowed down as it passed her house. *Mom must've asked one of her friends to keep an eye on the place while she was away,* she thought. She waved at the two figures in the car, but they didn't wave back.

39

Mortal love is but the licking of honey from thorns.

—Anonymous woman

When Jill returned from the store, she settled Marion on the couch for a nap, since the little girl was tired, and began carefully cooking for Craig. She would be prepared if he did come by, and if he didn't, she would send a plate to him with the person who delivered the files.

She read the recipe directions over and over to make sure she clearly understood what she had to do in order to make the meal edible. She prayed it would be delicious, knowing she was taking a big step of faith by cooking. She measured and remeasured.

No more serving Duck Inn food and passing it off as her own. No more pretenses—only raw honesty served alongside raw carrots. After lifting the heavy pan containing a sizzling pork tenderloin out of the oven, she basted the meat multiple times with apple juice before sliding it back inside and raising the temperature.

Then she pulled a firm acorn squash out of the brown paper bag and cut it in half with a large, sharp knife. She dug out the seeds and cut up the tender flesh into smaller pieces. A frying pan with butter was heating on a medium flame, to which she added brown sugar and the squash pieces for sautéing. As she stirred the contents together, she thought of how she liked the way her dinner for two was taking shape. The delicious aroma delighted her newly discovered culinary senses.

What was the fastest way to a man's heart? Whatever it was, she was covering all her bases tonight!

With her dinner under control, Jill decided to check on Marion. She had given her niece liquid Tylenol only an hour before, and Marion remained lethargic under its power. Her skin felt clammy and cool to Jill's touch. The little girl wouldn't be eating any of Jill's dinner this evening. Jell-O and chicken soup were on the menu.

Glancing at the wall clock, Jill saw it was 6:00 P.M. She rushed to set the table in the breakfast nook. Just as she was about to change into some nicer clothes, she heard little whimpering sounds coming from Marion.

"What is it, sweetie? Are you feeling sicker?" Jill stroked her head with the palm of her hand and said a little prayer.

"I hungry, hot dogs," Marion whined as she came to a sitting position while reaching her arms in the air for Jill to pick her up. Jill carried the child to the table and fastened her into the booster seat.

She poured apple juice into a cup for the little girl, then opened the refrigerator to look inside. "I don't see any hot dogs in here. How about some soup?"

"No, hot dogs!" Marion demanded, pounding the cup on the table and causing little sprays of juice to rain through the air.

Mom might have hot dogs in the basement in the big freezer. Her heart beat quickly just thinking about going down into the pitch darkness. "Are you sure you want hot dogs?"

"Hot dogs!" the cranky child repeated.

"Why must you be so hard to please tonight?" Jill gently teased with a grin spreading across her face. She went through the drawers, but she couldn't find any working flashlights. She wished she had replaced the broken one after her last trip down into the dungeon. She slowly opened the creaky door, turned on the light at the top of the stairs, and peered down into the basement. Somewhere in the darkness below hung a very skinny string that would banish any boogiemen hiding in the shadows. Leaving the door open wide for more light and, more importantly, so she could hear Marion, Jill took a deep breath and started down the steps.

"Auntie Jill is going to get your hot dogs, Marion. I'll be right back."

Creak, creak, creak. With each step she took, she shuddered as she felt cobwebs swiping her face and then clinging to her hair. She swatted her hand back and forth in front of herself to fend off those plump, fuzzy, water spiders that bred copiously in damp basements.

Finally her feet hit the cement floor. The light from the hallway above streamed down and stopped about two feet from the bottom of the steps. She shuffled her feet, like an old woman on fresh ice, while waving her hand around in search of the thin, elusive string hanging somewhere beyond the reach of the upstairs light. Finally she found the string. She pulled and breathed a big sigh of relief when the light came on. Now feeling brave, she stoically walked to the large freezer and pulled up the lid. Locked! Not remembering where her mother had said the key was, she searched the entire room for it, even looking behind the freezer and on the wooden ledges along the room. But all she found was lots of dust.

After catching sight of a hammer on the worktable, she gave the metal lock a few hard whacks. The lid of the freezer sprang open, and waves of cold air wafted up into her face.

Once it subsided, she saw two packages of rock-hard, frozen hot dogs and a large package wrapped in freezer paper right next to it at the bottom. The letters "FBI" were written in black marker across it. She couldn't believe her eyes.

"Dad's tapes!" Jill squealed. "Thank you, Jesus." She reached for the package of files, but suddenly the lights flickered and then went out, sending the basement into blackness. Her knees went weak. Hearing terrified three-year-old wails coming from upstairs, Jill dropped the tapes back in the freezer and slammed the lid shut.

"Mommy! I want my mommy!" Marion screamed. The little girl's voice seemed muffled and sounded like it was fading into the dark distance.

Jill reached out her hands and groped her way to the stairs like a blind person, chastising herself again for not replacing the flashlight she had broken. She shuffled her feet along in the darkness while feebly edging her way toward the direction of the steps.

"Auntie Jill is on her way, Marion. I'm coming!" she called up to the first story, which seemed like the top of the Empire State Building from where she stood.

Her toes reached the steps, and she fell hard on her knees, not having expected the steps to be right there. Pain shot through her legs from landing on the hard wood. She faced the invisible steps before her and slowly began to inch her way up on her hands and knees. Her palms and knees became gritty from the steps as she carefully felt her way along to make sure she didn't topple off either side of the stairs, since there was no railing. The steps were open to the cement below, and she didn't want to fall headfirst onto the hard floor.

She was at the top step when the door slammed shut in her face. She felt a wave of nausea wash over her. Why would the door slam shut? There was no open window, and Marion was buckled into her booster chair.

"Craig?" she cried hopefully.

As she reached forward, something came straight out of the darkness from behind her. A man's strong arm began pulling her back down the steps. She dropped to a sitting position to make it more difficult for the intruder to drag her back down to the belly of the basement. As she kicked her legs high up in the air toward the direction of the intruder, the other hairy arm grabbed her by the throat. She bit him hard and long, refusing to let go.

He backhanded her across the face, causing her to fall backward off the side of the steps and then headfirst onto the cold, unforgiving cement floor six feet below. She landed with a crack, and blood spurted from her head. She immediately felt the warm stickiness of it cascading down her face and rolling down her neck and onto her clothing. The pain was intense. "God help me!" she cried out.

Raising her arm toward the direction of the basement door, she mustered up a weak, "Marion, I'm coming." As she tried to sit up, the darkness encased her. She fell back to the floor, unconscious.

A bright light in the distance turned on and then quickly faded. She felt pain in her neck and head and back. *Marion. Marion. Marion.* She kept going back into the fog, and faces whirled and twisted around her. *Marion.* Outstretched hands reached for her. Voices, she heard familiar voices in the darkness. Suddenly everything faded to gray and then black again.

She didn't know how long she had been unconscious. She tried to lift her head. The blood had coagulated on her face;

she touched her fingers to it gently, but the pain was shocking and the blood felt pasty. Trying to get to her feet but still feeling very dazed, she fell back on her knees.

Curiously, the basement light was back on. Feeling painful waves like fire with each move she made, she ignored the feelings as she crawled across the hard floor to the steps. She pulled herself up on the first step and then collapsed. *Dear heavenly Father, help me!* She laid her head on the first step for a few minutes and pulled herself up again before crawling on the second step and then the third. She heard the buzzer from the oven going off in the kitchen and suddenly remembered Marion. She had to get to the top.

After what seemed like an endless struggle, Jill made it to the door at the top of the stairs. Listening intently, she only heard the silence. She reached out her red-stained arm and struggled with the doorknob, but it slipped from her bloody grasp. Again and again she tried to turn it. Finally she managed to get a grip; she turned the knob, and the door opened—freedom at last! Now she could call for help.

But he was waiting for her. She collapsed from pain and fear at his feet just inside the hallway. Even with the stocking mask she knew who it was. Barrows.

She looked up at him. "Where is she? Where's Marion?"

He responded with a sinister laugh and reached down to grab her by her hair, dragging her into the kitchen. Hearing the buzzer from the timer on the stove, Barrows dropped her abruptly and reached for a pan to toss at it. Following a loud crash, the noise ceased. Barrows turned his attention back to Jill.

"Who took Marion? Tell me where she is," she demanded while bravely looking up at the towering intruder.

"As soon as you give me those tapes, you'll get the girl back."

"But I don't have the tapes. I haven't found them."

"You lying witch." He began kicking Jill in the ribs with his steel-toed boots. She moaned as she writhed in pain on the kitchen floor.

"You'll give me those tapes now!" he yelled.

Overwhelmed by pain and fear, Jill felt confused but knew one thing for sure: If she gave Barrows the tapes, she would never see Marion again. Turning her head away from her attacker, she suddenly caught sight of Marion's empty chair and panicked to the point of bargaining.

"If you'll have Marion brought back here, I give you my word that I'll give you the tapes."

"You're not calling the shots," Barrows reminded her. "If you know where those tapes are, you give them to me now." He shoved a pistol against her neck.

"No! Not until I can see Marion," Jill repeated firmly, undaunted by the cold steel pressing into her flesh.

"I'll show you who's in charge," he raged. Surprisingly, he returned the gun to his shoulder holster and then stepped on her with his left foot in an effort to hold her down.

And then she knew. Terror filled her soul as she heard the whoosh of his belt slipping out of the loops of his pants.

Jill whimpered as she squirmed to escape from under the weight of his foot. "Please, God, please help me," she cried, but she was unable to move.

"Shut up! Shut up! There's nobody to help you now," he yelled. Breathing heavily, he bent down over her. Mustering all the strength within her, Jill retaliated, beating his chest with her fists and scratching his face with her nails. She pulled back her feet and thrust them hard into his belly, but the man wouldn't move. Angered, he reared his hand back and slapped her face so hard she saw stars.

She had no strength left to fight off her attacker; her eyes frantically searched the room for anything she might use as a weapon, but there was nothing within her reach. In desperation she waved her hands in surrender, whimpering, "Stop, stop! Please, no. Stop, I'll give you the tapes—just please bring Marion back to me."

He didn't respond. Tightly shutting her eyes, she prayed God would have mercy on her.

Suddenly a light shone from outside. Car lights flooded the kitchen, and then a door slammed; they both looked toward the kitchen. Jill was sobbing uncontrollably as Barrows sprang to his feet. At the sound of the knock on the door, he reached down and yanked Jill to her feet by her arm, shoving her to one side of the entrance. He threw her a dish towel to hold against her head to catch the blood trickling down the side of her face. *It must be Craig,* she thought.

Barrows moved across from her to the opposite side of the door. He pulled his weapon and cocked the hammer. Jill leaned forward. In walked Cornelia Southworth, carrying the files. Jill groaned. As Cornelia walked in, Jill's hope walked out.

"Hi, honey," Cornelia said, quietly closing the door against the cool night air. Jill's reply stuck in her throat like a burr, but Miss Cornelia didn't seem to notice as she continued chattering.

"Craig asked me to bring these to you," the older lady said, clutching the files to her chest. "He had to work late . . . deadlines, you know. He tried to call but your phone was out of order, so I volunteered to stop by with these. I've got to be on my way though. I'm covering the party over at the Grahams' house tonight. What do you think of my outfit?" She spun around to model her fuzzy, lime-green outfit with matching coat, shoes, and hat, stopping when she narrowly missed Jill's feet.

At last catching a glimpse of Jill's bloody and beaten face, the older woman screamed. "Yeeeeeeeeeek!"

The bloodcurdling sound climbed octaves as Cornelia's eyes darted from Jill to Barrows, and then back to Jill as Barrows pointed his gun at the women.

"Quiet!" he roared. "Give me the files, you old hag."

Cornelia dropped the bundle she carried. Barrows picked up the files and put them on the table. He then herded the two women into the hall closet and moved a heavy chest to block the door once the ladies were forced inside.

Inside the dark closet, Cornelia began to wail. Jill reached over and turned on the light switch.

"Oh, my. Oh, my," Cornelia gasped. "How do you feel, darling?" She patted Jill's face with her hand and then pulled it back quickly, horrified by the blood smeared across her glove. In a motherly gesture, the older woman reached up and pulled a coat off a hanger and wrapped it around Jill's shoulders. Jill took Miss Cornelia's hand and prayed silently. *Dear Lord, please protect us. Show us a way out of here. Please, Lord.* All of a sudden the prayer was interrupted by the sound of terse voices coming from outside the closet door. Then she heard the sounds of a struggle.

"It's Craig!" Jill whispered. "He'll save us."

Miss Cornelia squeezed her hand. "Oh yes, Craig did say he might drop by later. I forgot to tell you. It must be him!"

Both women started screaming his name and beating on the closet door as the tussle continued. They heard Jill's mom's fine crystal shatter on the parquet floor, and then the sounds of toppling chairs. Finally a shot rang out.

"Oh, please don't let it be Craig. Please, God," Jill begged. "Please don't let him die. Keep him safe in your arms. Please, God." She turned to Miss Cornelia. "We have to go get help!

Craig may have been shot. We can't just wait in here. Every second counts!"

"But what can we do?" The perplexed older lady shook her head.

"I don't know. Wait, do you have a cell phone?"

"Well, no. My Herman was going to buy me one, but—"

"Never mind, let me think a minute." Jill closed her eyes. Suddenly the answer came to her. "Why didn't I think of it before? There's a trapdoor in here leading to the porch! It used to be the opening for the firewood, but then Dad had it converted for a second coat closet. I think I can push it out and squeeze through it."

"But can I?" Cornelia asked as she considered her wide hips.

Jill kicked the trapdoor open and climbed out on the porch. A rush of cold air made her head begin to ache and her open wounds sting. She knew she had to squeeze Cornelia through. The older woman removed her coat, and Jill succeeded in pulling her out of the closet after several attempts.

"I think I left fifty pounds back there," an incredulous Miss Cornelia said as she sized up the hole she had just come through.

"Do you have your car keys?" Jill whispered.

"They're in my purse."

"Where's your purse?"

"Uh, in the closet." Cornelia bent down to go back inside, but Jill pushed her gently aside.

"Stay quiet and I'll be right back." Jill wiggled through the opening again and found the purse and fumbled for the keys.

When Jill got back outside, she whispered to Miss Cornelia. "Run for it!"

The two women ran for the car, and Cornelia jumped into the driver's seat as Jill slid through the other door.

"Step on it!" Jill screamed.

The big old Cadillac sputtered and then sped away with a jerk.

"Floor it, Miss Cornelia. We've got to get help for Craig and find Marion."

The older lady maneuvered the big car down the drive.

By the time they pulled into the main road, Jill's heart sank when she glanced into the rearview mirror and saw the patrol car behind them in hot pursuit. It was Barrows. She feared Craig had been shot and Marion was far away now even as they flew down the highway.

The police car was gaining on them.

Cornelia steered her trusty old Cadillac through the dark narrow road next to the river. They could see the bright lights of town in the distance as they headed onto the bumpy, country roads that would take them there. They were only a few miles from the police station.

Just then they were rear-ended by the pursuing car. Lurching forward violently, both women began to scream again. Another hard hit by the police car followed, but this time Barrows didn't back off. The patrol car was pushing their car toward the river embankment. Thoughts of her father and his last minutes on this same road flooded her mind.

Cornelia made a hard left turn to avoid being forced into the woods. Though she was pressing the brakes, the car no longer could remain on the road. Their bodies jerked violently as the car nicked the first tree. A second tree spun the enormous car about, sending it careening down the embankment toward the river despite all Cornelia's efforts to keep it from doing so. Jill felt as though she was reliving her father's death.

The force of cold steel broke through thick branches of

hundred-year-old trees as if it were a hunter snapping fallen twigs beneath his boot. Cornelia jammed the brakes all the way to the floor.

"Oh, dear God, save us!" Jill screamed in the dark car. Cornelia shielded Jill as best she could from the breaking windshield and the branches reaching in the car. There was a loud thud as the Cadillac came to a sudden stop.

The stillness lasted a few seconds, but then the car began to dip and turn in a seesaw manner. With utter horror, Jill realized the car had landed in the shallow banks of the river. Wildly glancing around, she saw the black water surrounding them.

The water began to move the car in a large circular motion, riding them toward the center of the angry grip of the river and then with the current to the lake. Their only hope was to get out as quickly as possible.

Words from Isaiah rang in Jill's ears. *"When you pass through the waters, I will be with you; and when you pass through the rivers, they will not sweep over you."*

She unbuckled her seat belt and then tried to make Cornelia's belt release, but the strap only tightened. They were in danger of sinking now as the car began to dip and tilt. Seconds mattered in their fight for life, and it was a fight for Marion and Craig's lives too, if they were still alive. Suddenly an eerie calm washed over Jill as the frigid waters rushed into the car. So this must be what happens when you're dying. With the little strength she had left, she tugged at the buckle on Cornelia's seat belt one more time, and at last it came apart.

She wasn't going to die! God was with them, right here. Until that moment Jill had been looking down at the problem, not up to the way out. The water showed her the exit. She pushed toward the weight of it as it spilled through the broken windshield.

"Kick your feet!" she shouted at Cornelia. "Swim."

Gasping for air and frantically kicking their way through the water, they finally broke the surface. Jill looked just in time to see the car turn on its side and sink beneath the surface. She thought she heard someone call her name amid Cornelia's screams but couldn't be certain.

"Help! I can't swim, Jill! I can't swim!" the older lady howled.

Trembling, with her teeth chattering, Jill clung to Cornelia tightly. She saw lights along the shore as the river's current continued to pull them slowly downstream. With one arm she held on to Cornelia and with the other she paddled hard as she frantically kicked her legs. Her wild efforts made little if any difference. Her heart raced as her mind searched for the solution.

Jill was freezing and knew Cornelia would not be able to tolerate the cold waters much longer. Just then they slammed into a large floating log. She held on to rest for a moment. It was the small reprieve she needed to go toward the lights on the shoreline and not in the direction the current was pulling them. She thought she heard someone calling her name again.

"Here!" she shouted with all her might, but her voice was the size of a murmur. She focused on the older lady. "Miss Cornelia, I'm going to need both arms to swim us toward the shore. I have a very important job for you. I want you to hold on to my back with both of your hands as tightly as you can and kick those feet of yours as if you were running a race. Can you do that?"

"I think I can," Cornelia said, speaking between gasps and tears.

With Cornelia holding on to her shoulder, Jill shoved them away from the log and swam in the opposite direction from where the river beckoned to take them. Cornelia began to sing "Jesus Loves Me" and coughed out the water that ran into her mouth. Jill imagined God's angels protecting them, cheering them onward.

The sound of the water rolled in her ears. Water rushed in and out of her mouth as she gasped for air. It tasted of dead fish and gasoline. She felt the tired muscles in her legs and arms begging to give up and surrender.

At long last, with one of her hardest kicks, she felt something solid under her. They had miraculously reached the shallow embankment. She dragged the heavy woman up to the shallows. Shaking badly, they collapsed onto the ground.

Lying on her back next to the whimpering older woman, Jill looked up at a night sky filled with stars. Tears glistened in her eyes.

We're alive! Thank you, God!

Suddenly off in the distance she heard her name being called again. It wasn't her imagination after all. She opened her eyes, and she saw him. He was running down the embankment to the river, right toward them. It was Craig, and he was alive!

"Craig!" she screamed. "Craig!"

"Here we are, Craig!" Miss Cornelia shouted. "We're down here."

Jill tried to stand, but her muscles felt like rubber and she fell to the ground. Reaching the women, Craig bent down on the bank of the river and held them in his arms, pressing them tightly against his chest. Jill could hear his muffled sobs of relief.

She wanted to tell Craig what had happened, what Barrows had tried to do to her. She needed to tell him Barrows had Marion, but then she caught sight of the blood on the front of his shirt. She wanted to ask him how he was, but the words would not come.

"Are we alive, Craig?" Cornelia gasped.

"Of course we're alive," he assured her. Taking his jacket off he put it around Jill, the more seriously injured of the two women, and then he fastened his down-filled vest onto Miss Cornelia. "I've got to get back up to the road to meet the police and the rescue units to let them know where you are. Will you be okay here?"

"No! No! Please don't leave us," Miss Cornelia wailed, clinging tightly to his ripped and bloodied shirt.

"Can the two of you walk up the embankment if I help you?"

"I—I'll try," Miss Cornelia whimpered. Jill nodded. Both shivered from the cold.

Cornelia looked back toward the river and began to wail again. "I lost my car, and I think I lost my hat too. Do you see my hat anywhere? It matches this outfit."

Craig shook his head and began to help the two women to their feet. Catching a glimpse of Jill's face in the moonlight, he gasped. He brushed a lock of hair from her eyes.

"Jill, we've got to get you to the hospital right away," he whispered with deep concern that seemed to breathe life into her.

"Oh, Craig, you're alive!" She put her head against his chest. "But they—they have Marion." She buried her head in his shoulder. "Oh, Craig, we've got to find her!"

"We'll find her, but you've got to save your strength. You're badly hurt."

"Was that you calling to me?" Jill whimpered deliriously. "I heard you. I followed your voice. Oh, Craig, I love you; I can say the words now. I thought you were dead, but you're here, and while I still have a chance to tell you—I love you!"

Craig touched the side of Jill's face and then wrapped his

arms more tightly around both women, pulling them closer. "Please hang on, ladies; it's just a few more steps."

"I thought you were dead," Jill muttered, clinging to him. "I thought you'd been killed, but you're alive!"

Miss Cornelia stared at his wound. "Are—are you hurt?" she stammered.

"Just a superficial wound," Craig explained. "Barrows was waiting for me when Gracie and I arrived at the Lewis home, and we got into a tussle over the gun. He fired and thought I was dead. I knew I had to find you before he did, but I couldn't risk him knowing I was alive. He was searching frantically for the tapes within a few feet of me. When he heard the car, he went after you, and I followed."

Craig looked at Jill. "Jill, did Barrows hurt you, or are your injuries from the accident in the river?"

She started to cry. "He beat me," she sobbed. "And he . . ."

"Jill, you've got to tell me. Did he rape you?"

"Oh, Craig, no, but it was so awful!" She began to cry hysterically. "God protected me."

"I'm sorry, Jill. I'm so sorry. You're going to be okay now."

The injured trio valiantly struggled up the steep bank, pulling each other along and grabbing tall weeds and tree trunks to help their climb. Finally, at last reaching the roadside, they could see rescue cars farther down at the spot where the Cadillac had gone into the river. Feeling that they were safe at last, the three began walking toward the vehicles.

But suddenly Barrows sprang at them from out of the darkness and pointed his gun in their direction.

"Forgive me for sounding repetitious, but I really do need those tapes. Tell me where the information is, Jill, if you want your boyfriend to stay alive. And I'm not through with you yet either." He smirked darkly, looking her up and down.

"Don't tell him, Jill. He'll kill us all if you tell him," Craig warned.

"But Craig, he has Marion somewhere! Where is Marion?"

"Far, far away," Barrows taunted her.

"I want to go home!" Cornelia wailed.

Ignoring them, Barrows aimed the gun at Craig and pulled the hammer back.

Appearing out of nowhere, Gracie jumped on Craig in greeting just as Barrows fired his gun. The dog howled in pain as she took the bullet for her master.

Craig lunged at the officer. The gun went off again, the bullet hitting the ground this time. Craig grabbed the gun out of his hand.

Jill screamed. "Please don't kill him, Craig! He's got Marion somewhere! We've got to find her!"

"Tell us where the girl is," Craig demanded, pulling back the hammer and pointing the gun at Barrows.

Barrows laughed and folded his arms across his chest.

"Don't make me use this!" Craig yelled. Barrows dove for the gun, but Craig turned the weapon around and hit him squarely in the forehead with the butt of it, rendering the man unconscious as he fell to the ground.

Craig turned toward Jill. She could feel the color drain from her face.

"Craig . . . Dad's tapes. . . they're in the basement in the free—" Before she could finish, her world went black.

All during the night, Jill tossed and turned, calling for Marion. The events of the day were whirling in her mind. Something within her memory was trying to tell her something, but she couldn't sort it out. The fragments melted together, and it was impossible for her to sort out the pieces one by one.

Two days later, she awoke with a migraine thumping inside her head as lines ran to and from her body to the machines that hummed and beeped at her bedside. Her whole body ached. With the fog lifting from her head, she thought of Marion and began to scream. "Nurse, nurse!"

A nurse rushed into the room. "What's the matter?"

"Is there any news about my niece, Marion?"

The nurse shrugged her shoulders and then shook her head. "I'm sorry."

"And what about Miss Cornelia and Craig?"

"They're both fine. Mrs. Southworth is in a room down the hall, and Mr. Martin stops by several times a day to check on both of you." Lightly touching the thick bandage wrapped across Jill's forehead, the caregiver explained her injuries. "You had a concussion, and it took over twenty stitches to close the wound in your head and another eight to sew up the damage done to your face. Mrs. Southworth is suffering from a mild case of shock, and her blood pressure is elevated, but you're both going to be fine."

"What day is it?"

"Friday. You've been sleeping for two days now. How do you feel this morning?"

She winced. "My ribs, they're killing me. It hurts when I move and even when I breathe. When can I get out of here?"

"We're going to move you to a room shortly."

"Meaning I can't go home today?"

"We're discharging your friend today, but you've got a concussion and you're pretty banged up, young lady. I've called the orderlies to wheel you down to your room."

Minutes after Jill was settled in her room and her doctors

gave their approval, FBI along with police officers swarmed in, all of them wanting answers to their questions.

Jill struggled with what she could remember, but the details hung like a thick fog in her memory. Feeling frustrated, she desperately tried to reach the information she knew was inside her head, knowing each moment was crucial. But she was of no help.

Finally alone, Craig appeared at the door, his arm in a sling, bearing an enormous bouquet of flowers.

"You're looking better, Jill. How are you feeling?" he inquired.

"Do you have any word on Marion?"

He sighed loudly. "Kathy and Jeff have practically camped out at the police station. Barrows is in jail and isn't talking. They've offered a substantial six-figure reward for Marion's return, and they put out an all-points bulletin. Her picture is on all the television stations, and her face is plastered on every newspaper from here to Chicago to Milwaukee, even up in Door County. All the border police have been alerted too. We'll find her, Jill."

"But will Kathy and Jeff ever forgive me?"

He squeezed her hand. "They're very concerned for you. How could they possibly blame you? Oh, and I finally reached your mother in France. She's on a flight out this morning."

"And Gracie? I'm sorry, my mind is in such a fog; I almost forgot about Gracie. Please tell me she's alive."

"Gracie is fine." Craig smiled. "I stopped by Kelsey's Veterinarian Clinic to check on her this morning before I came here. She saved my life. How can I ever thank you for that dog?"

"Don't thank me," Jill said with a smile, suddenly feeling better. "Gracie was strictly a God thing! The moment Mary Muelling gave me Gracie at the Bernese Mountain Dog Show,

I knew she was to be your Christmas present. After all, you're the one who assigned me to the dog show in the first place. God works everything out . . . every little piece to the puzzle fits, doesn't it?"

"And you've got to believe that's exactly what he will do with Marion too."

"Oh, Craig, I wish I could believe you, but I'm so worried. Most of these kidnappings don't have happy endings, and consider the people we're dealing with." She shuddered. "They wouldn't hesitate to do away with Marion."

"But there're so many people praying," Craig offered reassuringly.

"Did you find Dad's tapes? Anything that might lead us to the kidnappers?"

"The tapes are in safe hands now, and warrants for arrests are being issued. But it has nothing to lead us to Marion or to your father's killers. Barrows is our only hope. We still won't get Burke on a murder charge unless there's something in your father's tapes that personally implicates Barrows, or if he confesses and names his accomplices. But I do believe that we will get him."

Later, when Jill was alone in her room, her body rested but her mind raced like a computer. She sorted through information, sights, sounds, smells, and feelings from that horrible night.

Even the sight of Craig hadn't distracted her from her mission.

40

It doesn't matter who my father was;
it matters who I remember he was.

—Anne Sexton

Just past midnight, Jill was thrashing around in a fitful sleep. Lights blinked on and off in her mind. A loving hand reached out to help her, but suddenly it transformed into a gnarled and ugly stub. Barrows's hand. He was trying to attack her again. The sounds of Marion screaming resonated about the walls of her room.

The screams were replaced by unintelligible voices. She listened again. *Marion, Marion, Marion.* There was a familiar male voice, but it wasn't Craig. Whose was it then? She listened to more garbled words, and then there was light and then darkness again. The voice spoke again. *I heard a familiar voice as I lay unconscious on the cellar floor. But who was it?*

Jill bolted upright in bed, suddenly wide awake from her nightmare. She grabbed the phone on her bedside table, pushed the number 9 for a line out of the hospital, and then punched in the rest of the number.

"Hello, Craig here." The voice sounded groggy.

"Craig? Craig! Can you get over here right away and spring me from this place? I know where Marion is and who has her!"

"I'll be there right away." The phone clicked.

Jill set the phone back onto the receiver. She gingerly slid out of bed and tiptoed into the bathroom. As she took off the neck brace, she moaned, biting her lip from the pain. Her aching body longed for the safety of her bed. But little Maid Marion could not wait one moment longer to be rescued.

Jill dressed in her street clothes, refastened her neck brace, and cracked open the door to peek out into the corridor. She had forgotten about the guards. They were drinking coffee and talking amongst themselves. Slowly she shut the door. She looked around the room, noticing the window. She was certainly skinny enough to slip through. She looked out her second floor window and planned her escape route to the parking lot below.

Every inch of her body aching, Jill maneuvered out of the window. She jumped down a couple of feet to an overhang and then slid down it to the next level. Catching her breath for a minute, she stood back up and hobbled down the metal steps. Truck headlights whirled down the street toward her. Jill moaned in pain as she awaited Craig's arrival at the side entrance to the hospital.

When his truck pulled up beside her, Craig jumped out. "What do you think you're doing out here? Have you lost your mind? How did you get past the guards?"

"When God closes a door, he opens a window," she said with an effort at a smile. "We don't have much time."

"The window! What on earth were you thinking?" Craig said. "I'm taking you back to your room."

Jill refused to budge. "No way. I'm getting Marion back. Will you help me or not?"

He groaned. "I need to check myself into the mental ward for letting you talk me into this," he said while helping her into his truck. After he got back in on the driver's side he turned to look at her. "Jill, you look awful. Are you sure you're okay?"

"I'm okay. Besides, I don't have any choice. I have to find Marion."

He gently reached over to take her hand. "You haven't told me what Barrows did to you," he said with concern. "You're sure he didn't touch you?"

"I—I'm sure."

"You don't act so sure. Tell me what he did to you." Craig's brow furrowed, and Jill saw a flash of anger zigzag across his eyes. "Barrows will pay for this."

She broke down and cried. He reached over and put one arm around her.

"All I know is that when I cried out to God, Miss Cornelia came walking through that door."

Craig smiled at her. He gently rubbed her arm. "You've grown in your faith since I've known you."

"Thanks to you, Mom, Kathy, and all the others who prayed for me."

"You've just got to remember that those same people are praying for Marion too. She's going to be okay." He sat up in the driver's seat and started his truck. "Now tell me what this crazy notion of yours is. What are you asking me to do?"

"Drive."

"To where?"

"Egg Harbor, to Chuck's cabin."

Craig groaned, started the truck, and put his hands on the wheel. "I think you lost your mind when you fell. Chuck doesn't have a cabin. He lives in Delavan. You're confused. I'm the one who has a cabin at Egg Harbor, remember?"

"Chuck has Marion. I'm sure of it. He's there with her at his cabin, you'll see."

"Okay, I have my doubts, but I'm listening." He sighed and pulled out of the circular drive of the hospital and started down the dark road that would take them north to Egg Harbor.

"As I was on the basement floor floating in and out of consciousness, I know now I heard Chuck's voice," she explained. "Everything was scrambled up together and I couldn't understand it before now. But as I tried to sleep tonight, it all started to sort itself out. I remember hearing Marion screaming, and now I'm sure I heard two men's voices: Barrows and Chuck.

"My mind is clearer now. I remember a cabin with the rose trellises, and I know that cabin! It was Chuck's. He and my mom talked about it when he came over to our house on the night of the break-in and then again the night of the storm. He's there with Marion, I'm sure of it."

Craig sighed loudly. "Jill, I will drive up to Egg Harbor with you, but I've got to remind you that Chuck and Barrows were not on the best of terms. Chuck is a good guy. Explain to me why you think they worked together?"

"Their competitiveness was all an act to throw us off their path. Barrows has been arrested, and Chuck has Marion at his cabin and is trying to figure out what to do now. He's afraid that sooner or later Barrows is going to implicate him—so he needs to get out of the country.

"I believe they were hired by Senator Burke's crowd to kill my dad because he was about to turn in evidence. Somehow Burke got wind of it. When Dad finally got a guilty conscience, he compiled the evidence to give to the FBI. Senator Burke had to stop him and brought Chuck and Barrows in to help. They played off each other to divert the suspicion.

"My family has a history with Chuck, and I really did trust him. But do you remember the night of the storm when he said he was investigating a prowler? He said the neighbors called the police on their cell phone. There was no cell service; I know, I'd tried. I joked about what kind of service the neighbor must have had and said I wanted it! But now I think it was Chuck who was breaking into our solarium. If I'm right about him, he has Marion up at his cabin."

Craig pulled out his cell phone.

"No! Please don't call the FBI," Jill said, pulling the phone from him. "I want to make sure first that I'm right. And if I am right, then I don't want them to go in there with their guns firing."

Craig pulled back his cell phone and began to dial again.

"Please, I asked you not to call!" she pleaded.

"I'm calling Caroline."

"What on earth for?"

"Uh, I don't know how to tell you this," Craig stammered.

"What?"

"Caroline is an FBI agent."

"She wasn't your roommate?"

"Sort of. You see, both my cabin and the one next door were part of an FBI stakeout. Fred, the photographer, and Caroline and I are agents from the Chicago and D.C. bureaus. When your father became an informant, we moved our operation here. We've been trying to get Burke for a long, long time. When we found out you were breaking the story, we escalated our pursuit, but we began working on this covert operation long before you began your investigation."

"You knew my dad?" Tears welled in Jill's eyes.

"Very well. Your father and I became very close. I was

working in the Chicago agency when your dad decided to assist the FBI and called me. We arranged to meet in Chicago, and we worked together for a while before he died. It's hard to believe he's been gone for two years now. After he was killed I was assigned to Washington Bureau, where I worked on the Burke case until I was assigned to work with you back in March. Of course, you didn't get here until October."

"The FBI must have thought I was an idiot and that you were brilliant when I ran to you my first week on the job and asked for your help."

"Of course not." Craig laughed. "Definitely surprised, because we never dreamed our strategy would work so quickly. I guess you could say we had chemistry and bonded quickly."

"So Max knew too?"

"Yeah, but those were the only people—your father, Max, and Chuck Emerson."

"Is Chuck with the FBI?"

"No, but he's been working for us as an informant."

"So Chuck knew my father was murdered?"

"Actually, no. He investigated the accident and was convinced it was an accident, but we knew differently. Chuck has been a real asset to us; he may not be the best cop, but he's a great informant."

"A crooked one," Jill replied with conviction.

"That would surprise me. Chuck's been a big help to us."

"I hope you're right, because our families go back a long way, but I'm afraid that he may have sold out . . . just like my dad did."

"Jill, I must tell you, your father was a good man, and he loved you very much. He got involved in the adoption scandal before he realized all the ramifications. He was horrified over the operations, but it was too late to get out. When he tried to do something about it, he lost his life."

"Oh, Craig, thank you. I'm so glad he knew you and you knew him. That means so much to me."

"We'll discuss this more later. I've got to reach Caroline and call in some backup units and a helicopter. I'm trusting in your instincts."

"It's more than a hunch; I just know that God is leading me."

Craig dialed Caroline on the phone at the cabin. He left a message. "Call me on my cell phone." He dialed again and left the same message on her cell phone.

Next he dialed the FBI headquarters in Madison. "Craig Martin here. I need a helicopter and a couple of units, plus two EMTs up at Egg Harbor." He turned to Jill. "What's the name of the street?"

"I don't know the number," she said, "but it's the old Emerson cottage on Miller's Creek Road near the corner of Deer Trail and Trout Lane. They also have a home on Webb Way, but it's not that one; it's the cottage."

Craig relayed the information. "They'll be able to locate the street address if the cabin is still in the name of Emerson. Do you have his father's name?"

"It's Norman."

Craig turned back to the phone and gave the name. "Proceed with caution," he told the dispatcher on the phone. "Agent Jennings will be on site. My position is three and a half hours away. Thanks."

Dialing again, he left a message on Fred's phone. "Hey, buddy, head back to Egg Harbor ASAP. Miller's Creek Road."

Next he called Caroline.

"Get over to Miller's Creek Road. Our friend Chuck may have the little girl there. Stake out the house and wait, and make sure they don't leave. I'm on my way there, but it'll take three hours. Backup is on the way from Madison—air and ground. I'll explain the rest later, just trust me on this."

After hanging up, he glanced over at Jill. "Did you bring along some pain medication?"

She shook her head.

"I couldn't help but notice your two black eyes."

"Thanks for the news bulletin." She tried to quell those familiar feelings of affection that washed over her. Her mind was clearing now, and she suddenly remembered expressing her love to him. She felt her face heat up, but she quickly put it out of her mind. She had to focus; she couldn't let herself get distracted, not until Marion was safe.

A while later, Caroline called with an update. She had the cabin under surveillance.

"Does she believe you?" Jill asked after Craig hung up the phone.

"Well, there's no sign of any activity. Only Chuck's truck is there, which is pretty normal."

"But, Craig, don't you see? Chuck is there, just as I suspected. He told Mom and me that he hasn't been up to that old cabin in years."

"I know, Jill. I believe you, especially since his truck is there."

"Thanks. Can we drive any faster?"

"I'm going as fast as I can without putting our lives in danger."

———

An hour later, Jill and Craig pulled onto Miller's Creek Road. They drove past the cabin and noticed that Chuck's truck was still parked behind, just as Caroline had described.

Craig tried to reach Caroline on her cell phone, but there was no answer.

He tried radio contact, but her radio was apparently not turned on. "There's nothing to worry about; we'll just drive down the road until we spot her car."

As they slowly perused the houses on the road, they saw no sign of Caroline or her vehicle. Craig figured her SUV was hidden from view. He drove down the road slowly a second time.

"Where is she?" he wondered aloud. Jill sensed his concern and prayed silently.

"I'll go check it out. Wait here." He pulled out his gun. Jumping out of the truck, he moved swiftly and skillfully from window to window and then disappeared from Jill's sight. A few minutes later, he came back carrying Marion's shoes in his hand.

Jill couldn't move. Then her body began to tremble violently. "Where is Marion? Could he have killed her?" she asked with hysteria rising in her voice. "Why would he take her out without her shoes?"

"Calm down, Jill. There's no sign of anyone in the house. Chuck apparently isn't here, but he was earlier because there's still smoke coming out of the chimney. Marion's clothes were in the trash out back and so were the bags from several children's department stores. Chuck must've bought her all new clothes." He got back in the truck. "And there's something else."

"Tell me."

"Marion is now a redhead," he said, tossing an empty box of hair coloring at her. "Let's go look for Caroline again before we search the house."

Craig parked on the road so that the pine trees obscured the view of the truck. Jill opened the door and stifled her cry of pain as she got out.

"Jill, stay here."

"Not a chance."

"You have no business traipsing around in your condition.'

"This is my investigation," she reminded him.

He shook his head, probably realizing it was useless to persuade her to take care of herself.

They followed the path leading down to the lake. From there they made their way through trees and around stacks of piers piled up on lawns. The piers were still dry-docked. The lake path was quite narrow, and the earth was muddy. Fallen tree limbs suggested a recent rainstorm.

Craig moved easily through all the debris while Jill lumbered along, stopping from time to time to hold her side and catch her breath.

Craig turned around and scowled at her. "You should've stayed at the hospital. I need my head examined to have let you come along."

"I refuse to argue with you right now. Let's just keep walking."

There was no sign of Caroline anywhere. Suddenly Craig spotted fresh tire tracks in the drive of a home several doors down. Surveying the area, he next pointed out some broken glass near the tracks and picked it up.

"This isn't a good sign. Let's get back to the cabin and take a look around."

As they walked up on the front porch, Craig turned to Jill and put his finger to his lips. Then he ducked his head low as he hurried up beneath the wide expanse of windows across the front of the winterized cabin. He looked in the windows and then knocked on the door. Returning from circling the cabin, he held his arms up in the air. "There's no one here."

Jill picked up a rock. "Let's unlock the door and see what

we find inside." She threw the rock through the door's window. Craig reached in gingerly and turned the lock from the inside. He opened the door and allowed Jill to go in first.

Jill and Craig walked through the house, looking for any clues as to where Chuck and Marion and Caroline could be. As Craig looked through the living area, Jill entered the bedroom. She gasped when she saw a small iron bed with ropes tied to it. "Craig!" she screamed.

Craig ran to join her. "What's wrong? What did you find?"

Jill pointed to the ropes on the bed. Her voice trembling, she said, "Do you think he kept her tied up all this time?" She started crying.

Craig held her for a moment, then pulled away. He put his hands gently on her shoulders and looked into her eyes. "Jill, I know this is upsetting, but we've got to focus on finding Marion. Why don't you go through the garbage cans and see if you can find anything there. I'll finish searching the rest of the rooms."

Jill nodded and wiped away the tears. She went through the garbage in all the rooms and threw the contents together in the middle of the living room as if she were about to light a bonfire. She sat on the floor to carefully go through each piece as Craig sorted through papers near the phone and looked through kitchen cabinets.

Lord, show us the way, she prayed.

Then she found a crumpled up piece of paper. "Craig!" she called out. "They're on their way to Washington Island. Look, here's a piece of paper with a phone number on it. It says W.I. Ferry."

Craig took the paper from her hand and called the number. "Hello. I was wondering if you have any ferries running today to the island?" He scribbled on his notepad. "Okay, one at noon and one at 4:00 this afternoon. Thanks. Are there any cars scheduled to be transported today? Okay, thanks." He hung up and turned to Jill. "Two at noon and three at 4:00. We've got to alert the FBI before Chuck gets to the ferry."

She put her hand on his arm. "Craig, no. I want to get Marion first. If the FBI shows up, there's a chance she could be hurt."

"I'm taking this decision out of your hands. Washington Island is open to private boats, and they could get to Canada on one. We also have no idea which ferry they'll be on."

"Okay," she relented. "What did Caroline say to you the last time you talked?" she asked as they walked out to the car.

"She said that Chuck's truck was outside his cabin and there appeared to be no signs of movement. The guy obviously surprised her. He probably took her as a hostage. No border guard is likely to question a mother and father with their child. But on our side, the border patrol has received an all-points bulletin, so they're likely checking out every young female child. Plus, we've called in both Caroline and Chuck's descriptions. There's hope even if Marion has been disguised."

At 11:30 they pulled up to the ferry dock at the tip of Door County in Gill's Rock. Craig parked behind the fish hatchery and pulled his parka up over his head so he wouldn't be easily identified.

Looking for the SUV, Jill almost didn't notice the taxi that drove up. Two adults got out with a child. Only a handful of people milled about. It was not yet the busy season; every person there could be easily seen.

Jill waited from behind the parked cars, where she had a clear view of the bay. And suddenly she could hear a child squeal and cry. "Marion," she whispered. "Auntie Jill is right here. Just be brave a little longer, please. Please, Lord. Keep her calm. Keep Caroline safe. Give her wisdom."

She looked around frantically and saw Chuck greeting the boat pilot as he bought their tickets. She could hear his voice, but his words weren't clear. She knew Craig had told her to stay back, but now that Marion was so close, she couldn't help but creep closer and closer.

Chuck wasn't even looking around him. She believed she could get right to Marion before he even knew it. But she wanted to help Caroline as well. The woman looked frightened, and her body language told Jill she was protecting little Marion. *God bless Caroline.*

Suddenly the ferry captain started the engine. Only a few passengers stood on the top deck. Chuck began to walk toward it with Caroline and Marion. In the distance Jill heard a helicopter.

She rushed toward the ferry. Out of the corner of her eye, she saw Craig waving her away. She kept right on going. Just as she reached Marion, the little girl turned around.

"Auntie Jill!" She beamed and reached for her aunt.

Chuck turned and in one motion pulled his gun from his pocket.

Caroline screamed and knocked the weapon from his hands, and the gun bounced once before landing in the water. Before Jill picked up Marion and ran slapdash back to the truck, she saw Craig rush up and handcuff Chuck. Once she reached the vehicle, she saw the helicopter land and several agents disembark.

Jill held her niece close to her. "I like your red hair," she said softly, trying to interject calm in a frightening situation.

Marion didn't say anything, just clung more tightly to Jill.

Jill laughed shakily and pulled out her cell phone to call Kathy and Jeff. "Marion and I are on our way home!"

She then looked up to see Caroline running into Craig's arms. Watching the two of them embrace, Jill suddenly collapsed.

41

To a generous mind few circumstances are more afflicting
Than a discovery of perfidy in those whom we have trust.

—Ann Radcliffe

With a sudden jerk, Jill awakened from a surreal, drug-induced slumber. For a brief moment she had no idea where she was or how she got there. Sitting up in bed, she tried desperately to clear her head as scenes from the basement, Barrows's attack, the car going into the river, Cornelia, the hospital, and a terrified Marion spun around in her head.

The terror returned with intensity as the events of the past few days began whirling in her mind. They had Marion! She thrashed about under the covers, trying to get out of bed. But suddenly a comforting, familiar face came to her mind. It was Craig. He was smiling.

Feelings of love for Craig flooded her soul, but her sorrow quickly returned when she remembered Caroline and Craig's embrace. Everything from that point on was a blur—her mind was blank.

Despite her pain, Jill swung her legs around and off the bed.

"Just where do you think you're going, young lady?" Her mother's familiar tone floated in through the room.

"How is Marion?"

"Other than a little separation anxiety, she's fine. She's at home with Kathy and Jeff. You do remember that she was rescued—thanks to you?"

"I remember that, but nothing else. How long ago was that?"

"Two days ago. We brought you home from the hospital yesterday," Pearl explained.

"I had to go back to the hospital?"

"I don't recall that you were ever released!" Her mother smiled. "A little bird told me that you snuck out of there."

"And for good reason."

"Oh, Jill. If it hadn't been for you, Marion could have been—"

"Let's don't even go there. God heard our prayers."

"Yes, and he intricately wove all the pieces together leading you to Marion."

"And you were a part of that too. If you hadn't questioned Chuck about his parents' old lake cottage, I never would've known where to find Marion."

"God is good." Her mom smiled. "But poor Chuck. I feel so sad for his parents."

Jill folded her arms over her chest. "Well, I'm not feeling very sympathetic toward poor old Chuck. Mom, I don't know how to tell you this, but it's likely that Senator Burke's people hired him and Barrows to kill Dad."

Mom turned away from her. "Let's not talk about that. I couldn't bear for his parents to have to live with that knowledge."

Once again, her mother demonstrated she was the queen of denial. Quickly she changed the subject. "Do you remember coming home in the ambulance yesterday?"

"No, I don't. To be truthful, the last thing I remember is seeing Craig and Caroline embrace." She paused. "Mom, has Craig . . ." She was afraid to hear her mother's answer. "Has Craig been to see me?"

"No, darling, he hasn't, not since the first time you were taken to the hospital while we were still searching for Marion. He's probably very busy with the case. You know he's with the FBI?"

"Yes, I've known for some time. Obviously all I was to Craig was an important piece of the puzzle that helped him solve a big case." She feared the man she had learned to love and respect, her laid-back editor at the *Lakes,* was only an illusion. Jill didn't really know this Craig, this FBI agent.

"Well, darling, Craig did send two of these beautiful bouquets. And there's one from Annabelle and Rubric, and one from the staff at the *Lakes.* There's even one from David. I put the cards that came with the flowers along with all the other cards on the desk for you to look at when you feel a little better. The cards are from everywhere—your little escapade made the national news! And your father is a hero." Pearl smiled widely.

"Dad's tapes, of course," Jill remembered. "What was in them?"

"The transcripts are all right there on your desk, along with that stack of cards," her mom offered. "Craig had them sent over. Jill, I think he's in love with you."

"Mom, you're wrong about that. There's another FBI agent . . . well, they're pretty tight."

"You mean Caroline? So she's an FBI agent too?"

"Yep. She's one of Craig's partners—in more ways than one." She hobbled over to her desk. She opened the files and began flipping through the hard copies of the tapes. "Oh my goodness, Dad was a genius!" she cried, dropping the files and heading toward her bathroom.

"Jill? Jill?" her mom called out. "Where do you think you're going?"

"To Washington. There are at least half a dozen other names here. Senators, cabinet members, judges. Guess they all needed campaign money. And I want to be there to break the story!"

When she reached the bathroom, Jill could hear her mom mumbling to herself. "And I was hoping for a wedding."

42

Eyes what are they?
Colored glass,
Where reflections come and pass.
Open windows—by them sit
Beauty, Learning, Love, and Wit.

—Mary Coleridge

Jill turned her chair toward the window and occasionally stopped working on her laptop to look at the cherry trees blowing in the breeze. It was time to put the story of the adoption scandal to rest. Senator Burke had been indicted for several counts of fraud, extortion, and capital murder one, along with several other politicians and businessmen on various counts.

Jill said a silent prayer of thanks that her father had washed his hands of the deal before his death. *Good job, Dad.* She beamed as she typed his name numerous times into her article. "Annabelle is right, this is a Pulitzer Prize winner for sure, and it belongs to you and me," she said aloud.

Hours later, Rubric stopped by. He dragged a chair next to hers. "As soon as you finish this story, I'm ordering you to take some time off. You've had two major investigations and stories the past few months. You need some rest."

"I like it here. The soot and city is in my blood."

"It doesn't have to be. Why don't you take some time off and go to Chicago—see a few plays, browse the museums, and have dinner at some of the finest restaurants in the world? I know a great little steak house there."

"Chicago? You must be joking. If I were going anywhere, it would have lots of sandy beaches. You don't fool me for a minute. There's a certain FBI agent in Chicago you want me to see." She shook her head. "I never figured you for playing Cupid, Rubric. Sorry, but my heart is closed for business."

"So that explains why he sent you a letter?"

"Hey, how do you know about that? Oh, right, you must've bribed Johnny down in the mailroom." She shrugged her shoulders. "It was a note of congratulations, nothing more."

Rubric chuckled.

Jill spun around in her chair and opened her drawer. She pulled out Craig's note and held it up for Rubric to see. "Read it for yourself."

He scanned the note and then returned it to her. "Landry told me he called once a while ago and you pretended to be too busy to take the call."

"Can't a person get any privacy around here?"

"Landry also told me that he's never called again."

"Yeah, he finally got the message. I'm not interested, especially since he's in love with someone else. If only you could get that same message through that thick skull of yours." She affectionately rapped on Rubric's head.

"Okay, if you want to end up like Annabelle and me, be my guest. But you'll regret it one day."

She rolled her eyes. "Just because I'm not interested in Craig doesn't mean I'm not interested in a relationship. There are other fish in the sea."

"Well, it's time you went fishing again," Rubric suggested as he stretched and stood up to leave.

"Wait a minute. I didn't ask to be lectured about Craig, but I would like you to help me make a decision about my next investigation."

"I'm not discussing that topic with you until after you take some time off," Rubric replied sternly as he limped out the door.

Jill's phone rang.

"Jill Lewis," she barked impatiently.

"Are you having a bad day?"

Jill recognized Helen's voice. "I'm sorry, Helen. What can I do for you?" She tapped a pencil impatiently, anxious to get back to her work.

"Do you remember the sign that you tacked up on my bulletin board in the newsstand?"

"Of course I remember." Jill suddenly sat up straight. She had put up a notice about the sixpence when she returned to Washington. For some reason she still couldn't get those baby blue eyes out of her mind. "Did he show up?"

"He's on his way up to your office now," Helen said. "Says his name is John Lovell."

"Really!" Jill exclaimed, her heart racing. "Didn't I tell you he'd come, Helen?"

"You sure did. And guess what else? It's exactly like you said. He told me he was getting married and wanted to collect the sixpence for his bride's shoe. No wonder you're so good at your job. You have great instincts."

Jill's heart sank. *Wait a minute, Lord! How could the handsome stranger belong to someone else too?* She sighed loudly. *Oh, well, at least it'll be interesting to see him again. And maybe he has a twin brother.*

Jill dashed to the ladies' room to touch up her makeup and fluff her hair. When she returned to her office, the phone was ringing. She answered it breathlessly.

"This is Jill Lewis."

"Hi, Jill. There's a man out here to see you," Landry announced. "Shall I send him back or do you want to come up front to see him?"

"Who is he?" Jill asked nonchalantly, as if she didn't know.

"Some guy who says he's answering the ad you placed on Helen's bulletin board," Landry explained. "Says his name is John Lovell. Trust me. You want to see this guy . . . he's drop dead gorgeous," the receptionist added under her breath.

"Would you mind showing him back to my office?" Jill asked, figuring her corner office with a view would duly impress him.

A moment later the door swung open, and Landry motioned the man into Jill's office. The receptionist closed the door quietly but left it slightly ajar.

Jill's mouth flew open. It wasn't the mysterious stranger who'd come to her door. "Craig?" she gasped. He was wearing an expensive suit with a shirt with monogrammed cuffs, unlike his casual attire at the *Lakes*. On his head he wore an FBI cap. She had never seen him look so handsome. "What are you doing here? I'm, uh, expecting someone." She became so flustered she began to shake.

"This won't take long," Craig assured her.

"Excuse me a moment," she said politely and then ran to the door and caught Landry out in the corridor. "Don't let Mr. Lovell leave. Tell him I'll be with him shortly."

Landry looked confused. "Jill, that man is Mr. Lovell, or at least he claims to be," she whispered.

Jill turned on her heel and marched back into her office. She sat down at her desk, folded her hands, and cleared her throat. Trying to stay calm, she asked, "Is this your idea of some sick joke coming here pretending to be someone else?"

Without saying a word, Craig removed his glasses. Gone were his thick lenses and heavy black frames. When he smiled at her, the piercing cornflower blue eyes that had mesmerized her when she first encountered the stranger at the newsstand seduced her again. He then removed his cap. His hair was now sandy brown and grown out instead of dark brown and clipped flat against his head.

"Craig?" she gasped.

"Call me John. My real name is John Lovell."

"What on earth . . . ? What happened to your eyes? And your hair?"

"I tossed the glasses you hated and popped out those dark, tinted contact lenses. It was all a disguise."

"You're the same man who gave me the coin?" she asked incredulously. "Was it meant to be a bugging device?"

He shook his head. "That was very astute of Rubric to have it tested, but no, it wasn't a bug. It really was what I told you—a sixpence my grandmother had given me to give to my bride to wear on our wedding day. I was on my way to Delavan that morning after a meeting in this building when we met by chance at the newsstand. I had no idea that the woman who was standing in front of me was none other than Jill Lewis, the very woman who was the focus of my covert operation. We had just begun trying to lure you back to Delavan at that point."

"And I thought my mother had persuaded Max to hire me. Why did you want me back in Delavan?"

"First of all, we thought you might lead us to your father's files, and eventually you did. We were also trying to flush out your father's killers. We were using you as our decoy."

She could feel the temperature of the room rising. "So I guess I'm lucky to be alive . . . no thanks to you. You could've gotten me killed, you know."

"That's not true. You wouldn't believe how many agents were watching over you, your home, your mother, your sister, your niece, Jeff, and every move all of you made."

She stood up and put her hands on her hips. "Then how do you explain Barrows and Chuck getting into the house unnoticed, and Barrows almost killing Miss Cornelia and me? Not to mention Marion's kidnapping."

"Unfortunately, Chuck and Barrows murdered the two undercover agents who were on duty at your family's estate that night and dumped their bodies in the lake."

Jill winced. She didn't know what to say to him, and she had a difficult time looking into his deep blue eyes. She looked down at her desk and saw the sixpence. She picked it up. "Why did you leave this coin with me?"

"I hadn't planned on leaving it behind, but I didn't have any choice. When that guy at the newsstand interrupted us, I was stunned to discover that you were Jill Lewis. I didn't recognize you from your photographs."

"Oh, so that's why you disappeared? It makes sense, I guess. If I'd gotten a closer look and recognized you at the *Lakes,* it would've blown the whole undercover operation."

"It almost blew it anyway. When I reported the incident to my bureau chief, he wanted to take me off the job. But they determined I could pull it off if I was wearing a disguise. We altered my appearance with the glasses and tinted contacts to disguise my blue eyes. They also dyed and cut my hair. But it worked, didn't it?"

She nodded. "I had no idea you were the guy from the newsstand. His eyes, I mean, your eyes, are so distinctive—if those are your real eyes. I don't know what to believe anymore."

Craig smiled. "These are my eyes."

"And they're beautiful." Jill sighed.

"Thank you," he replied as he looked down modestly.

"So how did you happen to see my ad on Helen's bulletin board?"

"Strictly a God thing. It caught my eye while I waited in line."

She folded her arms across her chest. "Well, that doesn't explain what you're doing here in the first place."

"I have a meeting. The agency has some offices here."

Jill cleared her throat. "Okay. But if you had wanted your sixpence back, you could've just asked me. I would've given it to you."

"I did try to ask for it, but you didn't return my call. Besides, I never really needed the sixpence until now."

"Helen told me that you're getting married. Congratulations." The words stuck in her throat. "Anyone I know?" she croaked sheepishly, looking down at her feet, not wanting to hear his reply.

"Mmm, you know her very well."

"Caroline?" she said as she reached down to her desk to retrieve the sixpence, fighting back her tears.

"Caroline is one of my partners. We've worked together a long time, so naturally we're very close, but she's happily married and has been for several years."

"Married? Caroline's married? But I saw you hugging her when Marion was rescued. It didn't look like she was just a friend."

He laughed. "Jill, you have an active imagination. I suppose that's why you're such a great investigator. Caroline is just my partner. That was a hug of relief."

Then who on earth was he going to marry? Maybe his fiancée was the new obit girl he'd hired at the *Lakes*. Laura! That woman had set her sights on Craig the moment he appeared at her door.

"So tell me about this girl you're going to marry," she said, feeling like she already had the answer.

"There's not much I can tell you that you don't know already."

"Well, you certainly didn't waste any time, did you?"

"Oh, Grandmother always told me I would know my wife the moment I met her. She advised not to waste any time—life is too short."

"And did you know?"

"I guess I did. I can't really explain why, but I knew it the minute I laid eyes on her. I said to myself, 'I don't know how or when, but I'm going to marry that girl one day,' and I didn't even know her name. But I did know that God had miraculously brought us together."

"How romantic," Jill said stoically. "Well, here's your sixpence." She pushed the coin across her desk.

"No, it's yours," he said gently, refusing to take the coin.

"But you promised your grandmother you would give it to your bride to wear in her shoe on her wedding day. You wouldn't want to break your promise."

"I don't intend to."

"But why would you give the coin to me?"

And then she knew.

"Me?" she squealed as the realization sunk into her head and then her heart. "You want to marry me? I don't understand. Craig, uh, John, is this . . . is this a proposal?" She closed her eyes, afraid to hear the answer—afraid it wouldn't be the one she desperately wanted to hear.

"Not yet." He moved to her side and placed his finger to her lips. "Let's not spoil my surprise."

Her head was spinning. She wanted to take John Lovell by the hand and run down the courthouse steps to be married now, this very minute. But she knew she had to show some restraint.

Instinctively, men are hunters; they're the ones that like to do all the chasing. She bit her tongue as her mother's warning played out in her head. "But you do want to marry me?"

"Yes, I want to marry you, but I can't propose here. This isn't special enough for my gal." He cupped her cheek with his hand and looked her in the eyes with longing.

"Take her to Diamond Jim's Steak House," Rubric blurted out from behind the door. Shaking her head, Jill kicked the door closed with her foot.

Alone at last, John took Jill in his arms and kissed her with all the longing and passion of the kisses he had withheld from her for a long, long time.

Acknowledgments

Many thanks to the wonderful team at Revell. Heartfelt gratitude to acquisition editor Jennifer Leep, who gave us the opportunity to use our gift of storytelling, Kristin Kornoelje, project editor, whose skills enhanced our gift, and designer Cheryl VanAndel for her artistic talents. Appreciation to our exceptional agent, Chip MacGregor, and editor Marie Prys for their efforts on our behalf. Also a special thanks to Mary Garbe for her information on Bernese Mountain dogs.

Susan Wales is the author of a dozen best-selling nonfiction books including the popular Match Made in Heaven series, *Faith in Gods and Generals, Standing on the Promises, Social Graces,* and *The Art of Romantic Living.* As a Voice of Faith for Lawson Falle greeting cards, Susan writes the wedding card series, Happily Ever After. She and her husband, Hollywood producer Ken Wales, best known for the CBS series *Christy,* reside in Pacific Palisades, California, and are parents of a daughter.

Robin Shope, a twenty-year teaching veteran, is still active in the Lewisville schools near Dallas and has three teaching degrees. She lives with her husband of twenty-seven years and their two grown children, along with a cat and two dogs. Robin is the author of over one hundred articles and short stories for Sunday school magazines, educational magazines, and collections of short stories, including the Chicken Soup series. Robin writes of her hometown of Delavan, Wisconsin, where she lived through her teenage years. Several spots she mentioned in the story are places she worked as a teen.